HER
Last
CRY

BOOKS BY PAMELA FAGAN HUTCHINS

DETECTIVE DELANEY PACE SERIES

Her Silent Bones

Her Hidden Grave

PATRICK FLINT SERIES

Switchback

Snake Oil

Sawbones

Scapegoat

Snaggle Tooth

Stag Party

Sitting Duck

JENN HERRINGTON SERIES

Big Horn

MAGGIE KILLIAN SERIES

Live Wire

Sick Puppy

Dead Pile

KATIE CONNELL SERIES

Saving Grace

Leaving Annalise

Finding Harmony

Seeking Felicity

HER
Last
CRY

PAMELA FAGAN
HUTCHINS

bookouture

Published by Bookouture in 2024

An imprint of Storyfire Ltd.
Carmelite House
50 Victoria Embankment
London EC4Y 0DZ

www.bookouture.com

ISBN: 978-1-83790-306-1
eBook ISBN: 978-1-83790-305-4

To Tiffany, P1, and P2, who came into my life right as the you-know-what hit the fan, and for one challenging, beautiful year made it just barely possible for me to keep doing what I do, including writing the Delaney Pace books, most specifically this one. Thank you for your friendship, compassion, and love for all creatures great and small.
And to my husband, Eric—the hardest working guy I know—because of whom this book was written in Denmark, Maine, California, and Wyoming. Thank you for everything you do. You make a difference, to many more people than will ever know it, but most of all to me.

ONE

Annabeth Dillon twirled a straw in her gin and tonic. Absaroka Double Cask Gin 49. She'd anticipated a celebration and brought the limited bottle from the case she'd scored back home in Jackson, straight from the distillery. "Did you grow up around here?"

All she got was a one-shoulder shrug.

She put her drink down. "Fine, you're the silent type. Now what do you want me to do?"

Her intended lover slipped a blindfold over Annabeth's head.

Silk rubbed against her eyes. She adjusted the band and pulled some of her hair loose. "Oh, I like this."

A hand gripped her arm.

She jumped. Without sight, her other senses were heightened. "Strong *and* silent." A sound caught her attention. Outside the cabin, not in it. A knock at the window? She strained to hear, but it didn't repeat. "Did you hear that?"

She didn't get an answer.

More of the soft fabric slid in a loop over one wrist, then the other. Her skin tingled, a delicious feeling. Her lover took up slack, drawing one arm wide over her head. The fabric tugged at Annabeth's wrist as it was secured. She shivered. The feeling of giving up her power and control—two things she so jealously cultivated in her everyday life—was intoxicating in the right situations. This was one of them.

"You know you're restraining the future leader of the free world, right? A few years from now and this would be treason." The silk dug into her wrist. She bit her lip until the sharp metallic taste of her own blood coated her tongue. "How does it feel knowing that?"

A soft laugh was the only answer. Her lover adjusted the restraint on her other arm, putting her in a human T position, then moved to her ankles, slipping silk loops over them as well. In her mind's eye, she pictured it a rich scarlet color with long tasseled ends.

She began to writhe against the sheets. She would have liked it better if those were silk, too, but the old flannel had an appeal. Each nub vibrated against her clothes, grated on the skin it touched. Almost rough. Like the surroundings. A mountain cabin, snow falling outside, hundreds of miles from the gated estate where she lived, in mountains less populated and more uncivilized than her home range. A four-poster pine bed, to which her wrists were now tied. Low ceilings. A smokey fire in the old stone fireplace, burning her eyes even under the blindfold, tickling her nose. The expensive gin still tickling her tongue and circulating in her blood stream.

"Can I have another sip of my drink?" she purred. "You can pour some more for us if you'd like to share."

The hands at work on her legs stopped what they were doing. Footsteps. The sound of liquid sloshing.

She smiled.

Then the gin splashed onto her face.

She gasped. "What the hell?"

"Do you want it or not?"

"Yes, but not like that."

"This isn't about what you'd like. Open your mouth."

For a moment, Annabeth kept her mouth closed. Then, as a trickle of gin cascaded across her lips and down her chin, she relented. She licked it. The bite on her tongue was better than through a straw, with just a hint of her own saltiness. It was... perfection. She swallowed, then opened wide, greedily sucking it down. "Yes. Yes."

The liquid stopped. "That's all you get."

She pouted. "You're bossy."

"You're not the one in charge."

Oh, that's what you think.

The fabric tightened. Her body moved down the bed and her legs jerked toward each corner post. Annabeth couldn't see the room, but she could picture her body in a perfect X, fully clothed for the winter weather except that she'd taken off her boots and socks before she'd crawled up on the bed.

"How are you going to get me undressed now that you've tied me up?" she teased.

A snort. Something cold and hard pressed against her shin under her jeans. Then a snick-snick-snick, and the denim fell away. Scissors.

She wriggled. She was on fire from her head to her toes. "Good thing I didn't like this outfit."

"I said this isn't about what you like."

Every stroke of the scissors stirred something deep inside her. The sound of the metallic blade slicing through fabric. Steel under the band of her underclothing. Her lover's fingers brushing against her skin as they worked the tool. Soon every garment had been cut from her body, leaving her bare. Cool air prickled the skin of her shoulders. Warmth from the fireplace lapped at her feet. She arched her back, lifting her chest, desperate for human touch. When none came, she eased back, then tilted her hips in invitation. Still, nothing.

"Aren't you going to join me?" she said, her voice a husky moan.

Warm hands encircled her neck, squeezing firmly.

She tensed. She could still breathe, but the pressure was intense. A little too much. "Wait, I—"

"Relax." Her lover put a hand behind her head and lifted.

She softened and let it happen. More of the silky fabric slipped behind her neck and brushed over her face, under her chin, down to her neck.

"What is this?" She had an urge to lever her fingers under the band. To give herself space to breathe. Only her hands were tied to the posts at the head of the bed.

Fingers worked, fabric tightened. "Enhancement." Pressure lessened, then increased, lessened, then increased. It was... terrifying. *A slip knot?*

Despite her fear, she felt her excitement building. This was new to her. She'd dreamed about breath-play to heighten arousal, but she'd never asked a lover for it. Had never offered it to one either.

Wasn't she all about risk tonight, though? It seemed apropos. Suddenly, it seemed imperative.

She sighed and wriggled into the flannel sheets. *Let's just do this already.* But she wasn't going to beg. Wasn't going to rush it. In a cool voice she said, "There's something we need to talk about."

The weight on her body was sudden, warm, and insistent. "I don't think there's anything left for you and me to discuss."

And then the noose tightened around her neck, cutting off her air. Annabeth leaned into the sensation for a moment, anticipating her lover's touch. Yearning for it. Excited about it. Wondering in what way it would come.

Waited for it.

Waited.

Waited longer.

But there was none.

And without the pleasure, what was the point of the risk? Of the pain? Because there was pain. Not just the lack of oxygen that was starting to be uncomfortable, but the bite of the silk into her neck.

The fabric tightened again. It was more than a bite now. It was crushing her esophagus. Any harder and she was afraid it would break the bones in her neck.

Her lover breathed hot and fast on her face. "You like that?"

No! She wanted to scream it, but she had no voice. *This is not sexy. This is not fun.* She pulled at her wrist and ankle restraints, to no avail. She twisted her head from side to side. It did nothing to loosen the strap around her neck. She bucked and writhed, but the weight of her lover on top of her and the way in which her body was stretched flat made her efforts futile. *I'm trapped. Helpless.*

"How does it feel?" A soft laugh. The blindfold was released. "You don't have to tell me. I can see it in your eyes."

I'm going to die. Annabeth stilled. *Save your breath, stupid.* Her *lungs* begged for oxygen. Her mouth opened and closed like a fish, gulping nothing. *Surely there's humanity in there somewhere?* She looked her lover in the eye. Blinked. Tried to change panic to pleading.

Her lover laughed aloud and touched Annabeth's face with one hand, using the other to keep the noose tight. "I can't believe no one warned you not to mess with me. It's not a mistake you'll repeat."

A hand struck Annabeth across the face. Harder than she'd ever been hit before. *Why?* She couldn't cry out. She couldn't gasp.

Then a fist slammed into her nose. The pain barely registered with everything else that hurt.

Her lover studied Annabeth's face like she was a lab specimen. Walked away. *Just go. Just leave me here. Please, please,*

please. Came back with a water bottle and a smile. Held it up for Annabeth to see.

It was frozen, and ice had forced the top partially off. *What is that for?*

Her lover pointed it at the side of Annabeth's head.

Horror seeped through Annabeth. She wasn't going to draw another breath, much less become the leader of the free world or anything else. Her lover wasn't going to let her go. The water bottle cocked back and slammed into Annabeth's head. Annabeth's last thought before she slipped from consciousness was *How could I have let a killer in my bed?*

TWO

Off-duty Deputy Investigator Delaney Pace slammed the door to her car harder than she would have let anyone else get away with, then winced. The Chevelle SS—a legacy from the father murdered at the very bar she was parked behind—didn't deserve her frustration. But she had gone from being a single, childless woman to a guardian-soon-to-be-adoptive mother to her tween niece, Kateena, and seventeen-year-old crime victim, Carrie Hoff, in less than a year, and the journey was anything but a cakewalk.

"Why do I have to be here?" Carrie said, her voice in the register teenage girls used to irritate their targets into submission.

Because it's a surprise party for Leo, and he saved you from not one but two killers less than four months ago. Saying it aloud would be a waste of breath and make no difference, though. They were here to celebrate the birthday of the California transplant and interim sheriff, no matter what the younger members of her household had to say about it. And no matter how difficult it was for Delaney to be around him socially. Her head knew better than to give in to her attraction to him, but her heart and libido didn't make it easy. She valued their friendship and working relationship and her own independence—too much to indulge them. She was poison on relationships, plain and simple. And theirs would be no casual fling, of that she was certain. It would be a barn burning, take-no-prisoners relationship with a capital R ending in destruction with a capital D.

Delaney turned back to the girls. Carrie was leaning against the car, her fuzzy boots three inches deep in snow, straight pink hair hanging over her puffy jacket, and bling-pocketed Western jeans probably scratching Shotgun Shelly's pristine custom paint job. The girl let her head fall back against the roof of the car with a thunk and rolled her eyes. Kateena climbed out and stood beside her. Delaney squinted in darkness broken only by a light over the back door of the Loafing Shed. The girls had been running late when they'd left home, and she'd barely glanced at her niece. Now she took in thick black eyeliner, heavy eyeshadow, and lips painted a red that defied the meager illumination. Her black hair was pulled back severely against the sides of her head, but in the back the curls and volume she'd inherited from her African American mother were unleashed. The contrast of the too-adult look with her coltish frame in skintight ripped jeans made her look like a public service warning about sex trafficking.

She bypassed Carrie's question and zeroed in on her niece. "Kateena Pace, what do you have on your face?"

Kateena's hip popped, her shoulders shimmied, and her head bobbed. "Don't call me that. I've told you fifty bajillion times my name is Kat now."

Delaney sucked in a long breath through her nose. Had she acted like this with her parents? If so, maybe that's why her mother had run away and never come back before Delaney turned eleven. *But I am not my mother.* She pointed at the door. "Straight to the bathroom. Wash it off. All of it."

"But—"

"No buts."

"Everyone will think I'm a baby!"

"I don't care what everyone thinks. I care about you. Now go."

The child formerly known as Kateena stomped through the snow toward the door.

Carrie shot Delaney a look so snake-like that Delaney expected to see a forked tongue when she opened her mouth to speak. But of course, she didn't. Carrie was a teenage girl, not a serpent, no matter how similar the two sometimes seemed. She waited for Carrie to peel herself off the car then followed her into the back hall of the Loafing Shed, passing by the junker silver Toyota Corolla that she recognized as the car of Deputy Tommy Miller. Everyone in law enforcement was parking in back so the surprise for Leo wouldn't be spoiled.

Happy voices and laughter; the odor of beer, wet boots and clinking glass beckoned from the front of the bar, like an oasis. To reach it, Delaney had to walk the hardwood planks past the office, though—the site of her darkest memories. She shuddered. Hiding under her father's desk when she was Kat's age, hearing an altercation, then an unknown assailant stabbing him. Running into the hall and finding him, his blood spilling out and soaking into the wood floor. Calling 911, knowing even at her age that it was already too late.

She shook it off as she always did and walked faster toward the bright lights and the gathering of most of the people she cared about in the world.

"Delaney's here, everyone!" Mary Galvez, the curvy bar manager, beamed at her.

"Hello, everyone." She smiled at Mary and the rest of the crowd, but she scanned for Leo.

Her eyes stuck on a poster behind the group.

*WYOMING NATIVE MITCH STONEFIELD FOR U.S.
SENATE*

It detailed an upcoming fundraiser and included a picture
of a serious-faced Mitch with the Cheyenne River raging in full
spring melt behind him and the Bighorn Mountains in the
distance.

The man was a local legend in his own time. He'd won the
state chess tournament at the age of twelve and graduated from
the University of Wyoming at nineteen. He'd also been her
brother Liam's best friend back in the day, which was a shocker
since Liam had been born trouble and only gotten worse since.

Mitch had taken a different path than Liam and become an
attorney, then a Wyoming state representative, and finally the
state Attorney General. Delaney hadn't seen him in more than
a decade. Something about the poster caused her to take a
second glance and her mouth fell open. The fundraiser was
going to be *here*, at the Loafing Shed. This wasn't the right
forum for picking sides. Unless the event was for Leo. She
wondered if he'd decided whether to seek the party endorsement for sheriff.

She'd get Mary to cancel the event, later.

She resumed her hunt for the man of the hour. He wasn't
there yet, which was good. She wanted to be part of surprising
him. But most everyone else who'd been invited was already
gathered, and she took their hugs and handshakes one by one.
Skeeter Rawlins, the sometimes-nanny-sometimes-investigator
honorary member of the Pace household, looking burly and
casting hopeful gazes in Mary's direction as was his sad norm.
Grandfatherly Joe Tarver and his young partner, Tommy
Miller, both Kearny County deputies. Leo's elfin younger sister,
Adriana, a recent transplant to the area. Crime scene tech Sugar
Kuhk aka Sugar Cookie, sporting pink hair and nose rings. Dr.

Louise Watson, the county's on-call forensic pathologist. Clara, the administrative maven for the sheriff's department.

Other guests milled about, and Delaney's newly acquired mom-radar pinged on Katee... Kat—who had not washed her face or had only done a half-hearted job of it—with Leo's nephew Freddy. The two were increasingly inseparable but so far seemed platonic, *thank the Lord*. Something to keep an eye on. Carrie was making selections at the juke box, an addition Mary had made to the bar. Chris LeDoux's "Copenhagen" was currently playing, but if Carrie was picking the music, that would give way to hip hop soon.

"Can I get you anything?" Mary said.

Delaney noticed the sheet cake on the bar top. "HAPPY BIRTHDAY, SHERIFF," it read. Someone had crashed a white toy pickup truck into a little stump and stuck them in the icing, commemorating his mishaps since joining the department. "Nice cake. I'll have a rum and Coke. Hold the rum."

Mary smiled. "Coming right up, boss." Delaney was Mary's de facto boss, although Kateena had technically owned the bar since the death of her parents—the actual death of her mother and the *legal* death of her father. Liam Pace was still alive, somewhere, after faking his own demise so he'd be free to operate as "Jefe," dealing drugs and doing whatever he wanted. Most recently, that had included blackmailing a local developer, murdering the man's son, and breaking Kateena's heart again by using her as his human shield for his getaway. *Maybe a little eyeliner is the least I should expect from Kat after what she's been through.* Bringing her brother to justice was priority number one for Delaney.

Mary filled a glass and slid it to her.

Adriana leaned in to show Delaney her phone. "Did I tell you about the guy I've been talking to on my dating app?"

Ten thousand times. As flinty as Adriana was on the outside, she was eager—overeager—for a man to love her. "You did. Are things progressing?"

Adriana batted her eyes. "He wants to go on a real date."

"Do you want me to run a background check on him?"

She flicked a finger into Delaney's arm. "You're worse than Leo. No. I don't want the two of you to even meet him. Ever. It's impossible to date when guys find out my brother is the sheriff."

"If you change your mind…"

Adriana's phone chirped. She held it aloft. "It's Leo. He's parking right now. Everybody get ready."

"Get ready to what?" Skeeter had both hands wrapped around his rocks whiskey, like he was afraid it would run away.

Delaney punched his meaty shoulder. The whiskey sloshed, but Skeeter's death grip kept it safely in the glass. "To yell surprise."

"Oh, yeah."

"And sing 'Happy Birthday,'" Joe said. Delaney couldn't help but frown slightly as she looked at him. The older deputy's face was puffy. Clara had let slip that she'd had to order him new uniforms two sizes larger than the ones he'd been squeezing into for the previous few months. The man had been putting on so much weight that Delaney wondered if medication was causing it.

The front door opened, and in walked the man who, if there was a movie made about his life, would have played himself, because Hollywood couldn't have found anyone better looking or better suited for the role. Was it just Delaney's imagination, or was there a collective female sigh at the sight of him? Laser eyes an oceanic blue, dark hair curled at the ends. Facial hair, since he was trying to blend into Wyoming. A muscular yet lean build. Her eyes traveled down to his feet, clad in west coast appropriate casual boots, a brand Delaney took pride in not knowing the name of and one inappropriate for the snowy conditions. In her opinion, his goofy footwear was one of his only true flaws.

"Three, two, one," Adriana counted down on her fingers held over her head.

The room exploded with a collective shout of, "Happy Birthday, Sheriff!"

Leo grinned and put a hand to his chest. "Ah, shucks. You shouldn't have."

"Happy birthday, Uncle Leo!" Freddy was the first to hug him. He'd shot up several inches in the few months since he'd lived in Kearny. Lanky with floppy dark hair and big ice-blue eyes, the kid was on his way to being tall and handsome like his uncle.

Leo ruffled the boy's hair, eyes shining. "Thanks, kiddo. I'm so happy you're here to celebrate with me."

"Me, too."

"That's great. I love you."

"I love you, too." Freddy wrenched himself away and galloped back to Kat.

Delaney couldn't help but smile. The love and happiness in Leo's expression—she could relate. She'd never believed she had the capacity to love anyone as much as she now loved her niece, no matter how difficult the girl was becoming.

Leo's eyes rose and found Delaney's.

She tore hers away. *Nope. Not getting drawn in by that tractor beam tonight.* Her gaze landed on the man behind him.

Then her heart jammed up in her chest and stopped.

THREE

Delaney couldn't believe her eyes. The man behind Leo was shorter than her partner, but bulkier, with shoulders straining at his camo-patterned coat. Olive skin. Military-length hair. Eyes dark as pitch. It couldn't be. Could it?

He spotted her. The smile, oh, the smile, wide as his face, infectious. "By God, is that really you, Delaney Pace?" He waved, heading her way.

Leo cocked his head, frowning.

"Zeke Ochoa." Heat rose into her face. *I'm blushing. Stop it, Delaney.*

He reached her and immediately drew her into a hug. She was dimly aware of the crowd converging on Leo and offering him their well wishes, but most of her attention was consumed by Zeke's hard chest crushing into hers, digging the medallion she wore in honor of her father into her breastbone. Of the familiar scent of this man bringing back their one perfect night together.

Her mind rushed back to it. The people and the room around her kaleidoscoped away until it was seven years ago. She'd been engaged to a fellow long hauler. She'd picked up a load to southern California since it was off-season for an ice road trucker, and she'd decided to give herself a few days in the sun and sand before backhauling to North Dakota.

She'd wandered into a beach bar and lazily nursed a Sam Adams. Zeke had sat down beside her. Their attraction was immediate. Urgent. Animalistic. He was on a short leave between deployments, for a job with the Marines he wouldn't tell her much about that sounded dangerous and a lot like special forces. Sooner rather than later, they'd ended up at a nearby motel.

It had been, in a word, in-freaking-credible.

She'd awoken before dawn and walked outside with the rough sensation of his body still on her skin. Known nothing could happen between them and was fine with that. His job. Her fiancé. It had been a beautiful moment in time and nothing else. So, she'd kept walking—miles and miles—all the way back to the truck stop where she'd parked her rig Gabrielle for the night.

Fast forward six weeks. Things hadn't worked out with her fiancé. By then, Zeke should have been back overseas. She didn't know how to reach him, and she hadn't left him her number. The crossing of their stars intensified the magic of the memory. She chalked it up to fate and moved on.

Now, in the here and now of the Loafing Shed, he whispered, "I've social media stalked you so many times," in her ear.

She stepped out of his arms to get a look at him. Finally, she smiled. "Wow. How are you?"

"Gobsmacked. I can't believe I've finally found you in this nowhere town in a dump of a bar."

"Hey, don't badmouth my place. I was born and raised here. Not just in Kearny. In this bar."

"My bad." He laughed. "Leo said it's called the Loading Shed?"

Half the cowboys in northern Wyoming called it the

Loading Shed, as in the place they went to get loaded. But that wasn't its name, and Leo knew it. "The *Loafing* Shed. It's what people around here call horse shelters, and... never mind. What are you doing here? And how do you know Leo?"

"We're buds from our school days in San Diego. Just paying him a birthday visit. Back to the important question, though. Where the hell have you been?"

"Me? What about you?"

"Working for Uncle Sam all over the world." He shook his head. "You're as beautiful as the night I met you. Damn, Delaney."

"You've held up well yourself." It was an understatement. He looked like an advertisement for a fitness magazine. Or a military recruitment poster featuring the perfect soldier.

Leo appeared beside them. "You two know each other?"

Zeke didn't break eye contact with Delaney. "You could say that."

Leo frowned.

Delaney's cell vibrated in her pocket. Leo patted his hip and drew out his phone. She glanced at Tommy and Joe. They were pulling out their phones, too. She read a group text from the dispatcher.

Need a wellness check up in the mountains. Some Jackson Hole VIP is missing. Who's available?

Just as Delaney was thinking *Tommy and Joe!* Leo said, "Well, Zeke, sorry to cut out on you at my birthday party, but duty calls for Delaney and me."

"What do you mean?" Zeke looked a question at Delaney.

"I'm a deputy here," she said.

"Deputy Investigator," Leo said. "The one person I absolutely rely on in my department."

"I thought you were an ice road trucker?" Zeke looked confused.

"I was." A fleeting picture of her big black tractor Gabrielle flashed through her mind. Tires on creaking ice. Temperatures so cold that the cab never warmed over forty degrees. She'd loved it. The road had been therapy for the traumas of her childhood. She missed the life, but she'd been called home to care for Kateena, and she wouldn't change that for the world, even if Gabrielle was wasting away in storage on the other side of town. "I returned to my roots. I was in law enforcement before trucking."

Zeke winked. "A double badass. That's hot." He turned to Leo. "When will you have her back, Sheriff? I was going to see if the lady would let me drive her home."

"Delaney doesn't let anyone drive—"

"I'd love that," Delaney said, interrupting Leo, "if this turns out to be a false alarm. Give me your number. I'll text you." She and Zeke exchanged numbers while Leo ground his teeth. Then to her boss-slash-partner, she said, "Just let me work things out with the girls before we leave."

"I have to make my apologies anyway." He put his hand on her shoulder.

She walked out from under it toward the girls.

Leo climbed on a bar stool and whistled through two fingers. When the crowd had quieted, he raised both hands. "Duty calls. Thanks for coming, everyone. Mary, one round on me for anyone not driving."

He hopped down to whoops and cheers.

Delaney held the keys to Shelly toward Carrie. "I have to go with Leo. A work thing."

"Okay." Carrie took the keys.

"What about us?" Kat said.

"You can stay, but straight home in an hour. And Kat— Carrie is in charge."

Both girls whined but they didn't argue.

"See you at home." She kissed each of them on the top of the head and smiled at Freddy, who gave her a shy grin.

She turned back in time to see Leo give Zeke a complicated bro handshake. But the look he gave his friend was daggers and his voice venomous as he said, "Bye, *buddy*."

FOUR

"You sure I can't help?" Leo asked, watching Delaney hop onto the snowmobile trailer and feeling about as useless as a concrete parachute.

Damn, if the site of their wellness check wasn't a cabin high in the mountains, and, thanks to a foot of snow that day, unreachable with wheeled vehicles. This was his first season covering immense Kearny County during the winter. They'd be going deep into the woods through pitch dark with no street-lamps or even moonlight. Knowing this, Delaney—who had insisted on driving his truck—had dropped by the department for gear, chains, and a trailer with the two snowmachines on their way out of town. Maybe it would have been wiser to let Joe and Tommy take this call. He'd cut out on his own surprise birthday party after all. But he'd be damned if he was going to stay in that bar a minute longer watching his best friend from high school and Delaney make goo-goo eyes at each other.

"Thanks. But it's a one-person job." Delaney unfastened the first snowmobile, climbed on, and started it up. She backed it off, then repeated the process with the other.

He trusted Delaney out here. The woman was smart, with

an encyclopedic knowledge of the county thanks to her hobby of studying maps. She also had experience with the climate, expertise with all things mechanical, and she filled out a pair of snow pants like no one he had ever imagined. He'd grown up around outdoorsy girls, but most of them bordered on anorexic and were aspiring models, reality stars, or actresses. Delaney had a body built for performance. Muscular but feminine. Lithe but not skinny. Tall enough that she looked most men in the eye, although not him. Not quite. Tough enough that he secretly wondered if she could kick his ass in hand-to-hand combat. Hell, he'd let her just for an excuse to have her touch him. A black eye and broken nose would be worth it.

But it wasn't just her touch he wanted. He flashed back to Zeke's obvious play for her in the Loafing Shed, and his fists balled. He wanted to hold her hand and open doors for her if she'd let him. Tell her all his secrets and hear all of hers. Bring her flowers. Cook breakfast for her.

He was in love with Delaney, and it was eating him alive.

Enough. I'm the interim sheriff. She's made it clear nothing is going to happen between us. But his mind couldn't let it go. He'd been planning to move back to San Diego whenever the Drug Enforcement Agency released him from indentured servitude in Kearny, which Special Agent Natalie Amin had semi-promised would happen when he delivered Jefe to them. It wasn't his original assignment from them. That had been to ferret a dirty cop from the Kearny County Sheriff's Department, which was his punishment for the wrong turn his San Diego PD undercover assignment into the Bajeños crime syndicate had taken. Not that he'd done anything wrong, but it was impossible to disprove something for which there was no evidence in the first place. *You can't fight local bureaucracy, and you sure can't fight the DEA.*

But assuming he made good on the Jefe bust for the DEA, did he really want to leave Delaney? Adriana and Freddy seemed to be thriving here. Maybe he could run for sheriff. Stick around if he won.

Who was he kidding, though? The chance of a California transplant being elected to sheriff in a rural Wyoming county was slim-to-none. He'd put out feelers with the local party organization. They hadn't rolled out the welcome mat, but they hadn't slammed the door in his face either. What they had done was ask whether Delaney would be running. When he'd told them she didn't want the role, they'd said he should have her call them with her endorsement.

He would ask her soon.

Delaney turned off the second machine and hopped off. She grabbed helmets from the truck. "Remind me why we're the ones that had to make this wellness check?" Her tone of voice was more weary than irritated.

He held up his hands. "Apparently, Annabeth Dillon is somebody important in Jackson. The dispatcher said the Teton County sheriff called personally. Her husband is frantic. No one's heard from her in two days. The owner of the cabin is traveling and can't get up there to check it out herself."

She handed him his helmet. "I hope she's worth it. Carrie has to drive Kat home in Shotgun Shelly. Carrie, the same girl I had to pull out of school in Sheridan because she was throwing keggers."

Carrie had inherited the heavily mortgaged family home after her mother and twin brother had been murdered by the same man who'd left her for dead in a shallow grave. It was currently on the market, as a sale would be beneficial to the bank and might leave Carrie with a little college money. Leo had tried to talk Delaney out of letting the girl commute forty-five minutes each way to her old school in Sheridan, but Delaney had sympathized with the girl's need for something in her life to remain the same. Leo had seen trouble coming when Carrie had started asking to stay over and spend the night with friends after school. Their friend, Sheridan Deputy Travis, had been keeping an eye on the house, but it was a local real estate agent who'd caught the teens partying there. Leo hadn't said I told you so to Delaney, though. She was tapped out as it was, between Kateena acting out and Carrie acting up.

Leo said, "She has Kateena with her. She'll behave."

Delaney donned the helmet over her blonde-streaked long brown hair. She flipped the face shield up. "She goes by Kat now."

Leo laughed. "I'm sorry." He put his helmet on, too. It was tight and claustrophobic. He pushed up the face shield and tried not to look like he was gasping for air.

"It's about a quarter of a mile to the snow-tel."

"Snow-tel? How do you even spell that?"

"S-N-O-W-T-E-L. Just something the locals call these mountain cabins that get rented in the winter. I think it's also the name for meteorological stations that measure snowpack, but it's spelled differently."

His eyes had adjusted to the dark, and he looked around. Snow drifted in layer upon layer as far as he could see. "It fits."

"Anyway, there should be a cluster of them back there."

"Only one is supposed to be occupied, according to the owner." He hadn't been able to reach the woman himself, but that had been the information relayed to him by the dispatcher.

"Do you know how to drive one of these things?" She patted the handles of her snowmachine.

He climbed on his and stared blankly at the array of buttons and switches. She laughed. After she'd shown him how to turn it on and off, shift, accelerate, reverse, and stop, he felt better. Less like a flatlander, anyway.

"Just keep your speed up so you don't get stuck. And stay centered. They're sensitive to shifts in your body weight. Stay close and in my tracks." She straddled her machine and restarted it.

Leo planned on sticking to her like glue. Bears might be in their dens, but mountain lions didn't hibernate, nor did the Canadian timber wolves migrating to the area from their introduction into western Wyoming. As harsh as the winter was already in January—snowfall was tracking three times average with wind chill dipping down to -50 Fahrenheit and lower—the predators were bound to be hungry.

He realized Delaney had already put fifteen yards between them while he worried about becoming something's dinner. He squeezed the throttle and shot forward, closing the gap. Snow was flying up from behind her machine in a rooster tail, splattering his face and blinding him. He eased off the throttle, wiped his eyes, and pulled down the face shield. By the time he could see where he was going, Delaney had disappeared.

"Shit." The sound of his voice was eerie inside the closed helmet. His humid breath was fogging it up. He lifted it again. She wasn't close enough to spray him.

The beam of his headlight shone on the track of her snowmobile's belt. He followed it in a serpentine path roughly the width of a two-track through the trees, although when he glanced on either side of him there were openings of the same dimensions in different directions. Without her track, it would be easy to get lost back here. He gave the snowmobile more speed. The air was cold. He flipped the visor back down.

Come on, Delaney. Check behind you.

But she didn't. He drove through the dark with no sign of her light ahead of him. Even though he knew she couldn't be that far away, he'd never felt so alone in his life. If he lost her track, he could veer off and over a cliff. The whole reason he and Delaney were up here was because someone was alone and possibly needing help. They were supposed to be that help. *Oh, the irony.* If he needed assistance, Delaney was the only one who would be coming for him, which would put her at unacceptable risk.

"So, don't get lost," he said, fogging up the inside of his shield again. He raised it. Cold was better than blind.

He lost focus on Delaney's track for a split second. His veered ever so slightly off course and the machine wobbled out of the track into softer snow. He tried to correct it and instead caught a ski tip in deep snow. He relaxed his grip on the throttle. Too late, he realized more gas instead of less would have been the right move. *Like she told me.* The machine tipped over, dumping him in powder. It was unceremonious and quick.

With one side of his head submerged, Leo spit snow out of his mouth. "Son of a bitch."

The engine continued to hum even sideways with the belly exposed. Leo turned off the ignition, which also extinguished the headlight. Even buried in snow, it had been better than nothing. Again, a mistake. *I should have gotten out my flashlight first.* Utter silence met his ears, and chills raced up his neck. He tried to turn the engine back on, but it refused.

He inventoried his situation. He'd changed into snow boots and pants back at the truck and had on a good coat, gloves, and a wool hat. No injuries. The weather was clear and the temperature warm. Delaney had gone this way, so she'd come back this way, too. He was fine. He just needed to find a light, get the snowmobile upright, and restart it. But currently, the seat—which doubled as the lid to the gear box—was jammed in snow. As was he.

He shivered. He was out of his element.

He worked his leg out from under the machine, then stood, thigh high in drifted snow. He began the trudge from one side of the machine around to the other, fighting to keep his balance by grabbing the tip of an exposed ski and walking his hands along it. His lungs burned with every ragged breath of dry, cold air.

In the distance, he heard Delaney's engine rev. *Maybe she's turning around.*

Regardless, it was time to dig.

The snow shovel was strapped behind the seat with a bungee cord, unreachable, so he dug beside the machine with his hands, feeling ridiculous. In the past, his mishaps had been caught on film and shared via social media. At least all of Kearny County wouldn't see him in a humiliating position this time. The digging was hard work, and he built up a sweat in less than a minute. Just when he'd finished creating a flat space for the runners and stood to catch his breath, engine noise approached. He preferred that Delaney not find him floundering like a beached seal, so he grasped the seat to pull the machine upright. It didn't budge. He took hold of one side of the handlebars and put his weight into it, but that just landed him on his butt.

Delaney pointed her headlight at him. She raised her voice. "Was there a stump in the road?"

"Ha ha."

She hopped off—leaving her snowmobile running—and tromped over to him, looking more graceful than he'd felt. "You've got a good start, but we need to dig underneath it."

It only took him a second to understand. *Digging underneath helps it fall into an upright position.* He wished he'd thought of it.

As they dug, he said, "I can't get it started either."

She grunted with effort. "The engine floods when they're upside down. That's enough digging. Now, we'll pull on the skis to get them pointed in the right direction, so they aren't working against us, then we'll tip it over."

Together, they did as she suggested. One minute later, the snowmobile was upright.

Leo shook his head. "You made this seem easy."

"Easier. Because I've done it my whole life. If you aren't willing to dig, don't ride snowmobiles. Help me pull the front around a little more by the skis. All the way around facing the way we came in."

"You're sending me back?"

She laughed. "I'm not the boss of you. No, we'll just need to give the engine more time before we restart it. We'll ride double to the snow-tel."

They each took a ski tip and dragged the front end into alignment.

"You just saved me half an hour of frustration."

"I'm adding it to your list of debts." She climbed on her snowmobile. "Hop up. Let's get going before we freeze to death."

Leo climbed on behind her. He hadn't been cold until she'd mentioned it, but the sweat hadn't done him any favors, and he felt a chill.

"Wrap your arms around my waist or you'll go off the back."

He locked his hands in front of her waist and put his head to the side, so his helmet didn't knock against the back of hers. He could feel her body heat even through their bulky layers of clothing. He'd never had this kind of prolonged contact with her. Suddenly getting his snowmachine stuck and flooding the engine didn't seem like such a bad thing after all. Closing his eyes, he savored the moment.

Delaney pressed the throttle and her machine shot forward into the narrow beam of her light. At first, he squeezed her tighter, but her speed was constant, and the machine floated over the snow. After a moment, he relaxed, his earlier nerves now history. He trusted her. They were together. Everything was better. The drive, though, was short. Too soon she was killing the engine in front of a small, well-kept cabin with golden light streaming out a window. It looked like a Hallmark Christmas movie—not that he'd be caught dead watching one, but Adriana had streamed them nonstop during the holiday season.

He pointed at an SUV up to its frame in snow. "Looks like someone is home. Possibly just snowed in?"

Delaney shook her head. "No smoke from the chimney. These cabins run on solar and backup generators. I don't hear the generator, and it's been stormy out. They rely on the wood fireplaces and stoves for heat. I suspect the light is just a battery-powered lamp. I think something's wrong here."

"One way to find out."

The two of them stomped through the snow, unzipping their jackets to make their duty belts more accessible. At the door, both of them checked their weapons. Loaded, safety on, magazines full.

Leo stuffed his gloves in his pocket. Knocked. His RAP RAP RAP sounded muffled.

"If someone is in there, we're going to scare the spit out of them. They expect to be alone in a remote cabin, and here we are—two strangers at their door after dark." Delaney removed her gloves and put her hand on her gun.

But no one answered.

Leo knocked again. Harder, longer. "Hello in there. This is Kearny County Sheriff Leo Palmer. Can you come to the door, please?"

They waited. After another minute, Leo was fighting to keep his teeth from chattering.

"I think we're going to have to go in," Delaney said. "Want to jimmy the door?"

Leo sighed. "I'm told there's a spare key in the crook of the tree on the front left of the house."

Delaney went to the tree, reached up, and felt around the crook. Snow fell from the notch. She grasped something and backed away. "Didn't want to knock this in the snow or we'd be back to breaking in." She came to the door and inserted it in the lock, then turned the knob.

Leo took out his gun and pointed the business end in a low ready forty-five-degree angle downward.

Delaney pushed and the door swung open.

"Hello? This is the sheriff. Please let me know if there's someone in here." There was again no answer. He looked at Delaney. "Cover me?"

She answered by drawing her weapon. They both flicked off their safeties. Leo advanced into the room and moved to the side of the door. The space was split between a living area and a kitchen. There was an unlit fireplace in the middle of the back wall. A room was barely visible beyond it with a doorway beside the fireplace seeming to lead to it.

The front areas had a lived-in feel. A pair of socks hung on the hearth, as if drying, with boots below them. A quilt lay unfolded on a pine-framed couch. There were a few wine and liquor bottles on the wooden table. The makings of dinner were spread out on the counter—a box of pasta, assorted dishes and utensils, a jar of alfredo sauce, and a package of uncooked chicken. The interior was nearly as cold as the outside, so there was no smell of rotting food.

Delaney positioned herself on the other side of the door, which she closed behind them. "A bit chilly."

"Let's see where that doorway takes us."

"The cabins are one bedroom. They're all arranged around a center water well and fireplace with the bedroom in the back. See the well pump?"

He did now that she mentioned it. A handle and spigot through the floor beside the hearth. *Smart.* "You've rented one before?"

She grinned. "I've been *in* them before when I was a teenager. We didn't pay to stay here."

He walked across the living area. "Juvenile delinquent."

"Goody two shoes."

By unspoken agreement, Delaney again covered Leo as he

walked down a short hall—more of a connecting door with a large frame and jamb than a hallway—into the back of the house. The fireplace opened onto the foot of a bed with four thick pine posts. The bathroom occupied one side of the room. It looked like a modern addition. A small sink and mirror. A tub with a shower head extending above a circular rod and white curtain. A partitioned but open area with a composting toilet on a pedestal.

Leo liked the vibe. Under the right circumstances, walking into this bedroom with Delaney might have been cozy. Romantic. Exciting.

But not tonight.

Because tonight, a nude woman was stretched spread-eagle on the bed, wrists and ankles tied to the four posts, blindfold over her eyes, and scarf around her neck.

He fought an urge to say, "I'm sorry, ma'am," and avert his eyes to spare her dignity.

It didn't matter. If the blue tinge to her skin was any indication, she was beyond caring.

FIVE

Delaney slipped her hands into crime scene gloves from her duty belt, then pressed two fingers to the woman's carotid.

"Nothing," she said to Leo.

No pulse anyway, but the woman had been roughed up. Dried blood below her nose. A bruise on her cheek. Maybe additional injuries. Had she known what was happening to her? Cried out, in pain or pleasure? Or had she just lost consciousness and slipped away? She was past sharing her secrets now. Delaney stared at her, thinking. She didn't dare disturb the scene. Or cover the poor woman with a blanket. She'd wait for the crime scene techs and not risk messing up evidence collection.

"Is she stiff?" Leo said.

"No rigor mortis."

"The cold could have really slowed things down."

"Are we sure this is the woman we were sent to check on?"

He pulled out his phone and showed her the screen. "Here's the driver's license photo Teton County sent over. Annabeth Dillon. What do you think?" He was staring at the woman's face.

"It'd say it's her, but we'll need more. Or a real ID."

"Agreed."

Delaney scanned for a purse. A suitcase lay open on a collapsible luggage stand. She walked back into the front room. A hobo-type bag sat on a chair at the two-seater kitchen table. She fished through it, looking for phone numbers, notes, restaurant receipts. Anything useful. The woman kept it tidy, though, and, other than a wallet, there was nothing interesting. Not even a phone. She unzipped the wallet. The first thing she saw was a photo of a man. She pulled it out of the plastic sleeve. No name written on the back. Next she came to a driver's license and credit cards. She nodded. "Driver's license for Annabeth Mertz Dillon."

"I'll radio it in," Leo said, his voice coming through the cold fireplace opening.

"I wish we had some crime scene gear."

"I'll make sure we get everything we need brought up to us. Along with techs and an ambulance. This one is going to require the services of Dr. Watson." An elected coroner—the owner of the biggest funeral home in the county—handled most deaths. When homicide or unusual circumstances was suspected, the county had the option to call in the forensic pathologist, something they'd had to do far too frequently lately.

"And have someone check on Kat and Carrie for me. Please."

Leo appeared in the doorway. "Anything you'd like relayed to Zeke?"

Delaney side-eyed him. "No, thank you."

Sometimes she thought she was nothing to Leo but a friend and partner. Others, she believed he had feelings for her. Now, she was pretty sure the feeling he had was jealousy. Maybe one of these days they'd break down and talk it through. The thought was about as appealing as a lobotomy. Honestly, though, since they'd left the bar, she'd forgotten about Zeke. Death was more pressing than an old hook-up.

She'd call him tomorrow. He was still intriguing.

Leo keyed his mic and started transmitting. Delaney roamed the house, looking for evidence. She started in the kitchen. Two plates. Two bowls. Two forks. All unused. The chicken frozen. The alfredo sauce jar partially frozen and cracked. She opened the refrigerator, a propane model. A plastic container of grocery store blueberry muffins and a tub of butter. She closed it. At the table, two champagne glasses with dregs in them—a possibility for fingerprints and saliva. An empty bottle of Prosecco. Absaroka Double Cask Gin 49 with the lid off and two mostly empty glasses beside it—also full of possibilities for identification.

Whoever had been here, Annabeth appeared to have abandoned dinner preparations for bedroom activities. Which suggested she'd been enthusiastic about her partner. Combine that with the lack of signs of a struggle and what did that tell them—a new lover? An occasional hook-up? A steady partner who she'd been separated from? Leo had mentioned a frantic husband back home. Delaney needed to find out more about Annabeth, but sparse cell signal and no WiFi didn't exactly put information at her fingertips.

She knelt in front of the blocky Futon and lowered her head to look under it. Nothing but a few dust bunnies. Lifted the cushion. Clean. She checked the boots and socks at the hearth. Women's styles. A woman's coat, hat, and gloves hanging by the door. No business cards. No misplaced cell phone. No additional wallet or personal effects that would point to the second person who had been here.

She moved back into the bedroom and walked the bathroom area. One toothbrush. One hairbrush. One used towel. She paced to the other side of the room, opening drawers in a small chest and a bedside table. Empty, save a copy of the New Testament with no creases in its spine. The tops were bare of personal items.

Again, she lowered herself to the ground, this time to look under the bed. There was something there, but on the far side. She hurried over and pulled it out between two fingers. When she saw what it was, she was glad for her gloves. A condom. Used and full of evidence. Sex ending in death was bad enough. But something about the used condom made it worse. Wouldn't whoever-this-man-was have stopped when he realized Annabeth was in distress? Was dead? Of course, a decent human wouldn't have hit her and would have called for help or reported the situation, anonymously if nothing else. Delaney bagged and marked evidence with a growing sense of dread.

The last place to search was the suitcase. It was filled with women's items. Mostly winter wear, but a few pieces of barely-there lingerie as well. A tryst had been anticipated. She lifted the clothes aside and found a makeup bag, a blow dryer, expensive perfume, organic creams, birth control pills, and feminine deodorizers. Delaney scrutinized the deodorizer with a frown. Deodorizers specifically for *down there*? Was that something women did now?

It had been nearly a year since she'd had sex. What if she and Zeke ended up going down that road? Ugh. She didn't even want to think about it. If it required special products, she'd be better off staying home and playing Monopoly with the girls.

She straightened, pondering all she'd seen. Annabeth hadn't tied her own hands and feet to the bed and scarf around her neck. This was a homicide. Someone had been here who at best had fled the scene after a horrible sex accident, and, at worst, had taken Annabeth's life deliberately. There'd been no tracks or footprints outside from the direction she and Leo had come in, but fresh snow could have covered them since Annabeth's death. Or there might be some leading out in a different direction.

Then a thought raised hair on her arms. The perpetrator might still be in the area if he had been weathered in. They hadn't checked the other cabins. The doer could be watching them now. Could have them in his sights. She had to check it out, and most of what she could still do in this cabin would be done better once their equipment and help arrived. Semen, hair, fibers, fingerprints—crime scene techs would handle them.

"Leo?"

He was putting his radio away. "All good. Crime scene is on the way. Messages have been delivered, and I am told Carrie shot Clara a peace sign when she and Kat left, not too long after us."

"Good. I was just thinking about the other cabins."

"They're unoccupied."

She held up the baggie with the used condom in it. "Maybe. But we have a party of interest to find. A possible murderer. If I was him I would have high-tailed it off the mountain, but what if he couldn't?"

Leo took the baggie and grimaced. "We need to search the other cabins."

She tapped a finger to her temple. "Great minds thinking alike."

"What does your great mind think about keys?"

"That they won't be too hard to find, that we have an hour until the troops arrive, and that the cabins are small. But you could radio in and be patched through to the owner, vacation be damned. She'll need to be informed anyway."

Leo pulled his radio back out.

"While you do that, I'll be outside looking around."

"Wait for me."

Delaney headed for the door anyway. When they'd first started working together, Delaney had been Leo's superior. Deputy Investigator to his Deputy. Then Coltrane Fentworth had died in office, leaving a vacancy, and her old enemy Crispin

Allen became her new temporary boss. Crispin, too, didn't survive his term, although he would have been ousted for fraud if he had. Leo, Delaney, and Joe were probably the only people alive who knew that Crispin's suicide was more likely a hit, with Jefe behind it. The county commissioners had asked Delaney to step into the sheriff's role, but she had declined, to focus on Kat and Carrie. Leo had accepted the position when they'd offered it to him. It had changed the dynamic between them somewhat. Leo had other duties to perform that prevented him from partnering with Delaney as much as they had before, which meant she worked solo at times and alternated between teaming up with Joe and Tommy at others. She also deferred to him publicly, for the good of the team. But in their partnership dynamic, she still took the lead and even ignored or defied him, just as she had before the star on his chest was upgraded.

If it bothered Leo, he didn't show it, often. "Delaney, wait."

She rolled her eyes at him. "I'm an armed, experienced law enforcement officer."

But she couldn't help but shiver as she went out alone into the cold, cold, dark.

SIX

Leo muttered to himself as he walked away from the cabin where Annabeth Dillon lay dead. "What do you have against backup, Delaney?" The cabin next door was only fifty feet away, but through the deep snow it was slow going.

He stopped at the front door. No Delaney was out front. No lights were on inside. He tried the doorknob and it gave—had it been unlocked already or by his partner? He opened the door and poked his head inside. "Delaney?" He paused. No answer. "Anyone?" Again, silence. "This is Sheriff Leo Palmer." He always felt weird calling himself sheriff, but interim sheriff was too much of a mouthful and begged explanation.

He didn't have to explain it this time, though.

He stayed silent, listening for breathing or scuffling. He flipped on the light switch. The place was a dusty version of the cabin he'd come from, with covers over all the furniture. No wet or snowy prints in the dust to show Delaney had been through it. No disturbances at all, in fact.

He closed the door and went back outside, shining his flash-light on the ground. He should have done that in the first place, he decided. He swung the beam back over the ground he'd already covered. Definitely Delaney had come to this cabin and to the front door. He shone it toward the path to the third cabin. She'd also traversed that ground. A sense of urgency came over him. He broke into a high-stepping trot through the powder and hit the next door, panting.

He threw open the unlocked door and repeated the same song and dance as at cabin number two. "Sheriff Palmer. Anyone here?"

Same result, although this time there was melting snow on the floor. She'd gone in. Two sets of prints, identical to each other except one was exiting. He slammed the door, checked her snow tracks, and ran after them, sliding to a stop at cabin four, where the door was ajar.

"Delaney!" he shouted, adding a muttered, "Dammit."

He poked his head inside as he flicked the light switch. No light came on, so he turned the switch off then on again. Nothing. But there *was* light in the room, coming from the fireplace. Low light. A fire had been burning. Only embers were left.

Using his flashlight, he checked the floor, and his heart slammed in his throat.

Tracks everywhere. A scuffle. Furniture overturned. Broken glass on the floor.

And blood. Way too much blood.

SEVEN

Stupid, stupid, stupid, Delaney chanted to herself as she ran after the beam of her flashlight. Even if it had been too dark to see smoke from the chimney, she should have noticed the smell of smoke from the fireplace before she barged into the last cabin. The person hiding out in it had jumped her, smashing a lamp across her head before she could get her bearings. As she'd flailed her way to the ground, she'd knocked over a chair and end table. More like splintered the end table. She'd managed to grab an ankle and slow the perpetrator down, but they'd still gotten a serious head start before she regained her feet, decided the pain to her head wasn't life threatening, and gone after them.

Now she was charging after a phantom through the dark forest. Branches slapped her across the face. Obstacles buried in the snow tripped her up—logs, rocks, uneven terrain. She fought for stability, to keep from twisting an ankle, and was thankful for her winter rough terrain boots. Sweat trickled down her back. It was grueling, her head hurt, and she was shockingly lightheaded, but at least the tracks were easy to follow in the snow. Too easy. Which led to a worry. Her suspect wasn't using a light, so she couldn't see them. She could run up on them unaware. If they were armed, that would be bad for her.

There's a better way to do this.

She stopped and grabbed her radio. "Leo, I'm in pursuit of a suspect through the woods." She paused to gulp air. "Should be a clear path from the fourth cabin. Bring the snowmobile and catch up with me." She re-holstered her radio. Gulped more air. Would her words even be intelligible through her heavy breathing?

She pointed her flashlight downward. There were red drops in the snow. Was her suspect bleeding. But then she touched her temple where the lamp had hit her. She winced. Her fingers came away slick with blood—the source of her lightheadedness, and the drops at her feet.

Nothing I can do about it now.

She resumed her jog, her thighs and butt screaming in protest.

Leo's voice crackled through the silent forest on her radio. "10-4. I'm right behind you."

Seconds later, she heard the snowmobile engine roar to life. For a moment, she considered stopping to wait for him, but every second counted. She kept her legs pumping. Her lungs burned, her heart hammered, and her head screamed. The tracks in her beam never seemed to falter. Whoever the person was that had attacked her, they were uninjured and in good shape.

Delaney was no slouch when it came to fitness. Years as a trucker hadn't done her any favors, but when she'd come back to work as a deputy, she'd begun working out religiously. Her endurance and strength could be the difference between life and death—her own, a suspect's, or a citizen's. She considered it a job requirement, and it galled her that others in her profession, even her own department—with Joe Tarver a prime example—didn't always feel the same way. Leo's commitment to his fitness was one of the many things she respected about him. They occasionally worked out together, pushing each other, and it was good for both of them. He was planning to institute a health incentive plan at the department. She thought it was a great idea.

She realized her mind was wandering. *Focus on now.*

The snowmobile headlight suddenly brightened the forest around her, and the sound of its engine grew louder. She stepped aside, shoved her flashlight back into her belt, and bent over, hands on knees, back heaving. Leo pulled to a stop beside her.

She shooed him backwards. "I'll drive."

He scooted to the rear without argument. "You okay?"

She climbed on. "I'll be fine."

"You don't look it."

"Head wounds bleed like a mother."

"I think I lost your helmet. Take mine."

"Doesn't matter. I'm not falling off. Hang on tight." She goosed the throttle before he could argue.

He lurched and snaked his arms around her waist.

Accelerating, she squinted to minimize the impact of wind on her eyes. The branch slaps that had been irritating at a slow run became painful at the speed of a snowmachine. They'd leave angry welts. To combat the uneven snow and terrain, she crouched over the seat, absorbing bumps and providing steering leverage with her legs. In minutes, her upper body was as tired as her thighs from jerking on the handlebars.

Come on, come on. Where are you?

She realized that their path was gradually, steadily turning to the right. The suspect was looping. When she'd been running, the turn had been so gradual that she hadn't picked up on it. Either the suspect had lost their bearings, or they had a destination in mind, which would mean they knew the area.

Delaney knew it, too, but not intimately, and she'd lost her sense of direction in the slow speed chase.

She shot out of the trees and into a pasture that ran alongside a highway, accelerating along the now-straight trail through the open area. Suddenly she had no doubt where they were. In the summer months, cattle and horses grazed here as tourists drove by gawking and searching for moose and elk. Now, somewhere beneath the snow, were the deadly tops of fence posts with barbed wire strung between them. All she could do was keep an eye out for the hazards and hope for the best.

We should see the suspect by now.

She reached the road, which looked to have been plowed earlier but was covered by a few inches of fresh snow. "Do you see anything?" she turned her mouth toward Leo and shouted over the noise of the engine.

She felt Leo shifting and rotating his head behind her. Then, just as he started to answer, she spotted something.

He must have, too, because he pointed at the road. "Vehicle tracks. One set."

Delaney killed the engine and wiped her eyes. She climbed off the snowmobile, following Leo who'd slid to the ground ahead of her. Together they followed footprints across the road, where they ended beside wheel tracks, which led down the far side of the highway.

"Shit," Leo said.

Delaney couldn't have agreed more. "But we know one thing."

"What's that?"

"The vehicle was in the lane heading west." She pointed at the ground. "Our suspect got in on the passenger side."

She grabbed her radio and called in an Attempt to Locate on the passenger in a vehicle heading west through the mountains. No descriptions. It was the best they could do, and it seemed like nothing at all. What else could go wrong today?

Surly kids, a ruined birthday party, a dead body, a whack to her head, and a lost suspect.

But as soon as she had the thought she regretted it. Of course, more could go wrong. So, she wasn't surprised at all when she turned the key in the snowmobile's ignition... and nothing happened. Around her, snow started falling again.

They were five miles from the cabin. In the middle of the night. In a snowstorm. With a suspect on the loose who'd already assaulted her once.

EIGHT

"Where you been, dressed like that, partner?" The driver turned up the heater in his vintage pickup.

The passenger rubbed his hands on his jeans. He was just glad he'd already had his boots on when the unexpected visitor had caught him by surprise. Hitting her in the head had been instinctual. Sure, he'd heard the snowmobile earlier, but that wasn't unusual in the area. The Bighorn Mountains were a snowmobiler's wet dream, and the Mountain High Cabins were right on one of the major north side trails. He'd just finished stoking the fire—he was keeping it low, conserving wood, and trying not to betray his presence—when the knock had sounded. He'd grabbed the lamp and held it over his head. By the time the word "deputy" had come out of her mouth, he'd already clocked her, snatched up his coat, and tried to bolt. She'd nearly caught him, snagging his ankle, but he'd shaken her off and gotten the hell out of there, quite aware that he'd possibly committed an unintended felony.

Just one more night. That's all he'd needed. After being stranded, he'd been planning on trekking to his car in the morning. Damn Wyoming. Of all the luck.

He answered the driver. "Uh, hiking. Got turned around. Lucky I ended up on the road."

"At night?" The driver shot him a look, then trained his eyes back on the highway, which made the passenger feel better. Snow. Ice. Steep grades. Sharp turns. Pitch blackness. It deserved the man's full attention if they were going to make it anywhere alive, and he'd already cheated death or something like it once tonight.

"Hadn't planned to be but couldn't find my way back."

"No gloves. No water. You're not from around here, are you?"

"No. Afraid I'm not."

"Good thing I came along, or you mighta got yourself killed."

The passenger glanced at the driver, past the shotgun and rifle in the gun rack across the back window. The man smelled like chewing tobacco, had the tanned, weathered look of someone who worked outdoors, and the lean build of a cowboy, but his hair was gray. "What are you doing up here?"

"I have a few cows I couldn't find at the end of the grazing season. They refused to let themselves get caught once I did find 'em. Now I'm stuck throwing 'em hay all winter unless I want to kiss a few grand goodbye. And I gotta set it up like a photo shoot and post it to Facebook or all the do-gooders who don't understand ranching get in my business accusing me of animal cruelty and leaving the uncooperative dumbasses to die."

"Won't they freeze to death?"

"Probably not if the winter ain't too harsh. But nothing's certain in life 'cept death and taxes. I just do what I can."

"Where are you heading now?"

"Well, I figured since I was up here already I'd head down into Greybull. Got a woman there I been courtin'."

The passenger had no idea where Greybull was, but he'd take a ride as far as he could get. "That's where I'm going, too."

The driver looked surprised. "You have family there?"

"Nah. Just, um, heard it was a great town. Thought I'd spend a few days there before I move on."

"Want me to drop you somewhere?"

"Wherever you're going would be fine."

"No can do. You'd be competition for my lady."

"Any hotel. The cheaper the better."

"That'll be The Antler." The driver offered his hand to shake. "By the way, my name's Clem."

The passenger took it. He said the first name that came into his mind. "I'm Kevin."

"Pleased to make your acquaintance."

"Thanks for the ride. Do you mind if I close my eyes for a while? I'm wiped."

"Not at all. I'll wake you up when we get there."

The man whose name was not Kevin closed one eye and kept the other one open. He was expecting more trouble. Maybe even from the wary old cuss at the wheel beside him.

NINE

Three hours later, Leo and Delaney unloaded their snowmobiles and detached the trailer at the sheriff's department yard in Sheridan. Luckily, they hadn't had to walk too far earlier before they'd reached the crime scene techs by radio and gotten a ride back to their truck. They'd accompanied them to the cabin where Leo had tried to convince Delaney to go to the emergency room for her head wound, but she'd refused. Her compromise was letting one of the EMTs clean her up and close the cut with butterfly bandages. Delaney and Leo had left the group there to finish working the scene, with Dr. Watson examining Annabeth prior to moving her and the EMTs bringing her body down to Sheridan.

Then they'd picked up their snowmobiles and headed down the mountain.

Delaney had driven while Leo made notes on his electronic tablet. He'd started an investigation plan using a PDF template he'd created himself. One of his first acts as sheriff had been to procure identical tablets for the entire department. Then he'd issued a paperless reports procedure and introduced streaming video meetings, intra-department chats, and shared worksites for file storage and applications. He'd even loaded a special mapping feature just for Delaney. As long as he held the job, he'd make it his mission to bring the department into the twenty-first century. Or at least the twentieth. His next big move was to activate the tracking software on all the personnel's portable radio units, which was accurate within fifteen feet fifty percent of the time and thirty feet ninety-five percent. Their vehicles were already tracked, and that information was accessible to anyone within the department. But the radio information gave Leo exclusive round-the-clock access to the location data and history of his deputies, as long as they had their radios with them. Theirs was a big, rugged county, and it made him feel more secure about keeping them safe. And, given that his original assignment to Kearny had been to ferret out a bad cop in the sheriff's department, he liked having the data at his fingertips. Just in case.

Only he hadn't told anyone he'd done it. He wasn't sure how they'd take it. Helpful boss or invader of their privacy? He would tell Delaney, soon. Now was not the time, though.

"Why don't I drive now? I'd like you to look at the plan I started for the case," he said as they walked back to his truck from the snowmobiles.

She groaned. "Can't you just print it out for me tomorrow?"

He went to the driver's side and climbed in. His nose wrinkled. Something in the truck smelled like a wet dog. Something as in the two of them. When Delaney was settled, he handed her the notebook. "Think about the planet. It won't kill you to read a screen." His phone chimed with a text.

"What is the life cycle material and energy cost of that hunk of electronica? Prove to me this is better for the planet than paper," Delaney said.

Leo sighed.

"Fine. If I have no choice."

Leo checked his phone.

The text was from Joe.

Word from Sugar is your snowmobile was planted on a stump on the way into the crime scene.

He groaned and typed fast.

Wrong. Delaney and I just decided to ride in together... after I got stuck in a drift and the engine flooded. NO STUMPS.

Delaney held out the tablet.
"Leo, I can't even get this thing on the right page."
"Hand it to me."
He flipped to the plan and looked at all the blank spots.

Crime: Homicide of Annabeth Dillon
Victim: Annabeth Dillon of Jackson, WY
Known associates:
Family:
Work:
Previous residences:
Record:
Issues: bound, gagged, strangled during sexual contact; used condom found under the bed; no laptop, phone, or tablet at the scene
Online presence:
Phone records: submit request ASAP
Suspect: Man in cabin four who assaulted DI Delaney Pace and fled

To-do List:

- Interview husband, family, co-workers, and friends

- Obtain social media and email app logins from family, if available
- Obtain and analyze any fingerprint, DNA, and fiber evidence
- Find suspect who fled
- Review findings of forensic pathologist
- Boyfriend?
- Enemies?
- Medical conditions?
- Reason for travel?
- Talk to owner of cabins about occupancy, cameras, who has access

He glanced at Delaney. Her eyes were bloodshot and bleary. "The gist of it is that we don't know shit. We can talk about the rest tomorrow."

Delaney smiled and leaned her head against the seat, eyes closed. "I can get behind a plan like that."

Leo pulled out of the parking lot and pointed the truck toward the Pace homestead. "Are the girls safely home?"

"Ugh, I haven't even glanced at my phone. Winter mountain night driving pulling a trailer and all." She straightened and read her phone. "No texts." She shook her head. "They both quit sharing their location with me, as of tonight when they decided I was the worst excuse for an adoptive mother ever. So, I have no idea. But they'll lose their phones for unsharing with me. And be grounded if they're not home."

After a few months with Freddy under his roof and comparing what Adriana was going through to Delaney's situation, Leo was starting to appreciate how much harder girls at this age were than boys. Freddy stuffed his dirty clothes under his bed and forgot to brush his teeth most days. But he hugged his mother and told his uncle Leo he loved him every time he left the house. "What's the status of the adoptions?"

"We have our final hearing soon."

"Are you expecting any problems?"

"Other than the stink they've already raised about single parenting and the grave danger Kat has been in repeatedly since I took over her guardianship?"

Leo winced. "I'm sorry."

"I swear if I just marry the first schlub I see tomorrow, this will sail through. Even if he's a deadbeat."

You could marry me. The words in his head surprised him. He bit them back. "Let me know if you need any help," he said instead.

He gripped the steering wheel as emotion crashed over him like a wave off Black's Beach. He'd never wanted to be married. He didn't want to get married now, did he? Then a horrible thought hit him. Zeke was in town. What if Delaney proposed marriage to him? Zeke was a playboy. He might string her along to get her into bed. Or back into bed, if Leo's radar had pinged correctly at the chemistry and history between them. Leo would have to nurse her heart after Zeke broke it. Because he knew for a fact Zeke wouldn't marry Delaney. Leo might not be able to have her, but she wouldn't be Zeke's either.

"I will," she said. "Time for a subject change. Did you know Adriana is going to meet her online crush in person?"

It took him a moment to return from the wild path his thoughts had gone down, but when he did, he groaned. "She falls in and out of love faster than she can change shoes. The only relationship she's had that worked was Freddy's dad, and I'm not sure it would have lasted long term." Adriana's husband Jim had died in a house fire with their parents while he, Adriana, and Freddy were at Disneyland. He still couldn't figure out how in the middle of the day none of them had escaped. The fire department theorized there had been a carbon monoxide leak before the fire started. It was possible. But the house had sensors, so Leo had a difficult time buying it. Anyway, Adriana and Jim had been on the rocks before his death. "I pity any man she dates. The sucker is in for heartbreak." He turned left onto the highway out past the Loafing Shed and toward the turnoff to the Pace homestead.

"Speaking of relationships that hurt, I've been thinking about the guy we were chasing. I'll be interested in Dr. Watson's estimate of Annabeth's time of death. Doesn't it seem weird to you that a guy would kill a woman he was having sex with—"

Leo held up one finger, steering with the other hand. "If it wasn't an accident. Dr. Watson may tell us it was. Or even natural causes coincidental to the act."

"Okay, okay, doesn't it seem weird that the woman a guy was having sex with would die, and that he would leave her there and move into the third cabin down from her dead body? If he killed her or was afraid he'd be blamed for killing her, wouldn't he clean up any evidence and get the hell out of there?"

Leo flashed his lights at an oncoming vehicle using its full beams. The driver left them on—the nighttime motorist equivalent of giving him the finger. "That would probably be the normal response. But he didn't appear to have a vehicle."

"He could have used hers. Or walked. Or flagged down a ride, which is apparently what he did when he got away from us."

"So, maybe he was injured or sick and had to lay low."

"Maybe."

"Or he was obsessed with her or heartbroken and couldn't tear himself away. Paralyzed with grief and fear."

"He wasn't paralyzed by anything when I ran into him."

Leo tried a new angle. "It's always possible he's not our guy."

"Then why attack me?"

"Because you're as scary as a mountain lion and snuck up on him."

She snorted. "I announced myself."

"I'm serious. It could just be a coincidence he was there. He could have been hiding from debt collectors. The law, for something unrelated. From society, while he was writing his manifesto. From his ex-wife to avoid paying child support."

Delaney was nodding. "All true. And yet, I don't believe in coincidences."

"They're statistically less likely to occur but still possible."

"You can really be annoying sometimes, you know that?"

"Seems like you've mentioned it before. And you can really be a danger to yourself." Leo turned on the blinker and made another left, this time onto the country road that led to Delaney's place. "What were you thinking going into those houses alone?"

"That it was highly unlikely the person who killed Annabeth Dillon would still be hanging around. That I was just checking boxes on a list of things that had to be done. And that I'm highly trained and capable."

"How did that work out for you?" He pointed at the bandages on her head. "If I was a half decent sheriff, I'd write this up and stick it in your file."

Delaney laughed. "Thank God you're not half decent, then."

Leo turned into her long driveway. "Fresh tire tracks leading in."

Delaney frowned. "More than one set." She flipped her phone over. "It's midnight. I hope one of those is someone heading back out again. And not my girls taking advantage of my absence."

"Maybe it's Skeeter?"

"Possibly. I should have asked him to follow them home.

But he'd been drinking. This was his night off." She ground her teeth. "If they're having a party, I'm gonna kill them."

"Those don't look like enough tracks for a party."

"Friends over without permission is a party in my book."

Lights were on in the house. Of course, it was a Friday night. The girls might be staying up late. Or they could have left a light on for Delaney. Tire tracks and lights didn't mean they were entertaining unauthorized guests. He hoped not, for their sakes, and Delaney's.

Leo pulled around the back of the house. What he saw made him hit the brakes so hard that Delaney's upper body fell forward, caught by the shoulder harness of her belt.

"Ouch! What is it?"

Shotgun Shelly was nowhere to be seen. But parked outside the Pace home was a Range Rover. One Leo was recently all too familiar with.

TEN

Jefe studied his new face in the tarnished bathroom mirror as he washed his hands. Some of the changes had been easy. Hair color—from brown to blond. Eye color—contacts hid the green with blue, although they irritated his eyes, and he didn't wear them often. A pair of glasses made him look brainier. Height—lifts inside his high-heeled cowboy boots. His weight was a little harder—he hadn't been able to stand the thought of being fat, so he shredded instead. He never would have dreamed he could lose forty pounds, but he had.

He dried his hands on a towel. Other changes were difficult, expensive, and time consuming. He touched his cheek implants, his nose, which was straightened from an old injury and stream-lined at the nostrils. His lips, which had been lifted. His jawline, which was sharper. His chin, less jutting.

"I'm Brad Pitt's younger, slightly less good-looking brother." He grinned at himself.

No one, not even his own parents, would have recognized him. He'd already tested that theory by walking down the streets of Kearny, then stopping at the joint police station and sheriff's department, where he'd applied for a driver's license, loitering long enough for his sister Delaney and the interim sheriff with the checkered past to walk by. He'd made sure to wish them both a good morning. Neither had done so much as a double-take.

He strolled back to the kitchen table and the remains of his pre-dawn breakfast. Cold coffee. He touched his finger to the crumbs of a cinnamon roll he'd bought as part of a dozen earlier in the week, then licked the sweet bits off. Being home felt good after so long in Mexico. His work ethic had definitely taken a hit in Mexico. Keeping early hours he could do, but he needed something to get him motivated again. Something to put the fire back in his belly.

He wiped his fingers on his jeans, then opened his laptop, typed a message in a chat screen and hit send. During his three months away, he'd stayed on top of happenings in Kearny County and Wyoming through Ellen Day, who he'd deputized to act on his behalf. He chuckled. Deputized. Like his sister, wild child turned deputy.

Ellen was no deputy, but the county commissioner was sharp, trusted by the naïve public, and utterly ruthless. She'd set things up for his return—renting this house and procuring a new identity for him. And she'd left his sister alone while he was gone. Jefe wouldn't hesitate to kill Delaney if it became necessary, but only as a last resort. And he would be the one to do it. Him and only him.

He sent a request to FaceTime with Ellen.

She answered within seconds, as he'd known she would. Her Icelandic blue eyes, sharp features and short platinum hair filled the screen. The hair was mussed, like she was still in bed. If she held the phone any closer, he'd be able to count her nose hairs.

"Hello, lover." Her voice was a coo. "It's too early for a booty call."

The two of them had been bumping uglies since before he'd

left town. She'd visited him a few times during his transformation and recovery. The woman was tall and athletic. Inventive. Assertive. But he'd grown tired of her. He'd been crazy to mix business with pleasure, because there was no pleasure when it came time to separate the two. He'd put her off for the two weeks he'd been back, but she wasn't taking the hint.

"I need a status report," he said.

"On?"

"The upstart who is about to challenge for the U.S. Senate seat."

"I told you I'd handle it, and I did."

"Specifics?"

"The less you know—and the less our boss knows—the better, right?"

"My boss. There won't be any blowback?"

"None at all."

"All right. Any progress slowing the money that's flowing the wrong way lately?"

Her laugh was high-pitched. "Of course. That problem will be fixed real soon."

"Anything you want to tell me about that?"

"Same answer as before. Let me protect you."

He rotated his neck. Ellen was becoming a literal pain in it.

"I can take those kinks out for you, baby."

"Last issue. What have you been able to do to generate new income streams?" When local developer Hugh Pinehurst had gone on a crazed killing spree, it had tanked their plans for an entertainment complex in Kearny that would have cleaned their dirty cash and generated new funds for the cause. They needed a revenue stream to replace it.

"I think people underreport their business income in this county. I need to do some research on the best potential sources. I'll get back with you."

"Time is short. Our costs will be high."

"You're preaching to the choir. I handled this in your absence, you know?"

"We handled it together. Just like we're doing now. You report to me, I report to my boss. There's a hierarchy."

"Of course." She licked her lips. "I hear rumors your sister's boyfriend may run for sheriff."

"I assumed." Pending developing Leo as a contact, he'd need someone else on the inside. It sure wouldn't be Delaney. But he had an old contact he could resurrect. The time had come.

"I thought she would."

"She's raising my daughter."

"Which is the only good thing about that bitch. She and Leo have been nothing but thorns in my side ever since the Pinehurst fiasco. It's bordering on harassment."

He'd had enough of her. "My next call's coming in. I gotta go." He disconnected.

Blowing a raspberry through his lips, he leaned back in his chair. Was Ellen trying to protect him or was she trying to wrest control from him? Reaching out one hand, he flipped to his email.

His inbox held a message from his boss's private email account from the night before.

I met with Ellen while she was in Cheyenne last week. She's a go-getter. We seem to be on the same page. I'm glad we have her.

His blood boiled. Ellen hadn't told him about the meeting. He sent a reply.

Did you set the meeting up?

A minute later—during which he cursed and beat himself up for ever bringing Ellen in to help him—he had an answer.

> No, she was here and reached out to me. Used your code
> word. I thought you sent her.

Ellen had closed up his alter ego Larry Pilsner's affairs when Jefe had hurried out of Kearny. Electronics, files, his worldly possessions. He'd instructed her to destroy it all, unread. But what if she'd made copies? Gone through it? He snorted. There was no "what if." She clearly had. If the worst she'd done was secure a meeting with his boss, he might be able to forgive her.

But he was going to make her pay.

Oh, how she was going to pay. But in this moment, he couldn't show weakness. Couldn't admit she was working behind his back.

> *I meant did she call you ahead of time for you to set it up? Her*
> *role will be diminishing now that I'm back, but she's been*
> *useful. I'll update you later when you have time for a call.*

God, how he hoped his phone didn't ring in the next few minutes. He wasn't ready to talk to the big guy. He closed his email app. One of the things Ellen set up for his new identity was social media history. One of his tabs was open to Facebook. What he saw chilled him to the marrow.

PROMINENT JACKSON ACTIVIST AND BUSINESSWOMAN FOUND DEAD IN MOUNTAIN CABIN IN THE BIGHORNS

This was a much bigger problem than Ellen meeting with the boss behind his back.

ELEVEN

Delaney woke alone on Saturday morning, her eyes crusty and brain sluggish. For a moment, things felt normal. Like it was any other day. Then she remembered the night before and sat bolt upright.

Zeke was in her guest room.

She wasn't sure who'd been more shocked to find him at her house the night before—her or Leo. Leo had all but demanded he come in with her, but she'd sent him home. The look on his face, though. The day to discuss the boundaries of their relationship was drawing near. When she'd mistaken Adriana for his wife or girlfriend instead of his sister a few months earlier, it had hurt. It had hurt so, so much. But that was a turning point for her. She and Leo weren't going to happen, no matter how much she wished they'd met under different circumstances, in a different life. She was a relationship killer, and he was her boss, at least temporarily, and her partner for who knew how long. She couldn't ruin what they had. It wasn't fair to him or to her. She was going to have to move on from the idea of them together. What might be harder is that she was going to have to let him move on, too.

She just hoped she was strong enough when the time came that he did.

In the meantime, Zeke was here. Zeke, who she had once upon a time believed was the one who got away. She wasn't looking for permanence, then or now. He hadn't been either. That made him almost perfect. There would be no relationship for her to ruin. No one to hurt.

Last night when she'd walked into the house, the snow had been starting to fall in earnest. Zeke was sitting at her kitchen table, playing Apples to Apples with Kat and Carrie, like there was nothing in the world he would rather have been doing. Their sounds were raucous. Dudley, their manic French bull-dog, punctuated every laugh with his sharp barks.

Until they saw her.

"Aunt Delaney, your head. You're hurt!" Kat had said, jumping to her feet.

Dudley had barreled over to her, his low, portly black and white body wobbling like a Weeble. He put his front paws on her shin and licked her jeans.

"It didn't even need stitches. I'm fine." Delaney flapped her hand to show how little the injury mattered. "I see we have company."

"Zeke followed us to make sure we made it home okay. The roads were snowy."

"We told him we'd be fine, but he said this is what you and Leo would have wanted," Carrie added.

"How did you guys know he wasn't a stranger?" Delaney put her hands on her hips.

Zeke was grinning with his lips closed and eyes sparkling.

Kat said, "Adriana. She told us it wasn't up for debate, and that he'd been Leo's best friend since they were pimple-faced weaklings."

Zeke rose, shaking his head. "Hey, I was never a pimple-faced weakling. Leo was, sure, but not me." He walked into the kitchen. "We made apple cider. It's still hot. You're very well-stocked."

"Vestiges of my grandparents. I guess these days you'd call them preppers. Some of it rubbed off on me."

"You should see our cellar." Kat rolled her eyes. "We can vegetables and we buy ten of everything and keep it all down there."

"She's exaggerating."

"Plus, they were like religious freaks and made Aunt Delaney kneel in rocks until she recited Bible verses perfectly."

Her attempts to bond with her girls through shared trauma may have gone too far. "Kat, please."

"What? It's true."

"Sounds similar to my military training." Zeke smiled. There were mugs on the counter. He ladled cider into one and brought it to Delaney. "Tough call-out tonight?"

She finally smiled at him, grateful for the subject change. "Very tough. Thanks for making sure the girls were safe."

Carrie said, "Zeke called you an old flame. I told him you weren't *that* old."

Delaney's tiredness vanished. "Girls, bed. And say thank you."

"Thanks, Zeke," they chimed, then, giggling, walked down the hall bumping and jostling each other.

As much trouble as they'd been lately, just this simple interaction filled Delaney with a rush of love and gratitude. And she was relieved to see that Carrie, who bore the emotional and social wounds from a sexual relationship with a man older than her own father, wasn't reacting inappropriately around Zeke, as she had with Leo when she first met him. Months of therapy seemed to be helping, at least with that issue, although the therapist had warned Delaney upfront that the abuse could leave lasting scars.

"I hope you don't mind me being here. I can get going." Zeke's voice pulled her around.

"It was good of you to do this. I'm just afraid I'm not very good company after tonight. Homicide. Very remote area in the mountains. Snowmobile chase, foot chase.

"Assault."

"That. Tonight was—"

"Tonight was you being a sexy badass. Sit down. Let me take care of you. More cider?"

She looked in her mug. It was empty. "Sure."

He pulled a bottle out of a bag hanging from the arm of his chair. "And maybe a shot of this? Mary sold me a bottle at your bar when I asked for a recommendation." It was Koltiska Distillery's KO Original. A spicy liqueur made in nearby Sheridan.

Mary would have recommended iced tea if she'd known he was bringing it for Delaney, who wasn't much of a drinker. She'd never liked being out of control. Had seen too much bad behavior under the influence first-hand, growing up in and around a bar.

A shot sounded perfect now, though. "Sure. Just one."

He poured their drinks and took them to the coffee table in front of the couch. They sat down, starting on opposite ends. She felt nervous until they started drinking and catching up on their lives in the last decade. On their lives in general, really, since their previous encounter hadn't involved much talking. Before long they'd shed their footwear. Their jackets. Their socks. He was rubbing her fingers. Scooting closer. Kissing her hand. Lifting her hair. Complimenting her girly toenail polish and playing with the gold anklet with its dangling cross that she had kept hidden under boots, a long-ago gift from her mother. Stroking her cheek. Her skin tingled, partly from the second shot of KO she'd accepted and partly from the effect of his touch.

I'm sorry, Leo.

Then she felt something shake her shoulder.

Zeke's voice. "Delaney, wake up."

"What?"

"You fell asleep."

She was mortified. "I'm so sorry."

He'd laughed. "Don't be. I'm here with the most beautiful woman I've ever met and never got out of my head."

She groaned. "I have to work tomorrow. What time is it?"

"Two a.m. I'll get going."

"It's late. You're not familiar with the roads or the conditions. You shouldn't be out driving in this."

"What are you suggesting?" He looked hopeful.

"I have a guest room."

His face fell a little, but he soldiered into the bed on the other side of the wall from where she was now waking up.

She yawned and stretched. A scream pierced the air. It was from the living room. Delaney jumped out of bed. She'd raced to her gun safe and was punching in the code until she heard the girls giggling. Abandoning the gun, she put on a robe and slippers with her flannel PJs.

Her phone buzzed. She read the screen. It was only seven. Already a text from Leo.

Big Horn County picked up our guy last night driving into Shell in the only truck on the road. Made it even easier when the driver confirmed time and place of pickup. The suspect bolted but they caught him.

Her fingers flew.

You're just now telling me?

You were occupied. They held him in Greybull until the

storm broke. He'll be here within the hour. I need you
with me for interviews. His and the victim's husband
and other key witnesses.

The victim's husband—wasn't Annabeth Dillon from Jackson? That was a six-and-a-half-hour drive on dry pavement. Depending on how much snow had fallen—especially in the mountain ranges, of which there were two and change between Kearny and Jackson Hole—the journey could take ten hours. Maybe more. Had Mr. Dillon driven through the night? Or was Leo planning on the two of them heading west across the state?

She typed quickly.

Where?

Offices.

How'd they get here so fast?

They didn't. Video. Modern day stuff.

Delaney shook her head. At least she didn't have to navigate the technology without him. Still, she preferred in-person interviews. To see how people acted outside the camera lens. So much of what she picked up was non-verbal, like odor, body language, eye contact with someone outside the scope of a camera lens, and just the general vibe they exuded. But a video call did allow them to move this investigation forward, and it was better than just a phone call.

Fine. What time?

Do you have a conflict?

Zeke had been staying at Leo's house. Leo knew he'd overnighted at Delaney's.

On my way.

She stared at the phone, waiting for a reply from him. When none came, she went through a high-speed version of her morning routine in the bathroom. Back in her bedroom, she changed into her uniform. Strapped on her duty belt and gun. Drew her shoulders up and back with a deep breath.

"No big deal," she said to the woman in her dresser mirror. Then she walked into the kitchen to face her girls and her old fling.

TWELVE

Leo cleared his throat and straightened the papers on his desk. He'd banished the last vestiges of his office's last occupant, Crispin Allen, and restored it mostly to how it had looked when Fentworth Coltrane occupied it. Old West meets semi-modern law enforcement. Barbed wire and branding irons. FlexiCuffs and radios. The privacy and extra space were nice. The truth was, he missed sitting next to Delaney in the bullpen.

"Knock, knock." It was the woman herself at the door, then three feet across his desk from him before he'd responded to her. "Where's our suspect?"

Her green eyes bore into him. He scrutinized her for tells about how she spent the night. No bed head. No whisker burn. No love bites. *I don't want to know. I have to know. I can't ask her. I have to ask.* But he wouldn't.

His phone chimed, and he held up a finger as he read the message. "Waiting for us in interview room two. After you." He gestured at the door.

She strode down the hall in front of him. He shifted his eyes to the right over her shoulder, away from her shape and movement. *I can't run for sheriff and possibly end up stuck here subjected to watching her date other men.* His brain was in rebellion, refusing to think about all the things it needed to, focused on the one thing it shouldn't. Picturing Zeke and Delaney. A few months before, she'd dated Clint Rock-Below, an officer with the state police. He'd thought that was bad until his own childhood best friend had spent the night with her. Acid burned his stomach.

Delaney stopped suddenly and turned to face him. "I want the lead on this one." She pointed at the butterfly bandages peeking out of her hairline.

"You're emotionally impacted."

"I'm invested, not emotional."

Leo nodded. Delaney did excel at compartmentalization. "If you're sure, I'm good with it."

She gave him a crisp salute, then walked the last few steps to the door and jerked it open.

The rank scent of unwashed male met Leo at the door. A Big Horn County deputy sat across from a gaunt man with a fuzzy beard and short black hair. The suspect's eyes were deep-set and cast down at his feet. His hands were behind him, and Leo could tell he was cuffed. *Good.* He was not only a flight risk, he'd hurt Delaney.

Leo put his hand forward to the deputy.

The man rose and shook it, then did the same with Delaney.

"Thanks for the delivery," Leo said.

"No problem." He handed Leo some paperwork. "Can you sign for him?"

Leo clicked a pen from his pocket and scribbled his name. Then he leaned against the wall.

"All yours. I'll be going." The deputy grinned. "Gonna grab me one of those cinnamon rolls they make into French toast on my way out of town, over at the Cowpoke Café." And then he was gone, leaving them with their suspect and his stench.

Delaney yanked a chair from under the table. She pointed

at her bandages. "Thanks for the beauty mark. What's your name?"

The suspect didn't look up.

"Not in the mood to talk? That's okay. The sheriff can have you taken straight to holding pending charges of assaulting an officer. It's Saturday, and the judge is skiing at Big Sky this weekend, but I'm sure he'll get around to you first thing Monday morning."

The suspect grunted. "I'm warm. You'll feed me. Sounds all right to me." His voice sounded cocksure.

Leo's pulse quickened. The man was going to talk.

Delaney said, "Is that why you were in that cabin? For warmth and food?"

"It was either that or freeze to death."

"Why were you up there?"

He sighed. "Because the jackass I was hitching with dumped me out in the middle of the mountains. I was looking for shelter and saw the signs."

"When was this?"

"Two—no, three nights ago."

Leo and Delaney shared a look. Leo had called Shaina Pham, the owner of the Mountain High Cabins, early that morning. According to her, Annabeth had checked in three days ago. He needed to update Delaney on that conversation later.

"Did you see anyone else at the cabins?"

The suspect shifted his eyes down again. "No."

"That's funny. A woman checked in about the same time you got there."

"I wasn't exactly inviting people over for weenie roasts and s'mores."

"Now, why don't I believe you? Let me see. Oh, yeah, because I announced myself as a Kearny County deputy and you attacked me."

"You surprised me. And I was afraid you were there to arrest me since I broke into the cabin."

"Taking refuge from the weather? That's not a very serious charge. Assault is."

He raised his brows. "Which is why I took off."

"Listen, buddy—"

"Rufus. My name is Rufus Payne."

"Mr. Payne."

"Rufus."

"Fine. Rufus, you've got all the answers. But the fact is that a woman was murdered in cabin one, and you—"

Rufus leaned forward, frowning. "She was fine when I saw her."

For the first time, Leo saw something real in the man's eyes, and it was fear. *Good. He's not completely stupid.*

"So, now you saw her?"

Rufus hesitated. Leo could almost see the wheels turning in his brain. After a long pause, he said, "Yeah. Tall skinny woman."

Again, Delaney and Leo met eyes. This time her eyebrows arched. Leo kept his face neutral, but inside his pulse quickened. Their victim had been short and curvy.

"When did you see a tall, skinny woman?"

"It was late. I'd been asleep. I heard an engine outside and I looked out. She'd parked and was walking up to her cabin. I stayed away from the window so she wouldn't see me. But she was just fine."

Delaney was speeding up the tempo of the questions now that she had Rufus talking. "How was she when you went into her cabin?"

"I didn't go into her cabin or any other. I went back to bed."

"What about the short, curvy woman?"

"I didn't see a short, curvy woman."

"Did you see anyone else? A man? A moose? A bear? Anything?"

"Nothing."

"Tell me about this woman. What was she driving?"

"Didn't see it."

"This was before all the snow?"

"Before the big storm. There was snow on the ground, but the road was drivable if that's what you mean."

"Did you see any cars?"

"Nope. Doesn't mean there weren't any. Just means not from inside where I was, okay?"

"You said you went to sleep?" Delaney asked.

"After I warmed the place up, made some rice, ate, and showered."

"Mr. Payne, I mean Rufus, we have your fingerprints from Big Horn County. We will be taking a DNA sample. If you were in the cabin where the woman died, we'll find out."

"Take anything you want. The only thing I'm guilty of is squatting."

Delaney stood. "One last thing, Rufus. I'm about to look at your priors. What am I going to find?"

Rufus brushed his hand over his eyes. "Petty stuff mostly. A man has to eat."

"You said mostly. What's the one you don't want to tell me about?"

"I was charged. But I was acquitted." His face turned snarly. "Tell that to the people who live in my town. Once I was arrested, my life was over. And I didn't do shit. All the rest came after that."

"And what were you charged with?"

He looked away. The word came out with flying spittle. "Rape, okay? I was charged with rape."

THIRTEEN

"What do you think?" Delaney checked her phone. Nothing from the girls. Nothing from Zeke. He'd asked to see her that night. Wanted to surprise her with something that would blow her socks off, he'd said. *More like blow my dress up, I'll bet.*

Leo was booting up his laptop. "I think we're going to find his DNA and fingerprints all over that cabin."

Delaney pulled a chair closer to Leo's so they could fit both their images onscreen for their video interview of Annabeth Dillon's husband. "I don't think so."

"Why?"

"I don't think he's smart enough to lie. And his surprise about the murder seemed real."

"He was smart enough to make up a story about a woman who wasn't there."

"Why do you say that?"

"Come on, Annabeth had a hot date in a secret, remote location. We know the guy was there—we've got the used condom to prove it. Why would a woman show up in the middle of that?"

"You want me to come up with reasons?"

"Decent ones."

Delaney ticked ideas off, starting with her index finger. "Someone was spending the night after the date was over. A sister. A friend."

Leo gave her a thumbs down.

She ticked her middle finger. "She was coming over to join a threesome."

Another thumbs down. "The deed was done."

Ring finger. "She was seeking shelter, like Rufus."

Two thumbs down. "That place isn't a hotbed for vagrants."

Pinkie. "She was the boyfriend's wife or girlfriend, and she'd followed him."

He waffled his hand. "That's the only one that holds any water for me. But we've got to see where the evidence leads us." His phone chimed, then rang. He glanced at the screen and drew back. "It's Adriana. Do you mind if I take it?"

Delaney rolled her hand to tell him to get on with it.

"What's up, sis?" he said.

Adriana's agitated voice reverberated in the small conference room. "What's this shit in the paper about a recall vote?" Kearny had an actual newspaper that was still sold around town. The locals gobbled it up. Delaney hoped it never went out of business. It felt like a link to a past kind of life. A good kind.

"What vote?" Leo said.

"A recall. To force you out of office. One of the county commissioners has a bug up her ass about all the murders in Kearny County since you started with the department."

Delaney frowned. Leo wasn't unpopular, to her knowledge, even though he wasn't a county insider. And the murders had nothing to do with him. This smacked of an Ellen Day type of stunt. She'd been Delaney's and Leo's biggest critic ever since their testimony in front of the commission had resulted in a lengthy investigation into her pet development project, which had been revoked.

"Most of those predate my appointment as interim sheriff."

"Whatever. I don't think they care."

"Does it say when they'll hold the vote?"

Silence. Then, "No. I'm not even sure if it's happening or just being proposed."

"Okay. Thanks for letting me know."

Adriana sounded worried. "Are you going to lose your job? Freddy and I just got here."

"No. And the sheriff gig was only ever temporary. My job here is secure. Now, I've got to go. Say hey to Freddy for me."

"Ha. If he ever wakes up. It's like ever since he turned thirteen he has a sleeping sickness."

"Takes after his mom." Leo smiled. "Bye, Adriana." He ended the call. Then he raised his eyebrows at Delaney. "Well. This should be fun."

"It won't go anywhere. It's just politics."

"About that. Could I ask a favor?"

"No, I won't kill the county commissioner for you."

He laughed. "It's worse. Will you, uh, I mean would you consider endorsing me for sheriff? With the party?"

"You're running?"

"Maybe."

"Then maybe I will."

"If you aren't, I mean."

"Hmm. Let's see. Raising two orphaned girls alone and running for sheriff. Yeah, sure, I'll throw my hat in the ring."

"I'm serious. I need you to call them."

She finally smiled. "No problem."

He exhaled. "Thanks." He connected his tablet via USB to the computer. "I want to take some notes during the interview but I'm low on charge." His computer made a noise. "That's our call." Leo clicked a few keys.

A man appeared onscreen, his face splotchy and eyes swollen. Beside him sat Teton County Sheriff Ed Nickels. Delaney had met Ed at a conference earlier that year. He looked more like an accountant than a law man, but he seemed a good sort.

He said, "Sheriff Palmer, Deputy Investigator Pace—good morning. I've got Pete Smithers with me. He's—he was—Anna-beth Dillon's husband. Pete, these are the folks from Kearny County who found your wife." Ed gestured toward Leo and Delaney on his screen.

Smithers? Delaney had expected Dillon. Many women kept their own surnames when they married. Just not a lot of them lived in Wyoming.

"Sorry to meet under these circumstances, Mr. Smithers," Leo said.

"We're very sorry for your loss," Delaney said.

"I do want to confirm that you were shown her picture and positively ID'd your wife?"

Pete nodded. "It's here." His voice cracked. "What can you tell me about... about... how she... she..." He tapered off.

Leo nodded at Delaney.

She scooted just slightly away from him. His nearness was distracting. "It's very early in our investigation, Mr. Smithers. The forensic pathologist will give us her conclusions about cause of and time of death in the next few days."

"You aren't sure then."

"No, sir." And it was true. Just because she'd died with a scarf around her neck didn't rule out other causes.

"Do you have a suspect?"

"We can't rule out accident or natural causes yet." Delaney hurried onward, trying to gently redirect the interview and avoid giving him excess information. She respected his need for answers, but they didn't have much. And if it was murder, they had no idea yet whether Pete might be involved. "Can you tell us what she was doing in Kearny County and up at the Mountain High Cabins specifically?"

Pete shuddered. "Annabeth worked as a corporate attorney when we lived in Seattle. We just moved to Jackson four years ago. She decided to change her focus to nonprofit work here. Mostly environmental and wildlife organizations. Recently, she'd been approached about running for public office."

Delaney's pulse quickened. A public figure who died in a compromising position after a sexual encounter with someone other than her husband. This case was getting interesting. "Local or state?"

"Neither. The U.S. Senate."

Delaney was glad, for once, that an interview was being conducted on streaming video instead of in person. She leaned back in her chair to get distance from the camera, although that put her closer to the warmth of Leo. The man was a damn magnet. She relaxed her shoulders, hoping Pete wouldn't notice her physical reaction to such an ambitious leap. "Did she have prior experience in government?"

"A lot of nonprofit law is governmental."

Still. Delaney pretended to make notes. "Was her visit to Kearny County related to her candidacy?"

"Potential candidacy, yes. She was meeting with a big party donor."

"Do you know where and when that meeting was to take place?"

"In Kearny, three days ago. Apparently it went quite well. She was very close to saying yes. The meetings ran long, so she decided to stay over."

"Why was she staying up on the mountain if her meetings were in Kearny?"

His lip trembled. "I didn't think she was. I thought she was at the Holiday Inn Express."

"All right. Back to her meetings. Can I have the name of the person she was meeting with?"

"Brock Tucker."

"Does he live in Kearny?"

"I don't think so. But nearby. I think they picked Kearny as a low-profile spot to meet."

"And what does Mr. Tucker do for a living?"

"He owns an oil field servicing company. I can't remember the name."

"Was he the one who asked your wife to run?"

"I believe so."

"You knew him?"

Pete nodded. "Yes. He met with us both in Jackson."

"Anyone else she was meeting with here?"

"Just Brock, I think."

"When was the last time you talked with your wife?"

"About three o'clock on that day. The day of her meetings, three days ago."

"The day she extended her visit."

"Yes."

"Did the two of you know anyone else in the area?"

"Not really. We've kept to the Teton area. It's beautiful where we are."

Like the rest of Wyoming isn't? "Do you have children, Mr. Smithers?"

"From a previous marriage. Two boys and a girl. Annabeth wasn't able to have kids of her own, but, whenever they visited, she was very good to mine."

"How about your relationship with Annabeth?"

"What do you mean?"

"Your marriage. Was it solid? Did you have problems?"

He bristled. "We were good. We had disagreements like normal couples, but we loved each other."

"Was your wife faithful to you?"

"What kind of question is that?" He jumped to his feet, pushing the top of his head out of the frame.

Leo scribbled notes on his tablet out of sight of the camera.

Delaney raised her brows. She caught sight of herself in the little video box on the screen. She looked like a Pekinese, so she smoothed her features, hyper aware of Leo watching her in the same box. "I mean did she cheat on you?"

"Never. Annabeth would never. Her reputation was one of her greatest assets."

Leo motioned for Pete to sit, palm down. "We apologize if we've offended you, Mr. Smithers. These are standard questions, I'm afraid."

Suddenly Leo's notes from his tablet appeared. FU MEETING filled the screen.

"Nothing about this is standard to me." Off-screen, Delaney heard someone whispering.

Leo was looking down.

Delaney jabbed him. "Leo. Your tablet."

He glanced up just as Pete saw the words.

"FU meeting? Does that mean what I think it does?" Pete said. "That's about the most unprofessional thing I've ever seen!"

Leo jerked his USB cable out of the computer. His neck was red and splotchy. "Follow-up meeting. Follow-up. Sorry. I must have accidentally shared my tablet screen. Those were notes to myself. From earlier."

"About me?"

"No. Completely unrelated. I was just charging my tablet."

Delaney glanced down at the tablet. The tablet said FU MEETING WITH SHERIFF.

Pete said, "I don't like it. I want my lawyer to join this conversation."

Leo said, "Do you feel like you have a reason to need a lawyer?"

A third person appeared beside the sheriff and Pete. A woman of Asian descent, petite, white-haired, eyes blinking behind wire-framed glasses.

"Let's all just simmer down a bit," Ed said, his voice soothing. "Pete, I know this is upsetting, but I'd ask the same questions if I was in their shoes, even as much as I respect you and Annabeth."

The attorney and Pete put their heads together and whispered.

Ed mouthed, "I'm sorry."

Delaney reasserted herself as interviewer. "Mr. Smithers? A few more questions. Did Annabeth have any serious health condition that might have caused or hastened her death?"

The attorney, Delaney assumed, gave a barely perceptible nod at Pete.

"No. She was in perfect health."

"Do you know of anyone who might have wished your wife harm?"

Pete's face reddened. "Half the people in this state. The yahoos who don't care that they're destroying our environment and killing off our precious wildlife."

"I'm thinking more specifically. People who might have harassed her, made threats against her?"

He turned to his attorney. "Could I get sued for slander for this?"

Her voice was low and measured but not inaudible. "You are wealthy. You can and will be sued for anything and everything. Keep it to opinion or provable facts."

Delaney didn't like it that Pete hadn't introduced the woman. "Thank you, Ms... I'm sorry, what is your name?"

"Jade Li," she said.

"Nice to meet you, Ms. Li. Pete, can you please confirm she is your attorney?"

Pete said, "She is."

"Now, you were saying?"

"There's a few that come to mind. The worst of them is a woman named Alecia Black. She posts on social media about Annabeth. Stuff like that people who protect the grizzlies and wolves should be eaten by them. She's shown up at our house and thrown green paint on our gate. There's a man, too. I don't remember his name. Similar stuff, badmouthing her for being from out of state and throwing uninformed opinions around. He just hasn't shown up in person. You'd be able to find him on social media without much trouble, I think. Someone filed a lawsuit against the groups she supports. And lately there have been pieces in the paper about how she's bad for Wyoming. I suspect that's politics, though. You know. Basically, pre-emptive attack ads in the guise of op-eds."

"That's very helpful." Delaney scribbled quickly on a piece of paper. Leo did the same on his tablet. The lawsuit should be simple to verify. "If you think of the names of the man you mentioned or anyone who has published an op-ed or where, could you let me know?"

He nodded. His eyes seemed to lose focus. "When can I see my wife?" Tears welled and spilled down his cheeks. "I just need my wife. For a funeral. Cremation."

Leo leaned toward the screen. "It shouldn't be more than a few days until I can answer that question for you. We'll keep you updated as we learn more. Feel free to call Delaney or me any time." He gave Pete their contact information.

Delaney had an idea. "One last question, Mr. Smithers. Does the name Rufus Payne mean anything to you?"

Pete shifted, looked up, then at his lawyer before answering "He used to work for me. It didn't end well. Did that son of a bitch kill my wife?"

FOURTEEN

"Does that change your mind about Rufus?" Leo asked as he shut his laptop after the video call with Smithers.

Delaney threw her empty coffee cup in the trash. "It's a strange coincidence."

"From the woman who doesn't believe in coincidences. Rufus didn't tell us he knew Annabeth and Pete."

"We didn't tell Rufus who died."

Leo paused, thinking. She was right. "It's all over the news, though."

"It is now. It wasn't last night before he was taken in."

"True."

"Say—there's something bothering me, and it isn't about Pete or Rufus. How did the sheriff know Annabeth was at those cabins?"

"Huh?"

"Well, Pete said he thought Annabeth was at a Holiday Inn Express in Kearny. Didn't Ed call our department for a wellness check on Annabeth specifically up at the cabins?"

"Yeah." Leo pulled at his chin. "He did."

"How did Ed know where she was?"

"Excellent point." Leo hit the sheriff's number, which was in his Recents from when he'd set up the call with Pete.

Ed picked up on the second ring. "Leo. Been a minute."

"Hey, Ed. Putting you on speaker with Delaney and me." Leo set the phone on the desk and switched it to speaker. "Quick question."

"Fire away."

"Who called in the wellness check on Annabeth?"

"Me. I talked to your dispatch."

"No. Who called *you*?"

"Oh. Pete called me when she didn't show up at home. We didn't let grass grow on it, on account of who she is and all, so, I had one of my guys call her hotel. They said she'd checked out on the day of her meetings."

"Okay. Then how'd you know where to send us?"

"I'd love to say it was our fancy detective work, but it was actually an anonymous call."

Delaney's entire face puckered. She pressed the mute button. "He sent us up there without warning us it was based on an anonymous tip?"

Leo felt as irritated as she sounded. It was a reckless waste of another department's manpower.

"Hello? Kearny County, are you there?" Ed said.

Leo activated the speaker. "I don't recall that being part of the information relayed to us."

"Really? I could have sworn I told your dispatcher. But I confirmed the information with the owner of the cabins first."

"Shaina Pham."

"Yes. Shaina couldn't confirm whether Annabeth had shown up, given the location and that Shaina was out of town. Because there is no phone service at the cabins, none of us was able to call."

Leo was partially mollified. He still would have appreciated hearing the entire story. "Had you told Mr. Smithers where she was at that time?"

"I, uh—yes. We kept him informed of the status. He was surprised, but he thought maybe she'd been shortening her drive home. The cabins are on the road back to Jackson."

"When was that?" Delaney said. "When you told Mr. Smithers?"

"A few hours before I talked to you guys."

"In person?"

"Yes. At his home."

Leo did the math. Pete wouldn't have had time to kill his wife. A round trip from Jackson to the cabins was ten hours or more. And his best guess was that Annabeth was killed days ago anyway. "Do you have a record of the number the tip came from?"

"We do, and we followed up on it. It came from a burner."

Again, Delaney hit mute. "The killer called in her death?"

"Maybe the boyfriend wasn't as heartless as we thought. This may support the accident theory." He unmuted. "Male or female caller?"

"Impossible to tell. I suspect they were using one of those voice changer apps. Technology is getting to be the bane of my existence."

"Tell me about it," Delaney said, nodding at Leo's laptop.

He rolled his eyes at her. "If you think of anything else..."

"You'll be my first call," Ed replied.

The call ended.

"That was strangely disturbing," Delaney said.

Leo followed Delaney out of the conference room toward her desk. "I wish he'd been more forthcoming."

"Just when I thought I liked him."

Leo headed toward his office past the bullpen. Something caught his eye in Tommy's desk, and he slowed. Tommy's electronic tablet was propped against the cubicle wall with a photograph taped to it. Leo stopped, chagrined. Why didn't anyone in the department seem to understand that these tablets could improve their lives and the way they did their jobs? More efficiency could mean less mistakes and better solve rates. Save lives. He sighed as he leaned in for a closer look. The picture showed Tommy in what appeared to be a family photo. He was much younger—maybe his early teens. The resemblance ran strong, and the family was large, with lots of male facial hair and long, stringy hair on the females. One of the women was standout beautiful. Old enough to be Tommy's mother, but, based on the placement of a gray-haired man and woman in the center of the group, probably more likely to be a sister. A few of them were sporting T-shirts that read WESTERN PROUD.

Leo sighed and moved on.

Delaney settled into her own chair a few cubbies down. "Physical evidence will point us in the right direction. Have you heard from Sugar and the team on that yet?"

"They're still working on it."

"There's at least the used condom. I'm hoping for fingerprints or saliva from one of the glasses, too."

Leo was about to agree when he registered Delaney's tablet. It was face down on her desk with a water bottle on its back. *She's using it as a coaster?!?* "That's not good for your tablet."

"What?" She followed his gaze. "Oh. The rubberized back protects it. And this way my desk doesn't get water rings." She checked her phone.

"You expecting to hear from someone?"

She shot him a questioning look. "I have two girls at home, neither of whom has been behaving spectacularly."

"Zeke isn't still there?"

Delaney put her hands on her keyboard, waking up her computer screen. She typed in a password. "I don't think so."

"You haven't talked to him?"

"I've been interviewing witnesses. I believe you were with me."

"I just thought he might have texted or left a message."

She swiveled her chair, eyes narrowed. "Do we have a problem, Leo?"

Leo felt his insides turn over. He couldn't just tell her all that he knew. All that he thought. "Well, he did come to visit *me*."

She rolled her eyes as she spun back to her screen. "Are we going to fight over who gets to be best friends with Zeke?"

No, we're fighting over who gets to be best friends with Delaney. "How do you two know each other, anyway?"

Her fingers flew over her keyboard. "I have a homicide to solve. *We* have a homicide to solve." Her phone chimed. They both looked at it. Across her screen a notification flashed. Delaney's fingers paused then resumed their flight.

"Aren't you going to check your text?"

"No."

"It could be from Kat or Carrie."

She made a grumbly noise and checked it. Her cheeks and neck flushed.

"Was it Kat?"

"No."

"Carrie?"

"Leo! Stop. It was a text from Zeke. He's back at your place. Maybe you should run home so you guys can play Xbox or touch football or something."

Leo tried to stop his mouth, but it got the better of him. "Are you going to see him again?"

Delaney sighed so hard she growled.

Leo's blood was boiling. "I'll be in my office."

"Fine."

"Fine." He stalked away, punching Zeke's number for a FaceTime as soon as he was out of earshot of Delaney.

Zeke picked up after two rings. Leo could see his own dining room table. Zeke really was at Leo's house. Zeke yawned loudly, then said, "Palmer, yo. Want to grab some lunch?"

Leo's throat felt tight, and his voice came out strained. "No, you asshole, I don't want lunch."

Zeke scowled. "What the fuck, Leo?"

"What are you doing with Delaney?" he hissed.

Zeke waggled his eyebrows. "Trying for round two. She's the best f—"

"Leave her alone, Zeke. I mean it."

Zeke laughed. "What do you care? She's a big girl. She can make her own choices."

"That's beside the point."

"Wait—are you two a thing?"

"No."

"Then back off."

"You're misleading her."

"What, are you going to kick my ass to defend her honor?" Zeke snorted and shook his head. "I'll talk to you when you get a grip, man." He disappeared from Leo's screen.

Leo stood at his window, cursing his friend under his breath.

"Ahem."

He turned. Delaney was standing in his doorway. How long had she been there? "Sorry. I didn't know you were there."

She said, "Meet me at my truck."

"Why?"

"Because I found an address south of here for Brock Tucker, Annabeth's big donor. You can either hook me to a polygraph about my relations with Zeke or come with me. Your choice."

And just like that she was gone.

Leo thought about the polygraph. It was tempting. Then he ran to grab his coat and catch up with her.

FIFTEEN

Delaney turned into a gate under a giant metal "T Bar O" sign. The road had been plowed, which was a relief. There was still snow cover on the road and it was a bit slick but, given her upbringing and years driving the ice roads, it was like a Sunday drive to her. No need for the hassle of chains. "Maps says we're here. I'm guessing T is for Tuner and O for Oilfield."

"Maybe he's married to a woman named Olivia," Leo said, his expression deadpan.

"Or has a dog named Oscar." She was relieved to fall into their normal patter, the Zeke tension behind them. Leo had even updated her during the drive on his brief conversation with Shaina Pham, the owner of Mountain High Cabins, and they'd talked through an update to his investigation plan.

A large herd of pronghorn antelope milled in a field next to the entrance road. They appeared to be nibbling on the sagebrush protruding above the snow. Dark clouds had amassed to the north. With another storm, the forage would be buried, and the antelope would be forced to dig for it. Too many more storms, and their small hooves would be unable to pierce the crust, and they'd starve. Winter could be deadly for the slender ungulates.

Delaney crested a hill. A small creek ran—only partially frozen—behind a cluster of ranch buildings with a two-story house. A stand of trees stood to the south, notable because they were the only plant taller than sagebrush as far as the eye could see. *Probably planted by homesteaders long ago.* As Delaney neared the house, three Border Collies charged off the porch, their barks loud even with the engine noise. They leaped gracefully over snow berms around the driveway, a result of plowing.

Leo said, "I hope they're friendly."

"I wouldn't count on it until their owner appears." Ranch dogs filled many roles. They helped with livestock, entertained the kids, kept animals away from the house, and protected the property. Breaching their line of defense was one of the challenges of showing up unannounced.

"Great."

She parked between an SUV and a pickup. "Luckily, I put Brock's number in my phone back at the office." The call failed to go through. "Call dropped. No signal."

"Double great."

She beeped the horn twice. No one appeared at the house or any of the outbuildings. The dogs kept barking.

"It seems like no one's home," Leo said, eying the dogs.

"But we came all this way."

"Only half an hour."

"Each direction." She opened her glove box, pulled out a pouch and unzipped it, then poured a handful of dog treats into her palm. "This should ensure canine cooperation."

"I'll cover you."

"How about you just stay close to me, so I don't have to come to your rescue."

"Very funny."

Delaney wasn't joking. She climbed out and called to the dogs. "Come here, dogs."

The dogs slunk toward her, bellies low to the ground. The barking ceased as she coaxed them in.

Leo's phone chimed.

The dogs wheeled and retreated. The barking recommenced.

Delaney frowned. "Why do you have signal and I don't?"

"Because the universe knows I'm a better human."

"In your dreams. Turn your ringer off after you check that. Please." Delaney whistled softly. "Here, dogs. Come, dogs."

The pack started making its way toward her again.

Across the truck hood, Leo said, "It's Freddy. He wants to know if Zeke can take him and Kateena—I mean Kat—and Carrie to swim at the YMCA in Sheridan."

Delaney stiffened. "No one asked me."

"I assume Freddy is waiting on my answer before he asks them."

"What is your answer?"

"Fine with me."

She returned her attention to her mission. "Come here, you mutts." The three dogs were close now. Delaney held out her hand. The first two took the treats. The third hung back. "Don't be scared. I don't bite." Finally, it darted in and took the treat, and the three dogs scampered back to the porch.

An enclosed utility vehicle appeared from behind the house. It parked, and a man in winter-white camo emerged, twenty feet from Leo and Delaney. He rested the butt of a Mossberg 500 on the ground. The dogs swarmed him, forgetting all about the interlopers.

Delaney raised a hand. "Good morning. I'm Kearny County Deputy Investigator Delaney Pace."

Leo moved to stand beside her. "And I'm Sheriff Leo Palmer. Are you Brock Tucker?"

"I am. What brings you out to my place?" He started walking toward the house, carrying his shotgun.

Delaney and Leo followed.

"Have you heard the news this morning?" Leo asked.

"What news? I've been out hunting turkeys." He smacked a palm to his forehead. "Forgot to take my damn phone with me."

"Did you get any?" Delaney turned and craned her neck to check his UTV. She couldn't tell if there were any birds in it or not.

"I took a hen today. They were looking a little scrawny. Why don't you come in and tell me what's going on?" He threw open the door. "I'll be right there."

"Sure." Delaney stomped her boots then toed them on the porch mat but waited outside.

Leo did the same.

Brock returned to the UTV for the turkey, capturing the full attention of the dogs. Carrying the bird by its feet, Brock led the way into the house. He stowed the turkey in his kitchen sink and gestured them to the kitchen table.

"My wife would kill me if she saw this thing in here." He hovered a finger in front of his lips and winked. "She's on a girls' trip to New York, so I'll have time to clean up the evidence before she gets back." He washed his hands at the kitchen sink.

Delaney took off her hat and gloves and lay them on the table. "Fun. How long has she been gone?"

Drying his hands, Brock said, "Five days of exercising the credit cards. I'm expecting her home any minute."

Leo nodded at a framed photograph on a hutch of Brock and a stunning woman half his age and a head taller than him, somewhere on a tropical beach. Auburn hair. A smattering of freckles. She was posing for the camera, back arched. The picture looked worthy of the *Sports Illustrated* cover, except for Brock. "Is this your wife?"

Delaney expected Brock to answer that it was his daughter.

But perched beside it was a second picture with a woman of about the same age, a woman that looked like him in a way that was less than attractive.

He stopped at the picture as if to admire it. "That's Riley on our honeymoon."

"How long have you been married?" Delaney asked, but she was thinking: *Damn, oil field services must make some serious money.*

Brock took a seat. "Five years. And before you say it, I know she's too young and too good looking for me. She obviously has very poor taste. The picture beside it is me with my daughter, Jillian, who has told me as much. All right. Now what's this about?"

"We understand you had some meetings with Annabeth Dillon a few days ago. We'd like you to tell us about them," Delaney said.

He gave a firm shake of his head. "I'm afraid those were confidential until I get the green light from her. Which I'm still waiting on."

"For now, let's just confirm that they occurred—where and when."

"Tuesday of this last week. We borrowed space from a friend of mine who has offices downtown, while he was out of the country."

"And where were you that evening?"

"Uh, here at home with the dogs."

"What about Ms. Dillon?"

"What about her?"

"Do you know where she went that night?"

"We got through with our meetings a little late, so I believe she decided to stay over in Kearny before heading back to Jackson."

"Do you know if she had plans to see anyone else while she was in town?"

"I don't believe so. But she might have." He frowned. "Is this about Annabeth? Is she okay?"

Leo stood and walked to the bay window at the rear of the kitchen. It was a gorgeous view over snow-covered fields toward the Bighorn Mountains in the distance. "Are we anywhere near the hideout of the Hole in the Wall Gang?"

Brock's eyes cut from him to Delaney then back. "Near enough that I get sightseers lost on my ranch looking for it a few times a year. But what about Annabeth?"

Leo turned and spoke matter-of-factly. "Annabeth died Tuesday night."

Delaney watched Brock.

His eyes widened, his mouth opened, his shoulders rose then slumped. "I don't understand. She was fine when I left her."

"And when was that again?"

His Adam's apple bobbed. He swiped his hand over his mouth. Then he said, "I think I need my lawyer."

SIXTEEN

Ellen Day climbed out of her SUV and smoothed her skirt, high heels clicking up the front walk to Jefe's door. She fought down the nerves that she didn't want him to see. Being summoned without an explanation wasn't good. He was a dangerous man, and lately he was unreceptive to her attempts to keep him in her thrall. It had worked for a few months—while he was house-bound with his face wrapped in bandages. The way things had sizzled between them in Mexico, she'd expected him to wear all the skin from her body with his as soon as he hit town.

Maybe that's all this was. A ruse to get her in his bed. *I can hope.*

At his front door, she primped. Shiny lip gloss over lipstick. Hair fluffing. A two-handed breast lift. Then she closed her eyes, exhaled long and slow, and rang his doorbell. Cocking her hip, she waited. And waited. After a full minute, she rang it again.

What if something had happened to him? A thrill ran through her. What if something had *happened* to him? If there was no Jefe in between her and the big boss?

It brought a real smile to her face.

She tried the door handle, and it turned easily. Pushing the door open, she stepped inside. "Hello? It's Ellen. Anyone home?" When Jefe didn't answer, she said, "Yoo hoo, lover boy?"

She held her breath as she made her way through the house, hoping against hope. Maybe someone had figured out who he was. Where he lived. What he looked like now. She couldn't be the only person in this town who despised him. His sister and the sheriff didn't waste any love on him, that was for sure. Or on her, but it was nothing compared to how she felt about them. She had planted the idea of a recall vote for Palmer with a local newshound. A brilliant move, if she did say so herself. But it was Delaney she really hated. The woman had cost Ellen significant political capital. Jefe had made Ellen promise she would make sure no one took Delaney out. But she hadn't promised not to mess with her. And, oh, how she planned to mess with her. She shivered with delight. *So much to look forward to.*

She cleared the living room, kitchen and eating area, and the bathroom. No Jefe. And it was a tiny house. She'd picked it out for him. Only two bedrooms. She peeked into the first. He wasn't there.

"Are you hiding from me, you naughty boy? I hope you're saving up a very, very big surprise just for me!"

She crossed her fingers and mouthed a sacrilegious prayer that someone badder than him had blown his head off. If anyone on this planet deserved a slow and horrible death, it was Jefe. She pursed her lips. It would be gruesome if it had actually happened. What if she was about to find his body? She could handle it. Violence. Death. Gore. *No biggie.*

Poking her head around the corner with a smile she hoped was sexy, she said, "Come out, come out, wherever you are."

Behind her, a voice made her jump. "I was out back. Kitchen. Now."

Jefe. *Shit.*

She wheeled. "Darling!"

He'd already walked away. She grimaced. The man wasn't making this easy. She caught up with him from the back, swallowed her bile, and slid a hand around him and over his pectoral muscle. Not only did she hate him, but the fact that he was a different shape and looked like a stranger made touching him weird. His new face and body were attractive, but only if you didn't know the man on the inside.

He twisted away from her touch and took a seat. He pointed across from him. "Sit."

She gave a pretty pout and dropped into the chair. "You're no fun. I've missed you so much!"

His expression was stony. "Annabeth Dillon is dead."

She shook her head. "I heard that on the news. Such a tragedy."

Jefe slammed his fist into the table. "Don't bullshit with me, Ellen. Did you have anything to do with it?"

"Me? I heard it was a sex accident. County connections, you know." She winked. "Incredible timing, though. For us, I mean."

"Is it?"

"Sure. She hadn't announced her candidacy yet, and now she never will. Nice and clean."

"It had better be."

"Oh, Jefe, just relax." *As if.* The man never relaxed.

His stern look grew menacing. "You visited my boss without involving me."

Her heart caught in her throat. She didn't let it show in her face. "A spur of the moment thing. I was in Cheyenne anyway on county business."

"You used my code word to reach him."

Ellen held herself perfectly still. She'd anticipated this moment would come at some point. She was ready for it. "Jefe, it just blurted out of me on accident."

"You shouldn't have had it in the first place."

"I didn't mean to have it, I swear. But when I was closing up your place, I ran across it."

"On my computer."

"That was part of shutting down your old life."

"Excuse me if I find that hard to believe. I asked you to destroy it without going through it."

"I understand. But it's the truth. I have nothing to hide."

"Except your meeting, apparently, since you didn't mention it when we talked this morning."

"I was saving it for when we got together in person. And we finally have. I was beginning to think you were avoiding me." She tiptoed her fingers across the table.

He pushed them back. "Our personal relationship ends now. Your relationship with my boss includes me going forward. And any work you do, you report to me. No matter who in the organization assigns it. Are we clear?"

She knew she should look hurt. All she felt was relief that she would never have to be intimate with him again. On the other hand, how was she going to keep him close? *Maybe I don't have to. I impressed the big guy.* She would start working on a way to squeeze Jefe out—take him out, preferably —ASAP.

But, first, she had to pretend to be devastated.

"I don't understand. I thought we... we... we were good together."

"Were. And it was only okay." He touched his phone to check the time. "Goodbye, Ellen. I have a call."

She stood, wobbling on her heels, faking a lip tremble, willing tears to her eyes. "When you change your mind, you know where to find me."

But when she was safely out the door and walking to her car, she abandoned her subterfuge. "I hope you rot in hell, jackass, and I intend to have a hand putting you there." Then she pressed the new number she'd saved in her phone. "Starting now."

SEVENTEEN

Leo's phone rang. His screen identified the caller as Sugar. *It has to be about evidence from the crime scene.* He shook his head at Delaney and Brock Tucker. "I have to take this." He answered. "Just a minute, Sugar."

"No problem, Sheriff," she answered, her voice cheerful.

He held the phone at his side. "Mr. Tucker, feel free to call your attorney. We can wait." To Delaney he said, "I'll be right back. I'm just going to step outside for a moment."

Brock sputtered, then silenced.

Delaney nodded without taking her eyes off Brock.

Leo stepped out onto the front porch. The Border Collies didn't get up, although one raised its head for a moment. "Okay, Sugar. What've you got?"

"Fingerprints. Fibers from what we believe is clothing. Hair. Saliva. And, of course, the condom. This guy either wasn't trying to hide his identity or didn't have a clue how."

"Good. How long will results take?"

"Well, DNA will be a couple of days. With fiber analysis, I can give you some preliminary ideas now, but honestly for both the fiber and the DNA what we really need is a match to compare to."

He understood. Find a suspect, match the results to the evidence. "Tell me about the fibers."

"Denim and flannel."

He groaned. "The same thing every man in Wyoming wore that night. And most of the women."

"True. But you're looking for red flannel and a dark denim."

"Great. That narrows it down by fifty percent. Anything more definitive for me?"

"I thought you'd never ask. You're looking for dark hair going gray. Straight but coarse."

Brock Tucker's hair matched the description. So far, he was the last person they knew to have seen Annabeth alive. And he'd just asked for a lawyer. "Gender? Age?"

"Adult is as far as I can go on age. As for gender, we didn't find a sample with a root, so I can't give you that. But there's a second sample. Look for silky, straight blond hair."

"Our victim had red hair. Two perps?"

"Or bad housekeeping. We don't know when the samples were left."

"Shit."

"But we matched a fingerprint."

Leo pumped his fist. "Thank the good Lord. Give me a name."

"Don't you want to hear about my mad skills and our amazing luck first?"

"Quickly." He couldn't help smiling. Sugar's enthusiasm for her job was infectious.

"Fingerprints were numerous, but most were smeared. Did I mention bad housekeeping? There were a few good ones. Unfortunately, they belonged to the deceased. I finally found one that wasn't hers on a wine glass. Although the residue in it was Prosecco. I'm not sure whether that counts as wine or champagne. I'm more of a bourbon drinker myself."

"Sparkling wine."

"Good to know. We were able to identify the print because its owner is an adoptive parent who provided them as part of the application process, years ago."

"Skills and luck. A good combo. Now cut to the chase. Who does it belong to?"

"You're looking for Brock Tucker."

Adrenaline exploded through his nervous system. "You're sure?" It was good news.

"As sure as I can be which is never one hundred percent but pretty close."

An engine roared to life. Leo wheeled around. So did the dogs. A brand-new Dodge Ram 2500 sped from between the house and barn and shot out the driveway toward the interstate, fishtailing in the snow.

EIGHTEEN

Delaney watched the doorway from the kitchen into the hall, waiting for Brock to return from calling his attorney. She tried not to get excited about it. Lots of people called attorneys during questioning, especially if they felt like they were under suspicion. Brock was a wealthy, connected man. This might be a normal precaution for him. A standing instruction from counsel on retainer to never talk to cops without them.

She glanced at her phone and noticed she'd acquired signal and had a backlog of texts from Kat and Carrie. She scrolled through them. They became progressively unhappier as she failed to immediately answer their request: could they go to the YMCA in Sheridan. The last one from Carrie said:

We ARE going to the YMCA in Sheridan with Freddy and your old boyfriend so Adriana can go on a coffee date with her online crush.

Delaney would have said yes anyway, but it was too late. She sent:

Sorry, have fun.

Then the front door flew open, and Leo shouted to her. "Is Brock with you?"

She jumped to her feet. "No. He went to his bedroom for privacy to call his attorney."

"Unless he's decided to do that talk in person, I think he's making a run for it. A black Ram just drove away from here like a bat out of hell."

"Dammit!" Delaney shoved her phone in her pocket, scooped up her hat and gloves, and sprinted toward Leo. She grabbed their coats from a rack by the door, pausing to shout, "Brock? Mr. Tucker?" Her voice was loud enough to reach him two counties over.

There was no response from him, but a woman said, "Who are you and what are you doing in my home?"

Delaney turned. Brock's wife stood in the doorway, clearly recognizable from the photo in the kitchen, only without the bathing suit and come-hither smile. "Mrs. Tucker?"

"Yes? And I'll repeat—who are you?"

Delaney pointed to the star on her uniform then to Leo behind her with a thumb. "Deputy Investigator Delaney Pace. This is Sheriff Leo Palmer. We were here talking to your husband. Have you seen him?"

"I waved to him when we passed each other on the driveway a moment ago."

"Do you know where he was headed?"

"Excuse me, but what is this about?"

Leo said, "Our apologies. I'm sure he'll fill you in later. Deputy Pace and I need to go now."

He moved past the woman, out the door. Delaney hurried after him. She ignored Mrs. Tucker's shouted questions on repeat.

To Leo, she said, "Which way did he go?"

"He turned south on the interstate. He was kicking up snow the whole way or I wouldn't have been able to tell."

They made a dash for her truck. The dogs chased after them, agitated by their hurry and Mrs. Tucker's shouts.

Delaney said, "Get back," in her deepest alpha voice.

They hesitated just long enough. Leo and Delaney hustled into the truck. Seconds later, Delaney had them barreling down the road.

Leo turned on the wig wag lights and keyed his radio mic. "This is Sheriff Leo Palmer of Kearny County with DI Delaney Pace. We're in pursuit of a late model black Dodge Ram 2500, believed to be owned and operated by Brock Tucker of Kaycee and last seen exiting Tucker's property toward the interstate, heading south. I need a license plate number and an Attempt to Locate on the vehicle, and we could use some backup. Also, the driver is a suspect in a homicide investigation. Officers should exercise caution if they attempt to pull the vehicle over. Consider Tucker armed and dangerous."

The calm, disembodied voice of their dispatcher replied. "10-4, Sheriff. Hold, please."

Delaney navigated the right turn off the ranch road onto the access lane for the interstate without slowing down. The back wheels lost traction for a moment before gripping pavement. "Strap in, Leo."

He did, and Delaney accelerated rapidly. She steered with one hand and pulled up a map on the truck's screen with the other. She wanted a bird's-eye view. She knew this area in general, but nowhere near as well as Kearny County.

"You're killing me," Leo said.

"I don't plan to." She'd prepped her vehicle for winter driving weeks ago. Switched out her summer tires for studded winter ones. Loaded a thousand pounds of sand over the back wheels in the truck bed. Added a snow shovel and chains to her survival kit. Not that she expected to need the last two items today. The pavement was cold and the snow fluffy and fresh. Ice and compressed snow shouldn't be an issue. Of course, the interstate between Kaycee and Casper was notoriously hazardous in the winter. Not as bad as I-80 in the south of the state, but bad enough. With luck, it would trip Brock up and end this pursuit quickly.

The dispatcher came back on. "Sheriff Palmer? I've got Johnson and Natrona counties responding with units on the interstate but based on their locations you're on your own for the next twenty minutes."

"Thank you," Leo said. "Understood."

"The ATL has been issued. And Mr. Tucker does own a new black Ram." She recited a license plate number. "What else?"

"Add that license plate number to the ATL?"

"Already done it."

"That's enough for now. Thanks for your help. Over and out."

"Over and out."

Leo dialed the radio to the MAT1 mutual aid channel. "This is Kearny County Sheriff Leo Palmer. Looking to connect with the Natrona and Johnson county units assisting in pursuit of a new black Ram truck." He added the plate number.

Delaney said, "I still don't see him."

"He might have turned off somewhere."

She shook her head. "I've been following his tire prints."

Leo scowled. "How can you even tell which ones are his?"

"He left clear ones in his driveway and on the road out to the interstate. I've just kept my eyes on the trail."

"Okay, eagle eyes."

"Our traction is good. We need to close the gap."

Leo glanced over as she accelerated. The speedometer crept up to ninety-five miles an hour. "Good thing I went to church last Sunday."

The radio crackled with responses. Natrona was moving north from Casper, nearly seventy miles away. Johnson County, unfortunately, was halfway between Buffalo and Kaycee, further from Brock than Leo and Delaney. Then a familiar voice came over the line. "This is Deputy Joe Tarver. Sheriff, I was visiting family in Casper today. I'm about fifteen miles south of Kaycee northbound. I haven't seen your vehicle, but my guess is I'll be the first to catch a glimpse if he stays on the interstate."

Leo whooped. "Great news, Joe. Keep us posted."

"What's this about?"

Leo screwed up his face, as if considering how much he could say over the radio. "Our mountain death."

"Oh." Joe paused. Then he repeated, "Ohhhh," dragging the word out. "Gotcha. Thanks."

Leo released his mic. "Well, at least we've got good help."

"Any idea where Brock's going?" Delaney asked Leo.

He rubbed his chin. "The airport in Casper, maybe?"

"He has to know we're following him."

The radio crackled again. Joe's voice sounded amped-up this time. "Your black Ram just turned off the interstate heading east on Long Canyon Road. I have to find a place to turn around then I'll start pursuit."

"We're close," Delaney said, tapping the map screen. "Less than a mile to the exit."

Leo radioed. "10-4, Joe. We may be first in line."

Delaney made the turn off the interstate thirty seconds later. She crowed. "And there are his tracks."

"The snow looks deeper here." Leo's forehead bunched.

She caught a glimpse of an SUV in her rearview. "Joe behind us."

Leo nodded, his mouth set in a line. "I don't know what made him run, but Sugar confirmed his fingerprints were in the cabin, and they found hair that matches his description there."

"He knew what we'd find. And you did use Sugar's name on the phone with her in front of him. Everyone in the area knows Sugar Cookie after that piece *Cowboy State Daily* ran on her. She's as famous around here as the *CSI* actors now."

He sighed. "You're right. My bad."

"Do we arrest him for manslaughter or murder, though?"

"I don't think we have enough for murder."

"She was roughed up. And he's running."

"Yeah. Maybe. We can only follow the evidence."

Delaney caught a glimpse of shiny black in the distance. "I see him!"

"Do you want to wait for Joe to catch up to us?"

She gave him an incredulous look. As she took a curve, she saw Brock's truck again. It was far closer than she'd expected. Too close.

And not moving.

Or right side up.

NINETEEN

Adriana freshened her lip gloss. She wanted to look natural. Too much makeup really stood out in Kearny, and almost any amount was too much. And her silk scarf was already pushing it, but she loved the pop of hot pink with her dark hair. Her social life in Wyoming had been nonexistent. It was official—she was lonely, and she didn't want to mess this up. It wasn't just that, though. Paul was unlike any of the men she'd dated since her husband Jim passed away. Most of them bailed when she told them about Freddy. With Paul, she'd mentioned her son in their first conversation. If Freddy was a deal killer, she didn't want to waste her time. She was tired of the game.

Paul hadn't reacted negatively. In fact, he hadn't reacted *at all*.

"Sorry about that. Don't let your coffee get cold because of me." Back from the bathroom, Paul eased down in his chair, flashing her a white smile. He had perfect teeth. "Thanks for meeting me. You're even prettier in person than in your profile picture."

Teeth mattered to Adriana. A man could get a good haircut, take a shower, and put on clean clothes. Those were short-term fixes. If he didn't take care of himself all the time, his teeth would rat him out.

She wrapped her hands around a thick, white oversized mug. She didn't spend money on fancy coffees, and she'd never been in the Java Joint before. Homey expressions painted on board hung on dark paneling. Not her style, but cute. She sipped. And her latte was fantastic.

"Still warm." She smiled back at Paul. "And thanks. Did you have a long drive to get here?" There was so much she didn't know about him, but she didn't want to be too pushy; like *give me your address so I can start cruising your house.*

Paul emptied two sugar packets into his own mug. "Not too bad."

"I'm just around the corner. I live with my brother. It's not a forever thing, but my son enjoys it. Saved me from having to find a place on the fly. We moved here on a whim, sort of."

"Are you always that spontaneous?"

She laughed. "My brother would say yes. But my husband died young. It's true what they say. You only live once. I want to live."

"I couldn't agree more. What made you move here?"

She leaned in. "My brother used to work undercover with the police. Bad people in the drug trade got too close to us. I *had* to leave."

His eyes widened. "Holy smokes! Your life is much more exciting than mine."

"I probably shouldn't have told you that." She giggled. "Leo would kill me. But it's the truth."

"Well, sounds like it's a good thing you moved to Wyoming. Where was this?"

"Southern California. And it's been much better here. It's not like cartels are a big problem in Kearny."

"I hope not. One of the reasons I moved here was to get away from big city issues."

"Where did you live before?"

"Denver. Too many people. Too much traffic. But don't tell anyone. I think people here hate Coloradoans almost as much as Californians."

"What's up with that anyway? I'm a nice person, but when people hear I'm from California they get weird on me."

"I think the locals want things to stay the way they've always been. Code of the West and all that."

"I don't even know what that is, but I'm cool with them keeping things like they've been. Except that they really do need more charging stations for electric cars."

He nodded. "There's only one place to charge them in Sheridan. None in Kearny. It's uncivilized."

"People here don't seem to understand that we all have a responsibility to take care of the planet." She giggled. "Where will they hunt if we let the earth be destroyed, right?"

He nodded. Laughed. "You're so right." Then he reached across the table and touched her fingers. "I didn't think I'd find anyone with beliefs like mine here."

She flipped her hand over and let their fingers intertwine for a moment, then, not wanting to seem too eager, slid hers back to her mug. "Living here has even changed my brother, I think. That and having a big, fat crush on his co-worker."

"Is he still in law enforcement?"

She tapped her fingers on the white porcelain. "Get this. He's the *sheriff*. Of the whole county! It's an interim thing, but he's thinking about running for the permanent job."

"Does he think he can get elected?"

"I guess it's all about who you know and who gets behind him. And this deputy he has the hots for is pretty wired in. Born and raised here and all that."

Paul lowered his voice. "Workplace scandal?"

"Oh, no. They're not really together. You could cut the

tension between them with a knife, but they're both so noble and all 'not my boss, not someone I work with.'"

"It could hurt him for election though. Getting involved with a subordinate."

"Maybe. But, if I was them... well, I already told you. You only live once."

He lifted his coffee mug. "To living." His blue eyes met hers and held her gaze for several electric seconds. When he spoke, his voice was low and husky. "How soon is too soon to see you again?"

Shivers ran up her spine. "I'm not in a hurry right now."

"I'll get my car." He stood and his Adam's apple bulged as he swallowed. "By the way, love the scarf."

TWENTY

Leo's heart lodged tight in his throat as Delaney hit the brakes and spun the steering wheel. The truck turned perpendicular to the road and slid straight toward Brock's overturned truck. Just off the road, the ground took a steep, rocky dive. He grabbed the hand grip above the window, praying silently.

And then he realized the truck had stopped. They hadn't crashed into the pickup. They hadn't flipped. They hadn't plunged.

"Shit," he said.

"Shit," Delaney agreed. "I don't smell gas or see smoke or flame. Or Brock Tucker."

He called for an ambulance over the radio. Then he said, "How in the world did you do that?"

She unbuckled her seat belt. "Snow can be your friend sometimes. I used it to our advantage to slow us down and keep us on the road."

"Well, I'm glad you were driving."

"Always," she said.

He jumped out and ran toward Brock's truck. Not only did he have a duty to provide aid, but the man in that truck was a murder suspect. He needed him alive so they could figure out what happened to Annabeth Dillon. The snow was deep, though. Leo pitched forward. Caught himself on bare hands buried a foot under and ended up with a cold, wet nose.

Delaney walked slowly up to him, each step deliberate, high-kneed, and stable. She was wearing gloves and a wool cap and carrying the emergency kit. "You look like a bad 80s movie. Face covered in cocaine."

He climbed to his feet. "It's my first Wyoming winter."

"I wish I'd taken a picture."

He brushed away snow, thankful she hadn't.

She passed by him. "Cover me in case he's armed. I'm going in to check on him."

Leo was glad that for once Delaney was evaluating risk and asking for help. But his hands were like ice blocks. He cupped them over his mouth and blew on them. That would have to be good enough. "Got you. I haven't heard or seen him yet." He drew his weapon and pointed it down, safety on. With the treacherous footing, he didn't want to risk another fall and an accidental discharge.

Delaney kept advancing on the overturned truck. "Mr. Tucker? Can you hear me? Are you okay?"

Leo didn't hear an answer, but she was closer. "Anything?"

"Nothing. I don't see any gas leaking. I'm going in after him."

Leo positioned himself to one side as Delaney kicked out the jagged remnants of broken glass on the driver's door. The roof was partially caved in, but the space seemed big enough and stable. She crawled into the upside-down vehicle.

In seconds, she was back out, her face puzzled. "He's not in there."

"What?"

"He's not in the truck."

"I don't see any footprints. Maybe he was thrown clear?"

"I'm going to walk a perimeter."

Leo scanned the ground leading up to the crash then called after her. "Anything?"

The truck blocked his view of her. "Nothing. Dammit!"

"I'll check the road." Leo walked heavy-footed, his eyes sweeping the ground. No indentations, no footprints, no disturbed snow except what the two trucks had kicked up.

Joe stopped beside him, window down. "What's up?"

"Truck rolled. Tucker's not in it. Can you back out and search from the intersection?"

Joe shifted, nodding. "On it."

"Thanks."

Delaney reached Leo just as Joe accelerated backwards. "I don't think this was an accident. We need to find him and go after him, but we're on foot from here on out, and he's got a head start."

"This would be a good time for a snowmobile."

She was already trotting up the right side of the road. "Not deep enough. Now would be a great time for a horse, though."

Leo took the north side. "I'd think he'd be headed some-place particular. Back to town or to someone's house."

"You're probably right. He doesn't look like the type to survive a cross-country escape in this weather." She pulled out her phone. "I've got signal. You keep looking. I'll check Maps and see what's out here."

Leo grunted and trudged onward, shoulders hunched and face down. The wind had picked up, and the blowing snow burned his ears, pelted his cheeks, and stung his eyes. He shoved his hands in his pockets. About fifty yards away, Joe was walking toward him in a similar bowed posture. Suddenly, the snow on Leo's left seemed different, although it was hard to see it well to figure out why. He squinted and shaded his eyes. That did the trick. The smooth surface of the snow looked roughed up, like something had been tackled on it. *Or like someone jumped from a moving truck?* He looked past the disturbance. Were those footprints leading away from it?

Delaney shouted, "There's a house just north, up a creek. It's the closest shelter. Maybe he knows whoever lives there."

"I think I've found where he got out of the truck."

Delaney jogged toward him. Leo shouted for Joe's attention then waved for him to join them.

"What do you think?" Leo asked Delaney.

"I think that's his trail, and we follow it."

"There's got to be a way to drive to that house, though."

"Sure, if that's where he's going. Let's send Joe and Johnson County by vehicle."

"Don't I get the easy job since I'm the sheriff?" Leo muttered.

Joe leaned over, hands on knees, breathing hard. "What's up?"

"These are his tracks. Delaney and I will pursue by foot. We think we know where he's headed. We need you to try to intercept him."

Joe straightened. His face was bright red. "Point me in the right direction."

Delaney motioned him over and showed him her screen.

"I'm going back to the truck for my gloves and hat," Leo said.

Delaney glanced up. "Grab us waters and Powerbars." Then she went back to her conversation with Joe, who was nodding.

Leo walked in his own prints back to their truck. After he'd gathered the items he needed, he noticed a pair of snow boots in Delaney's back seat, with wool socks stuffed in the left boot. He picked one up. They were his boots. Delaney had brought them without telling him. He shook his head. If he survived his first Wyoming winter, it was going to be because of her.

In warm, dry footwear, he rejoined his deputies. "Thanks for the boots, Delaney."

She winked at him. "I was forged in the frigid winters of Wyoming and tempered on roads of Canadian ice. I'll rub off on you eventually."

Leo laughed. *She already has.* "Joe, you good?"

"I know where I'm going and how to get there. I'll radio Johnson County." Joe waved and headed back to his vehicle.

"Ready?" Delaney said.

Leo handed her a Powerbar and bottle of water, then stared across the bleak, snowy landscape. It looked like a scene from a John Wayne movie, right before disaster struck. Of course, that was Hollywood, and the Duke always prevailed.

This was Wyoming, where Mother Nature held the upper hand.

A terrible sense of foreboding settled over him. It was all Leo could do to force himself to start down the slick, rocky descent.

TWENTY-ONE

Delaney strode through the snow. Brock might be leading them on a merry chase, but now that they were on his trail, he wasn't hard to follow. The snow made it impossible for him to hide his tracks. Unfortunately, the terrain would have been challenging even in summer conditions. Boulders. Sage brush. Old fence. Steep slopes and sudden elevation changes. It made the going slower. Speed could lead to injury, which might stop them completely. She hated it, but Brock had the same handicaps.

She and Leo reached a creek bed.

"The water is running. I thought it would be iced over," he said.

"Not this early in the winter. It takes a lot of sustained sub-freezing weather for moving water to freeze." She held out her arms for balance as she made her way across from rock to rock. "It's plenty cold though, so don't fall in."

"Great." Leo picked his way over the rocks. He threw his arms over his head and wobbled.

She reached for his hand. "At least the water is low. Looks like he cut back up this hill. I'll bet he's trying to stay hidden from the interstate. But this is going to be rough sledding."

"We're sledding?"

She put her hand over her mouth to hide her smile. "It's an expression that means this won't be easy. Obviously not one used in San Diego."

"We're short on any vernacular related to snow."

"Brock's tracks cut up the hill. It appears he's aiming to cross the ridge in that saddle."

Leo slipped as he started climbing up after her. Rocks tumbled down the slope behind him.

"Careful. You're too heavy for me to drag out of here."

"You insisted I come overland with you."

Delaney scrambled up the last ten yards and peeked over. The ridge was narrow and dropped off almost immediately on the other side. A puff of snow was still dissipating on the edge. *We're closing in on him.*

She put a finger over her lips, then mouthed, "He's just on the other side."

Leo nodded.

She crept forward to the far edge and lowered herself to a crouch. The animalistic scent of a frightened creature hit her nose. She looked down.

Brock Tucker had himself in a pickle. The northern descent of the ridgeline ended in a cliff at his feet. Not an especially high one, but not one to hop off either, even with snow to land in. He turned to look for a different way down and their eyes locked. He froze.

She flipped open the closure on her holster and put her hand on the grip of her Staccato handgun. "Mr. Tucker, I'm sure we can find a safe way down together. But I'm going to need you to take a few steps away from that ledge, nice and easy."

He wheeled to look out over the expanse again. She felt Leo's presence as he climbed up to crouch beside her. Brock glanced at them again. Just when it seemed like he was about to give in and walk toward them, the rock beneath his feet collapsed, and he screamed as he disappeared from view.

TWENTY-TWO

Joe Tarver had never dreamed a place like this ranch compound existed near tiny Kaycee, Wyoming. A palatial house on a gorgeous piece of property with killer views and an actual manned guard gate that had taken five minutes to talk his way through, all shrouded in a cloak of secrecy. He still didn't know who owned it. He'd asked and been given a company name. It was unfamiliar. Probably a limited liability company to protect owner finances and identity.

He parked in front of the two-story rock and log structure— a larger version of the Duttons' place on *Yellowstone*—and peered back to the south. He didn't see the suspect, Leo, or Delaney making their way across the barren terrain.

"May I help you?" The voice was deep and familiar.

He turned, expecting an acquaintance, and instead recognizing an actor, one of the most famous in the world, whose movies he'd shelled out cash to see in theaters for twenty years, many of them set in the West. The man was almost as famous for his environmental activism and the incendiary documentaries and infomercials he funded and starred in. Not exactly someone whose politics would earn him an invite to his neighbors' tables for dinner. But for the life of him, Joe couldn't remember the guy's name.

"Sorry to bother you, sir." *Would it offend a star not to be recognized, or would it be a relief?* Well, he recognized him. He just didn't know what to call him. "I'm Kearny County Deputy Joe Tarver, from just up north of here. We have a suspect fleeing arrest who's believed to be moving northward across your property." He gestured back toward the south. "Two officers are pursuing him on foot. Have you seen any strangers on your property in the last half hour?"

"Besides you?"

Joe felt his cheeks redden. "Of course. And the two Johnson County deputies who are probably at your gate right now."

The man stared to the south. "Nobody. But I think I see movement up on that ridgeline. Do you have binoculars?"

Alice, Joe's high school sweetheart and wife of thirty years, was a birder. Every one of their vehicles had a full birding kit including binoculars that set him back a week's pay per set. That wasn't counting the birding clinics and conventions she went to all around the world. The special gear. The perfect clothes. *Who cares what you're wearing to bird watch? Certainly not the birds.* All of this after she'd quit her job as a nurse. She had champagne and caviar tastes. He had a ramen and Busch Light job. His doctor said his recent weight gain was due to stress eating. That, and the doughnuts he put away during the extra shifts he worked.

"Absolutely." He fetched the binocs, then trained them on the ridge. "Well, I'll be damned."

"What is it?"

"It's our suspect. And my sheriff and colleague are talking to him. Looks like they'll be—" He had been about to say they'd be bringing Tucker in, but then the front of the rock face on which Tucker had been standing sheared off the mountain, taking Tucker down with it. His scream seemed to echo off the buildings behind them.

"Holy shit!" the property owner yelled. "Did he just go down in a rockslide?"

"I think so." *Tucker might be dead.* Wouldn't that solve a lot of problems—the state wouldn't even have to pay to prosecute him. An open and shut case.

"I've got a Can-Am four-seater. The back folds down to extend the bed. I'll go get it."

"Do you have a medical kit handy? And some blankets?"

"Sure. Give me five minutes. I'll meet you back here."

Five minutes was a long time, but it wasn't as long as it would take to double back for the things they didn't think to bring and discovered they needed once they reached the suspect. Joe sent a quick group text to the sheriff and Delaney.

> *At the ranch house. Saw Tucker go off the ridge. Loading emergency gear and heading out there in owner's ORV. Are you guys OK?*

Then he got on his radio to redirect the EMTs and ambulance. He didn't know the address, but the Johnson County deputies at the front gate could supply that information.

Leo responded.

> *We're fine. Can't get to him. Have to hike down and around. He's not responding to us verbally.*

> *Roger that.*

He thought about sending one more text—he could make some money off this situation—but decided there was no time and headed to his SUV instead. He kept a fairly good emergency kit in the back. He hauled it out then grabbed Alice's birding bag, too. Could be something useful in it. Lastly, he added another layer beneath his jacket and switched out of his driving gloves into heavier ones.

The actor pulled up in the ORV. Joe threw his gear onto the passenger floorboard and climbed in after it. Then they sped straight across the pasture toward the jumble of rocks at the base of the ridge. Joe tried to buckle the seat belt, but it wasn't set long enough to close around his midsection. The bumps made it impossible to adjust it, and he gave up quickly. The visibility was terrible driving into the blowing snow. He should have worn sunglasses to keep it out of his eyes.

The vehicle went airborne, and he wedged his feet hard against the floorboard.

"Sorry," the actor said.

Joe bit his tongue as they landed. "No problem."

A few bumps later, they stopped at a wire gate. Joe was about to lever himself out to take care of it, but the actor held a hand up to stop him.

"I've got it," he said. "It's a tricky gate."

He didn't have to tell Joe twice. He was already feeling battered, bruised, and tired from the violent ride. With the vehicle stopped, his visibility improved. The rock fall was only about twenty yards away. He squinted. A shadow was moving. Not a cow or horse. Something upright. Was it Brock? The figure materialized out of the whiteness. It was a man stumbling toward them.

Then he pitched forward face first and didn't move.

With renewed energy from adrenaline, Joe jumped out and sprinted past the actor, who'd just moved the gate aside. "Catch up with me. I see him."

"Will do."

Joe reached Tucker and fell to his knees. He probed the man's neck, feeling for a pulse at his carotid and wrinkling his nostrils at the coppery odor of Tucker's blood. Leo said they'd confirmed Tucker was on the scene of Annabeth Dillon's death. The man was on the run, which screamed of guilt. Trials were uncertain, expensive, and took too long. *Is it wrong to hope there's no pulse, for everyone's sake?* Tucker's pulse was steady though, rendering the question moot.

Joe said, "Sir, can you hear me?"

Tucker moaned. "My head. My stomach."

"I'm rolling you over. We're going to get you fixed up and take you to the hospital." He pushed the man's body over. Tucker's head looked to have a pretty sizable cut on one temple. The blood was profuse, but most head injuries bled like a mother. His midsection didn't appear to be bleeding, but he could have internal injuries.

"I didn't do it," Tucker said.

"Do what?"

"Kill... anyone."

Joe hadn't arrested him yet, thus he hadn't read him his rights. He could let Tucker incriminate himself. But not if he was just going to blather on about what he didn't do. "Save your breath, Mr. Tucker."

"My wife."

"I'll call her."

"No. Don't tell her."

"Don't tell her you're injured?"

"Don't tell her about Annabeth. I love her."

"You love Annabeth Dillon?"

"No. I love my wife."

A little late to be thinking about that now. "What you tell your wife will be up to you."

The actor crouched beside them. "I think the ambulance just pulled up at my gate. I'm not sure it can get out here."

Joe nodded. "His pulse is strong. He's talking. I saw him walking. I think we should load him and drive him over to meet the EMTs."

Tucker said, "Corey."

The actor gasped. "Brock! What are you doing out here?"

"Long story."

"Damn. That rockslide could've killed you. What were you thinking? Never mind. We're going to get you to the hospital."

Now that Brock Tucker had used the actor's first name, Joe remembered his last one. Castle. Corey Castle. "You two know each other, Mr. Castle?" Joe said, trying it out.

"Yeah, we've found ourselves on the same side of some issues and funding requests. Small community."

"On my count." Joe grabbed Tucker under his arm pits.

Corey secured his grip around Tucker's knees. "Okay."

"Three, two, one, and lift."

Joe and Corey hefted Tucker. Tucker screamed. The sound stopped abruptly, and Joe knew he'd passed out. The few steps to the ORV were difficult in the snow, but they made it without falling and maneuvered him onto the little pickup bed. Joe wished he'd had on his uniform. Alice wouldn't appreciate the blood on his clothes.

Just as they were about to take off, Joe saw Delaney and Leo only ten yards away, running toward them. "Hold up. Those are my colleagues."

Corey called, "We're taking Mr. Tucker to the ambulance. Grab any spot you can."

Leo and Delaney vaulted onto the bed on either side of Tucker. Leo crouched beside him and held onto the Can-Am. Delaney knelt and braced herself.

Joe said, "Delaney and Leo, this is the property owner, Mr. Corey Castle. Mr. Castle, this is Deputy Delaney Pace and Kearny County Sheriff Leo Palmer." He purposefully shortened Delaney's title. She could be a little big for her britches. Any chance to keep her on the same level, he took. It wasn't that he disliked her. He just didn't like their unequal status. He was years older than her. Law enforcement was a third career for him. But still.

"Thanks for your help, Mr. Castle. Nice to meet you." From the look on Leo's face, it was clear he knew who Castle was.

"Likewise." From the look on Delaney's, it was clear she didn't.

"Nice to meet you both." Corey chuckled. "I don't usually get this much attention from law enforcement unless I'm in trouble. Hold on."

He accelerated more carefully this time and drove back around the pasture fence on a two-track. It was far less rough. Tucker didn't make a peep.

The ambulance reached the house at the same time as the Can-Am. Corey drove straight to its rear doors. The EMTs transferred Tucker to a stretcher while Joe gave them a rundown on the man's condition. He was still out cold.

Leo stood at the head of the stretcher. "If he's stable, take him to the hospital in Kearny, please. Our sheriff's department will pick up the tab for the longer haul."

The two men loaded the stretcher into the back of the ambulance.

The driver said, "Yes, sir. We'll let you know either way."

Then they drove away, lights flashing but no sirens.

Joe turned to Corey. "Nice to meet you, Mr. Castle. Thanks again." He offered his hand, and the two men shook, then Castle did the same with Leo and Delaney.

The actor said, "Just remember what a helpful guy I am if we ever run into each other again."

Leo said, "Are you expecting trouble?"

"Occupational hazard."

"What kind is that?" Delaney asked.

Corey looked amused. "How refreshing. You really don't know."

Delaney looked from Leo to Joe. "What am I missing here?"

"Mr. Castle is an activist. And an Oscar winner." Leo put his hands on his hips. "Is something big coming our way, Mr. Castle?"

"Nothing unnecessary."

"I can't wait." Leo's voice was dry.

"I have a call," Corey said. "If you don't mind, I need to get back inside."

"Not at all. We'll be on our way shortly."

Castle waved and disappeared into his enormous home.

Joe said, "Why don't you guys warm up in my SUV? I'll just be a minute and can give you a ride back to your truck." The two of them were covered in snow, mud, and blood. They looked beat.

"No argument from me." Leo headed for the passenger side door.

Joe turned and pressed speed dial. An answering service picked up. *Dammit.* "Brock Tucker was caught in a rockslide during apprehension. He's in custody for Annabeth Dillon's murder and headed to the hospital in Kearny."

Joe turned back toward his vehicle and nearly plowed into Delaney.

"What was that about?" Her face was dark and suspicious.

She heard my call. Joe cleared his throat. "I promised a scoop to a reporter who's done me a few favors." He grimaced. "Don't tell the boss?"

Delaney frowned. "I don't like it."

"I'm not doing anything wrong."

She narrowed her eyes. For a woman who liked to color outside the lines herself, she was such a stickler about certain things. Protecting Leo was one of them. "I'll let you know if I decide to tell him. Give you a chance to do it first."

He nodded. "I guess that's the best I could ask for." He kept his voice friendly. Grateful. Deferential. But inside he was thinking *Why does Delaney have to be such a bitch?*

TWENTY-THREE

Leo huddled with Delaney and Joe outside Brock Tucker's hospital room. The EMTs had honored Leo's request to bring Brock to Kearney, and he was due back from his MRI any moment. Leo hated being here. Everything from the odd mixture of dirty mop water and antiseptic to the squeaky shoes in the corridor reminded him of losing his parents and brother-in-law. While his father had died in the house, his mother had survived several hours and his brother-in-law nearly a day in the hospital. The emotions of that day would never be washed from his psyche.

His phone rang. Caller ID told him it was Dr. Watson. He took two steps away from his colleagues to answer. "Dr. Watson, how are you?" After three months in the sheriff role, he didn't dare refer to her by her given name Louise, as the sheriff who'd hired him had—Delaney's mentor, Coltrane Fentworth, may he rest in peace.

"Hello, Sheriff. I'm wrapping up for the day. I'd hoped to see you and Delaney for the autopsy."

"We'd planned to be there but ended up chasing a fugitive."

"Oh, my. Well, my verbal report will have to suffice for now, then."

"Ready for that verbal report." He raised his eyebrows at Delaney in question—should he put Dr. Watson on speaker?

Delaney nodded at Joe then shook her head *no*. He understood and agreed. Despite his assistance that day, Joe wasn't on the case with them, and, besides, a hospital corridor wasn't exactly the location for this type of conversation.

"Where shall I begin?" Dr. Watson asked.

"Most important question first: natural causes or foul play?"

"Definitely not natural causes. Asphyxiation from strangulation, including a broken hyoid bone in the front of her throat. That's a lot more force than is necessary for so-called breath-play, where one partner chokes another to supposedly heighten sexual arousal. Interestingly, she wasn't drugged although her blood alcohol level was twice the legal limit. So, she was impaired, but not incapacitated."

"Any signs of struggle?" Leo remembered the bruises and blood he'd seen on Annabeth.

"In these cases, it can be hard to draw the line between marks left in consensual sex and a struggle, because minor bruising is consistent with vigorous sexual relations up to and including erotic asphyxiation. But this case is suspicious."

"What makes you say that?"

"The number of injuries, for one, the location for another. Bruises on the wrists, upper arms, and neck and abrasions on the wrist and ankles from the restraints. These are where one would expect to see them with the use of restraints and with breath-play. She had a bloody nose, which could have been accidental or a blow to the face. She doesn't have injuries on the thighs, abdomen, or buttocks. If she had, it would have steered me toward sexual assault and rape. I don't think that was what was going on here. Taken altogether, though, the injuries she did have are a lot. The most troubling of which was a blow to the side of her head. A serious blow with something quite hard but smooth. No identifying marks or residue. I honestly have no idea what it was."

"Hard enough to knock her out?"

"Certainly. I can't say whether it did, of course. Possibly hard enough even to kill her—although it didn't. She died of asphyxiation. It's very hard to draw the line between an incapacitating and a killing blow. Either the person who struck her didn't care if the blow killed her or wasn't aware that it could have been fatal."

"Could it have been accidental? Like from a fall?"

"Possibly. But I find it more plausible that if someone continued sex play after she was incapacitated that the incapacitation was intentional rather than accidental."

Leo nodded, then, realizing she couldn't hear him, said, "I think I'm following you. Did the blow occur before she was restrained?"

"Impossible to say for sure, as the injuries appear to have occurred at roughly the same time, but the blow bled profusely so was clearly before her death."

"If you had to guess, how do you see this whole thing happening?"

"It's speculation, but I'd say Annabeth didn't consent to the restraints or the asphyxiation. That someone struck her in the head to gain her compliance or subdue her or to intentionally injure her. Whether her death was then manslaughter or murder is a harder call."

"Go ahead and guess. I won't hold you to it."

"She was hit in the head, restrained, and strangled to death. The killer didn't report it. That's plenty for the county attorney to prosecute as manslaughter. But I think it was intentional. I've never seen a true accidental erotic asphyxiation with a broken hyoid bone. In fact, breaking a hyoid bone is less common than you'd think even in strangulation. It's hard to do and only occurs about a third of the time."

"Can you identify the killer by anything you found?"

"We can identify a person who was in the cabin with her by the fingerprints. I believe you've already picked up that suspect, according to the radio reports I'm hearing."

"Yes."

"I'm sure Sugar told you, but there are unidentified fingerprints all over that cabin."

"Unfortunately, it's a rental and gets a lot of traffic. But the fact that she found a clear print on an item used that night gave us what we needed. What about DNA?"

"You'll have to wait a few more days."

Leo wanted everything nailed down yesterday. But they'd at least be able to get a warrant and search Brock's house for clothing that matched the fibers in the cabin. "Okay. Thank you. This has been very helpful, as always. Nice doing business with you, Dr. Watson."

"Anytime, Leo. Good luck."

Leo walked back to his deputies as he checked the time on his phone.

"Well?" Delaney asked.

Leo kept his voice low. "I think we have enough to move from manslaughter to murder."

Joe shook his head. "That bastard."

"We need to arrest Tucker and have someone stand guard outside his door. I don't see any way we're getting to transport him to the jail tonight."

"I can do it," Joe said.

Delaney shot Joe an irritated look. *What was that about?* "Did you see all the media out front? *Somehow* news that we have Brock Tucker here in relation to Annabeth Dillon's death has leaked out. With what we learned from Brock and Annabeth's husband about her political aspirations, I think this story is about to blow up. People are going to be trying to get into his room to interview him, too."

Leo pulled at his chin. "Joe, you've already worked a half day during your time off. Tommy's on-call this weekend. I'll bring him in."

Joe shrugged. "Suit yourself. I can at least stay until Tommy gets here to relieve me."

"Thanks," Leo said.

Delaney looked like she wanted to say something, but just then they were interrupted by two orderlies wheeling Brock down the hall on a gurney. He made fleeting eye contact with Leo as he passed by. The orderlies closed the door to Brock's room behind them. Leo strained to hear any conversation behind the door, but it was muffled and seemed perfunctory.

The orderlies stepped out of the room.

"Excuse me," Leo said.

"The doctor will be here in a moment," one of them said. With a brisk nod, she walked away with her colleague.

"Well, okay then, thank you very much," Leo muttered under his breath. He gestured for the deputies to enter the room. "They didn't tell us to *wait* for the doctor." He checked that his body cam was activated, then followed them and shut the door.

Brock opened his eyes, then narrowed them. He was wearing an ice hood over the bandages on his head. Was this a man who would incapacitate a woman, kill her, have sex with her, and leave her discarded like garbage? Anger surged in Leo at the thought of what Annabeth had gone through.

He kept a blank expression on his face. "How you feeling, Mr. Tucker?"

Brock said, "I'll be fine."

"Good. Because you're under arrest for the murder of Annabeth Dillon."

Brock pushed himself up further in bed. His cry was sharp. "But I didn't kill her."

"Hold that thought." Leo recited the Miranda warning,

then held up a hand to keep Brock shushed. "Do you acknowledge that I have advised you of these rights?"

"Yes. Yes."

"Do you understand them?"

"I do."

"Normally, we'd take you to jail and book you in, but that's going to depend on what we learn from the doctor."

"They said I'm staying here. But you don't understand. I'm being set up. I didn't hurt Annabeth."

"Set up. In what way?"

"I don't know. I—I admit I had a relationship with her." He shook his head, then winced.

"Why'd you run this morning if you didn't do anything wrong?"

"I was scared. I didn't know what to do. I made a mistake."

"What kind of mistake?"

"Maybe I should just wait for my attorney to get here in the morning."

Leo stared at him, letting the maybe play out.

Brock frowned. "I can't wait. I need you to know something. I heard you talking to that CSI person."

"Sugar."

"I assume you have or will have fingerprints and DNA that put me up at the cabin."

Leo nodded.

"I, um, I had sexual relations with her there. But it was consensual. Oh God. My wife is going to find out." He lowered his face into his hands for a moment, then took a deep breath and lifted it. "But I cared about Annabeth. It wasn't the first time we'd... been together."

"You were having an affair?"

"A relationship, yes. But neither of us was planning on leaving our spouses."

Leo was intrigued. Annabeth had been having an ongoing

affair with Brock Tucker. What if Pete Smithers *had* known about the cabin—and about the affair? *Don't lose focus. This is your guy.* "Go on."

Brock's face was white. "I don't know how anyone knew she'd be up there. Annabeth had only booked the cabin that day. The owner is sort of a friend of hers. Part of one of her secret activist groups."

"Secret?"

"The mainstream activist groups have to follow the rules. Some people like to get more aggressive about their goals. Means-to-an-end type of people. Less concerned about the law. They fly in the shadows of the public facing groups."

Leo's pulse quickened. A law-breaking element of environmental and wildlife activism—could any of that be related to Annabeth's death? *But no. We have our perp.* He was lying on the bed right in front of them. The evidence said so.

The door clicked open.

"What's the meaning of this? Who told your lot you could be in here?" Their accuser was portly, gray, and red in the face.

"Mr. Tucker consented." Leo held out his hand. "I'm Sheriff Palmer."

"I'm Dr. Baron." The doctor took his hand, grudgingly.

Leo introduced the deputies.

"Are you new?" Delaney asked. "I don't believe I've seen you before."

"I'm covering vacations."

"A traveling doctor?" she asked.

He nodded. "But I care about my patients no matter where the road takes me. This man has sustained a bruised spleen and a concussion. He needs to rest, especially his brain."

Leo nodded. "He's also under arrest for murder. When can we interview him?"

"Murder?" The doctor's face blanched. "Um, uh... tomorrow, assuming I give him the all-clear in the morning."

"Fine. We'll have a deputy posted outside his room until he's released to us. He'll enter the room once an hour to verify Mr. Tucker is still in his bed. Mr. Tucker will have to remain handcuffed to the rail except when he has to leave his bed, and then he'll have to be supervised by a member of our department."

"As long as your deputies don't try to interview my patient, we're good."

"I want to talk now. I have information that can exonerate me, in exchange for immunity," Brock blurted out.

Leo shared a glance with Delaney then caught sight of Joe. His eyes were wide. "You think you know who killed Annabeth?"

"I think I know who wants you to think I did it. And that it is someone you'll definitely be interested in."

Dr. Baron stepped between them. "I've seen this song and dance before. They want an interview from you, Mr. Tucker, when your attorney isn't here. I warn you, a concussion can sometimes cause you to say things you wouldn't otherwise."

"Good thing they hand out law degrees with medical diplomas," Delaney muttered.

Brock frowned. "Hell, I don't know what to do."

Leo tapped his finger in the air, almost like he was pointing at Brock, but not quite. "We'll see you when you're released, Mr. Tucker. But just know I can't approach the county attorney about an immunity deal without more to go on. And not if someone else comes to me with information first."

"If I decide I want to talk to you later, will you come back in?"

"Like I said. It may be a horse race. We'll just have to see what we see."

The stricken look on Brock's face told Leo his words had the desired impact. He expected to hear from his suspect sooner rather than later.

TWENTY-FOUR

By the time Delaney entered the homestead gate, she was exhausted. Texts to Kat and Carrie had gone unanswered. Zeke had called, but she hadn't picked up or listened to the voice mail he'd left. She would, in a little while. First, a shower.

But when she pulled up behind the house, she saw that she wasn't alone. Zeke's Range Rover was there again. She lifted an arm and sniffed under it. *I need a shower.* She wanted to be thrilled—and she did feel flattered—but she needed a re-set, not a rendezvous.

Layers of delicious aromas met her nose as she opened the door. Garlic. Something tangy and creamy. Bread. A fishiness. The music rocking from the stereo wasn't contemporary teen girl, for once. Instead, it was "Kryptonite," a song from her own high school days.

"Hello?" She hung her coat. A vase of red roses anchored the kitchen table. A bottle of white wine stood beside it.

Zeke walked out of the kitchen wearing an apron over a T-shirt that showed off his muscles. "Hi, honey. You're home."

"Zeke. Wow."

He held up a slotted spoon. "I put the pasta on to boil when I heard your truck."

"Where are the girls?"

He grinned. "Kat is at Freddy's. Adriana offered to keep her for the night. Carrie is staying over with a friend. I wrote the name and phone number on a piece of paper. It's on your nightstand."

It took Delaney a moment to process the information. Zeke had stashed the girls away without asking her. Granted, he'd called, and she'd ignored him. But... the girls knew better. And Carrie—the last time she'd been allowed to go on a sleepover, she'd thrown a rager. She hadn't been grounded per se—not anymore—but she was on probation.

"I hope that's okay? I wanted to do something special for you."

He won't be here forever. Recovering, she said, "Yeah. Sorry —I'm a mess. I need a shower, and then I'll be half human."

He waved the spatula. "Go. Dinner's on your schedule. Shrimp fettucine alfredo, garlic bread, Caesar salad."

"You made all that?"

"Well, I bought the bag version of the salad. And dessert is pre-made strawberry shortcake. But the rest is me."

"I'll hurry."

He disappeared into the kitchen. As she walked to her room, she heard him singing. She shucked her duty belt, locked her gun in the safe, chose a change of clothes, and sequestered herself into the bathroom.

She leaned back against the door and closed her eyes. This was a seduction scene. Was she ready for intimacy with Zeke? With anyone? "Honestly, I'm not sure," she said aloud.

After a quick shower and dry shampoo in her hair, she returned to the kitchen. Her stomach growled loudly. She pressed a hand into it. "Oops."

Zeke winked and handed her a glass of wine. "An Oregon Chardonnay."

Delaney couldn't remember the last time she'd had alcohol two nights in a row, but she took it from him. "What can I do?"

"Besides save the world from crime? Warm a seat. I'll just plate up and dinner is served." He bowed.

It felt odd to be waited on in her own kitchen. Even as a girl—before her father died and she was dumped into foster care—she'd always helped, and one night a week dinner was solely her responsibility. Wednesdays. When her grandmother had Bible study.

Zeke set a bowl of salad beside her place mat then a steaming plate of pasta and garlic bread in front of her. "It smells delicious."

"Wait until you taste it. It's my specialty."

"So, this is how you woo all your women?"

He put his own bowl and plate down. "All my women? And you'd get this impression how?"

She took a sip of the wine, stalling. "A lucky guess."

"How do you woo all your men?"

She attacked the pasta, spearing a shrimp then twirling fettucine around the tines of her fork. Salad was filler in her world. "Taming girls is my life."

"Leo said you dated a state cop?"

"For half a minute. My last serious boyfriend was before I moved back to Kearny, and he was a waste of a year."

"Did you marry the guy who kept you away from me?"

"Nope. Dodged that bullet. How about you?"

He flashed his bare ring finger.

"Never?"

"Never."

They ate in silence for a few minutes. She'd mowed down the pasta and nibbled at the salad because he'd gone to the trouble of making it.

"It's all delicious," Delaney said.

"Is your wine okay?"

She took another sip. A tiny one. "Wonderful. I'm just not much of a drinker."

He laughed. "When I met you, you were."

"That was a symptom of an underlying issue. Bad fiancé." Needing a quick subject change, she said, "Are you headed back overseas?"

"Eventually. I just finished a stint."

"Anything you can tell me about it?"

"I survived. Anything else, and I'd have to kill you."

"I mean what do you do?"

"Let's just say I have a very exciting job that requires me to stay mentally and physically ready."

Has to be Special Forces. What did they call them in the Marines? Raiders? It was sexy as hell, especially when combined with his culinary skills. He could woo with the best of them.

He held the bottle over her glass.

She put her hand over it. "I'm good."

"Dessert?"

She patted her belly. "In a little while. That was a lot of food."

He took their plates to the kitchen.

"I'll get cleanup."

"Nope. This is all on me tonight. You relax. Put your feet up."

"I can pick us out a movie."

Zeke gave her a bemused look. "Uh, sure. You do that."

Butterflies cavorted in her belly. And lower. She went into the living room and used the remote control to scroll a streaming channel, taking her time, dismissing most of the choices. *Nothing romantic. Nothing erotic. Something funny. Or violent. Or both. A Marvel action adventure.* "Have you seen *Infinity War*? It's one of the Avengers movies."

Zeke slid his arms around her waist from behind and spoke so close to her ear that his lips and breath tickled it. "Is that really how you want to spend tonight?"

Her mouth went dry.

TWENTY-FIVE

Joe sat across from Tommy in the hospital cafeteria. The mashed potatoes were dry and the meatloaf greasy, but it was this or Alice's specialty—petrified chicken breasts. He was glad Tommy had talked the floor nurse into keeping an eye on their guy so they could eat.

"Anything I should know about this guy?" Tommy took a bite of his hamburger.

Joe chugalugged his milk, wiped his mouth with his hand, and covered a belch. "Leo doesn't want anyone talking to him. Treat it just like an overnight in jail."

"No visitors?"

"Only hospital staff. And if he has to pee, you have to go with him."

"Great."

"He's probably not going to do much. He fell off a cliff today. I think his head really hurts."

"What did he do?"

Joe checked for anyone in earshot in both directions. None. He leaned in and whispered, "Leo didn't tell you?"

Tommy shook his head.

"Murdered that woman from Jackson. He denied it."

"Nobody admits it."

Joe chuckled. "He even asked for immunity. Said he'd give us bigger fish to fry."

Tommy tilted his head, chewing. "Wow. Did he name names?"

"Supposed to tomorrow morning. The doc wouldn't let him talk to us tonight because of his head injury."

Tommy groaned and clutched his stomach.

"What's the matter?"

"I've had a gripey stomach today."

"Can you stand watch? If not, I can cover it."

"Yeah. I just took some stuff for it. I'll be fine."

"You're sure?" Joe thought about Alice at home. She planned to show him a brochure for a Galapagos Islands cruise she wanted to go on. Without him. He'd get to pay for it, though.

"Yeah. Well, maybe if I could just make one more trip to the bathroom."

"Take your time."

TWENTY-SIX

Brock Tucker adjusted the ice pack bound to his abdomen. He'd become numb to the hood, but the cold on his stomach was still too much. But he could handle it. What he couldn't imagine was how he was going to bear up to becoming public enemy number one in his adopted home state. He'd been a big fish in a small pond. His company a huge success. His much younger wife beautiful, popular, and admired. His ranch the envy of the county. His status as political king- and queen-maker secured.

It had been just one indiscretion. Just one affair.

Annabeth.

The woman had been like a fever dream. From half an hour after they'd met, they'd been tearing each other's clothes off. In public bathrooms. In cars. In the laundry room of her house with her husband down the hall. Was she beautiful? Was she someone he liked? Those things weren't even a consideration. Nor was his wife, who was the polar opposite of Annabeth. Riley Tucker was measured, exacting. A woman who doled out sex like a commodity. No, like a vending machine that only took one-thousand-dollar bills.

Annabeth was brash and ambitious. After their first time,

she'd bitten his ear lobe and told him she wanted to be a U.S. senator and she knew he was the one to make it happen. He cringed. Had that been why she'd wanted him? Could she have been faking it with him as a means to an end?

The thought felt like a horse stepping on his chest. The humiliation. Her manipulation. But he'd always known it was possible, even though she had sworn her desire for him was separate from her lust for power.

He just hadn't cared because with her he was virile and alive and a god. A fucking god, literally. Their trysts became wilder. More out of control. Closer to the edge. In retrospect, she'd been controlling him by letting him control her.

"She got what she wanted," he muttered.

"This has to be the last time," she'd panted, while he was inside her at that damned mountain cabin.

It had taken him a few seconds to stop. To ask, "Why?"

"An affair with you would wreck my credibility as a candidate."

"After you're elected then."

She'd shaken her head. "Brocky, don't you want to see how far we can take this?"

For a moment he thought she was talking about their relationship. *Yes I do,* he'd thought. "What do you mean?"

"A cabinet post? Or what if I could be the first female vice president? Or even president?"

Rage had exploded inside him. "Then let's make this one neither of us will ever forget," he'd said.

"Yes," she'd screamed. "Yes!"

She'd wanted him. She had. She just hadn't wanted him more than she'd wanted to be elected.

A knock sounded at the door. He assumed it was someone on the medical staff. His guard dog wasn't going to let anyone else in. And the criminal defense attorney his business lawyer had called for him wouldn't be able to visit until the morning.

Jenn Herrington was a former ADA in Texas and came highly recommended. Thank goodness he'd been able to take her call before his phone had been confiscated. She'd promised they'd talk through a strategy to make this all go away.

But it would take more than a superstar attorney to remove the stain. This would ruin his marriage and his political career. Maybe his business.

The door opened. He recognized his visitor and sighed. "You. Hello."

"The nurse asked me to give you this." The visitor handed Brock a cup of liquid.

"What is it?"

"I didn't ask."

Brock shrugged and downed it. Cranberry juice with a bitter aftertaste.

"How are you feeling?"

"Like I fell off a cliff in a rockslide. But I'll survive."

The visitor took the empty cup. "I wouldn't be so sure about that."

TWENTY-SEVEN

Leo paced the floor of his bedroom. For the last hour, he'd been researching the leads Pete Smithers had provided. The people harassing Annabeth. The op-eds against her. He hadn't found anything useful enough to keep his attention, which was no surprise as they had the probable murderer under arrest at the hospital, and the guy Leo liked second best for the crime awaiting arraignment for assaulting Delaney.

Jangly noise blared from the television in the living room. Kat and Freddy were playing something Hogwarts related on the Xbox. He heard Kat whoop and Freddy shout, "Sick!"

It reminded him of the thing he was trying to distract himself from—Adriana was keeping Kat overnight so Zeke could try to seduce Delaney.

His phone rang. He didn't recognize the number, but it was a local area code, so he picked up. "Hello?" His voice was snappier than he'd intended.

"Is this Leo Palmer?" a woman asked.

"It is."

"This is Bethany Willett. I conduct child welfare interviews for the state. I believe a Delaney Pace works with you?"

He frowned. "Yes. What's this about?"

"She has an adoption application pending. Or, two of them, I believe."

"I'm aware. And did you realize that it's a Saturday evening?"

"I did, and I apologize. Some information has come to light about her applications that has put us in a bind, given that the hearing is coming up. Time is of the essence. Could I have a few minutes of your time?"

"Sure. Monday morning, at my office."

"I'm just right outside. I could pop in if that's okay?"

Leo pulled the phone away from his ear and mouthed, "What the hell?" Anything to help Delaney and the girls, though. He returned to it and said, "Fine. I'll meet you at the door." He ended the call and marched through the house.

Adriana was at the kitchen table, typing on her laptop, a big smile on her face. *The new boyfriend, I'll bet.* In the living room, he turned off the TV.

"Uncle Leo!" Freddy's dark hair hung over one eye. Gaming was a favorite pastime of his. He had a zest for life that included sports, reading, outdoors, music, and cake decorating. In fact, there was a culinary masterpiece in the kitchen at that moment that Freddy had created with Adriana the day before. A San Diego Chargers football helmet, sculpted and iced. Freddy refused to acknowledge the team's move to Los Angeles. The kid's diverse interests amused Leo. As did his SoCal tween attitude, which to some kids in Kearny made him a pariah. Luckily, Kat seemed to think he was cool.

Leo chucked him on the arm. "A woman with the state is coming to interview me about Delaney's adoption applications. I need you guys to go to your room and keep it down."

Kat's mouth dropped open. "Why is she here?"

"I'm not sure yet."

"But—"

The doorbell rang.

"That's her. You guys stay out of sight, okay?"

Kat nodded, but she looked rattled.

"Come on," Freddy said, touching her elbow. "Gotchoo. People have been giving me grief about Uncle Leo getting recalled from sheriff because he's a loser—"

"Hey!" Leo said.

"But we know he's fire, right? That's how it is with your aunt, too."

He was still talking as Kat followed him and his clomping boots out. Leo smiled. The kid had taken to wearing them to fit in at his new school. None of them in his family could get used to the change from Reef sandals to Tony Lamas.

Leo opened the door.

"I'm here for Mr. Palmer?" a voice said. The woman outside was standing off the step and so short that he literally hadn't seen her at first.

It irked him that she was here, that she was bringing problems about Delaney, that she was dumping them on him—or expected him to dish—yet she didn't even know who he was. It wasn't like he expected people to kiss his ring. But her interruption of his Saturday night meant she could do better.

So, he answered her in a manner and tone that was out of character. "Kearny County Sheriff Leo Palmer, yes."

Her eyebrows rose. "Sorry. I thought you were just Delaney's co-worker."

"I am. Also, her friend. And her boss." Even if Delaney didn't treat him like a boss and he didn't supervise her like one. "What's this about, Ms. Willett?"

She stomped her feet. "It's cold. Do you mind if I come in for us to talk?"

"For a few minutes. It's Saturday night. I've been working all day. I'd like some time with my family." He stood aside to allow her in.

In the living room, she removed her coat. He didn't offer to take it from her, nor did he offer her a drink or a seat. After a few moments of awkward silence and intermittent eye contact, she sighed. "Mr., uh, I mean Sheriff Palmer, it's come to our attention that as a single guardian, Ms. Pace works long hours and leaves her niece in the care of the town drunkard. A Mr. Skeeter, um, Skeeter..."

"Skeeter Rawlins. A local private investigator. He does work for me occasionally as well."

"Really? And you're aware of his reputation and penchant for drinking?"

"I'm aware that he's sober when he works for me and sober every time I've ever known him to work for Delaney."

"Surely you'd agree that with a girl Kateena's age his is not the best influence? And a male nanny with a girl of her age? Well, that's just asking for *trouble*."

Leo cocked his head. "Actually, no, I would not agree. Skeeter loves Kat and would protect her with his life."

"Which we have heard is part of the problem. Ms. Pace's occupation has put Kateena in danger many times. And now she is asking to adopt a juvenile delinquent as well."

Kat burst into the room, fists balled, eyes flashing. "Skeeter is the best babysitter ever. And Carrie is not a juvenile delinquent. You're just saying all this to make my aunt sound like a bad mother so she can't adopt me, and you don't even know us. Aunt Delaney is the best aunt and mother in the world. She's my only family besides Skeeter and Carrie. And you, you're just a... a... a... hater."

Leo walked over and put his arm around the girl's shoulders. "Ms. Willett, this is Kat Pace."

The investigator puffed up. "Well, if this doesn't just prove my point. What awful behavior from a young lady her age toward an adult."

Freddy jumped in between the investigator and Kat. "Just because you're a fossil doesn't make it okay to be so rude."

Leo's tight chest felt too small to contain his pride at his nephew's defense of his friend. This is how Delaney felt about Kat, he knew. He'd always loved his nephew, but he'd never had the chance to live with him and see up close the fine young man he was becoming. "And this is Kat's best friend, my nephew Freddy. I think it's time for you to go, Ms. Willett. You won't get what you want from us anyway."

She huffed. "You didn't tell me Kateena was here."

"You didn't ask."

The woman stared at him, her mouth opening and closing, until Leo pointed at the door and repeated his instruction. "Out. Now."

She whirled and nearly fell as she jerked the door open. It slammed behind her.

TWENTY-EIGHT

Delaney's phone rang, which gave her a chance to put a few inches between Zeke and herself. She checked caller ID. It was Leo. "I have to take this."

"Are you sure?" Zeke trailed his fingers down her arm.

She smiled at him but stepped into the kitchen, aware that she felt relief. *I'm not ready. At least not for Zeke.* In Delaney's mind's eye, her grandmother's pinched face appeared, and the pious woman's sanctimonious voice resounded in her head. *The Lord works in mysterious ways.*

Into the phone, she said, "Yes?" Out of her peripheral vision, she saw Zeke checking his own phone.

"How's it going?"

Her eyes narrowed. Kat was spending the night at Leo's house. Zeke wasn't there. Was Leo interrupting things on purpose? "Fine. Is Kat okay?"

"Um, yes, but listen, I just had a visit from a Bethany Willett, an investigator with the state. She was here about your adoption applications."

"What? On a Saturday night? At your place?"

"Yeah. And it didn't go well.

"Start from the beginning."

"She was asking about your work hours and Skeeter's drinking."

"You've got to be kidding me."

"That's not all. She brought up Carrie's... issues, and then Kat came running in and went bonkers. Freddy, too." He paused. "Shit. I've got a call coming in that I have to take. Hold on."

"You can't put me on hold when you're in the middle of something like this!" But Delaney realized she was talking to dead air. She paced and fumed as she waited for Leo to return.

"Everything all right?" Zeke had walked into the kitchen and was staring at her intently, a look of concern on his face.

"Yes. I mean, no. I—"

Leo was back. "I'm sorry, Delaney. That was Tommy. Can you meet me up at the hospital?"

"Is something wrong?"

"You could say that. Brock Tucker is dead."

TWENTY-NINE

Tommy wrung his hands and rocked from side to side.

"Take me through it from the beginning," Leo said, thinking: *Man, I'm glad I have the body cam footage of our meeting with Brock.*

"I relieved Joe about seven o'clock. I let Brock up to go to the bathroom, then he got back in bed, and I handcuffed him to the side rail. It was quiet up here, so I asked a nurse I know to call on my cell if he got loose. Tildy. She said she would. I mean, he was hooked to the bed, right?"

Leo wanted to chew out the young deputy for defying a clear instruction in the first five minutes of his assignment. He'd had one job. That job was to stay outside Brock's door. But taking a piece of Tommy's hide wouldn't help now. Leo needed information, so he nodded. "Right."

"I made a pit stop then met Joe down at the cafeteria to grab dinner and some drinks and snacks to get me through the next few hours. I was only gone twenty minutes. A half hour, max. Everything was fine when I left." Tommy's voice was ragged.

"Well, he didn't get loose."

"Right. Right."

"When did you find out he was dead?"

Tommy bit his lip and nodded. "A machine was beeping, and people were running down the hall when I came back up. I went into his room, but there was nothing anyone could do."

"I'll talk to the medical staff, but do they know what happened? Was it his spleen? Or a heart attack?"

Tommy's face whitened. "No, sir. No, sir. I wish. It was... it was..."

"Just spit it out, Tommy. It's not your fault."

"But that's just it. It was. He shot himself. With my gun."

Leo closed his eyes. *Shit.*

THIRTY

Zeke idly poked around Delaney's living room. It was cozy, if a little dated and worn. And the alcohol situation was dismal. Briefly, he considered rummaging around a bit. *Delaney has always been mysterious.* Did he dare try to learn a few of her secrets? Even the evening and morning before, he hadn't had a chance, since the girls were with him. When he'd arrived today, he'd started cooking from the jump. But Delaney was a trained law enforcement officer who probably did low tech James Bond-type shit. Tape under drawers to show if they'd been pulled out. Strings that broke if doors opened. He was no slouch, but she'd probably bust him. He decided to give it a pass.

She'd promised to text him when she was on her way back from the hospital. That was a good sign. If she wasn't going to let him in her bed, she'd have sent him home. At least that was what he figured. She wasn't making it easy, though. But he had no idea how long she'd be, and he was bored out of his mind. He knew he wasn't going to get her drunk, but that didn't mean he couldn't be. He only had a week of freedom left. Time for this one last fling. In two weeks, he'd be married and back in the desert. *No whiskey, no women, no song.*

Yeah, he was going to get his drunk on. Then he was going to spend the night getting reacquainted with every square inch of the body he'd never forgotten before he made a vow to forsake all others, forever.

Not that he was sure he could. Make the vow—yes. Keep it... well, forever is a very long time.

He pulled his keys from his pocket and tossed them in the air as he walked out to his car. It had snowed again. How did people live in a place like this? He enjoyed skiing—and ski bunnies—as much as the next red-blooded guy, but only when he was bundled up and even then only in short bursts. The rest of the time, he let his inner iguana soak up the sun.

His feet sank into the white stuff and snow spilled into his shoes.

Cursing, he got into the car, turned on the engine, and jacked the heater up to high. He backed up and reversed direction, fighting the steering as the rear of the Range Rover lost traction. He eased off the gas. The last thing he wanted was to get stuck out here. He turned onto the road and headed back toward town.

His thoughts touched on Leo for a moment. Zeke had expected this visit to his old friend to go differently. He'd figured they'd hang out, drink a few twelve-packs, and reminisce. Leo was living outside the civilized world, after all. It wasn't like Zeke had expected there to be places to see and things to do. *Not counting Leo's birthday happy hour as either.* No way had he imagined Delaney as part of this picture. Maybe later Zeke would regret the missed time with Leo, but they weren't the "Bros before Hos" kind of friends. Zeke would have expected Leo to drop him in a nanosecond for the right woman.

He pulled onto the highway toward town, but town wasn't his destination. A quarter mile later the neon lights of the Loafing Shed came into view. He used his blinker, then laughed at himself. There were no headlights behind him or in front of him. He counted the vehicles parked in front of the roadhouse. Five. Well, he wasn't going to have trouble finding a barstool.

Inside, the atmosphere was boisterous, though. The jukebox was cranking with something twangy. The five cars must have been filled like they were on the way to a clown conference, because the bar was almost full. He sidled his way through the crowd up to the bar. He took a stool between a canoodling couple and a blonde a few years older than him.

"Hey, you're Leo's friend, right?" the bartender asked, setting a bowl of peanuts in the shell in front of him. He remembered her sexy curves but not her name. "The one that knew Delaney from back when."

"Zeke. Yes." He scooped out a peanut, popped it in his mouth, and sucked the salt off the shell. The he cracked it between his teeth. He spit the shell out. This seemed like the kind of place where shells went on the floor so he dropped them by his feet, then chewed the nuts.

She touched her chest, right above her cleavage. "Mary. How did you know Delaney?"

"We met in a beach bar. The rest is history. Or maybe a little bit of right now." He winked.

Mary laughed. "What are you having?"

"I'm in the mood for whiskey. What do you pour?"

Beside him, a husky voice said, "I wouldn't if I were you."

He turned. It was the blonde. "Wouldn't what?"

"Drink the house swill." She lifted a glass. "I'm having Skrewball Peanut Butter Whiskey."

"Sounds gimmicky."

"But delicious." She lowered her lashes. "Or do you have to swear off everything that tastes good when you sign on with special forces?"

"Who says I'm special forces?"

She laughed. "Oh, come on. Tell me I'm wrong."

He let it go. She was right, after all. "Skrewball, huh? If you vouch for it..."

"I do."

Zeke held up two fingers. "Another of those for her and one just like it for me."

Mary flipped a glass. "Coming right up. Want to open a tab?"

What Zeke wanted was to get a booty text from Delaney. He put down a twenty. "Nah, I'll stick with cash."

When Mary had turned away, the woman said, "Thanks for the refill. It was a double."

"Uh oh."

"No, it's all good." She leaned closer. "I know Delaney. I used to be real close to her brother."

"I didn't know she had a brother."

"He's dead to her now."

Zeke arched his brows. "Gotcha. Was she a hellion back when?"

Their drinks came, glasses clanking on the wood.

"Thanks," Zeke said to Mary.

But she was already on to another customer. A tall, heavyset man he'd seen at Leo's soiree.

"Let's get a table and I'll tell you all about her," the woman said.

No one else was vying for his attention. He shrugged. "Sure."

He followed her to a table in a back corner. A text came in on his phone. *Delaney?* The anticipation set his skin on fire and a surge of blood to his best places. He hadn't wanted a woman this badly in a long time. But when he checked his phone, it wasn't her. *Buzzkill.* In fact, it wasn't someone he wanted to hear from at all.

He shoved his phone back in his pocket, then set his drink down. "Gotta hit the latrine first, if you don't mind."

She waved her hand. "Be my guest."

He was back within a minute. Small-town bars—no lines in bathroom. It was one thing to like. Standing by his chair, he tossed his double back.

The woman applauded. "That's one way to make sure you don't taste it and lose your man creds."

He had tasted it though. She wasn't wrong. It was tasty stuff. He started to signal Mary for another.

"Oh, my," the woman said.

He glanced down at her.

"I'm not feeling so hot." She was staring at her empty glass.

"You've had four shots of that stuff since I've been here."

"Yeah, well, I had more before you came."

"Do you need to call an Uber?"

Her nose scrunched up. "Uber? Where do you think you are? There's no Uber here." Her voice grew singsong. "No Lyft. No cabs. No buses. No trains. This is small-town Wyoming."

"Do you have a friend that can give you a ride home?"

She made a sad face. "I came alone."

He started to suggest that she call someone. *Don't be a dick, Zeke.* He was here, she was Delaney's friend, and she needed help. "I can give you a ride. If you'd like."

"Really?" Her voice was starting to slur.

"Really."

She smiled, stood, and swayed.

"Watch yourself." He caught her and held her upright.

"I need to go to the bathroom. You can warm up the car. What are you driving?"

He described the Range Rover and left to get the heater cranked, sighing. Why did being a good guy feel like such a shit idea? He pulled on the wool cap and gloves he'd borrowed from Leo. As long as he was free when Delaney texted, it didn't matter how he spent the evening until then.

THIRTY-ONE

When Delaney joined Leo and Tommy, both men looked like someone had kicked their puppies. "Sorry it took me so long to get here. I'd ask who died, but I know it was Brock."

Tommy covered his eyes with one hand. Two Kearny City Police officers emerged from a hospital room, waved, and kept walking down the hall away from them.

"What? What is it?" she asked.

Leo said, "Brock got hold of Tommy's gun and shot himself."

"Holy moly!" Delaney had expected to hear Brock died of a heart attack after his stress and injuries. Not suicide. And she couldn't believe Tommy had allowed his gun to be stolen. Or that Brock had the skills to take it from him.

"You showed up right as we were talking about it. We still have to go through the details, don't we, Tommy?"

"Yes, sir." Tommy didn't look up.

Delaney said, "I thought Brock was eager to meet with his attorney. It seemed like he believed he could stay out of jail. I mean, he was upset his wife was going to learn about his affair, but he wasn't acting like he'd given up on life."

Leo shrugged. "I didn't think so either. But it could have just been smoke and mirrors. Maybe the reality of life in prison and all he would lose was too much for him."

"Or he could have had an attack of remorse," Tommy said.

Delaney thought about the man she'd chased around Johnson County the day before. The one who'd spun his story in his hospital room. Not once had he expressed grief about Annabeth passing. She patted Tommy's shoulder. "Don't beat yourself up. Learn, and move on."

"Let's work on that now," Leo said. "The learning part." He pointed at Brock's room. "In there."

Tommy blanched. "But he's... it's..."

"Gruesome. Yes. But I need you to take Delaney and I through what happened."

Tommy shuddered, but he ducked under the crime scene tape and led the way.

Leo whispered to Delaney, "You take the lead. He's pretty shaken up."

"Yet you're sending him into the death scene."

"He needs thicker skin."

"Wouldn't you be the more sensitive interviewer?"

He smiled. "Usually. But I want to be thinking instead of worrying about his feelings. This isn't going to go well for our department."

She thought about the potential recall vote on Leo. He was right. "All right." She hurried to catch up with Tommy, Leo right behind her.

The room was empty except for the obviously dead body of Brock Tucker. Blood and brain were splattered on the wall behind him. *Hollow points,* Delaney noted. The ammunition of choice in a cop's handgun, designed to do maximum damage inside a target rather than to pass through. Brock's hand was in his lap. The gun had landed on his body a few inches from his fingers.

"I think I'm going to be sick," Tommy said.

"Not in here, you're not." Leo's face was blank but firm.

Tommy started to head into the attached bathroom.

"Not in there either."

Tommy's eyes darted from Delaney to Leo and back. His Adam's apple bulged.

"You need to go find a place?" Leo said.

He shook his head with minimum movement. "I'll be fine."

"All right," Delaney said. "Then let's start at the beginning. What time did you get here?"

"I guess about six-thirty. A little after, maybe."

"Then what?"

"I already told the sheriff. I took Mr. Tucker to the bathroom, hooked him back up like he is now, got Tildy to watch Brock's door, then went with Joe to the cafeteria. When I came back, he was dead."

"Let's back up. Assuming Brock took your gun when you were in here—"

"But he didn't."

"How do you know that?"

"I had it on me in the cafeteria."

"You're sure?"

"I, uh—I had to take my belt off and leave it with Joe."

"Why?"

He lowered his voice. "Bathroom issues. The gun gets in the way."

"Oh, I know. I don't have the luxury of standing up for number one."

"Uh, yeah."

"So, the gun was still in your belt when you got it back from Joe?"

"That's the thing. I was in the bathroom a long time."

"How long?"

"Ten minutes? Fifteen?"

"And?"

"I was in a big hurry when I came out. Joe met me at the door to the bathroom, handed me the belt, and said Alice was upset with him and he had to leave."

"Okay. And then what?"

"And then I came up here."

Delaney frowned at him. "Go on."

"Alarms were going off. I ran into Brock's room. My gun was in his lap."

"You're saying that Joe...?"

"I don't know what I'm saying." Tommy's voice was shrill. "I handed my gun and belt to Joe. Fifteen minutes later he handed my belt back without my gun in it, and Brock Tucker was dead."

Delaney's jaw dropped. Had Joe given Brock Tommy's gun?

THIRTY-TWO

Leo pulled Delaney aside in the cafeteria. The two of them huddled in a corner. He'd sent Tommy home on suspension pending an investigation into misuse of his firearm. He'd questioned the staff that were around. No one had seen a gun until it was discharged and lying in Brock's lap. Leo had tried calling Joe in, but he was forced to leave a cryptic voice mail since Joe wasn't picking up. It had been all he could think of to do.

Honestly, he was rattled.

Delaney pulled her hair back, stretching her face. It made her look as tense as he felt.

"I did a thing," Leo said.

Delaney waved for him to continue speaking.

He opened the radio tracking app on his phone. "I have an app that shows me where our radios are."

Delaney's face scrunched. "You mean where *we* are."

"If you have your radio with you, yes."

"I thought only our vehicles were tracked."

"*You guys* only have access to each other's vehicle information. I know the location of your radios."

"But that's invasive."

"Delaney, I can see where Joe is."

Her expression eased. "Where his radio is."

"Yes."

She peered at his screen. "His radio is at his home address. Maybe he and Alice are asleep."

"Do you sleep through calls from me?"

"I only wish."

Leo nodded. "Either something is wrong or he's not there."

"What about earlier?"

"What do you mean?"

"Can you tell where he was when Brock shot himself?"

Leo nodded and accessed the history. "I can try."

"How accurate is it?"

"Ninety-five percent to within thirty feet."

"Show me."

Leo tried to, but he quickly ran into a problem. "I can see Tommy and Joe were both in the hospital when Brock shot himself. But the cafeteria appears to be nearly directly below Brock's room."

"So, we can't tell whether Joe was up there."

"No. And even if we could—"

"We don't know where the gun was."

Leo nodded. "We've got to find Joe."

Delaney gestured for Leo to follow her. She stopped in front of the coffee vending machine. "Want one?"

"Good idea."

Delaney pressed a few buttons. "There's something you need to know. About Joe."

Leo groaned. "Why do I sense this isn't the good kind of something?"

"Because you're smarter than the average good-looking guy. I'm pretty sure Joe is on the take, feeding information to reporters."

"And you're just telling me this."

"Like you just told me about the radio tracking."

"Touché."

"I only had reason to suspect this for the first time earlier today. But it makes sense. He's been acting super stressed. Gaining weight. It could be guilt."

"Well, shit. All the more reason to pay him a visit."

"Shouldn't we interview that nurse first? The one keeping an eye on things for Tommy?"

"Tildy. Good idea. Maybe we'll have something definitive before we talk to Joe."

When they both had their coffees—Leo's light and sweet and Delaney's black as road tar and smelling about the same— the two of them returned to the second floor and the nurse's station. Leo asked the nurse at the desk for Tildy. She looked frightened but pointed down the hall. A woman was consulting a tablet outside a patient's room.

Leo headed toward her. "Excuse me. Are you Tildy?"

"I'm Tildy Parrish." Her face was grave. "Is this about Mr. Tucker?"

"Yes. Do you have five minutes to speak to us?"

She nodded. "How about we go to the breakroom? We'll have some privacy there."

"Good idea," Delaney said.

The three entered the breakroom and sat around a Formica-topped table. Delaney glanced at Leo.

He nodded. To Tildy, he said, "My colleague Delaney Pace has some questions for you."

After she'd obtained the basics from Tildy about her job and personal information, Delaney launched into the events of the evening. "Our deputy, Tommy Miller, said he took a break at about seven o'clock and that he asked you to call him if Brock left his room."

She nodded. "More like about six forty-five. We have a floor meeting at seven."

"Where was that held?"

"Here in the breakroom. It only lasts for fifteen minutes."

"Is this a regular thing?"

She rolled her eyes. "Yes. Our supervisor likes to hear herself talk. Every morning at nine, every night at seven."

"Was anyone watching Mr. Tucker's room during that time?"

"No. But he was handcuffed to the bed." Her face took on a panicked look. "Tommy didn't say I couldn't leave. Am I in trouble?"

"Oh, no. You're fine. We're just building a timeline. It wasn't your responsibility. You were doing your job."

"Thank God." She fanned her face with her hand.

"You called him Tommy. Do you know each other?"

Tildy blushed. "We've gone out a couple of times. It's nothing serious."

Leo scribbled on his tablet and didn't look up at her. Tommy hadn't mentioned he was dating the nurse. He wasn't sure if that mattered. But he didn't like it.

Delaney cleared her throat. "When was the first time you knew anything was wrong with Mr. Tucker?"

"I came back to my station. I decided to check on him since Tommy wasn't back yet. And... and he was slumped over and there was blood on him and behind him and everywhere. Then I checked his pulse. There was none, of course. And I called for help. I didn't know what had happened. My boss came. She found the gun on the floor."

"It was on the floor?"

"Yes. She handed it to me, and I put it in Mr. Tucker's lap. It felt wrong to leave it on the floor, you know? I called Tommy, but he was already coming into the room by then."

Again, Leo made a note. Tildy's fingerprints on the gun—had she picked it up so there'd be a legitimate reason for them to be on there?

"I'm sorry. It sounds like it was horrible."

A tear slid down her cheek. "It was. Tommy was so upset, too. He saw the gun and realized it was his, which didn't make any sense. He isn't going to get fired, is he? He's such a nice guy."

Leo smiled at her. "Don't worry. We'll get to the bottom of what happened."

"What about Deputy Joe Tarver?" Delaney said. "Did you see him at Brock's room?"

Tildy smiled through her tears. "Uncle Joe. Yes. He was here until Tommy showed up."

Delaney nodded. "Joe's your uncle?"

"Oh, no. It's just what we called him. His wife Alice used to work this shift. She retired about six months ago. We sure do miss her. Uncle Joe used to drop by sometimes to see her. Such a nice old guy."

Uncle Joe knows Tildy. Tommy dates her. She found the body. Her prints are on Tommy's gun, which Joe had while Tommy's belt was off. Leo's brain spun trying to connect the information in a way that explained the events.

"Did Joe come by again after Tommy showed up?"

"Not while I was at the desk. But if it was while we were in our meeting, I wouldn't have known it."

"Did you see or hear anything from the time Mr. Tucker arrived until now that seemed strange to you? A person who shouldn't have been here? Someone saying something that felt wrong? Noises? Smells? Anything. Anything at all that we haven't already talked about."

She frowned. "You think someone else was here?"

"I don't have any reason to, but it's our job to gather evidence without making assumptions. So, I ask a lot of questions."

She bit her lip and looked away. Then she sighed. "Everything was off. I mean, we don't have murderers handcuffed to their beds every day. Cops in and out. Calls for Mr. Tucker, which were routed to us, since he was, you know, under arrest. Reporters."

"Who called for him?"

"Well, the reporters for one thing. They've been really aggressive. Our security won't let anyone into the hospital without a valid visitor's badge, but they keep trying."

"Did Mr. Tucker have visitors?"

"I don't think so. Not that I saw. And we weren't supposed to let them in if he did. That's what Uncle Joe told us."

"Who besides reporters called Mr. Tucker?"

"His wife." She leaned forward and lowered her voice. "She sounded really upset."

"Did he talk to her?"

"No. This was before Uncle Joe told me he couldn't have calls, so I asked Mr. Tucker if he wanted to talk to her. He said to tell her he was asleep." She didn't look like she approved.

"Anyone else?"

"Other people who wouldn't give their names. Probably more reporters."

"Male, female?"

"Both."

"Anything else you'd like to ask, Sheriff?"

Leo stopped taking notes. He had jotted down a follow-up question. "Are there any video cameras in the corridor outside Mr. Tucker's room?"

"No, sir. I wish there were. Families or even patients don't always treat us very nice. They're upset, I get that, but they can be abusive. And sometimes they lie about us. But the hospital administration feels like it's an invasion of privacy." She leaned in. "I think some of them are also worried about liability."

"I understand. Thank you, Tildy."

"You're welcome."

"Just be sure to contact us if you think of something else." Delaney lay a card on the table and stood.

As she and Leo were walking out, Tildy said, "What do we do with Mr. Tucker's things?"

They'd already taken his personal belongings after they arrested him, as with any detainee. They'd been secured at the jail. "What did he have?" Leo asked.

"There was a phone on the rolling tray in his room. I put it in the nurse's station so nothing would happen to it."

Leo froze. He'd personally seen Brock's phone taken from the hospital in an evidence bag earlier. Leo had learned the easiest way to beat security at an airport was to bring two of any contraband. When they found the first one, they quit looking. Had Brock had two phones on him? And why hadn't the Kearny city cops taken it as evidence?

Shit, shit, shit. "Take us to it, if you don't mind."

THIRTY-THREE

Zeke drove carefully following the woman's verbal directions.

"Left here." Her voice didn't sound slurred anymore. That was good. Hopefully that meant no vomiting and that his job would be done when he dropped her off.

"You live even further out of town than Delaney."

"Everyone lives out of town in Wyoming" she said.

This state was weird. "Tell me about Delaney as a kid."

"Tell me about your relationship with Delaney now."

He was a little taken aback. She was brash, that was for sure. Or maybe still drunk. But he guessed he had to establish his bona fides if he wanted insider scoop. "We know each other from years ago. I'm only in town for a couple of days. We're making the most of it."

"You're serious about her?"

I'm serious about sleeping with her. But he wasn't going to say that to a family friend. "Yeah, I guess I am." He kept his tone light, trying to sound as if a heavy conclusion had taken him by surprise in the most delightful way. *Like friggin' Mary Poppins. Or Pinocchio, in my case.*

The woman golf clapped. "Take a right."

Zeke turned onto a rough, unpaved road. Snow-covered, of course. He hoped he didn't end up with damage to his Range Rover because he'd gone all Good Samaritan.

Without warning, his hand slipped off the wheel and his vision blurred. "Whoa." He readjusted his hand, but it slid again. His head lolled. He stomped on the brakes. He had to get a grip. "Sorry."

"Something wrong?"

He shook his head, but that made the wooziness worse. "I made fettucine alfredo with shrimp tonight. Must have been some bad shrimp. Never buy seafood in a landlocked state."

"You cooked that for Delaney?"

His head slumped forward on the steering wheel.

"Put it in park!" she screamed.

"Huh?" Zeke saw her hand reach for the gear shift. *Four on the floor,* he thought. But no, that was a long time ago, when his dad had taught him to drive an old truck. No one drove manual transmission anymore. *Three in the tree. No, not that either.*

The car jolted to a stop. "You were about to plant us head-first into a tree and deploy the airbags, you idiot."

"Hostile, much?" Zeke said. Or did he? He'd thought it. He'd tried to say it. But something was wrong with his tongue. So much was so wrong so fast. Why was she mad at him, anyway? He'd brought her home halfway to Montana.

"I hate that bitch," she said.

Zeke barely registered her words. He could hardly feel his tongue.

"But no one is supposed to touch Delaney. Oh, no. She's special. And double that for Kateena. God forbid. But no one said anything about boyfriends. *Lovers.*" She said the word with a mocking lilt in her voice. She didn't sound drunk anymore. At all. "The universe just dumped you in my lap tonight. A consolation prize for all I've put up with."

"Did... didju... didju gimme somethin?"

"Just a little roofie, GI Joe."

What kind of woman carries roofies? What kind of woman gives them to him? "Dohn unnerstan. Why. Why. Why...?"

"You don't need to worry your thick pretty head about it."

Zeke felt a wild desire to laugh. He'd been roofied. After all his training, the years of staying on high alert, watching his back and everyone else's. He'd let his guard down in a little Wyoming town. A civilian was taking him out, and he had no idea why. *Fight, you dumbass, fight now.* The words in his brain were a torrent, an explosion. A last-ditch effort. But when his arm translated them, it was with a feeble movement that ended with his hand falling in his lap.

The driver's door opened. He felt a tugging.

"You're a lot heavier than Delaney or Kateena would have been."

His body slumped onto the ground. Something cold and wet pressed into his face. Down his collar. *Snow. I could learn to hate snow.* A hard edge scraped against his cheek. He was moving. Being dragged in jerky fits and starts.

"Gotta. Get you. To the. Edge," the woman huffed.

A few seconds later, he felt himself rolling. Then falling. Then landing on something hard.

Then... nothing.

THIRTY-FOUR

Without knocking, Jefe let himself in the back door of Ellen's house with the key she'd given him before he left for Mexico. He'd never used it—the woman acted like they'd been in a torrid love affair, which was laughable. It had never been more than convenient sex.

But he was glad he'd kept the key.

He entered through the dark kitchen, careful not to make any noise. He stood, listening for sounds that meant Ellen was awake. A TV. A phone conversation.

It was dead quiet.

He strained to see signs of the faintest of lights, but nothing broke the inky black except the red clock on the microwave. He nodded. Once he'd heard the news that Brock Tucker died in the hospital after his arrest for the murder of Annabeth Dillon, he'd driven by this house three times until he'd seen Ellen's car and knew she'd be home. She'd been out late. Probably celebrating that someone had snapped a picture of her going into the boss's office. It raised her stature. It raised Jefe's ire.

He needed to hear from her exactly what was going on with Annabeth and Brock. It was his job to fund his boss and pave the way for his campaigns and agendas. It was also his job to ensure that nothing ever blew back on him.

Jefe had a bad feeling about blowback this time.

He touched his hip, checking the tools he'd brought. Duct tape. A knife. A pistol. A bandana to use as a gag. Not that he would need any of them necessarily. But he was prepared. Ellen might not be glad to see him. He would make sure they talked, one way or the other.

He slunk silently through the main floor of the house, opening doors and shutting them gently, but not to the point of latching. A bathroom, smelling strongly of rose petals. One guest room, unoccupied. An office. The living area. Stairs to a basement. He ignored them. Ellen would be in the primary bedroom. He took the stairs to the second story, sliding one hand along the wood banister. A stair creaked and he held himself perfectly still, waiting.

When he was sure nothing in the house was moving in response to his noise, he crept the rest of the way up. A night light in the hallway made the upstairs brighter. He found another pristine but empty guest room—this one with its own bathroom inside—and, at the end of the hall, what he hoped was Ellen's bedroom. He stood to the side of the doorway and peered in.

The bed was unmade. *Bingo.*

"I saw you drive by." Ellen's voice. Behind him.

He turned.

She was pointing a shotgun at his head.

"You were in the basement."

"If you wanted to get together, all you had to do was ask."

"Consider this my request."

"Is this a social or business visit?"

He snorted. "It's not a booty call, if that's what you mean."

She motioned him downstairs with her head. "I'll follow you."

Jefe didn't smile on the outside, but inside, he was grinning. She wanted him to walk past her in the tight hallway? He could do that.

She pushed her back against the wall and drew the shotgun across her chest. The look in her eyes said she'd realized her error too late.

He took two quick steps.

"No, I'll go—"

He wrested the gun from her hands before she got the sentence out. With one hand on the barrel and the other on the stock, he jammed it under her chin.

Ellen gurgled, her eyes bulging. Her breath smelled like a distillery.

"Don't ever point a gun at me again, Ellen, or it will be the last thing you do."

Her chin knocked the gun as she nodded. "You scared me. An intruder. A woman alone has to be careful."

"It's good to know you're not completely stupid. Now, let's have our business chat. First, where were you tonight?"

"Managing things."

"What things?"

"Putting some pressure on law enforcement."

"What does that mean?"

She licked a drop of blood from her lips. "Who are you most afraid of?"

His sister's green eyes popped into his mind. He didn't answer.

"I'm dividing her focus. Taking her mind off work."

"Do not harm my sister or my daughter. We've had this talk before. Am I clear?"

"Crystal. No one touches Delaney but you. And I definitely didn't touch her." She smiled.

He'd let it go. For now. "Are you responsible for that picture that ran in the paper?"

"What picture?"

He applied pressure across her neck.

She gasped and gurgled.

"Did you stage and leak the photo of you and Mitch to the press?" He eased up so she could answer.

"I—yes. It's good for my career."

He'd figured as much. She was a climber. As soon as he was sure he had everything he needed from her, he was going to sever her ties with the organization. Permanently. "Was that so hard? Now, what the fuck happened to Brock Tucker at the hospital today?"

"My sources tell me Brock ate his gun."

"Did he have help?"

She shrugged. "It's hard to talk with this thing crushing my larynx."

He gave her some more breathing space.

"The cops had his confession to an affair with Annabeth Dillon and confirmed his presence at the cabin where she died. They already had fingerprints, and they'll have DNA and I'm sure all kinds of other evidence as well."

"Did he kill her?"

"Annabeth broke up with him that night. I've been told there's a recording on her phone, which was left in her hospital room. I'm sure the police have it now."

Jefe glared at her. "What aren't you telling me? You can't keep secrets from me. Not about going behind my back to meet with our boss, and not about Annabeth or Brock. If you did something that is going to hurt us, tell me now."

She licked her lips. "My sources tell me that Brock denied killing Annabeth, of course. That was no surprise. But he did ask for immunity and told the sheriff and Delaney that he had someone he could hand over to them."

"The person who killed Annabeth?"

"Could be. Or possibly it could be... you."

"Me? No one knows about me but you and the boss. No one."

Her teeth raked her bloody upper lip. "Aren't you forgetting the sheriff, your sister, and your daughter? And God knows who else they've told."

"Aren't you forgetting I disappeared, got a new face, and have a new identity? I'll repeat, no one but you and the boss know about me. What are you not telling me, Ellen?"

"I haven't told anyone else about you. But I may have let a few people know some of the things Annabeth was up to. Like with Brock."

"Are you responsible for their deaths, or not?"

She stared back at him, defiance in her eyes.

THIRTY-FIVE

Delaney rapped her knuckles on the storm door at Joe and Alice Tarver's house. She'd already called and rang the doorbell. Leo was out back, to make sure Joe didn't bolt.

"Who is it?" Joe's voice was muffled through the door.

"Delaney. And why aren't you answering your phone?"

He opened the door, revealing a T-shirt straining and failing to cover his belly before it reached the waistband of his flannel pajama pants. His gun hand pointed his service pistol at the ground. "My charger crapped out on me. I was going to pick one up in the morning."

"We've been trying to reach you for hours."

"You and the sheriff?"

"Yes." Delaney keyed her mic. "Leo, I'm out front with Joe."

"Where is he?"

"At your back door."

Joe pushed greasy, matted hair off his forehead. "You might as well come in. It's freezing out here."

"I'm not sure we should have this conversation where Alice can overhear."

He rolled his eyes. "She wears industrial strength earplugs to bed. Nothing wakes her."

"If you're sure."

Leo tromped across the yard and joined them at the door.

"Hello, Sheriff. And, yeah, I'm sure. Come on in." Joe swung the door wide, flipped on a light switch, and led them to chairs at a dining room table only a few steps from the entrance. Delaney had never been in his house, but she was able to draw some quick conclusions about his and Alice's style from the ornate flowered wallpaper with gold scrolls and heavy hutch with blue and white china inside. "Now, what's this about?"

Delaney took a seat.

Leo woke his tablet and nodded at her.

She said, "Brock Tucker died of a gunshot wound tonight in his room."

"What?" Joe's jaw fell.

Delaney was no human lie detector, but his surprise seemed genuine. "You didn't know?"

"Why would I—has it been on the news? I went to sleep as soon as I got home. Today wiped me out. But what's going on? Who did it?"

"Preliminary evidence suggests he did it himself. With Tommy's gun."

Joe stared at her, then turned to Leo. "Tommy's gun? But that doesn't make sense."

Leo said, "Take us through your handover to Tommy, from the time he arrived until you left the hospital."

Joe nodded, rubbing his chin. "Sure. Sure. Okay, let me think. I'm a little groggy."

"Do you need a water? Some coffee?" Delaney said.

"Uh, no. This conversation is waking me up. I'm fine. Let's see. Tommy came about six-thirty. I took off for my car, but he texted me before I got there and said he was grabbing a quick dinner in the cafeteria if I wanted to join him." He grimaced. "That was a no brainer. Alice is many things, but she's no chef."

The house smelled like lima beans and chicken to Delaney. Vestiges of her childhood. She would have preferred cafeteria food, too. "So, you met him in the caf?"

"I did. He wasn't feeling well and went to the bathroom. I stayed with his chow so the staff wouldn't throw it out."

"He left his belt and gun with you?"

Joe shook his head. "No, just his burger and fries."

Delaney raised her eyebrows at Leo.

"What?" Joe said.

"How long was he gone?"

"Quarter of an hour. I was worried about him, and I needed to go home, so I boxed up his food and took it to the bathroom. He was just coming out."

"Is that when you gave him back his duty belt?"

"No. I already told you. I never had his belt. What's this about?"

"At any time after you went to the cafeteria did you ever return to Brock's hospital room?"

"No."

"Did you leave Tommy's belt or gun in the cafeteria?"

"I never had it!"

"Did you give Tommy's belt or gun to anyone?"

"What the hell are you going on about? I never had the gun."

"Who did?"

He frowned, his face confused. "Tommy, I guess. I never even thought about it. Why, what did he say?"

"He said he gave it to you. And that the next thing he knew, Brock was dead."

"He can't have said that. It's not true."

Delaney looked at Leo. His face was grim. *Two trusted colleagues. And one of them is lying. But which one?*

THIRTY-SIX

Delaney knocked on Leo's office door. The two of them had returned to the station to get organized after they left Joe's half an hour earlier. "Are you close to calling it a night?"

Leo rubbed his eyes. "Soon. My brain is spinning."

"Do you think Tommy is making this up to try to get out of trouble for losing his gun?" Delaney walked behind his desk to a jar on his credenza that had originally held leftover Halloween candy. It seemed to get replenished every week. She took a miniature Snickers bar. As she unwrapped it, she caught sight of his computer screen. A browser tab was open to Top Ten Cities for Law Enforcement Careers. It was like a blow to her solar plexus. She popped the candy in her mouth and moved away, not wanting him to know she'd seen it.

"He could be. And I don't see how we're going to get to the truth of it." He groaned. "What if it's Joe that's lying?"

"You know I don't trust him."

"Joe might have lost the gun. Or Tommy could have. One of them is maybe trying to cover up an innocent but serious mistake."

"Or one of them could have assisted Brock's suicide. Or

killed him." Dr. Watson was taking a look at Brock's cause of death for them, even though it had appeared straight forward—the cause, not how he obtained the gun. Without a witness, they couldn't rule out murder.

"That's a leap. Where's the love, lust, loot, loathing? No motive for either of them." He snapped his fingers. "Dammit!"

"What is it?"

"Remember the DEA sent me here in the first place because they had reason to believe there was someone dirty in Kearny law enforcement?"

"How could I forget?" Leo's secrets—his DEA assignment and the existence of his sister and nephew—had nearly ended their friendship.

"Right. Well, what if one of them is dirty?"

Delaney tapped her lips. "I think Joe's taking money from a reporter. But Tommy is Mr. Earnest. He's like the last person on earth who'd break the rules."

"Which makes him the most likely." Leo tented his fingers.

"Okay. I'll run with that. Maybe one of them is connected with the activist groups."

He tilted his head. "Go on."

"Retribution against Brock for them. Annabeth was their girl."

"It's worth looking into, for sure. A bad cop. I sure would hate that, for all of us."

"Brock Tucker most of all."

Leo nodded. "We should check whether one of them has some kind of personal beef with Brock."

"Why don't I take the lead researching the activist groups and you track down the Mountain High Cabins owner, Shaina Pham?"

"Okay."

"And I'll look for ties between Brock and Joe or Tommy, if you can get me in that phone from Brock's room, too? We need to know whose it is and what's on it. That background photo didn't give anything away." It had been a picture of mountain wildflowers. Beautiful, but generic.

Leo felt a little guilty that he hadn't turned the phone over to the Kearny police. He'd send it to them after he'd copied the data. "I'll just update the investigation plan with all of this."

"Of course, you will. You'll be happy to hear I plotted the events today on my map. Expanding out of Kearny County. I'll need a second cubicle."

"Or you could use your tablet mapping app."

She smiled, then frowned. There was a newspaper on Leo's desk. On the front was a picture of a familiar figure. She turned it around. Ellen Day shaking hands with Mitch Stonefield in the doorway to his office." "Did you see this?"

"What is it?"

Delaney read aloud. "'One can only guess at the topic of conversation between Kearny native Mitch Stonefield and Kearny County Commissioner Ellen Day behind closed doors at his office in Cheyenne. Does the commissioner have aspirations for higher office? Repeated calls to both politicians returned nothing but: *no comment.*'"

"She's ambitious."

"She's obnoxious. And I wouldn't be surprised if she's the one behind the move for a recall vote against you."

"That, too."

"At your birthday thing, I saw Mary had a fundraiser scheduled for Mitch at the Loafing Shed. I've been meaning to talk to her about it. I don't like it."

"Don't like him?"

"That's not the point. I don't think a bar should be choosing sides."

"Annabeth Dillon would have made an interesting opponent for him."

His words ignited a thought. Delaney sat down hard in the chair in front of his desk. "And now she won't."

Leo cocked his head. "What are you getting at?"

"Who stands to benefit from Annabeth's death?"

"Possibly her husband if he inherits. Which we need to explore." He scribbled on his tablet.

"Right."

"Anyone in a dispute with her. Like on opposite sides of public issues."

"Correct."

Leo grinned. "And Mitch Stonefield, who doesn't have to run against her." He made another note.

"Bingo." Delaney's pulse quickened. "And who benefits from Brock's death?"

"If it wasn't a suicide."

"Regardless."

"His trophy wife. He seems loaded." Leo wrote on the tablet again.

"Agreed."

"Business rivals."

Delaney smiled. "You're getting warmer."

"Political rivals."

"And who was Brock backing and funding?"

"Annabeth Dillon."

"Which puts him on the opposite side of the fence from our boy Mitch." Delaney checked the time on her phone. "The bar is still open. I'm calling Mary. I like this fundraiser less all the time." She pressed the number for Mary's cell.

Mary's voice was cheerful. "Hey, boss. We had a busy night tonight. Your friend was here. I'm kicking stragglers out now."

Mary was a treasure. The Loafing Shed was in the black for the first time since Delaney had returned to Kearny. "What friend?"

"Zane. Leo's buddy."

"Zeke." She felt Leo's eyes drill into her at her mention of the name.

"Yeah, Zeke."

"Is he still there?"

"No, he took off an hour or two ago. He wasn't here long."

"Okay. Listen, I saw a poster up for a fundraiser for Mitch Stonefield. How did that come about?"

"Ugh. Yeah, they shamed me into it since we no longer make contributions to his campaign. They said it's what your brother would have wanted. And I pretended like I cared." Liam had tried to have Mary killed out of fear she'd realize he had faked his own death in a car crash. Mary hated him.

"What contributions? Wait, let me put you on speaker so Leo can hear this."

"No problem."

"Okay, we're ready."

"Mitch's rep said Liam made a standing contribution of five thousand a month from the Loafing Shed to Stonefield's campaign."

"You're kidding."

"No. And he was right. When I took over, we weren't making any money, so I stopped paying it. They noticed. Said I could make it square with a fundraiser."

"You don't have anything to make square. This is BS. There will be no fundraiser."

"Want me to call Ellen?"

"Who?"

"Ellen Day. She's the one who set it up. She was in here tonight, in fact."

Delaney shook her head. *Unbelievable.* "She doesn't seem like our normal clientele."

"She came in to be sure we were on track for the event. Zeke talked to her for a little while."

Leo snorted and wrote: *Another name for our list.*

Delaney said, "You just take the poster down. I'll handle Mitch and Ellen."

"No problem, boss. Have a good night."

"You too."

Leo put a King Ropes ball cap over his curls. "Our list isn't getting any more manageable. Hey, are you picking up Kat tonight?"

"No. Adriana texted me that she was asleep on the couch. I'll get her in the morning. She had a rough night, too. I can't wait to deal with this investigator who's stirring up trouble with the adoptions."

Leo looked away from her. "Are you meeting Zeke?"

Delaney was too tired for this conversation. "Not your business, Leo."

Leo leaped to his feet and leaned on the desk with both hands. "Zeke is engaged, Delaney. He's getting married next weekend."

The blood drained from her face. "What?"

"He's using you as his last fling."

Was this true? If so, why hadn't Zeke mentioned it? It seemed like their conversation about relationships and marriages had been the opportune time to bring it up to her. Unless Leo was right. Zeke was hiding his engagement from her because he was using her.

And Leo, her best friend and her boss, had known it and was only telling her after she'd nearly ended up in bed with Zeke two nights running.

Anger flared in her. "And you knew."

"I did. But I didn't know you and Zeke had a past. That you'd be all over each other."

"We're not... we haven't been..." She dropped the thought. "You knew. *And you didn't tell me.*"

"Delaney, I never saw you and Zeke coming. And then I thought for sure he'd tell you. But he didn't, obviously."

"I spent one night with Zeke, a long time ago. I've spent nine months with you. I would have thought for sure that you cared enough to tell me."

"I do care! That's why I'm telling you now!"

"You have a funny way of showing it, Leo." She stomped to the door. And then she left. Walking fast, then trotting, then running to her truck.

THIRTY-SEVEN

Leo rolled out of bed at seven a.m. after a sleepless night. Zeke hadn't come back to the house. Leo rubbed his face with both hands. Apparently Zeke was a shit friend who didn't care what Leo thought. And Delaney didn't mind being used. *Fine.* Except that it wasn't.

At least he'd been productive during his emotion-fueled insomnia. He'd emailed the judge for probable cause warrants on Brock's phone and the one found in his hospital room. Even better, he'd researched the nonprofits Annabeth had been involved in. He'd found three. Western Wyoming for Wildlife Conservation. Western Wyoming Against Carbon Producers. Western Wyoming for Environmental Preservation. All three had the same executive director. Elana Holowitz of Sheridan, which was odd, since Sheridan was north central—a few hundred miles away from the area most people would consider western Wyoming. But awfully close to where Annabeth had died.

All three organizations were embroiled in lawsuits. Interestingly, they'd been sued by the same plaintiff. Abe Dunkirk, a Wyoming landowner seeking a permit to mine his property. Leo had emailed an article about the suits to himself, with the promise to read it in the morning.

Morning had come.

He zombie-walked the five feet from his bed to his desk chair. The office he'd kept in the spare bedroom had relocated into his to make a bedroom for Freddy. Adriana had hers out of the sunporch on the back of the house. He thought about Kat asleep on the couch. The air mattress in the dining room that Zeke had planned on using as his bed, until he reunited with Delaney. The house was crowded. He was making decent money. Maybe it was time to upgrade to bigger digs. The conversation with Delaney from the night before replayed in his head. *Or to move on.*

He quickly added his research results into the investigation plan. The case had gone from feeling solved yesterday to a hydra overnight. And now there was Brock's death. He filled in a preliminary plan.

When he was done, he rubbed his forehead. It was a lot, especially with Tommy on suspension and Joe under suspicion. But maybe talking to the witnesses he'd identified overnight could shed light onto Annabeth's relationships within the activist community. He didn't usually hope for dead ends, but this time he did. He wanted to wrap the two cases up, with Brock Tucker as Annabeth's killer and himself as a suicide. Simple and tidy. Was that too much to ask?

He clicked on the link from his Leo-to-Leo email. The article about the lawsuits popped up on his screen. His tired eyes were unfocused. *I'm only thirty-six. It can't be time for readers.* He blinked several times then tried again with more success. The gist? Abe wanted to mine for coal on his land. All three organizations claimed irreparable harm to the interests they championed. He was facing stiff opposition to his permitting requests, with the triumvirate of western Wyoming groups spearheading efforts against him.

He went back to the Annabeth investigation plan and jotted in notes.

The house was still quiet when he finished. He checked his email for a response from the judge. Nothing. It was Sunday morning after all, so he hadn't expected one. It would have been nice, though, because it was time to crack the phone from Brock's room and get to work on its contents. If they were very, very lucky, the information on it would point them in the right direction. Or at least cut off avenues that would waste time and resources. He hoped no one would ever try to determine when he'd accessed the phone, but he would erase his tracks and turn off the Screen Time app, if it was tracking usage. And it's not like he'd be sending out messages. Yet. Because he certainly wasn't opposed to doing whatever he had to do to track down Annabeth's killer.

Delaney's rubbing off on me. But that wasn't true. He'd ended up in law enforcement after recreational college hacking had earned him a semi-voluntary stint in the Coast Guard as an alternative to a completely involuntary stint in state prison.

Hacking a phone wasn't hard with the right equipment. The sheriff's department didn't own most of it, but Leo's private stash had all he needed. He connected the phone to an external hard drive and ran his passcode cracker, an app he'd written himself back in the day and kept refreshed as technology evolved. In minutes, he was in and making a backup of the device.

Annabeth Dillon's device.

He felt an old, familiar satisfaction. At one point in his life, he'd thought nothing could top this type of high. He'd loved his job in special ops for the Coasties. He'd thought he'd be happy there his whole career, getting paid to do what he would have done for free, but that had all ended with the death of his parents and Jim.

He'd never regret coming home for Adriana and Freddy.

But everything had gone haywire after his return. The disastrous undercover assignment with the San Diego PD. His banishment to Wyoming. His failure to hunt down the criminals the DEA had sent him here to find. Delaney's rejection.

Still, if he was being honest with himself—not something he wanted to make a habit of—he had found practicing a new type of law enforcement invigorating. Being a real cop out in the field. Adventure. Danger. The sheriff gig. An effective partnership with Delaney.

Maybe not everything was bad.

Returning his attention to the phone, he pursed his lips. This had been an easy jailbreak. For a woman having an affair with the top contributor to her soon-to-be-announced U.S. Senate campaign, she didn't employ much security. Was she naïve? Was it deliberate?

Leo hoped he was about to find out.

His phone chimed.

A text from Delaney.

I'm out front.

The horrible ending to their interaction the night before crashed back down on him. Was it too much to hope she'd forgive and forget? Instead of answering, he slipped on a pair of jeans and a T-shirt and padded barefoot to the door, careful not to wake Adriana, Freddy, or Kat, who was snoring softly on the couch.

He took a deep breath in and let it out slowly as he opened the door.

The woman on the steps took his breath away, just as she'd done the first time he'd seen her, when he'd pulled her over for speeding. How was he to know then she was a deputy investigator in pursuit of a suspect, when she couldn't produce a driver's license and was oh-so-beautifully out of uniform and wearing high-heeled sandals—with red-painted toenails he'd never forget—and figure-hugging jeans? Snowflakes sparkled in her hair now. Her green eyes were lit from a glow inside her. They always were. And even though a Carhartt jacket covered her jeans, he had long since memorized all of her curves. Her face was fresh. She rarely wore makeup that he could tell. Today her lips were bare but still rosy and full.

She opened them and spoke, and he was ready to tell her again he was sorry, if she gave him the chance. "I'm here for Kat."

"Of course. But she's still asleep." He pulled the door shut behind him, not caring that it was snowing and way too cold outside for his bare feet and T-shirt. "I made good progress on the case. It's Annabeth Dillon's phone. I have it open if you want the pleasure." A peace offering. Delaney loved to be the first to dive into fresh evidence.

She gave him a strange look, then said, "Is Zeke here?"

He felt his forehead bunch in consternation. "No. I thought he was with you."

She shook her head. "He wasn't at my place when I got home last night. I've texted and called but I haven't heard from him. Maybe he left town?"

"Did you... have words with him, about... you know—what we talked about?"

"No. I didn't mention it. I was saving it for in person. Should we worry?"

Leo bit his lower lip. There was no way Zeke would skip town without a word to either of them, not when he thought he'd almost reached his goal with Delaney.

Yes, we should worry.

THIRTY-EIGHT

Delaney walked out to the barn after getting Kat settled with Skeeter, Duds, and Carrie. The teenager seemed like she was suffering from the kind of hangover that was worse than any punishment Delaney could dish out. Delaney nodded in satisfaction. It served the girl right.

Despite the roads, Delaney was taking Shotgun Shelly into the department today. She did it every chance she got. The snow had stopped falling, but the temperature had dropped further. She wasn't surprised when the refurbished Chevelle SS refused to start. Luckily, she was prepared for this winter phenomenon, and she opened the hood, took off the cover to the carburetor and air filter, and sprayed a few three-second bursts of starter fluid into the carburetor's primary intake. She pumped the gas throttle a few times then turned the key. The engine caught and she gave it more gas until it was running smoothly. One more trip out to replace the cover and close the hood, and then she was off to town.

Today was going to be a long day. Normally, she treasured Sundays at home with the girls. Luckily, working Sundays was an exception, not the rule. Working weekends at all was unusual. But in their small town, when it came to homicides, it was all hands on deck. The Annabeth and Brock cases were doozies. She was worried about Zeke. Upset with Leo. Apprehensive about her upcoming showdown over the adoption. There would be no rest, no relaxation, no family time.

She locked Shelly's doors in the parking lot at work and trekked in kicking snow. Murder in a small town. In her small handful of years as a patrol deputy before she'd pursued self-sanctuary on the ice roads, there'd been very little violent crime. Murders were unheard of. Why the recent change? There were fewer than twenty murders annually in the entire state of Wyoming, including the notoriously dangerous Wind River Reservation. But just last year, there'd been *nine* in Kearny County. Well, not nine that were recorded as murders on their death certificates. Two went down as accidents— Coltrane Fentworth and a Kearny city cop. Another as suicide —Crispin Allen. Delaney knew the truth about those three, though, even if she couldn't prove it beyond a reasonable doubt. That truth led back to her brother and his involvement in every single case. Even with only six official murders in their county, it threatened the state's average for the previous year. This year wasn't off to a better start, either. Annabeth. Brock, if his death wasn't suicide. That was two in January alone. Would that mean twenty-four by year-end? She hoped not, for the sake of their citizenry as well as for her Sundays at home.

She toed snow off her boots then pushed through the door and wiped her feet on the mat inside the vestibule.

Clara smiled as Delaney walked through the lobby. "Good morning."

"What are you doing here on a Sunday?" Clara kept the most regular schedule of anyone in the department.

"Leo's letting me trade some hours. I have dental surgery this week. I didn't want to take unpaid time off."

Delaney wasn't in the mood to award Leo a humanitarian medal. "Ouch. Sorry to hear that."

"It will be okay. Have a great day and go catch some bad guys."

Delaney waved goodbye. To get to her desk, she had to pass Leo's office. He'd betrayed her trust—again—no matter his reasons. She kept her eyes straight ahead. She had to work with him, for now at least. She had six more years with Kat at home, so hopping in Gabrielle and returning to the road life wasn't an option.

Maybe she'd apply for a job in Sheridan. Or even with the Kearny cops. Or just wait for him to run away back to California or one of the other Top Ten Cities for Law Enforcement Careers or whatever that bullshit he'd been reading last night was called.

"Delaney?" he said.

Busted. She turned back and stopped on the near side of his door. "Yes?" Looking at him hurt, deep in her chest. Why couldn't she hate him? Why did he have to make her *feel*?

"I talked to Zeke's, um, fiancée. She hasn't heard from him. Isn't expecting him back until Tuesday."

"Okay." The news hit her funny. Zeke didn't seem like the kind of guy to run off without telling anyone. But then, she hadn't thought he was the kind of guy to try to seduce her without telling her he was getting married in a week. She wracked her brain again for any reason he would have left. She hadn't told him she knew about his upcoming marriage, and Leo said he hadn't spoken to Zeke either. Obviously, his fiancée hadn't called him back on an emergency. And if war had broken out and his unit had reeled him in, his fiancée would have known something about it and told Leo. *It makes no sense.* "Do we treat him as a missing person?"

"It hasn't even been a day."

"Time frames are guidelines. We—you—know this guy."

"Yeah. I say we give it until noon. In case he's sleeping it off somewhere."

She nodded. That was reasonable. Maybe he'd gotten bad news. A military buddy's passing. A bad test result from a doctor. She started to leave.

"Wait. Let's talk about next steps. On Annabeth and Brock." He held up a phone.

"What's this?"

"Annabeth's phone."

"Warrant?"

"Listen to you, talking about following rules like you ever have before. But yes, I got the go ahead from the judge this morning."

"Any prints?"

"I had that checked last night. Just his."

"But not hers."

"Yeah."

"Like it had been wiped."

"Exactly."

"Why would his prints be on a wiped phone that was in his hospital room after we thought we'd relieved him of all his possessions and the city cops had been through it?" Leo had told her his theory about Brock having two phones. It made sense, but he also might have had a visitor who left it there, when Tommy and Joe were in the cafeteria and Tildy was in her meeting.

"The million dollar question."

"What's on the phone?"

He looked at his desk. "I saved that for you." He put the phone down and held out a thumb drive. "Everything's on here. Now I need to walk the actual phone across the building to our city counterparts."

She narrowed her eyes at him. Exploring virgin evidence, especially a phone, was something they both loved to do. Was he trying to get back in her good graces? It wouldn't work, but she'd take it. "Thanks." She snatched the drive from him. A thrill of excitement ran through her.

Leo said, "I looked into the activist groups last night, too, and found some potential leads. A few people to interview anyway."

She listened as he told her about Elana Holowitz and Abe Dunkirk and ran her verbally through his investigation plans.

He said, "Elana is in Sheridan. Let's see if we can set up an interview today. And with Shaina Pham—she lives there, too. Not sure about Dunkirk, but if nothing else, we can stream him. I'd like to get Stonefield and Day nailed down, too."

She nodded. "I'll see when we can talk to Mitch. He's planning on being in Kearny tonight for the fundraiser at the Loafing Shed. We could always ambush him there if I don't tell him it's canceled. And, of course, Ellen Day is local, so we have some more flexibility with her."

"And we need to talk to Riley Tucker and do a follow-up on Dillon's husband. I've filed for a warrant on his financial and insurance records. I think I'll start there with him."

"Our dance card will be full."

"But there's something else you have to look into, right?"

For a moment she drew a blank, then she remembered. "Tommy and Joe."

"Better you than me."

She snorted. "I was going to ask you to do it."

"Perks of being the boss."

She hurried to her desk with the thumb drive, buoyed by the possibility of discovery and a sense of forward momentum on the case.

A voice stopped her. "Hey, Pace. What are you up to?"

She didn't even turn around. It was Joe. She couldn't believe he'd come in with all that was going on around Tommy's gun. "Reviewing some evidence."

He leaned over her shoulder. "A thumb drive."

"Yep."

"Fine. Be mysterious."

She turned around. "Tell me about your relationship with Brock Tucker."

Joe's mouth gaped. "What relationship?"

"Did you know him before this case?"

"Not at all."

"And Annabeth Dillon?"

"Same. What's this about?"

"Pretend I asked better questions. What aren't you telling me about your connection to them or people in their lives?"

Joe's face flamed. "Back off, Delaney. I already told you. I don't know them. You're barking up the wrong tree."

"How much are you getting paid to leak stories?"

His glare was lethal. "Listen, Miss Holier-Than-Thou. I haven't broken the law. I'm doing the best I can. You worry about your own self."

She heard his stomping footsteps recede. His answers didn't negate actual research, but they'd been worth a try. Wiggling her fingers, she eyed the thumb drive. "What have you got for me, beautiful?" Almost reverently, she inserted it in her laptop, then started going through the data, in reverse chronological order.

The most recent items were texts, dated the probable night of her death. But how had she sent them from a location with no cell signal?

To Brock:

I'm sorry. Thank you for everything.

He'd replied:

Don't worry. This won't affect your campaign.

That was attention-grabbing. What was the deal there? Could it be potential motive to take Annabeth's phone? If so, he would have also had motive not to let it get into police hands. She frowned. But the texts sounded like they were sent *after* he left. She looked at the times. The exchange had occurred at nearly eleven p.m. How could he have killed her during sex if he was gone and she was still alive? Maybe he'd come back for a second round?

It was perplexing and something to ponder.

To her husband Pete:

It's all taken care of. See you tomorrow. I love you.

He hadn't replied. He also hadn't told Delaney and Leo about talking to Annabeth that night.

To Elana:

If any of this shit lands on me, you're fired.

There was no reply. Didn't sound like that relationship was healthy. Could it relate to the lawsuits?

To Shaina:

Thanks for letting me stay. Consider us even.

A reply:

Fine.

But even for what? Another relationship that didn't sound as great as Delaney would have thought it would be.

Maybe Elana and Shaina weren't aligned with Annabeth on her causes.

To Ellen:

You're too late. I have a press conference scheduled to announce that I'm running.

Ellen Day—the Kearny County Commissioner? Delaney scrolled back in the correspondence. Annabeth was responding to Ellen's earlier text:

I have a proposal for you. It involves how you don't spend your next few years.

If that was what it sounded like, Ellen was more heavily involved in state-level politics than Delaney had given the county commissioner credit for. She remembered the picture in the paper of Ellen meeting with the state AG and that Ellen had set up the fundraiser for Mitch at the Loafing Shed. *Maybe she's an up-and-comer.*

To a 307 area code number:

Just give me a settlement figure and cut the shit.

No reply. That had to be Abe Dunkirk. If not, it was a witness to add to their list.

To her sister:

You're texting with the next U.S. Senator from WY.

Her reply had been:

Who's got the big head, little sis?

Nothing there. They could circle back to the sister if none of the leads pointed to Brock or panned out. Or to Rufus, who was still in jail for assaulting Delaney.

All in all, it felt like they were definitely on the right track with the interviews she and Leo had discussed setting up. *But we need a timeline.* And now she sounded like Leo.

The next most recent file she came to was an audio file. She opened it, and it began to play.

A woman's voice, one Delaney had never heard before. Delaney winced. She was... exhorting a lover.

A man's voice. This one she recognized. Brock. And he was indicating enthusiastic agreement. Delaney shuddered. Things were getting dirty. She was going to need a shower after this. She turned it down, not wanting to assault everyone else in the building with it. *Please, God, don't let this be just a sex tape.* More moaning and dirty talk. Five minutes of it, including smacky mouth sounds that made Delaney want to stab her ears with a fork.

Then, Annabeth said, "This is the last time, Brock. After tonight, it's all about getting me in the Senate. No distractions. No scandals waiting to trip us up. Okay?"

Brock's response was a panting roar. "You tell me this while we're having sex? Right when I'm about to—"

"Don't let me down here. Let's end on a high note. You can do this."

Delaney heard shuffling covers and stomping feet. Brock's voice seemed to get further away. "The fuck you say. You end this on a high note for yourself. Which is what you'll be doing with your campaign, without me."

"Oh, Brock, that's where you're wrong," Annabeth Dillon cooed.

THIRTY-NINE

Leo listened to the audio as Delaney replayed it. She'd given him a full update on Annabeth's phone, then hit him with the recording. He gaped but shook his head. "So, did Brock kill her or not?"

"Not while Annabeth was recording him. And I checked her phone. I didn't find any other, um, sex recordings."

"I'll bet she was recording him as insurance."

"Or to prove to someone else she did it."

Leo made a face. "Like her husband? If so, she'd have to make him listen to a recording of her having sex with another man."

"True. Maybe not her husband. But this is just evidence. Of what, I'm not sure. It doesn't prove who *didn't* kill her. The only way we know that is when we know who did."

"And it still could have been Brock, later."

"He would have had to come back after their text exchange."

Leo rolled his eyes. "Damn. If he did it, he was sloppy. Leaving a used condom?"

"If it's his. We don't know that yet either."

"Good point, although even more smarmy."

She lifted her shoulders in a shrug. "Just when we thought it couldn't get any worse."

"Still, it's something. A lot of little somethings. I didn't make as much headway as you did, but I tracked down Elana. I think we can catch her at a clean water rally later today, between here and Sheridan."

Delaney said, "I questioned Joe. He was here in the office."

"Why?"

"He didn't say, and he left after I talked to him."

"I should have suspended him. I'll do it later today. Punchline?"

"He claims he didn't know Brock, Annabeth, or any of their people."

"I guess that's all we could expect him to say."

"What about the other people to interview?"

"We'll need to do Dunkirk with a video call, but I like the element of surprise. I'll get the sheriff's help on that. I talked Riley Tucker into visiting us here. She has to come to the hospital because of Brock's death here anyway. I didn't try Ellen or Mitch yet—I like your idea about ambushing them tonight. Shaina may be our biggest challenge. Her outgoing voice mail says she's traveling."

Delaney tapped her lips with a finger. "I think we should verify that."

"Good point. We'll pay her a visit, too." He put her address in the mapping app on his phone. "She doesn't live too far from the rally."

His phone rang. "Dr. Watson." Sadly, the forensic pathologist had been busier with suspicious county deaths than she ever had been in the past. He'd hoped that his time as sheriff would be homicide-free. And it had been, for three whole blissful months. He answered. "Hello. You're on speaker with Delaney and me. What's up?"

"You two have time to come to the hospital?" Her voice had a somber tone. She was often serious, but this was different.

Delaney nodded her availability.

"We can, but can you give us a preview?"

"I think it's better we have this conversation in person."

Dr. Watson ushered Leo and Delaney through the door of her autopsy suite and into the sterile world of stainless steel and refrigerator temperatures. The odor of death never got any easier to take, at least not to Leo. He'd tried cotton in his nostrils, even foam earplugs up his nose, but nothing really worked. He'd decided his best strategy was to lean into it as the smell of solving cases. Today he was leaning in as hard as he could. His stomach lurched, but he looked at Delaney's smooth, untroubled face, and he swallowed the saliva pooling in his mouth.

Dr. Watson's shoes chirped across the floor. She pulled back a sheet, exposing Brock's ruined head and one intact, fixed eye.

Lean harder.

She said, "Thanks for coming over so quickly. I hope you had time for a bite to eat?"

Not before an autopsy. "We're good. This is the most important thing we've got going on right now."

"I wish I had better news for you." She cleared her throat. "But let's do this right. The victim, Brock Tucker, is a 56-year-old well-nourished Caucasian male who was suspected to have died from a self-inflicted gunshot wound to the head but otherwise appeared to be healthy. He came to me with a time of death already established due to a witness who heard the gunshot and another who found his body only minutes later. I am told his fingerprints were on the gun."

"Yes. His were the only prints on it," Leo said. Sugar had

confirmed that information with him that morning. "Which is troubling. The gun belonged to one of our deputies."

"Yes. Suicides don't often take the time to wipe down their death instruments before they use them. Not out of the question, but odd. As is this." She led them to a microscope. "I found these fibers on the bridge of Brock's nose."

Leo and Delaney took turns at the eye piece.

Leo said, "What are they?"

"I had my assistant retrieve the bedding from his hospital room. They're like those from the case covering the pillow on his bed. I referred to the photographs from the scene. His head was resting on a pillow."

Delaney said, "Is it unusual for someone to have pillowcase fibers on their face?"

"No, but they're more common in the hair on the back of the head or on the cheeks of a side sleeper. Hospital beds don't allow for stomach sleeping, which is how fibers would most easily get on that part of the nose. My assistant did confirm the head of his bed was elevated. The fibers could have ended up there innocently. Except the concentration was higher than I'd expect from sleeping or incidental contact."

"This isn't looking good."

"It gets worse. The presence of these fibers guided me to look for other physical signs, which I found." She returned to Brock's body and shone a penlight into his eyes. "See those tiny splotches?"

"The red ones?"

"Yes." She pointed the light at his cheeks and neck. "They're hard to see, but they're present here as well. They're called petechial hemorrhages. We expect to find them in his lungs as well when we crack him open." She opened his mouth with a tongue depressor and aimed the light into the back of his throat. The trajectory of the bullet hadn't damaged the lower half of his head.

Leo bent down to get an optimal view. "What am I looking for here?"

"Foam."

"I see it."

"That's mucus from the lungs mixing with air."

"What causes it?"

"His struggle to breathe."

"Son of a bitch. He didn't die from a gunshot wound."

"He was recently dead or dying when the bullet entered his head. From suffocation. Brock Tucker was smothered to death with a pillow. Even injured as he was, he was a strong man. He would have fought back. This took someone with strength, who was determined and knew what they were doing."

Leo shook his head. *Shit.* "Someone who was possibly carrying Annabeth's phone to plant in the room when the deed was done."

FORTY

Kat skipped a few songs on Spotify then turned up the volume. Olivia Rodrigo: "good 4 u." She just loved that song!

Carrie rolled her eyes and turned down the volume. Of course, she took the front seat. "Adele, please. None of this bubble gum caca."

Skeeter pulled to a stop at the drive-through window of the doughnut shop. "Turn it all the way down, or I'm not getting anything for either of you."

A teenage boy stuck his head out of the first window. "What can I—oh, Carrie, hey. Wassup?"

Carrie shrank back. "Nothing."

Skeeter said, "I need half a dozen chocolate glazed, one cinnamon roll, one bear claw, two apple fritters, and three blue-berry cake. Heated up, please."

The boy looked stung by Carrie's rejection. He rang their order in and recited a total in a dead voice. "Pay and pick it up at the next window."

Skeeter pulled forward.

"Why were you mean to him?" Kat said.

"He's been texting me. I'm not into him. Now, turn the music back up." She reached for the stereo.

Skeeter stuck his arm out. "Not until we have our breakfast. And I mean it, Carrie," he added as she tried to push past him. He pulled a twenty out of his wallet and handed it to the woman at the next window. The smell of doughnuts coming out of it was heaven to Kat's nose.

"Pull up and to the right. Someone will be out with your order when it's ready."

"Warmed up," Kat reminded her.

Skeeter did as the woman instructed then shifted into park.

Kat used her phone to turn the music all the way up. Not Adele. More Olivia.

Carrie started dancing in her seat. "Fine, little weirdo."

Kat laughed.

Knuckles rapped on Skeeter's window.

He rolled it down. "Sorry about the noise." He grinned. Then his face fell. "Where are the doughnuts?"

A Kearny cop stood outside the door. "Step out of the car, Mr. Rawlins, and keep your hands where we can see them."

Kat whipped her head around, looking for a second officer. A woman stood by the trunk of the car.

Skeeter looked confused, but he complied. "What's the matter?"

"Put your hands on the roof of the car and stand with your feet shoulder width apart. Do you have any weapons?"

Skeeter nodded. "I carry a knife on my belt. There's a handgun in my glove compartment."

"With minors in the car?"

"I have a license to carry, and I keep it locked up."

The officer frisked Skeeter, removing the knife. He cuffed him, read him his rights, and had the other officer retrieve the gun from the glove box.

Carrie crossed her arms. "This is bullshit. We were just

sitting here waiting for our doughnuts. He didn't do anything. Our mom is a deputy, too. He's our nanny."

"Your mom?" the cop said.

"Yeah," Carrie sneered. "Our mom. The adoptions are almost final. Call her."

"She's my aunt," Kat added.

"Out of the car," he said, opening one passenger side door while his partner opened the other. "Bring your things. You're coming with us."

Kat shook her head. "No way. Aunt Delaney trusted us with Skeeter. We're staying with him."

"Sorry. Skeeter Rawlins is headed to jail. And, unless there's someone at your house when we go to search it, you're heading into a CPS foster home."

"NO!" Kat shouted. She pressed her aunt's number, and it went straight to voice mail. Panic rose inside her. She ended the call without leaving a message. "Carrie, stop them."

"This ain't right," Skeeter said. "You can't just take me to jail. I didn't do nothing."

The officer said, "We have a tip about child pornography being conducted by you at the Pace home. We have every right to arrest you and take you in."

"I never. I never ever EVER!"

"Skeeter is the best," Kat said. "He would never hurt us."

The cop held out his hand. "Give me your phones, all three of you."

"You can't take them," Carrie said. "So, kiss my ass." She reached for Kat's hand. "Come on, Kat. Let's go to the station and find Delaney."

The officer shook his head. "You have a mouth on you. You should start using your brain before you open it. Everything is being done by the book. If you try to resist custody, we'll be within our rights to restrain you."

Tears rolled down Kat's cheeks.

Skeeter glanced back at them as the cop loaded him in the back seat of a city car parked behind them. "We'll get this sorted out, girls. It's all a mistake. Just do as you're told. I don't know what in heck is going on, but your aunt Delaney will be along soon."

Kat crawled out of the backseat and joined Carrie in the parking lot.

The teenage boy walked over, a doughnut box in his hand. "Here's your order."

The female cop shooed him away.

Carrie grabbed the box. "We paid for this." Then she lowered her voice to a whisper. "Can you please call Deputy Delaney Pace at the Kearny County Sheriff's Department and tell her Skeeter is in jail and we're going to CPS?"

His eyes were wide. He nodded.

Kat mouthed, "Thank you," and followed Carrie and the officer to the car, its blue lights strobing on the roof.

FORTY-ONE

Ellen sank lower, rested her head against the air pillow in her bathtub, and sighed. Bubbles and warm water lapped at her neck. A lavender-scented candle burned, for peace and tranquility. Her phone played an Ava Butler ballad, part of a curated list of songs for moments like these. It had been a stressful week, and she deserved her Sunday morning ritual. Right now, per the confirmation text she'd just received, the next part in her multiphase plan to ruin Delaney Pace's life was underway. She had managed to plant the right seeds with the right people to ruin Annabeth Dillon's as well, or, rather, to end it. And, through an unimaginable stroke of luck, the same force that had taken down the Senate candidate had done in her lover as well. Even the campaign to recall the sheriff might have some legs, because of the murders of Annabeth and Brock.

Ellen adjusted her gel undereye patches. They were cool and lovely against her skin. The face mask—one of those goopy press-on sheets in a tear-top packet—was slipping around over her eyes and mouth, but a Vitamin C infusion would pay dividends later.

She closed her eyes, concentrating on her breathing. Four

slow beats in, hold it, four slow beats out. Meditation. Something she didn't do often and wasn't good at. But she needed it now.

All her dreams were within reach. The relationships she'd built one upon the back and shoulders of another. Jefe being just one example, the ruthless, despicable toad. A man whose time was almost up. And she was going to be the one who stopped his clock. She would enjoy that oh so much. She'd finally convinced him the night before that she hadn't given him up to Brock Tucker, but for about half an hour, she'd been sure he was going to deprive her of the pleasure of killing him, by killing her.

Truth be told, she had hinted at Jefe's identity to Brock. It was all she'd had left after she'd tried diplomacy, manipulation, pressure, and blackmail with him—none of which had worked. She'd given him enough that Brock would have figured it out eventually.

Jefe had dodged a bullet when Brock died before spilling his guts to the cops.

At least she'd made the most of her servitude to Jefe. She'd leveraged and climbed until now she was working directly for the boss. Well, not *working* directly, but in direct contact, and the rest was only a matter of time now that she was proving herself indispensable. Tonight's quaint fundraiser would be like a coming out party for her. A slap in Jefe's face, too. His old bar. His family. His boss.

Her coup.

She counted to four, paused, then backed her breath down. She didn't know how many more repetitions she had left in her. How did people stay still for so long when there was so much to do? She opened her eyes to check her phone, which was propped up on a hand towel on the tub ledge near her feet. She'd set the timer for the masks.

Only thirty seconds to go.

One more breath cycle and she was done. One-two-three-four, hold it, one-two-three—

"Ellen."

She startled, splashing water out of the tub. A man's voice. Familiar but not *the* voice, the one she was terrified of. Jefe.

This man was in the bathroom, but behind her head. A past hook-up, maybe? She looked into the mirror and goose flesh pimpled her arms.

He was wearing a mask. One of the thin balaclavas, like she wore under a snowmobile helmet. It covered his hair, his face, his neck. He locked eyes with her and waggled fingers encased in surgical gloves. The other hand hung by his leg. In it was a gun.

All the air went out of her lungs. She was cornered. The closest things she had to weapons were a Venus shaver and a plastic shampoo bottle.

She faked bravado. "Yes?"

"Get the crap off your face."

"Excuse me?"

"Take those things off your face and wash it." He stepped into her line of sight and held out a bag. "Drop them in here."

"Why?"

He raised the gun. "Because I said so."

She peeled the eye patches away, trying hard not to tremble. She dropped them in the bag then removed the face sheet and balled it up. "Do I know you?"

He shook the bag.

She dropped the sheet in. Splashed bubbly water over her face, scrubbed it. Did it several more times, slowly, until the mask residue was completely gone.

"Turn off the music on your phone."

She sat up, one arm over her breasts. Picked up the phone, set it aside. Grasped the towel and wriggled her hand in it to dry her fingers. Set the towel down. Pressed the phone to stop the music.

"Toss the phone toward my feet."

"It will break."

He snorted.

It was a brand-new iPhone. She slung it as gently as she could, hoping it would land on its back and slide. It didn't. *Such a waste.* Then she realized how ridiculous she was being. A broken phone was the least of her worries. She dropped her arm. Her bare A cups weren't an issue either.

"If I don't know you, why are you here?"

He kept his gun and eyes on her as he leaned over, grabbed her phone, and added it to the contents of the bag. "I didn't say you don't know me."

"I repeat—why are you here?"

He blew out her candle. It went into his bag next. He dropped the bag on the floor. "We can do this easy, or we can do this hard, but one way or another, we are going to do this. Which do you want?"

Then she recognized the gun. It was hers. From her night-stand. She whispered a prayer of repentance and prepared for it to go the hard way.

FORTY-TWO

Delaney and Leo walked side-by-side into the throng of people at the clean water rally in downtown Sheridan. During their drive north from Kearny, she'd put the ATL out on Zeke. She'd called Mary to ask her to close the Loafing Shed an hour before the erstwhile fundraiser. Then she'd tried to locate Tommy using Leo's radio and truck trackers, now that they knew Brock had been murdered. Both trackers showed as unmoving at Tommy's home. But he didn't pick up her repeated calls.

"We need clones," she'd said.

"We need Tommy and Joe," Leo had responded. He'd called Joe from the road and informed him he was on suspension pending investigation.

Now they had a singular focus. Find Elana. Thanks to her strong online presence and the fact that she was wielding a megaphone and leading the crowd in chants, she was easily recognizable. Pippi Longstocking pigtails, freckles, and a gaunt, hungry look.

"What do we want?" she screamed.

"Clean water," the crowd screamed back, their number

filling the closed road between a fly-fishing store and a coffee shop. Delaney winced as she watched protestors lurching and slipping. Snow had started falling again, thick and fast. The street looked like it was ready for a downtown skijoring competition, which was one of Delaney's favorite events of the year. Horses sprinting at full gallop on snow-covered streets with kamikaze skiers attached to them by tow ropes. What wasn't to love?

"What will we get?" Elana screamed.

"Clean water!" her followers replied.

"Do you think she knows she's preaching to the choir here?" Leo said. "I've never lived in a community that cared more about preserving nature, water, and wildlife."

Delaney waved her hand at the cameras trained on Elana. "My guess is this is about the optics. And painting a red state with tar and feathers. The facts aren't as important as getting the message to the masses. Ready to see if we can separate her from the herd?"

"Somehow I don't envision this going well," Leo said. "But, yes, sure. You go first."

"The lamb to slaughter," Delaney muttered. But she picked her way through the crowd.

There were no familiar faces, and her "excuse me, pardon me," was met with hostile stares, expletives, and references to pigs. When she was standing in front of Elana, a big smile spread across the woman's face.

"This is a peaceful protest. We have every right to be here. Freedom of speech!" The strain in her voice was grating. The decibels through the megaphone at close range were cranium-splitting.

Delaney smiled back at her. "Absolutely. But I'm Kearny County Deputy Investigator Delaney Pace. I need to speak with Elana Holowitz on a matter unrelated to the rally, if you're her."

She didn't remove her mouth from the megaphone. "Unrelated, my ass!"

The crowd laughed.

"Hell no, I won't go!" she shouted.

"Hell no, she won't go!" the crowd responded.

A shopkeeper was leaning in a doorframe. "They're hurting my business. Send them all home or to jail. Please."

Delaney looked behind her for Leo. He was hanging back, out of the line of fire and cameras. She returned her attention to Elana and prayed the crowd couldn't hear her. "This is about the murder of Annabeth Dillon. Just a ten-minute break, please, and then you can get back to this. Maybe let someone else do the screaming for a few minutes?"

Elana dropped the megaphone. "Can't it wait?"

"Brock Tucker was murdered last night. We believe there's a connection between the two."

Elana's face blanched, emphasizing the geography of her freckles. "The news said he shot himself."

"Fake news. I take it this resonates with you?"

Elana's lips moved like she was talking to herself. Then she shoved her megaphone into the hands of a young man.

He eyed it like he'd been handed a rabid cat.

"Take over for me," she said.

"But I—"

"If you won't do it, I can find another second lieutenant."

The megaphone rose so fast it clanked against his teeth. "What do we want?" His voice cracked.

But the crowd was on his side. "Clean water!"

"Let's go." Elana was already moving down the alley beside The Mint Bar.

Delaney waved for Leo. He nodded and came after them.

Elana stopped behind The Mint, out of sight of the protest, within sniffing distance of the dumpster, which Delaney guessed wasn't emptied on Sundays by the stench of it. "What the hell is going on?"

"One step at a time. You're Elana Holowitz?" Delaney asked.

"I wouldn't be back here with you if I wasn't."

Leo trotted up. "Kearny County Sheriff Leo Palmer." He put out his hand to shake.

Elana didn't touch it or even look at him.

Delaney said, "What's your occupation?"

"I'm the executive director of several pro-environment and wildlife groups."

"What's your relationship with Annabeth Dillon?"

"She's a dear friend and a great supporter of our causes."

"So, the two of you were on good terms."

"The best."

Delaney read the text from Annabeth's phone aloud. "If any of this shit lands on me, you're fired."

"That's a private communication."

"Validly obtained from Ms. Dillon's phone pursuant to a probable cause warrant."

"Well, it's a violation of my fucking privacy!"

"Whoa, whoa, whoa. This is a *murder* investigation of someone you supposedly consider a friend. I would think you'd want to help."

Elana crossed her arms.

Delaney took that as assent. "Can you tell me what that text was referring to? What shit was she afraid would land on her?"

"Why don't you steal some more of our communications and then you tell me?"

"We'd prefer to hear it in your own words."

Elana patted her jeans pocket, then her chest, found a pack of cigarettes, and pulled a cig out. "Do you mind?"

"I don't, but the environment might. Is that a CO_2-free cigarette?"

That earned her a dirty look. With shaking hands, Elana produced a lighter from the same pocket. After a few puffs, her tremors subsided. "Do I need a lawyer?"

"Only if you've done something wrong, but it's your right to have one, of course. And I know you're big on rights."

Another dirty look.

"You're not under arrest, if that's what you mean."

Elana took a deep drag, slowly blew it out, then sagged. "Annabeth had lofty ambitions. She was afraid some of our goals and methods were too aggressive for her to win the middle ground. Mind you, she had no problem with any of it before she hooked up with Brock and decided to run for senator or president or whatever she had her sights on."

"President?"

"I just mean she saw herself as presidential material."

"What kind of goals and methods was she disassociating from?"

Elana shrugged.

"Would it have anything to do with the lawsuit against Abe Dunkirk?"

"That dickhead? He's a rabble-rouser."

"What's the lawsuit about?"

"Google it. There are no secrets."

"In your own words."

"It's about greed and disregard for our planet and the creatures living on it."

"What is he alleging?"

"That we somehow kept him from getting permits to rape the land." She held up both hands and waggled her fingers in the air. "Like I have the power."

"Did Ms. Dillon block his permits?"

"Not to my knowledge."

The questions about Abe weren't going anywhere. "What did Ms. Dillon mean when she said, 'you're fired' in her text?"

"I didn't work for her. But I had no doubt that with her money and rising star she could get me fired if she wanted to."

"Can you think of anyone who would want to hurt her?"

"Half of Teton County. The half with no money. She didn't pretend to be poor."

Delaney couldn't imagine someone with no money traveling across the state to stage a sex accident. But it wasn't impossible. She filed the idea away. "What about Abe?"

"Maybe. But he was mostly mad at me and his county."

"Brock?"

"Why? She was his golden girl."

"Her husband, Pete Smithers?"

She snorted. "She was his trust fund baby. The money dies with her."

"I thought he was independently successful."

"Appearances can be deceiving."

"Their relationship, how was that?"

"Annabeth didn't talk about him much. But he always showed up wherever she went. They held hands. He looked good in photographs with her."

"Was Ms. Dillon faithful to him, to your knowledge?"

Elana laughed. "I doubt it."

"Who was she unfaithful with?"

"That I don't know. Just that she hinted at getting her itch scratched and it wasn't by Pete."

"When was the last time you spoke to Annabeth?"

"In person?"

"In any form."

"That text."

"Why didn't you answer it?"

"Who says I didn't?"

"Me. I have her phone."

"I was thinking about how to respond. And then she died."

"Was murdered. Do you know Shaina Pham?"

"Yeah."

"Would she have it in for Ms. Dillon?"

"Why?"

"If Ms. Dillon was disassociating herself from the public activist groups, I'd think she'd cut all ties to the extremists, like those Shaina ran with."

Elana looked over Delaney's shoulder. "Sounds like you know more than me." She pretended to glance at the time on her Apple watch. "That ten minutes is up." She backed away down the alley. "If you need anything else, you'll be talking to my attorney."

FORTY-THREE

Adriana glanced up from her laptop at the kitchen table. Freddy had fallen asleep reading a book on the couch. From the giggling she'd heard the night before, he and Kat had been up until the wee hours. Their friendship was sweet. But they were fast approaching the age where even supervised sleepovers would become a problem. She wanted to put that time off as long as possible, though. The time when she had to say no. The time when she couldn't pretend he was her little Freddy-boy anymore. The time when he'd become a young man, then a real man, and someday would leave her completely alone.

Losing her husband at such a young age had been hard, but she'd always had her son. In some ways, losing Freddy to adulthood would be harder. As independent as she was and as feisty as most people believed her to be, she needed *connection*. A man. She missed it. She deserved it. She didn't believe it was asking too much out of life to want it.

She'd turned the sound off on her laptop so that Freddy wouldn't become curious about her chat conversation. Better for him to think she was just surfing the web for shoes and moisturizer. Since she'd looked away, Paul had sent her three more messages.

The first:

I can't stop thinking about you.

The second:

Best first date ever.

The third:

Most beautiful woman in Wyoming.

Back in California, while Adriana had always known she was good looking, she'd felt ordinary pretty. Here in Wyoming, she rose like cream from milk. It's not like she had her choice of men, but close to it. It was just meeting them that was the problem. Her job as a court reporter didn't put her in contact with many eligible men—mostly just drunks, minor felons, and deadbeat dads—and she wasn't into church or rodeos, which seemed to be the social events of choice locally. Online dating was a necessity.

She replied.

Stop, don't stop. ;-)

Are things crazy at your house with all these murders in the county?

What do you mean?

Didn't you say your brother is the sheriff?

Oh, yeah. It's kept him busy. I have the house nearly to myself.

Can you FaceTime then?

Sure.

Her phone vibrated almost instantly. She bit her lips to give them some color, fluffed the crown of her pixie hair, and answered as she fast-walked to her bedroom. "Hello?"

His handsome smile filled the screen. "Are you going out somewhere?"

"No, why?"

"You look so good, I figured you must have a date with some other guy."

She laughed. "Oh my god, no. I don't even have on any makeup."

He shook his head. "You're out of my league, Adriana."

If only he knew what a hot mess she was. Or, rather, if she could only keep him from finding out. He was handsome, made great money, gave compliments, and hadn't run when he learned about Freddy. "Please. It's the other way around. What are you up to today?"

"Trying to think of a reason not to see you again already. I can't come up with one."

"Good. Because it would be cool to see you again, too." Her calendar was clear. Freddy was old enough to stay by himself a few hours at a time.

"Unfortunately, I already have plans today. But maybe I could swing by on my way and say hello?"

It took all her willpower not to ask him what plans he had and with whom. "It's just Freddy and me hanging out."

"Just for a few minutes then. To drop something off, ask you out in person. That kind of thing."

She instantly forgot about his other plans. "I'll be here." The doorbell rang. "Hold on a second." She didn't want Freddy to answer it, so she trotted down the hallway. One peek through the peephole and her heart sped up. She wrenched the door open, unable to keep the smile off her face. "That was fast."

Paul's answering grin made her stomach flutter. "I wanted to surprise you."

"Well, you did."

"I hope in a good way."

"Very good. Come on in."

Freddy was stretching, with his arms over his head, torso twisted, face scrunched. "Hey, Mom."

Adriana took a deep breath. She hadn't planned on introducing Freddy and Paul this early. "Hey, sweetie. This is my friend Paul, er, I mean Mr. Lester."

Freddy said, "Hey. Nice to meet you."

Paul pulled a bouquet of red roses from behind his back. "Hi, Freddy. Nice to meet you. Adriana, these are for you."

"Oh. My." She took them from him. "They're beautiful. Thank you."

"Not half as beautiful as you. Is the rest of the family here? I'd love to shake your brother's hand. Thank him for working as a public servant."

"No. He's on the job."

"Oh, well, you can pass along my sentiment then. Has he talked about these recent murder cases? Pretty exciting stuff."

"He really hasn't. But he's been gone most of the time since they, um, happened."

"Say, how would the two of you like to go snow skiing with me tomorrow?" Paul said.

Adriana wasn't into winter sports. Moving here had been about getting away from the bad people after Leo, not about an interest in Wyoming. But she wanted to be with Paul, and she found herself saying, "That would be so much fun! School doesn't start back up for Freddy for another week."

The look her son gave her was dubious. "Um, can Kat come?"

Paul frowned.

Adriana saw his expression and jumped in. "Not this time. We're all just getting to know each other."

"Okay, I guess." Freddy left the room.

Paul took a step closer to Adriana and whispered. "I don't think he likes me."

"He'll warm up." She felt his nearness. Smelled his musky scent. Wanted him to touch her again. "Um, what time tomorrow?"

"Do you have skis?"

"No."

"Then how about I pick you up at eight-thirty? We'll have to rent equipment for you."

Adriana hadn't thought about the cost of equipment rental. Plus the lift tickets. The last time she'd been skiing was before Freddy was born, and even back then it had set her and Jim back five hundred between the two of them. "Oh, gee. You know what? I don't get paid until Friday. Can I take a raincheck?"

"I invited you guys. I'm picking up the tab."

"But it's so expensive. And there's two of us."

"This is Wyoming. You'll be shocked how much cheaper it is than in California. Besides, it's a small price to pay for a day with the two of you."

"If you're sure?"

"I've never been surer of anything in my life. Just promise to wear that pretty scarf you had on when we had coffee."

Adriana tingled all over. She'd never been surer of anything either.

FORTY-FOUR

With time on their hands after their eye-opening interview with Elana, and before their scheduled video call with Abe, Leo and Delaney dropped by Shaina Pham's house. Leo called ahead. As expected, she didn't pick up. Her outgoing message didn't provide any clues to her whereabouts.

Delaney parked the truck in front of a sprawling restored two-story in the historic district of town. "She's doing all right for herself if she lives here. Keeping these old houses in shape must cost a fortune."

Leo climbed out. "New front walkway." The fresh concrete hadn't yet buckled under the tumult of Wyoming winters. It was also shoveled nearly clear, except for the most recent snow that day. "And someone is taking care of it while she's gone."

He rang the bell. It let off a peal of chimes that seemed to echo inside the old house. They waited, but no one answered the door.

Leo rang again, then started knocking loudly. He put his mouth next to the door jamb. "Kearny County Sheriff's Department. Can you open up, please?"

"Nada," Delaney said. "Nadie."

Nothing. No one. "Since when do you speak Spanish?"

"I learned a lot of it on the road. It leaks out occasionally."

Leo answered her in fluent Español. *"Crecí en San Diego. El español fue prácticamente mi primera lengua."*

"I got about fifty percent of that. Anyway, no one is answering this door."

"Agreed. Want to look around?"

"Sure, I do. But I wouldn't think you would. Maybe you'd like to wait in the truck with your eyes closed for deniability?"

"I didn't say let's break in through a window."

"Nor did I. But I'd like to see if she's bringing in her mail."

"Delaney, opening her mailbox without a warrant is a federal crime."

She ignored him. "Peeking in a few windows would be good."

"Trespassing at the least. Voyeurism if there's someone in there."

"Like I said, maybe you'd be happier in the truck?"

"Our footprints in the snow will make it pretty obvious we've been here."

"Mine. See you in a minute."

"Delaney..."

"I won't leave tracks in the snow. None that can be identified, anyway."

Leo walked to the truck. When he looked back, Delaney was peering into the front windows on tiptoe. Then she used her elbow to lift the lid on the mailbox, barely even breaking stride across the porch as she went by it.

A text came in from Clara.

Report from Paintbrush Lodge of an abandoned vehicle on their property in the mountains.

He texted her back.

*Can you send someone up to take a look? Get a plate and
run it?*

Will do.

Delaney hopped in the truck.

"Anything?"

"Mailbox is full. House is spotless. Kitchen tidy. I think
she's traveling."

"Do you think she lives alone?"

"I couldn't tell. But I don't think anyone is staying in the
house right now." She pulled away from the curb. "But I'm
pretty sure that everything we just did was caught on a security
camera."

"Great," Leo said.

She shrugged. "Your hands are clean. Mine are only slightly
smudged."

Back at the station, Leo set up their connection to Sheriff Ed
Nickels, who'd texted ahead to confirm that a deputy was
bringing a very consternated Abe Dunkirk in momentarily for
the meeting.

"Hello, Ed," Leo said.

"What's going on, Leo? I thought you found the murderer
and he committed suicide." Ed had baggy dark circles under his
eyes. *Join the club.*

"Delaney's here with me." Leo motioned her over.

She scooted her chair beside Leo's, and their heads
appeared on screen next to each other. *So close and yet so far.*
"Hello, Sheriff."

The sheriff nodded politely. "Delaney."

Leo went back to the question. "It's complicated. Turns out

our suspect didn't kill himself. And there's no direct evidence that he killed Annabeth either."

"Stirring up a hornet's nest though, aren't you? Sure would be more tidy if you could close it out. I hate seeing Jackson on the news every night. Every story leads and ends with the average home value in the county and the wealth disparities in our citizenry. It's not a good look for us."

A wave of irritation surged up in Leo. *Not a good look? Try having the murders occur in your county and a deputy's gun involved in one of the incidents.* "You up for re-election this year and worrying about your campaign funding, Ed? Otherwise, I'd think you'd empathize."

Delaney bristled. "Next time, keep your more infamous residents over in Teton County, then you can control the narrative. Or try to."

Leo took a deep breath. Delaney's interjection had given him the pause he needed. Even when they were at odds, she was a better teammate than he'd ever worked with. "We can't leave a killer out there. But strap in tight—this case is growing more high profile by the minute."

Ed raised his hands in defeat. "Okay, okay. I'm on your side."

Leo hoped so, but their interaction bothered him. He couldn't trust anyone, except Delaney. "On to Abe Dunkirk. There seemed to be some bad blood between him and Ms. Dillon."

Ed shrugged. "They see things differently. Saw. But his beef was with the activist groups, not Annabeth."

"Aren't they one and the same?"

"What do you mean?"

"She was synonymous with them. The executive director all but said most of their funding came straight from her trust fund. And if Mr. Dunkirk is right, someone with serious pull blocked his permits. Pull like Ms. Dillon had."

"The way I hear it, there was no way he was going to get those permits, with or without Annabeth's opposition."

A knock sounded off-screen.

Ed stood. "It appears Abe has arrived. Give us a second."

Leo heard shuffling and muffled conversation in angry tones.

Delaney pressed mute. "What's up with Ed? I don't like his vibe."

He nodded. "I'm sure he's under a lot of pressure, but I don't like it either." Pressure sure came with the job.

She nodded and pressed unmute.

A man appeared on screen, his face too close for a moment as he sat down, showing longish nostril hair and oversized pores. His eyes were narrowed and his mouth tight. One cheek bulged with what Leo assumed was chewing tobacco.

Ed took the seat beside him. "Sheriff Palmer, Deputy Pace, this is Abe Dunkirk. Abe, this is Sheriff Leo Palmer and Deputy Investigator Delaney Pace. They're from Kearny County."

Abe glared at them. "This is harassment. I'll sue over this. Don't think I won't."

Leo said, "Oh, I don't doubt it for a second."

Ed put a hand on Abe's shoulder "You're not a suspect, Abe, so just calm down. One of our Teton citizens was murdered."

"Is that what you call them? The rich out-of-staters buying up the county and trying to impose their will around the state on those of us who've been here all our lives? Citizens? If Annabeth Dillon was a citizen, what does that make me?"

"You're both property owners."

"So, you have to own property to be a citizen? I'll bet your voters would be surprised to hear you saying that."

"Now, that's not what I meant, and you know it."

"Whatever, Ed. It's clear some property owners have more rights than the rest of us. She gets to move here and tell me what I can and can't do with my land."

Delaney leaned toward the screen. "I'm a fifth generation Wyomingite, Mr. Dunkirk. I hear you."

He aimed watery blue eyes at her. "Rich city folks who want to impose their rules on the rest of us. It's not right. They don't understand what it takes—what is has taken—to survive out here, insulated in their big, gated houses and surrounded by staff who take the hard work out of living in Wyoming. Property taxes are eating me alive. I have to mine my land just to afford to keep it. Otherwise, I'll lose it to someone like her."

"I understand. I'm hanging on to our family homestead by a thread."

He turned to Ed and threw his hands in the air. "See?"

"Listen, as many problems as you had with her, it's Leo's and my job to find out who killed Ms. Dillon."

"It wasn't me."

"Can you confirm your phone number for us?" She read out the 307 number she'd found in Annabeth's texts.

"Yeah, that's it. Why?"

"Did you receive a text from her that said, 'Just give me a settlement figure and cut the shit?' She would have sent it the night she died."

"I did. My attorney told me not to answer it."

Leo stepped in. "Had you and Ms. Dillon texted before?"

"No. I was surprised to hear from her."

"But you knew it was her?"

"Who else would it be? Besides, I'd called her before. I recognized the number."

"Why'd you call her?"

He shifted in his chair. "She'd blocked my permits."

"Did you talk to her then?"

"Yes."

"What did you say?"

"That, uh, that I knew it was her and didn't appreciate it,

and that it was my land, and I was going to mine it one way or another."

"What was her response?"

"She said there were people who would make sure I didn't."

"Who did she mean?"

"She called them 'people more ruthless than me' and said I'd have nothing left when they were done with me."

"Did Ms. Dillon ever offer you money? An actual dollar figure?"

"No. She just offered to buy my place so I wouldn't have to worry about the property taxes anymore. I hear tell her husband is driving up and down Jackson Hole making the same kind of offers to all the locals in the valley. I told her to go fuck herself, of course."

"Abe..." Ed said.

"It's an exact quote. I believe in speaking the truth, even if other people don't like it."

Leo said, "Then what happened?"

"Then someone contacted me who had real pull. Told me he'd get my permit for me if I sued Annabeth and her activist proxies. So, I hired a lawyer to give 'em a taste of their own medicine. I'm going to shove it up their asses, like a big fat suppository of law and justice."

It was crude, but Leo understood the point.

"Son of a bitch!" Abe jumped to his feet, his phone in his hand.

"What is it?"

"A neighbor just texted me. Those environmental terrorists are parked out by my property shouting on a bullhorn."

"About what?"

"Well, it sure as shit isn't going to be to give me a man of the year award." He disappeared from the screen.

"Wait, where is your property? Jackson? Cody?"

His face popped back into the screen, in extreme close-up.

"Where the hell'd you get that idea? It's just south of Kearny. On the face of the Bighorns."

"But you're in Teton County."

"Who'd want to live on a piece of property that's getting mined?"

If he heard the irony in his own statement, he didn't stick around to discuss it.

FORTY-FIVE

Delaney checked her phone. Again. Not only was she hoping to hear Zeke was okay, but neither the girls nor Skeeter had checked in with her in hours. She'd sent them a group text earlier, too. *Do you guys miss me?* It had been a dumb thing to send. Begging to be disappointed. Kat and Carrie were not at an age where they'd give her a warm fuzzy answer, and Skeeter would stare mutely at the screen unable to figure out what to say to a question like that. She thought about sending another. Something they'd have to answer.

Instead, she woke up her laptop screen. She was still avoiding the deep dive into connections between her colleagues and the murder victims. She had a few minutes before Riley Tucker was due in for her interview to chip away at it.

Her phone rang. Her heart leaped. The girls? But when she looked at her screen, she saw the name Shaina Pham. "Deputy Investigator Delaney Pace."

"This is Shaina Pham. You were peeking in the windows of my house." The high-pitched voice sounded like the woman was holding her nose. Obviously her security video went to the cloud, and she'd reviewed it. It was one way to get a person of interest to call in, even if the woman had apparently been ignoring Delaney's actual phone calls.

"Ms. Pham, thank you for calling me back." Delaney wished Leo was with her. It was always better to have two people in interviews, for corroboration as well as interpretation and collective memory. Plus, Leo kept records. She hated admitting what a benefit his investigation plans and notes were, so she wouldn't. Not to his face, anyway. "I believe the sheriff has called you as well. When we couldn't reach you by phone or in person, we were concerned."

"I'm sure."

"I'm calling about Annabeth Dillon."

"I figured as much. Can I have my cabin back now? This is costing me money."

"Not quite yet. As you can probably imagine, we're trying to figure out who murdered your friend."

The line went silent.

"Ms. Pham?"

"What do you mean, my friend?"

"I mean Annabeth Dillon, who you knew from your activist work, and who others in her life have characterized as your friend."

"She was *not* my friend."

"You rented your cabin to her on short notice."

"I lent it to her. And that was because she expected people to kiss her ass."

"Why?"

"She thought tossing money around gave her privilege."

"Did it?"

Shaina's voice rose. "People that really care about our planet give their time and their lives for it. They don't expect to be repaid for money in favors. They expect to be reviled and endangered and imprisoned for their efforts."

"I take it you don't think she really cared about our planet."

Her voice cracked. "She was all about the cause until she wanted bigger things for herself."

"The Senate campaign?"

"Yes. She had the nerve to demand use of my cabin after she didn't have the balls to tell me herself that she was cutting all her ties with us."

"Us? Who is us?"

"Listen, I hope you find the person who killed her. I really do. Because they deserve a medal from the rest of us for ridding the world of a hypocrite like her."

"Who do you work with?"

"The good guys."

The call ended, leaving Delaney listening to dead air. She put her phone down. *All right, then.* After she typed up notes of the call and emailed it to Leo, she checked the time. *Crap.* Riley was probably waiting for her and Leo out front.

She fast-walked down the hall, stopping to stick her head in his office. "Brock's wife was due here five minutes ago. I'm heading out to get her."

"Wait. I have news."

"I don't want her to give up on me."

"This will only take a second. I got a very strange phone call. From Annabeth Dillon's trustee."

"On a Sunday?"

"It's a big trust. And he's very concerned about the balance."

She dropped into a chair. "That sounds ominous."

"Only because it is. He's missing several million dollars."

"What? When did it go missing? And how?"

"In the last month. A series of transfers to an offshore account. The who and the how they don't know but will get investigators on the case. However, it hasn't escaped my attention, or his, that Pete Smithers is a supposed financial guru. And that he would get nothing if he divorced his wife. Or if she died."

"And suddenly, right after the money goes missing, she ends up dead." She snapped her fingers. "Annabeth's audio recording. The text to her husband. He knew about the affair."

Leo smiled and lifted his shoulders. "And his former employee was hanging out in a cabin, right next door, unregistered."

"Time for another chat with Rufus."

"Agreed. After Riley." Leo snatched up his tablet. "I'll meet you in the conference room."

"Good stuff. See you there." She leaped to her feet and resumed her march to the reception area. A woman was perusing the photo gallery on the wall. It was a new collection, purchased the year before from local wildlife and outdoor photographer Steve Bourne, and it showcased the rugged beauty of the area. The woman's ash-blonde hair was rolled into a chignon, her tall, thin body encased in a black pantsuit with a heavy fur coat draped over one arm. Wedge-heeled boots—Sorels?—elevated her height to well over six feet.

"Ms. Tucker?" Delaney said. "I'm Deputy Investigator Delaney Pace."

She turned. Her familiar features looked more delicate in real life than in the photograph at her home. She extended a hand. "Riley Tucker. You were at my house, before..."

"Yes." Nails scratched the back of Delaney's hands. Red. Hard. Fake. "I'm so sorry for your loss."

"Thank you. It's a sad and confusing time."

Delaney found herself looking up to keep eye contact with Riley, which didn't happen to her with many women. Given her height and body type, Riley could have worked as a model, if she'd lived nearer a fashion center. Wyoming wasn't famous for runways or couture. "I'm sure. If you'll follow me, we'll join Sheriff Palmer."

Delaney badged herself in from reception, then led Riley into the conference room. Leo stood and introduced himself. Riley put her coat over the back of a chair and took a seat next to it.

"Can I get you coffee?" Delaney asked.

"No, thank you," Riley said.

Delaney was happy to hear it since she would have had to make it in the break room. After dispensing with preliminaries, she launched into the heart of things. "You've met with Dr. Watson about your husband's death?"

Riley nodded.

"He died of suffocation before he was shot."

"With a gun from your department."

"And after his arrest for the murder of Annabeth Dillon."

She nodded again. Her expression didn't change.

"Your husband admitted to an affair with Ms. Dillon and to his presence at her cabin on the night of her death."

She winced. "Yes. As I said to you earlier, it's a sad and confusing time."

"Had you known about the relationship?"

"Brock has never been faithful."

"He's had other affairs?"

"Since before we were married. I don't know if he realized I was aware, but I'm not stupid. He loved me. Sex was about money and power to him. Money and power were part of what attracted me to him. It was hard to separate the good from the bad without changing who he was. I confronted him about it the first time. After that, well, I just decided to enjoy the life I'd chosen."

Delaney thought the whole arrangement sounded terrible. "Mr. Tucker said you were on a girls' trip this last week."

"Yes. I'd just gotten home when I encountered the two of you at our ranch."

Delaney stood and walked to a credenza. She took a pad of

paper and pen out of a cabinet and brought them to Riley. "If you could write down the names and phone numbers of your traveling companions, as well as the hotel information, please. Oh, and the dates and times of your flights."

"Excuse me? What's this about?"

"Just confirming alibis."

"I'm a suspect?"

"You're the spouse. Standard procedure."

"Okay." She started writing.

Delaney and Leo stayed silent and motionless.

When she finished, she pushed the pad to the center of the table. "There."

Leo smiled at her. "Who inherits your husband's estate?"

"Unless he's changed his will, it goes to his daughter, with a life estate to me in our ranch."

"Meaning you can live there during your lifetime, and after that it is hers to dispose of as she sees fit?"

"Yes, although she has the option to buy me out. Brock's idea was that either way I'd have a place to live or the money to buy a new home."

If Riley turned up dead, Jillian would make the list of suspects. But with a life estate to her stepmother, Jillian didn't stand to gain from her father's death in Riley's lifetime. "The two of you don't have any children?"

"No. And Jillian was an adult when we married. She lives in Georgia. I barely know her."

"Nothing else goes to you?"

"Not a thing."

"Do you work outside the home?"

"I do not, unless you count charity work."

Delaney looked at Leo. He was writing quickly. The conversation so far was snappy and fast. "I don't mean to press a sore point, but how will you support yourself?"

She inspected her nails. "Life insurance. Brock bought a policy with me as the beneficiary."

"Oh, that's good."

"Yes."

Delaney slipped back into the lineup. The hardest questions always came last. "Where were you last night at seven p.m., Ms. Tucker?"

"At home trying to reach my husband at the hospital. His attorney had called me to let me know where he was."

"Were you alone?"

"No. The dogs were with me."

Delaney smiled at her. "I mean is there anyone else who can confirm your whereabouts."

Riley stood. "No one."

"Do you have security cameras that record entry and exit from your ranch?"

She scoffed. "No need for them. And I hope that doesn't keep you from figuring out who was in my husband's hospital room at about that time smothering him with a pillow."

"It won't be a problem for us. One last thing. Did you and Mr. Tucker have a prenuptial agreement?"

She gripped the back of her chair. "We did. I didn't come from money. His lawyers wanted to be sure I wasn't a gold digger."

"What were the terms?"

"If we divorced, I would get a lump sum of half a million dollars, no matter the reason."

To Delaney, that sounded like a lot of money. But for someone living like Riley with a husband as wealthy as Brock, it was a mere rounding error. "If you could send over a copy of his will, the insurance policy, and the prenuptial agreement, that would be a big help."

"I'll have my attorneys take care of it." She collected her coat.

"Thanks for coming in. Again, my condolences. Shall I walk you out?"

Riley was already at the door. She pointed to the exit only steps away, through a door that Delaney knew would automatically lock after her. "I'm fine." Then she stalked away, again bringing to mind a runway model.

Delaney turned back to Leo. "Well?"

He fanned himself. "I think she's not going to be single very long if she doesn't want to be."

Delaney rolled her eyes.

"Seriously, she doesn't seem broken-hearted."

"Not at all."

"And I've seen her somewhere before."

"On a photograph in her kitchen."

He shook his head. "Not just there. I can't remember, but it will come to me if it's important."

Important like how good-looking she was? Delaney felt an irrational urge to punch her partner.

FORTY-SIX

Kat kicked the seat of her chair with her heel. THUMP THUMP THUMP. How long were these dumb people going to leave her and Carrie in this place that smelled like dirty diapers? "I don't understand why they won't call Aunt Delaney!"

"Maybe she's working and hasn't been able to answer?" Carrie wrapped her arms around her knees, feet in her chair, pink tail hanging down her back.

Kat shook her head. "She always checks in with us." She used to think it was annoying how much Aunt Delaney texted her. And the texts were always so goofy. But now she'd give anything to have her phone back and get a message from her.

"She's super busy. People are getting murdered."

It didn't matter. Tears stung Kat's eyes. She missed her real mom. But Lila Clement hadn't risked her life for Kat. Aunt Delaney had. More than once. For Carrie, too. They'd repaid her by being mean to her. And now these stupid people were trying to keep her from adopting them. Her tears spilled over.

The door opened. The woman who'd bad-mouthed Aunt

Delaney, Skeeter, and Carrie at Freddy's house walked in. "I'm—"

Kat jumped to her feet. "I know who you are. I want to call my aunt. I want to go home."

The woman turned away from her to Carrie. "I work for the state of Wyoming as an investigator in family cases. My name is Ms. Willett."

Carrie looked away and didn't reply.

Ms. Willett said, "I'm really sorry it had to come to this, girls. I know you've had a tough time, and you deserved better."

Carrie snorted. "We got the best with Delaney."

"I mean you deserve better than to be dumped with an unfit babysitter—"

"What did he supposedly do wrong, anyway? The cop wouldn't even tell him."

"That is no business for children."

She dropped her feet to the floor. "I'm seventeen. That hardly makes me a child. And why won't you let us make a phone call?"

"We're taking care of that for you."

"I want to call Delaney Pace. She is my legal guardian, and she is Kat's blood aunt. And she's a deputy."

"Right now, all that matters is keeping you safe. She's at work, and you were put in the middle of a dangerous arrest. There's a search warrant pending for her house."

"Our house!" Kat shouted.

"Yes, well, if she's cleared of wrongdoing, there will be a fitness hearing in a few days. Everything will be decided there."

"What about letting us call Leo? He's the sheriff."

"I don't think so. He has a conflict of interest."

Kat's voice strained and her eyes bulged. "This is total bullshit!"

"I won't tolerate that kind of language, young lady."

"Total fucking bullshit," Carrie said.

"It breaks my heart the things you two have learned under such a bad influence.

"I learned those words from my mother."

"I'll leave the two of you until you can behave more appropriately. In the meantime, I'll be finalizing places for each of you to stay until the hearing."

"Places? As in plural?" Carrie said.

"Yes. One for each of you."

"Why can't we be together? We're sisters." Kat began to sob.

"Actually, you aren't, and it's very difficult to place teenage girls at all. You should be very grateful anyone will take you in."

"We're sisters in every way that counts." Carrie grabbed Kat's hand and squeezed it. "And we had a place where someone wanted both of us. We'll be going back there. You'll see."

The investigator shook her head and left the room.

FORTY-SEVEN

"This had better be important. I've got a press conference in five minutes, then I'm getting on a plane to Kearny for my little fundraiser," Mitch Stonefield said.

Standing in his tiny kitchen, Jefe pressed the phone against his ear so hard he was probably crushing cartilage. If he hadn't been friends with Mitch since they'd both grown up as the poorest kids in school, would he put up with his shit? Once upon a time, they'd been partners. It had been Jefe—Liam—who, at Mitch's request, had done whatever was necessary to buy into the lucrative side businesses that seeded Mitch's law school tuition and first campaign. When Mitch had asked him to fly under the radar, afraid of their relationship and business dealings becoming public as his career became more high profile, Jefe had conceded. It had cost him his identity, his wife, his daughter, and the last ties to his family home and business.

He believed in Mitch. Or, more to the point, he believed in Mitch's future and Jefe's place in it. It had been a necessary gamble. Jefe didn't need his name in lights. He had a role, a powerful one, that would get nothing but bigger as Mitch set his sights on the Senate, the Cabinet, and the White House.

Over the last year, though, things had changed. Mitch didn't make time for his old partner. He didn't include him in all the big decisions. Didn't update him on important events. Like Mitch thought he was better than Jefe. Like he was squeezing him out. And then there was this crap with Ellen. Mitch never should have let Ellen compromise him with a face-to-face meeting. It was short-sighted. Bad judgment. Borderline betrayal.

And now Jefe was calling to help him. To help Mitch. Always to help Mitch. And how did Mitch respond? Like Jefe was a pest.

It came down to one thing to Jefe—Mitch owed him. Owed him big. The Wyoming Attorney General didn't seem to remember that essential fact. Or that Jefe knew *everything*. Where every single body, both figurative and literal, was buried in the graveyard of Mitch's past.

But he'd just brought up something that was news to Jefe. He opened the cabinet and pulled out a bottle of Wyoming Whiskey. "What fundraiser?"

"The one at your old family bar. Ellen set it up for me. It's the least your sister could do after cutting off the donations to me."

Jefe swallowed down the bile of his poisonous thoughts. He cradled the phone between his ear and shoulder as he retrieved a cocktail glass from the cabinet. The door stuck and he had to jerk it harder than he intended and nearly dropped the phone. "We have a potential problem."

"You will fix it. That's your job."

Technically, Jefe didn't work for Mitch, although he called him boss, and everything he did was about furthering their power structure. Jefe ran the empire that funded Mitch's dreams. But, yes, he did fix things.

Uncapping the bottle, he kept his tone neutral. "Of course, I will. Already did. We had a rat."

Mitch lowered his voice. "Name? Or do I want to know?"

"Ellen Day. She leaked my identity and possibly my relationship with you to a... competitor." *Or that's my theory anyway.* "It's possible that information has been contained, but I couldn't let her continue to compromise you or me." He poured two fingers, paused, then added two more. Lifted the glass and sniffed. Smelling the whiskey did almost as much for him as drinking it.

"She was a rising star. Tell me you didn't do something you can't undo."

Why was this man blind to her machinations? Or was he blind to anyone who blew smoke up his skirt? "I fix things. I fixed this thing. You're welcome." He toasted the air with his glass then took his first sip. The burn in his mouth spread warmth through his arms down to his fingers.

"Is it that, or is it that you were threatened and neutralized a threat—a rival?"

Another sip. *Stay calm.* "A rival for what?"

"For your *job*. Not only did she perform it well while you were in Mexico—"

"That was me, Mitch. Me the whole time."

"—but I've been giving her special assignments, and I have every reason to think those had gone perfectly, too."

Jefe squeezed the glass until he was afraid it would crack. "What kind of assignments?"

"Now that you can't have a face and a name, I needed someone who could act under the color of my office."

"Hire an admin."

"Like setting up the fundraiser at the Loafing Shed. Not exactly something you could do, is it? Forming alliances with the enemies of my enemies."

"What do you mean?" Then he tossed back half the contents of his glass.

"She was going to push a permit through on my behalf for a Kearny County landowner who Annabeth Dillon had blocked from mining his own property. She obtained compromising information on a candidate and donor and made sure it ended up in the hands of the right people."

Jefe set his glass down, gritted his teeth, recapped the bottle, and put it away. "Are we talking about Annabeth Dillon and Brock Tucker?"

"I don't know, are we?"

"I'd already asked her to stand them down."

"I was doubling up."

"You realize they were both murdered, don't you? And that it doesn't take a rocket scientist to realize how much their deaths benefit you?"

"So?"

"So, who killed them, Mitch?"

"I don't know, and I don't care."

"If it was your new pet, I think you'd better start caring a lot."

Mitch went silent on the other end.

Jefe leaned his hands on the countertop as he pressed his advantage. "As for Ellen, she was no threat to my role in our plans. She didn't have our thirty years history."

Liam heard someone whispering to Mitch and his reply of "one minute."

Then, to Liam, Mitch said, "Change can be invigorating. A lifeblood."

Jefe laughed, but it was without mirth. "Oh, jeez. Tell me you didn't sleep with her."

"I was invigorated by her mind and her ambition, not her body. She had a future in Wyoming politics."

"Her ambition was her downfall. She was insubordinate and dangerous. I just hope you'll have deniability if her sins ever come home to roost with you. I'm working to ensure they don't."

"I have to go. But this conversation isn't over."

"What conversation?"

"The one about change." Mitch ended the call.

The hell it wasn't. Jefe picked up his glass and threw it sidearm at the sink. Glass exploded, liquid splashed. He was one hundred percent certain that he and Mitch would never have this conversation again.

FORTY-EIGHT

Delaney rang the bell at Ellen Day's house. Her stomach growled. Lunchtime had passed two hours ago with no food. *This is the day that will not end.* When had Leo's party been? Two nights before? She'd worked nonstop since then. "I need food."

Leo nodded. "Me, too. When we're done here."

She nodded and stared through the panes of glass in the door. She also needed a break to think about her job and Leo. To connect with the girls. To see if she could figure out where Zeke had gone. *No, the ATL has been issued. He's a grown-up, engaged to be married. Just let him go.* She couldn't get over a sense that things with him were not right, though.

She rang the bell again. "Déjà vu. Just like at Shaina's house. No lights on either."

"Let me guess. I should wait in the truck."

Delaney tried the door handle. It wasn't locked, and the latch gave way. "No. I'd like you to enter with me."

"We're trespassing."

"I think I heard a scream. This is a wellness check."

"She's a minor witness from a coincidental text."

"In a case that makes no sense and has already spawned two deaths." Delaney stepped inside.

"Which may or may not be related to each other." Leo sighed and followed her. "She's going to come after us with both barrels for this. Hello, recall vote. And for something that may not be relevant."

She wrinkled her nose. "The woman likes her plug-in room deodorizers." Then she raised her voice. "This is the Kearny County Sheriff's Department. Ellen Day? Are you home? Are you okay?"

There was no answer. She and Leo swept the ground floor and basement quickly. Delaney kept a sharp eye out for anything related to Annabeth Dillon or Brock Tucker. What those items would be, she had no idea. But still she was surprised when she found both of their business cards on the kitchen counter by Ellen's purse.

She pointed at them. "What do you make of that?"

"That Ellen is upstairs asleep?"

"No, I mean the business cards."

Leo moved closer to them. "She's a political animal."

"Yet she was photographed with Mitch Stonefield only days ago."

"Playing both sides of the fence?"

"Maybe." Delaney took a photograph of the tableau. Then she headed for the stairs. Her skin started to tingle as she climbed. "Something has my sixth sense on high alert." She stopped in the upstairs hallway.

Leo frowned. "Me, too."

"Let's start with her room." Delaney entered the room. "She doesn't make her bed." Pillows were askew. The comforter was bunched up.

"Two doors. Closet or bathroom?"

The bathroom was ensuite. A remodel for a house this age. Probably a former nursery or second closet. "Bathroom." She pulled open the door to a large, tiled space. *No, it's probably a converted bedroom.* White and black with accents of red. Awfully contemporary for an old house in Wyoming.

But then dread seeped through her. The red splashes weren't intentional contemporary styling. They were blood. Blood so fresh it was still oozing down the walls around the tub.

And the source? The gaping throat of a blonde woman lolled over in pink bath water.

FORTY-NINE

"When do I get my damn phone call?" Skeeter pounded the bars in the holding cell. It wasn't his first time in Kearny lock-up, but it was his first time there sober. He knew they were jacking him around. He should have gotten a call hours ago.

"Keep your pants on. This is a Sunday. Things don't move fast around here," the officer on duty said, his feet resting on the desk, eyes on his phone. He laughed and flicked the screen.

"Phones work on Sundays."

"I don't know why you're in such a hurry. We've got forty-eight hours to charge you. Ain't no judge coming in to do arraignments today. Settle in, son."

Skeeter shook the bars. "I don't even know why I'm here."

"That's easy. For whatever you were arrested for."

"Well, now, it would be, if I'd been told what that was."

The officer frowned and looked up from his TikTok or cat videos or whatever he found so interesting. "Nah, man. You don't get arrested for nothing."

"You can look it up, can't you? On your computer?"

He sighed. "I guess. What's your name again?"

Skeeter spelled it for him, first and last.

The officer typed, then he started reading with his lips moving. "Huh. Well, it says you were picked up for possession of an illegal gun."

"Untrue. I have a license for concealed carry, and the gun was locked up in my glove box."

"Don't shoot the messenger, bucko. Just telling you what it said. Looks like they're executing a search warrant at your place of employment."

"At Delaney's house? What does that have to do with me?"

The officer read some more. "Suspicion of fencing stolen property."

"That's malarkey. My employer is a deputy with Kearny County."

"Yeah, I didn't figure there was more than one Delaney in these parts. But you know she was trouble when she was younger. I think everybody's been half expecting her to backslide."

"She hasn't been backsliding. There is no stolen property. No fencing. No illegal guns."

"You'll get your chance to prove all that later."

"Listen, these are serious charges. I need to call a lawyer."

A second man who'd been sleeping in the cell with Skeeter lifted his head. He groaned. "Dude, they aren't going to let you make your call. Give your pipes a rest and let me sleep."

"Did you get to make a call?"

"Yeah. But it wasn't fast."

"What are you in for?"

"Well, here's a coincidence. I'm accused of assaulting your boss."

Skeeter wheeled on him. "You attacked Delaney?"

"It was a misunderstanding."

Skeeter balled his fists.

"Listen, she seems like a nice enough lady. I didn't mean to hurt her. I've been thinking. I have something to tell her that might make things better for her. If you could get her a message."

"How can I get her a message? They won't let me make a call."

"Well, just in case you do. Could you tell her something for me, see if she wants to talk to me again?"

"What is it?"

"Tell her Rufus was working for Pete Smithers, and I was there to take pictures of his cheating wife."

"Is that going to mean anything to her?"

"Yeah. But be sure you tell her that's all I did. And I'll testify against him if they want. You got it?"

"Got it." Skeeter banged on the bars again. "Hey, did you hear that? When do I get my damn call?"

The officer fished a pair of earmuffs from a drawer. "No offense, man, but I can't stand listening to you anymore."

Skeeter pulled at his hair and slumped to the bench.

FIFTY

Delaney watched the crime scene team bag and tag evidence. The bloody knife retrieved from a pool of splatter on the bathroom floor, below Ellen's open palm. A wash rag. The leavings from sweeping up the bathroom floor. She sniffed. It smelled like lavender with a hint of smoke. Had Ellen been burning a candle? She didn't see one, though.

"She didn't seem the type to kill herself." Leo stroked his beard.

Delaney moved aside for a tech with bags in both his hands. "Right? Her star was on the rise."

"I hate that there's no note."

"No note yet. Maybe we'll find something that explains all this in her office or on her electronics."

"I'm still asking myself who would want her dead." He lowered his voice. "Besides one of us."

Delaney raised her eyebrows. "Lucky you have me as an alibi." She checked her phone.

"Anything from Zeke?"

"I'd tell you." She squinted at him, irritated. But also

worried, and not just about Zeke. "I'm concerned I haven't heard from Skeeter or the girls."

"Take a minute. Call them."

"I have. Repeatedly."

"We should wrap it up here, let the team do its work. We could drop by your house."

She shook her head. "The canceled fundraiser for Mitch at the Loafing Shed."

"Ah. You're right."

"Do you want me to take my own car?"

"Let's stay together. If you're driving, I can—"

"I know how this partnership goes. I drive and think, you collate and update."

"And research."

"Yep. As long as we can stop at the Burger Barn, I'm good."

Leo got out his phone. "I'll call our order in ahead."

Half an hour later, Delaney parked Leo's truck behind the Loafing Shed. She been able to wolf down fries on the drive, but that was it. Leo hadn't waited for her. She hoped he had permanent grease marks all over his tablet screen.

She gathered up her remaining food. "Did you come to any earth-shattering conclusions while you stuffed your face?"

Leo bagged his trash. "Just more questions. Supposing Ellen didn't kill herself—who would want her dead? And given her connections to Annabeth and Brock, could it be someone who also wanted them out of the way?"

Delaney exited the truck. "Wyoming politicians are big fish in a very small pond. Everyone is connected. It could mean nothing."

"Proximity and time frame, though. Plus, it would be ideal to wrap this up all with one murderer."

She unlocked the bar and held the door open for him. "On

what planet does ideal get served up to law enforcement? I'd like to relocate there."

He laughed.

In the office, she fished a piece of paper out of the printer tray and wrote a message in block capitals.

MITCH STONEFIELD, LET YOURSELF IN. YOU KNOW THE WAY TO THE OFFICE. MEET ME THERE.

She signed her name. "Make yourself useful while I eat." Delaney handed the note and a roll of tape to Leo.

"You don't want me to just wait outside for him?"

"Suit yourself."

"I'll do both."

Delaney attacked her burger and strawberry milkshake as soon as Leo left, with her stomach singing the *Hallelujah* chorus. Just as she was swallowing her last bite, the front door opened, then muffled male voices reached her. Two of them. And footsteps.

Suddenly, the worst kind of déjà vu gripped her.

She was a girl again. Waiting on her daddy in his office. *On the Banks of Plum Creek* was open on his desk. She'd been reading it for the umpteenth time. Daddy had gone to talk to someone out front. She heard two voices. His and another. He didn't sound happy. They came closer, close enough that she saw her dad, but in his bulky winter clothes, he was blocking the view of the other person.

Someone said, "I've told you this. It's just not happening."

But was that her dad in her memories? Because that's what she remembered him saying. It sounded like Leo though. Like it was happening now.

The other person laughed, then spoke in a whisper she could barely hear. "That's where you're wrong."

The world split in two. The real voices in the hall played on top of the remembered voices from her past. And after more than two decades of not recognizing it, she realized that she did know that other old voice. Alarm bells clamored in her head. *I recognize it, but I can't place it.* Chills rose up her arms and neck. *Can't place it... or can't face it?*

Mitch's camera-ready face appeared in the doorway, breaking her out of the weird juxtaposition of memory and the present. "It's been a minute, little sister." She hadn't remembered he'd called her that until he said it. But as Liam's childhood best friend, Mitch had always teased Delaney that she was the closest thing he had to a little sister of his own. He held out his hand. "You grew up pretty as a picture."

"Mitch." She stood and shook his hand to keep things cordial. As cordial as it could be.

He moved closer, filling up the office space. He was bigger than she remembered. "I flew up for a shindig. Now your sheriff is telling me it's canceled. Tell me he's wrong."

She kept her feet. "He's not. I never approved a political event."

His face darkened. "Would have been nice to hear about this a few hours ago. Is the bar yours now?"

"It belongs to my niece. I'm her guardian, so it's my responsibility."

"And as her guardian your objection to it is what, exactly?"

Delaney stepped closer to him and leaned her tush against the desk, arms crossed. "That we don't drive away customers by taking sides. Politics and religion. Not in the bar."

"Oh, come on now. Some of my best events are in bars and churches."

"I also don't like being strong-armed. As in, you used to submit your payola, now you don't, thus you owe it in kind."

Mitch held up his hands and took a step back, bumping into Leo. Leo didn't budge. Mitch moved to the side in the frame of the door. "I can assure you that was never my intention. This event was set up by a local county commissioner."

"Oh, I'm aware. Under your color of authority. But I don't pay to play. And there will be no events for you here. Got me?"

"Loud and clear."

"As a deputy, though, I have objections as well. Your name keeps coming up in relation to some homicide investigations."

"What?" He shot Leo a glance, but Leo's face gave nothing away.

"Annabeth Dillon. Brock Tucker. Ellen Day."

Mitch's face went slack and pale.

"What's the matter, Mitch? You look a little peaked."

"Ellen Day—she's dead?"

"We just came from her house. Found her in the bathtub with her throat slit. You hadn't heard?"

He cleared his throat. "No."

"Hmm. Well, what about Ms. Dillon and Mr. Tucker? You heard about their murders, I'd guess?"

"I, um, yes."

"Tell me about that."

"Tell you what?"

"Your connections to them."

"None, really. Annabeth hadn't announced yet, but I'd heard she was planning to run against me for the Senate seat. Brock was propping her up. Money and campaign management."

"Good thing for you they're out of your lane."

"Not good enough to kill them over. Sometimes it's better the devil you know. A new candidate will take Annabeth's place."

"Where were you last Tuesday night and Wednesday morning?"

"Seriously? You're asking for my alibi?"

She gave him a pointed look.

"I was speaking at a fundraiser in Laramie. About two hundred people can confirm it."

Not that she expected him to do his own dirty work. She remembered Rufus's claim that a tall, thin woman had gone into Annabeth's cabin. The description matched Ellen Day. And it was ever clearer that Ellen had been close to Mitch. But Mitch still had to answer the question like everyone else, if only to get him to commit to a story, and to piss him off. "And seven p.m. Saturday night?"

"Same song second verse. Fundraiser. Cody. A few less heads there, but the plates went for a higher dollar. Still well worth the trip."

"Did Ellen Day kill Annabeth Dillon or Brock Tucker?"

"Not to my knowledge."

"Did you ask her to kill them?"

"No."

"Did you ask her to have someone else kill them?"

The slightest of hesitations. *What had she not said?* "No."

"Did you ask her to do anything with regard to them?"

He sighed. "I asked her to talk to them. To find out their intentions. And to see if there was any way to get Brock to switch sides."

"And?"

"She said she tried."

"Did you get Abe Dunkirk a permit for his mining operation in exchange for him filing a lawsuit against Dillon and several nonprofits?"

He frowned. "Why would I do that?"

"Did you?"

"No."

Delaney wadded up her hamburger wrapper and pitched it in the trash by the door, right beside Mitch. He shied away. The wrapper went in. "Leo, anything else?"

Leo winked at her behind Mitch's back. "Nope."

"Mitch, anything for us?"

His glare was malevolent. "Your brother would hate what you've become."

"Thank you. I hate what he became. And while I haven't seen you in years, the two of you were friends. It gives me pause."

"We were young. Our paths went in different directions."

"Yet he still gave you sixty thousand dollars a year. Sorry you wasted your trip to Kearny."

"It wasn't a total waste."

"Why's that?"

"They say keep your friends close and enemies closer. I guess that means I'll be seeing a lot more of you, *little sister*." He nodded to Leo as he turned to go. "Sheriff."

"And we'll be watching you, Mitch. Watching you like a hawk." Delaney slurped the last of her shake. It was only then that she noticed her hands shaking and the voices from earlier were still in the background on repeat in her head.

She felt so close to identifying her father's killer. Could it be Mitch? She didn't think so, but something about hearing his voice had triggered her like nothing ever had before.

FIFTY-ONE

Delaney was so dazed after the Mitch meeting that she decided to let Leo drive.

"Should I take you to the ER?" he said.

"Very funny."

He struck the steering wheel as he turned out of the parking lot. "I forgot to tell you. When I went out front to meet Mitch, I saw Zeke's Range Rover parked out there."

Delaney closed her eyes. A memory came rushing back to her. Mary telling her she'd seen Zeke the night he'd disappeared. She opened her eyes and speed dialed Mary on speaker.

"Hey, what's up?" Mary said by way of answering.

She was too tired for the niceties and got straight to the point. "Do you remember anyone Zeke might have been talking to when he came into the Loafing Shed last night?"

"Yeah, as a matter of fact. Just one person. Then he left. He bought Ellen Day a drink."

Leo whispered, "What the hell...?"

Delaney tried to make sense of it. "Did they leave together?"

"I don't think so. Why?"

"Because Zeke is missing. And Ellen Day is dead."

Delaney was beyond exhausted by the time Leo dropped her at her car. She was zombielike when she pulled Shotgun Shelly around back of her house fifteen minutes later, her mind still unable to put the connection between Zeke and Ellen together in a way that made sense. But she couldn't wait to see her girls. Couldn't remember the last time she'd been unable to reach them all day. It gave her a burst of energy.

But then she realized what she was looking at. She mashed her brakes, throwing her body forward. Skeeter's car wasn't at the house. But there were two Kearny City Police vehicles. Her girls! Skeeter! Something had to have happened. Why else were there cops here? But why had no one called her?

She slammed the car into park and barely remembered to turn it off before jumping out and running to the house with only her phone. Despite the cold weather, only the storm door was closed at the back of her house.

She dashed inside, breathing hard. "Kat! Carrie! Where are you?"

Dudley came barreling at her. He yipped and barked and bounced.

"What's the matter, Duds?" She tried to shush him.

A Kearny city officer hurried from down the hall. Delaney had seen him before, but he was new since the death of Ted Cross in a fiery crash with Sheriff Coltrane Fentworth nine months previously. His name tag read *Andy Bean*. She'd been looking forward to meeting him. She was aunt-and-soon-to-be-mother to one of the few black kids in this part of Wyoming. It made her happy in a way she didn't know how to describe to see a black officer take a job as a Kearny cop.

"Stop, Ms. Pace," he said.

Dudley turned on the officer in a full-blown Frenchie fit. Bean backed off a step.

Anger flared. This was her house. Her family. He was giving orders to her? And dropping her title when she was in uniform? "My name is Deputy Investigator Delaney Pace. And this is my home. Where are my girls?"

"The girls weren't here when we arrived with the search warrant."

"Where. Are. My. Girls?!"

"I'll find out for you if you'll call off that dog."

"Dudley, come." She grabbed his collar then dragged him to the door where his leash was hanging. She snapped it on his collar. "I kept my end of the bargain."

"While I do that, would you like to read a copy of the warrant?"

She held out her hand reflexively, the one not holding the end of a leash. She didn't want to read a warrant. She wanted to hold Kat and Carrie in her arms and know that they were all right. "Skeeter Rawlins, too. I need to know where they are, what happened, that they're okay." Her voice cracked.

Officer Bean turned his back on her and spoke into his radio mic. Dudley growled at his back. The paper trembled in her hand, but she didn't read it.

After a few minutes of whispered conversation, Andy turned back to her. "Skeeter Rawlins is in holding. Kateena Pace and Carrie Hoff are with Child Protective Services. I am told they are fine and awaiting pick-up by foster families."

"CPS? Skeeter in holding? What the hell is going on?"

Dudley picked up on her escalating emotions and let Bean hear how he felt about it.

Bean had to raise his voice to be heard over the dog. "It's on the warrant, ma'am."

She forced herself to read the words. The officers were searching for stolen property, pursuant to a tip that she and

Skeeter were running a fencing operation out of her home. "This is total unmitigated crap." She shook the paper in her fist. "And what are city cops doing where county belongs?"

"You'll have to take that up with the chief."

Just then, two officers walked by holding boxes of electronics that she'd never seen in her life.

If Dudley had been upset before, now he was apoplectic.

"Hush, Duds. It's okay." *But it isn't.* Delaney shook the leash. "Where did that come from?"

"Your cellar."

"I don't keep anything down there but canned goods and prepper stuff leftover from my grandparents."

The officers kept walking without responding.

She ran after them with Dudley straining against the leash ahead of her. "Let me look at that. At least let me see what I'm being framed with before it's gone forever."

They glanced nervously at each other but stood still.

She frowned and mouthed the words on the packaging. "It's addressed to Ellen Day."

"Yes, ma'am. She reported the theft. She saw Rawlins take it off her porch."

Oh, my god. Ellen—who was now dead, and the last person seen with Zeke—had accused her and Skeeter of criminal activity? The same week she'd tried to push forward a recall vote on Leo? And now her kids had been taken? *What is in motion here? And why?*

She hit Leo's number on her speed dial.

FIFTY-TWO

Zeke blinked his eyes open. His skull felt like it was crushing his brain. His vision was murky and red. Where the hell was he? He pushed himself up to his knees. Something shifted under him. Rocks? And he was as cold as his basic training drill sergeant's heart. How could he be so cold and still alive? He became aware of white even though it was pitch black around him. White everywhere. Heavy white. He lifted an arm and moaned. It felt like an anvil. The white shifted and fell away, leaving his arm so dark it blended into the sky.

His murky brain struggled to feed him some information. The white stuff was thick. Dry. Heavy. Snow. He was covered in snow.

It didn't snow in southern California. He must be somewhere else. *Ya think, idiot?* But the last thing he remembered was Janeen's warm, fluffy duvet, her soft skin smelling faintly of fake tanner—God, he hated that stuff—and her screech as she said, "Oh, my god, Zeke, we're getting married in ten days!" Her words had woken him up and then some. He'd jumped in the shower, packed a bag, and driven away as she protested that there was *so much left to do* and *you're an asshole for leaving it all to me again just like always while you're off playing soldier and I'm keeping our lives going.*

Where had he gone? How long ago was that? *Maybe I'm back in theater.* There were mountains there. There was cold and snow. But he hadn't been due to go back until after the wedding. And he definitely didn't remember getting married. He glanced down at his arm. And he wasn't in military garb. No snow camo.

He shifted, trying to stand, and dizziness hit him so fast that he vomited on his legs. Or on the snow on his legs. The smell made him retch again. He scooped clean snow into his hand— he was wearing gloves, that was good—and rubbed it into his mouth. His parched lips and tongue begged for more even as his stomach heaved again. He told his stomach to shut the hell up and went with hydration. Slow and steady. Then he brushed the already-nearly-frozen vomit off his pants.

Gloves. He pulled the left one off. *No ring.* That helped narrow things down. He hadn't gotten married yet. Maybe he was on the trip he'd taken. Taken to someplace cold. He touched his head. A wool cap, sticky. Blood. While he was patting, he tried all his pockets, looking for his phone. He wasn't surprised when he didn't find it.

He stood, hands on knees as he steadied himself. Vomited again, this time not on himself. *Damn, I must have banged the crap out of my head.* It wasn't the first time. Or the tenth. Hazard of the job. He'd had a few memory losses, growing longer each time, and he couldn't let it panic him. *Trust it will come back.*

He needed to find shelter of some kind. Buy himself time to orient. He looked around. He seemed to be in some kind of ravine. Maybe a creek bed, although he wasn't wet and didn't hear any water. The chances of him hiking out here by himself in the middle of the winter were slim. The most likely scenario was that he'd been in a car wreck. He didn't see a car, but he might have been thrown clear, although he usually wore a seat belt. Maybe he'd had it off for some reason. Obviously there was no road down here. No bridge. No people, no cars, no houses. Nada.

Nothing left for him to do but climb out.

He scanned the slope in front of him. It wasn't a deep ravine. He could see the top. And it wasn't crazy steep. He took a deep breath and started up. Immediately he cursed his shoes. He had on leather ankle boots—social wear. Another clue. Definitely he hadn't been planning on being out in the elements. His feet felt like ice bricks. He'd be lucky if he didn't lose a few toes to frostbite. His legs were warming up as he climbed, though. The coat he had on had kept his core warm, with a little help from a snow blanket. The coat wasn't his. He must have borrowed it from Leo.

The name struck him out of the blue, and he smiled. At least he now knew where he'd gone. Wyoming, to visit his old buddy Leo. Patience and distraction always worked to give his brain time to get back on the track.

But what he still didn't know was how he ended up in this predicament.

He scrambled the last few feet to the top of the incline. He took a moment to look around. He was in a forest. Lots of rocks. Snow, of course. There was a break in the trees ahead of him. He tromped the ten yards to it. A flat clearing two vehicles wide stretched in both directions.

A road, of sorts. But no cars on it. Had he driven himself out here? Where from? Where was the vehicle? And was he alone? His stomach lurched again. He hoped he hadn't just left someone to die down in the ravine. *No, I didn't see anyone else. No lumps. No tracks.*

Decision time. Left or right to search for shelter and help?

An image formed in his mind. A face. Short light hair. Blue eyes. A feral expression. He remembered feeling sick. Not sick.

Drugged. And being dragged through the snow. His eyes clos-ing. The sensation of falling, then tumbling.

Shit! Someone had tried to kill him.

He shifted his eyes skyward. No moon. No stars. The sky was dark and overcast. He was going to have to choose a direc-tion and start walking with no more than a mental coin flip to guide him. If he chose wrong, he could walk to his death in this unpopulated wasteland. He'd learned enough about Wyoming to realize it had a lot of ways to kill you.

But he wouldn't let it come to that. He was fit and highly skilled in survival tactics. Daylight would arrive in a few hours. He'd orient himself then. In the meantime, he had a 50/50 chance of choosing the right direction, and walking would keep him warm. It would keep him alive.

As long as he didn't run into the person who wanted him dead.

FIFTY-THREE

Leo closed the door behind the last of the officers to leave Delaney's house. She paced the living room and kitchen in frantic figure eights, occasionally sipping at the hot tea that was sloshing over the sides of her cup. He'd spent the last hour on the phone trying to sort things—which included a screaming match with the police chief for cutting Leo out of what should have been a county operation based on the location of Delaney's home. Mara Yellowtail was a recent hire. There was a battle brewing between them for another day. Ellen Day had given him a parting gift before her death—an allegation that he couldn't be impartial since she'd gone public asking for him to face a recall vote. It was a stark reminder that once the wheels of bureaucracy were in motion, it was almost impossible to bring them to a halt.

He hadn't been able to do much about Skeeter who was stuck in jail and would be until the next day other than arrange for an attorney to be there first thing in the morning for him. He'd done better by Dudley. Mary had picked him up fifteen minutes before for a sleepover. She and her toddler son Juan Julio were big fans of the little bulldog.

At least he'd learned that Kat and Carrie were safe, albeit unreachable, spending the night with foster families. A hearing about their placement was scheduled for later in the week. Delaney had nearly had an aneurysm about that. She was going to have to fight the stolen property battle in the legal system during normal working hours, before she could even attempt to get her girls back.

He glanced at his phone. Ten p.m. Monday morning seemed like an eternity away. While he was looking at it, it rang. It was Clara's number. He answered. "You're still working?"

Clara said. "I'm making up my dental surgery time, remember? I have something for you."

He put the phone on speaker. "What is it?"

"That abandoned vehicle up at Paintbrush Lodge? It's registered in Teton County to Pete Smithers. Isn't our victim from there?"

Leo looked at Delaney to see her reaction, but she wasn't paying attention. What the hell did this mean? *Rufus Payne.* Maybe the man who'd worked for Annabeth's husband hadn't been hitchhiking like he'd said. His ties to Pete and Annabeth just grew stronger, as did Pete's possible connection to his wife's murder. "Do we have fingerprints?"

"No. I can pass the request to Sugar, though."

"Please do. And thanks. Now go home, Clara."

"Good night, Sheriff." She ended the call.

"I just don't get it." Delaney's voice was an angry hiss, which was calmer than earlier, when she'd been shouting. Screaming. Crying. "How could this happen?"

Leo decided to update her about the vehicle in a minute. She had every reason to be focusing her thoughts and emotions on her own situation. "What did you do to piss off Ellen Day so much?"

"She was after you, too, so I suspect we brought this on together with our investigation into that zoning variance. But, dammit, she's not even alive to put a stop to this insanity. Or to ask what the hell happened to Zeke. And I've been so caught up in the cases today that I didn't notice I had a new message on voice mail. Clara put a kid through. Turns out Kat asked him to call and tell me she and Carrie were headed to CPS and Skeeter to jail. Hours ago." She slammed her teacup down. "So much planning and coordination went into this. Who planted those boxes in my cellar? How? When?"

"When was the last time you were down there?"

"A week ago. Maybe two."

"Let's check your cameras."

"Unless it was in the last twenty-four hours, there won't be anything on them."

"You don't pay for the cloud storage? After everything that's happened out here?"

She held up a hand. "Save the ass chewing for another time, please."

Simultaneous text notifications sounded. Their hands reached for their phones.

Leo read the message. It gave an address for a property southwest of town, in the foothills.

Explosion and fire called in by onsite facility manager. Injuries reported. Fire, EMT, law enforcement response needed ASAP. Fire, coordinate with Trish Flint of the National Forest Service in Sheridan.

Delaney was grabbing her purse and coat. "Shit. I know that area. It's pristine national forest all along the western edge of the private property out there. Lots of feed for a fire."

"Are you sure you're up for this?"

"There's nothing for me to do here tonight but rage and mope."

He would have felt exactly the same in her shoes. They raced to his truck together.

The fire site was only ten miles from the Pace homestead. Delaney and Leo were the first responders to arrive on the scene, although firefighters were converging quickly from multiple locations. A wall of flame was moving from a complex of blazing buildings up toward the mountain and the national forest. It sounded like an angry beast, and even from a distance the smell of smoke and burning wood, metal, and fuel was strong.

"My god. It's an inferno." Leo looked out the windshield with his lower jaw gaping.

"It's moving away from us." Delaney parked the truck fifty yards away from the complex. "But I don't trust it." She licked a finger and held it in the air. "No wind. But that can change in an instant."

Leo shielded his eyes. Even from this distance, the heat was incredible. And terrifying. "We should wait for the firefighters. We don't want to create more work for them by putting ourselves in a situation that requires more rescue."

Delaney ignored him and started toward the complex.

"Really?" Leo muttered.

She turned. "Someone called in this fire *with injuries*. I promise, I don't want us to do anything stupid. But they may not have much time."

Leo flashed back to Coltrane Fentworth engulfed in flames after a fiery crash. Neither Delaney nor Leo were trained or dressed for fire work. That hadn't stopped her then. He wouldn't be able to trust her now. He ran after her.

She talked as she sped up. "I've seen an aerial of this place before."

"Of course, you have."

"But a lot of it looks new to me. Industrial."

A man emerged from between burning buildings, waving his arms. "This way."

Leo ran harder and was still barely able to keep up with Delaney. His lungs were burning now, from heat not exertion. His face felt like he'd spent too long on the water with no sunscreen. They reached the man.

Leo took his elbow. "Are you hurt?"

"Not me. The two assholes who lit us up. I should have just let them burn. Come on." He whirled and limped toward the fire.

"Shit." Leo stumbled and Delaney grabbed his arm. They caught up with the site manager quickly. "This was an intentional fire?" Leo shouted.

"Hell, yes. Goddamn environmental terrorists."

"Whose place is this?"

"Abe Dunkirk. I'm the site manager. Robby Platte."

"Oh, no. We talked to him earlier. Is this about the mining?"

"It's gotta be." Robby gestured at the burning structures as he trotted forward. "They set explosives around the new equipment. But they overdid it, as you can see. We're going to be lucky if they don't burn down the entire Bighorn National Forest. Anyway, the woman was screaming when I found them, so I dragged them clear. She seems to have a broken leg. The man is unconscious, but he's breathing. Here they are."

Smoke swirled around a prone man and a woman sitting up and holding her leg. She was rocking and weeping. Her sooty face didn't hide the fact that she was beautiful.

Leo knelt beside her.

Delaney remained standing, staring at the man on the ground. "He's the owner of that ranch in Kaycee. The one where Brock did a dive off the crumbling cliff. What's his name?"

"Are you okay, ma'am?" Leo said to the woman. "An ambulance is on its way."

Delaney poked Leo's shoulder. "His name was Corey something-or-other."

The woman shot Delaney a glare. "Corey Castle."

"Yeah. And he warned us about this, Leo. You asked if he had anything big in store for us and he said, 'Nothing unnecessary.'"

Leo shook his head. "I thought he was joking."

"Damn," Robbie muttered. "Corey Castle. I thought he looked familiar. A celebrity blew up our mining operation. That's just great. It's going to be all over the news."

"My fucking leg is broken, and my boyfriend is unconscious. Maybe in a coma. You're all focusing on the wrong issues," the woman said.

Delaney cocked her head. "I know your voice."

Corey's eyes popped open. "I can hear you. It's a miracle."

The women said, "You should know it. We talked on the phone this morning." She turned her attention to Corey. "It's going to be okay, baby."

Leo was confused. "What's going on?"

Delaney put her hands on her hips. "Leo, it doesn't seem like anyone is about to die around here, so let me introduce you to the woman you're about to arrest. Meet Shaina Pham, the owner of the Mountain High Cabins and former conspirator with Annabeth Dillon."

She tossed a long black ponytail over her shoulder. "Former is right. Bitch isn't around to stop us now. We can do whatever—"

Corey reached out and gripped her leg. The broken one.

She screamed. "What did you do that for?"

"Shaina, love. I think now is a good time to exercise our right to be silent."

Leo got to his feet. "Corey Castle and Shaina Pham, you're

under arrest for arson and felony property destruction. And I can assure you we'll be talking very seriously about the death of Annabeth Dillon as well."

Delaney smiled at them. "And when Trish Flint with the National Forest Service gets here, I think we'll be adding a few more felonies. She takes burning down her forest very seriously."

FIFTY-FOUR

Zeke's crappy boots reached pavement about the time the sun cast a brilliant orange and pink glow over the horizon to the east. It didn't matter which way he turned now. From his drive to Kearny, he remembered that towns in Wyoming averaged about sixty miles apart. He might not hit true civilization for quite some time, but he was bound to reach a house or pass a car before too long in either direction.

He turned west. Easier on the eyes without sunglasses. His biggest worry, besides how badly his head hurt, was encountering the wrong people. More of his memories had returned as he had trudged through the snow, alone with his thoughts in the dark. Not completely alone. There was the red fox that had crossed the road in front of him, the skunk that thought about spraying him, and the giant moose that had lumbered out of the forest and looked more surprised than him. But alone enough to appreciate the immensity of the landscape he'd been dropped into. He'd felt this way before, outside the wire in Afghanistan. It was no less dangerous here. People had been trying to kill him every time he left the forward operating base. He didn't know which ones and had to assume it could be anyone he met. It was no different here. And in both places, it was highly frowned on to shoot civilians first and ask questions later. When he had a gun, that is, which in Wyoming at this moment he did not. He'd picked up a good-sized rock and pocketed it after the moose. That would have to do.

He walked briskly. Nothing to do but think, so he let his mind continue freewheeling. His gun—if it hadn't been stolen—was in the glove compartment of his Range Rover, locked in a mobile gun safe. His Range Rover was God knew where, as he'd been driving it at the time he'd been dumped off a cliff by a blonde Amazon woman who'd befriended him by claiming a connection with Delaney and her brother. He wasn't even sure that connection was real. He could only guess she'd done it because of his conversation about Delaney with the bar manager.

Delaney. Another thing he'd remembered. The gorgeous, magnetic woman who had been starring in his dreams for a decade. His amazement at seeing her here, with Leo. *Leo is in love with her.* Did it matter? Zeke had known her first. He wanted her. Had been wooing her hard. He frowned and actually stopped walking for a few seconds. He hadn't told her about Janeen or the wedding. Was what was happening to him some kind of karmic punishment? Delaney was a free spirit, like him. But maybe he should have been more open. She'd given him the chance to tell her, and he had consciously decided not to. Almost dying had given him perspective. If he got the chance again, he'd make better on that.

He resumed his march away from the sunrise. Was the murderous Amazon a random psychopath or did she have something against him in particular? Their meeting couldn't have been anything but pure chance. That lent credence to the random psycho theory. Or to her particular interest in him being because he mentioned Delaney. He nodded. That felt more likely. Either in objection to him being with Delaney or... what? He tried to think of a different motive. To punish Delaney? Someone Delaney had harmed or who hated her?

Every conclusion spawned more questions. He stopped for a few handfuls of clean snow. It didn't melt down to much water in his stomach, but he'd been doing it regularly and it was keeping dehydration at bay. He restarted his march. If Janeen had known what he was up to with Delaney—or trying to be up to anyway as he hadn't charmed Delaney's pants off yet—she would have come at him head-on, guns blazing. She wouldn't have had someone else do her dirty work. Definitely, the attack had not been about him and Janeen. A sick feeling roiled through his empty stomach. *How long was I unconscious?* If he'd been missing more than a few hours, Leo might have called Janeen. If this was about Delaney, would it all get back to his fiancée? Was she possibly waiting for him back in Kearny, one part worried and one part ready to eviscerate him?

Things could get really ugly.

But he couldn't worry about Janeen yet. Right now, his focus and energy needed to be on a safe return. If the attempt on his life wasn't random, there could be more than one person involved. The tall blonde might show up out here to make sure he was dead. She might bring reinforcements. Or send someone he wouldn't recognize. Maybe it would be safest to avoid vehicles altogether, then?

The road turned north. Exhaustion crept over him. He moved like a sleepwalker, barely noticing where he put his feet. He became aware that the snow had been plowed. The going became easier. His stomach started growling and wouldn't stop. He scooped more snow, but leaning over made him dizzy. His head injury needed medical attention. He thought about sitting down for a rest but was afraid he wouldn't get back up again.

Time and many more steps went by. The sun was halfway over the horizon. He stumbled and realized he had nearly fallen asleep.

A vehicle pulled up behind him and beeped its horn. He hadn't even heard it. The wind. The sound had been muffled by the wind. He put his hand in his pocket, felt for his rock. Hoped for the best and turned to face the car.

It was a Kearny County Sheriff's Department truck. With the sun in his eyes, he couldn't see who was behind the wheel.

FIFTY-FIVE

Delaney stalked into the CPS office at the stroke of eight a.m. Monday morning after waiting on the sidewalk outside for fifteen minutes. She'd just finished listening for the hundredth time to a voice mail from Kat. She'd called while Delaney was out of cell range at the Dunkirk property.

"Aunt Delaney, they took my phone. They wouldn't let me call you. I'm sneaking on the phone at the house where they're making me stay. I don't understand why they took Skeeter. And why I can't come home?"

In the background, Delaney heard a sharp female voice. "Get off that phone. I did not give you permission to use it."

"I have to go. Bye." The message ended with a click.

There'd been no number on her caller ID. It made Delaney ill that she'd missed her and couldn't call her back.

But she was going to find out where she and Carrie were now.

A man at the front desk glanced up as Delaney entered the office. "May I help you?" His expression was wary. Delaney guessed it was about fifty-fifty for people coming into CPS happy versus unhappy. Often extremely unhappy—like her.

Delaney pointed at her badge. "I'm Deputy Investigator Delaney Pace. I have applications pending to adopt Kateena Pace and Carrie Hoff, both of whom reside with me. Yesterday while I was at work, they were taken from my babysitter and placed with foster families. Since it was a Sunday night, I was unable to get any information."

"Who did you say you were?"

Delaney glared at him. "Someone who needs to talk to whoever is in charge, right now."

He continued to stare at her without moving.

She took a card from her wallet and slapped it down in front of him.

He picked it up with two fingers. "Wait here." He walked away with the speed of a three-toed sloth.

Delaney ground her teeth. She waited with arms crossed by the glass doors until her phone rang. She didn't recognize the number, but she picked up, just in case it was news about Zeke or Skeeter, or a call from one of the girls. "Deputy Investigator Delaney Pace."

"Hello, Deputy. This is Attorney Wesley James from Sheridan. I got a call from Sheriff Leo Palmer last night, and, as a result, I now represent your employee Skeeter Rawlins."

Delaney broke in when he took a breath. "Is Skeeter all right?"

"We'll get this straightened out. He requested that I assure you he's fine."

"It's my fault. I made the wrong person angry. We were framed."

"That's what the sheriff said and what I explained to Mr. Rawlins, who was immensely relieved. But there was another thing. He asked me to tell you, and I quote, 'Rufus was working for Pete Smithers taking pictures of his cheating wife.'"

Delaney had expected Skeeter to comment on his arrest. Ask about the girls. Maybe even demand to be released from his nanny duties, since it was Delaney who'd brought trouble on him. She had *not* expected to hear the name Rufus from him and his attorney. Rufus, as in the man who'd assaulted her at Mountain High Cabins? The one who claimed to have seen a tall, blonde woman enter Annabeth's cabin late that night. The one who Pete Smithers said used to work for him in Seattle. But instead of "used to" apparently it was "still does."

She said, "Rufus Payne?"

"Yes. Mr. Rawlins and Rufus were in holding together. Rufus found out Mr. Rawlins worked for you and asked that he share that message. Rufus also said that taking pictures was the only thing he was guilty of and that he had nothing to do with murder."

Delaney's heart rate accelerated. Did that mean Rufus had pictures of the woman he'd seen? Or of the killer?

"Miss Pace?" The man from the front desk was back.

She held up one finger. Into the phone, she said, "Thank you, Mr. James. For this information and for helping Skeeter."

"It's no problem at all. While we often find ourselves on the opposite side of issues as defense attorneys and law enforcement, I hope you'll remember that I am at your service should you ever need me."

"Thank you." She ended the call and faced the CPS employee. "Yes?"

"You'll be receiving a call about your hearing, which will be scheduled later this week. You'll be able to see Kateena and Carrie at that time, and you'll be allowed to plead your case for them to be returned to you then as well."

"I need to speak to someone about straightening this out *today.*"

"I'm sorry, but that won't be happening. I can assure you the girls are safe and well taken care of."

"That is not the point. They should be home. I've done nothing wrong. They certainly haven't."

"I'll let you see yourself out. And, in the meantime, we at CPS wish you the best of luck clearing up the charges against you."

"Charges? I haven't been charged with *anything*."

He returned to his desk and began typing, eyes glued to his computer screen.

FIFTY-SIX

Adriana opened the door to Paul's truck for Freddy, who climbed into the back seat of the crew cab. She nudged him to remind him of his manners.

"Hey, Mr. Lester." Freddy's voice was a mumble.

"Hi, Freddy. Ready to have some fun today?" Paul said.

Adriana arranged herself uncomfortably in the front seat. Long johns under her loose jeans. A puffy jacket over a thick sweater and shirt. At Leo's recommendation, she'd bought and emptied a spray can of Scotchgard to waterproof hers and Freddy's clothes. The intense chemical smell of the spray filled the cab. It was embarrassing, but there was nothing she could do about it.

"Wow," Paul said. "You are beautiful."

She didn't feel beautiful. She felt like a tree trunk. But she wasn't putting that thought in his head. "Thanks. You look pretty great yourself." And he did. But he didn't look dressed to ski. More like to grab another cup of coffee. "Where are your ski clothes?"

"In my bag." He jogged his head at the back seat. "I'll put all that on when we get there. Maybe I should turn on the air conditioner for you two, huh?"

"Oh, no, we can shed a layer." Adriana struggled out of her jacket then handed it to Freddy. "Take your coat off, too, hon. We have a long drive."

"An hour," Paul said. "Make yourself comfortable."

Freddy stuffed the coat in the floorboard. "Mom, can I call Kat? She's not answering my texts."

Paul pulled onto the interstate heading north. "Kat? Who's Kat?"

"My best friend."

"Oh, yeah. You mentioned her before."

Adriana bit her lip. Leo had told her that CPS took Kat and Carrie from Delaney and hadn't let the girls keep their phones. Something about it being too disruptive if they were just texting and calling Delaney the whole time. She hadn't told Freddy yet. She hadn't wanted to upset him before their getaway. But if he was going to be worrying about why Kat wasn't answering him the whole time, it would have the same impact.

She turned to Freddy with a bright smile. "Oh, gee, hon. I don't think she has her phone."

"Why?"

"She's staying with an, um, family, and she had to put it away. Just temporarily."

"What family? Delaney is her only family."

"Um, friends of the family."

"I don't understand. Where's Delaney?"

"Delaney is working really hard. You know. Some people have done some really bad things."

"So? Kat has Carrie and Skeeter. And us. She should have come with us."

"That wouldn't have solved the problem. We can talk about this later. Just for now know that she is perfectly all right."

"Doesn't sound all right to me." Freddy put his earbuds in.

Good. His music will distract him. And I can talk to Paul in private.

Paul glanced at Freddy, then said to Adriana, "What's the story? CPS took her away from her own mother?"

"Delaney is her aunt, although she's trying to adopt Kat." She lowered her voice. "My brother said someone framed Delaney and their nanny for fencing stolen merchandise. Leo thinks he knows who it was. There's a hearing at the end of the week. Kat and Carrie should be able to come home then."

"That's bullshit!" Freddy yelled.

Adriana winced. *And the mother of the year award goes to... me. Not.* Apparently his music hadn't been turned on. "Everything will be okay, Freddy. You'll see."

"Yeah, right."

Paul shook his head. "Wow. That's quite a scandal for this little town."

"I know, right? Big city worthy." Adriana smiled at him. "I feel terrible for the girls. But especially for Delaney. She's having a tough time all around. She'd hooked up with this friend of Leo's who's visiting us, and he disappeared Saturday night. Just vanished. Leo is pretty worried about him."

"Wait—I thought Delaney and Leo were a thing?"

"No, even though they should be."

Paul winked at her. "Okay, just between us, who did it?"

"Who did what?"

"Who framed Delaney and the babysitter? You left out the best part of the story."

Adriana didn't need to get on Leo's bad side. She was living rent free, and he was standing in as Freddy's father figure. He was a great brother. She loved him. But Paul was right. The frame-up was the best part of the story. "You can't tell anyone. You either, Freddy."

"Of course not," Paul said.

When Freddy didn't answer, she said, "Freddy, I know you

can hear me. I'm serious. This could cause problems for Delaney with Kat and Carrie."

Her son's voice was just a hair shy of snotty. "I wo-on't."

Adriana took a deep breath. "Leo said there's a county commissioner who has it in for him and Delaney. Like she's the one who started some BS trying to get Leo recalled."

"She's behind the frame-up?"

"Leo thinks so. The way he figures it, she ordered a bunch of electronics, stashed them in Delaney's basement, then called in a tip about Delaney storing property that Skeeter—he's their nanny—stole and was fencing."

"That's terrible." He frowned, exited the interstate, then turned toward the silhouette of the mountains and the town of Ranchester. "Wait. Who is this and why does he think she would do something like this?"

"Ellen something. Leo said she was in cahoots on a sketchy land deal, and he and Delaney got her investigated for it. Ever since them, she's been on their asses." Paul was nodding, his mouth open. The rest of the story came tumbling out before she could think better of it. "Get this. Yesterday, they went to interview this Ellen about all the recent murders. You know—that woman from Jackson and the rich guy she was having an affair with?"

"Yeah. What does a county commissioner have to do with any of that?"

They were already through the little town. Adriana would have liked to stop for coffee, but she hadn't asked. "I don't know. But when they got to her house, she was dead."

Freddy was now leaning over the console in between them. Adriana hoped he wouldn't have nightmares about all this. But it wasn't anything the kids at school couldn't read about on social media. They'd all be talking about it.

"What? That's crazy. Murdered, too?"

"No. They think maybe suicide."

Paul whistled. "This town. I think things were calmer in Denver."

They drove in silence past snow-covered fields. Cattle clustered around bales of hay. Tall cottonwoods marked the twists and turns of a river. Bald eagles perched on alternating limbs of a tree by the road.

Then she felt a warm presence between her head and the door.

Freddy whispered in her ear. "Uncle Leo doesn't like us to talk about his work."

Anger and shame rushed through her in a silent skirmish. She faced the window. "Shh."

The truck bumped over a bridge and entered a picturesque little town with mountains looming over it.

"Where are we?" she said.

"Dayton." Paul's voice was strangely atonal.

"Can we stop at a bathroom?"

His lips were moving, but she couldn't hear any words. He passed up a gas station, the kind with the green dinosaur logo. She waited, thinking he would respond or pull over at the next one. Only, after a few more curves, there hadn't been a next one. The truck whizzed past a high school then started climbing.

"Paul?" she said.

"Yeah?"

"Bathroom?"

He shook his head. "We're meeting a friend of mine, and we're running late." Cold. No apology. No smile. The change in his demeanor made no sense. Nothing had happened. Had it?

She really needed a bathroom. "Well, if we make up any time and pass a place..."

He drummed his thumbs on the steering wheel.

"I can't get any cell service, Mom," Freddy said.

"Try turning airplane mode on and off."

"I already did."

"Turn your phone off and on."

"Mo-om, I already tried that, too. There are no bars."

Paul's voice cracked like a whip. "We're in the mountains. What do you expect?"

The silence from the back seat hurt Adriana's heart. Freddy didn't deserve that. "Paul—"

"I need silence."

"What?"

"I. Need. You. And. Your. Spoiled. Son. To. Shut. Up. Do you think you can do that?"

"What did we—I don't understand." She turned and saw Freddy's frightened, pale face. She didn't know what had gotten into Paul, but no matter how much she liked him, Freddy came first. Calm and quiet, she said, "Paul, take us home, please."

He ignored her.

She put starch in her voice. "Turn this truck around and take us home, right now."

Paul took several long, slow breaths. His face relaxed. "I'm sorry. I don't know what came over me there for a second." He shook his head. "That's not true. I think it's your relationship with your brother and his with Freddy. I lost some family members recently. I miss them. And it just triggered me. I've been looking forward to this. No more talk about murders and kids taken from their families and bad stuff."

Adriana almost reminded him he was the one who had pushed her for the details about all the "bad stuff," but he looked sincere and very repentant. She glanced at her son. He shrugged. If Paul lost it again, she would give him no more chances. Today or ever. "Okay. Let's go have an adventure."

FIFTY-SEVEN

Leo's stomach roiled with coffee and stress. Zeke. Delaney and her girls. The possibility that either Tommy or Joe was dirty. The burning national forest in his county and the arsonists connected to the murders who had started it. And, of course, the homicides. Working these murders was bad enough. Being the guy in charge as they happened one after another? Down by two in his core headcount. Three, actually, with Delaney out this morning.

He pushed back from his desk and whirled to face the magnificent view out his window. With all the snowfall, it looked picture perfect. Pristine. Talk about a delusion. He turned back and leaned over his blotter on his fingertips. If he had it to do over again, would he turn down the interim sheriff position? Did he want to stay in Kearny or leave? Would the DEA even let him leave?

He didn't have any answers for himself. He wanted his life in order. To introduce a healthy dose of Boolean logic to the messed-up situation like the ones and zeroes in well-written code. All he could do was impose it on the cases he was handling. And that meant update his investigation plans.

Update Annabeth and Brock. Line out new ones for Zeke's disappearance and Ellen's death. The frame-up of Delaney and Skeeter. He shook his head. With what extra time?

New plans first, prioritizing by severity of crime. He opened a fresh template on his tablet and filled it in. As was the norm, seeing evidence—or lack thereof—collated into his normal format stopped the misfiring neurons in Leo's brain. They'd already searched Ellen's home and should have results from Sugar's team soon. The next most likely place to find appointments, notes, mail, or electronic files was the county building. He sent an email to the judge asking for a warrant for her office.

Nothing to do but keep moving forward until he heard from the judge. That led to Zeke and preparing an investigation plan for Zeke's case. Could this have something to do with his job in the Marines? It was hard to believe with Zeke working in Afghanistan that military enemies would have found their way to Kearny, Wyoming, but it wasn't impossible. He'd have to contact his unit.

He decided to save Annabeth for last—so much had happened that day that the thought of updating it overwhelmed him—and read through Brock's plan. After he was done, his lips were pursed. The big issue was the two deputies. But he also needed to perform an alibi check on Riley Tucker.

Too much to do, too little help, too little time. But he had the present. He looked up the names and numbers for the other women on Riley's girls' trip. Dialed the first one.

It rang, and a woman answered in a booming voice. "Liza Wells. Who am I speaking to?"

Leo introduced himself. "Riley Tucker said you just had a girls' trip last week. I'm just following up to verify her whereabouts. You were with her the whole time?" Her reply was garbled. "I'm sorry, our reception was bad for a moment. I've put you on speaker. Do you mind repeating your answer?"

"Hello. Well, I was saying that Riley was with us the whole

294 PAMELA FAGAN HUTCHINS

time, but I didn't share a room with her. She called off sick two of the days. We felt terrible for her. Food poisoning. She was weak as a kitten the rest of the trip."

"Do you remember what days those were?"

"Well, it wasn't the first day or the last day. Actually, it had to have been the second and third days, since we had tickets to see *Hamilton* on the fourth night, and we got our hair and nails done before the show. She was with us then."

"She flew home on Saturday."

"Yes. We flew to the city on Monday and home on Saturday."

"So, her sick days would have been Tuesday and Wednesday?"

"Yes. That's right."

"And you didn't see her at all those days."

"No. But I talked to her. What a crappy way to spend her precious days away."

"Did anyone in your group see her?"

"Well, one of the gals took her some chicken soup and crackers, but Riley wouldn't open the door."

"Who was that?"

"Kate Benson. She left soup by the door for her. Riley was so embarrassed."

Leo had Kate's number, from Riley. "Thanks. What else can you tell me?"

"I feel so bad for Riley. Losing Brock. Anything I can do to help."

"You two were friends?"

"Yes. Good friends."

"How was her relationship with Brock?"

"She loved that man to pieces. They were a real partnership. She never said a bad word about him."

"So, she was faithful?"

"Oh, my goodness, yes. She came from nothing, you know.

Dirt poor. Big family. Parents died young. That was a scandal. I didn't know her before her marriage to Brock, but even I'd heard about it. The Wyoming version of Ruby Ridge, you know."

"I'm, uh, not from here. Tell me about it."

"Her parents had all those kids living rough in the foothills. They had some kind of quasi-military compound, and the ATF raided them. Suspicions of anti-government activity. Illegal weapons. That kind of thing. Turned out that it was partly true, but not on as big a scale as the feds suspected. When they raided, it was just Riley's parents and her brothers and sisters. She was the oldest, and they sent her down into the cellar with the kids and had a shootout with the cops. Both of her parents died. She was old enough to live on her own, but the others ended up split around between foster families. It was quite a mess, I tell you. I know they were a bit odd, but around here, people believe in live and let live, and, well, if the feds had left well enough alone, those kids would have been better off."

"Wow. That's quite a story."

"You can imagine how Riley looked up to Brock and appreciated the life he gave her."

"I can't."

"She didn't deserve more tragedy. And I sure as hell hope you catch whoever did this to Brock."

Leo ended the call and dialed Kate Benson. He left a message for her to call him back.

Then he tapped his stylus on the blotter. Decided to stick with Riley and her background. He ran a Google search. Browsed the results.

"Riley Miller marries multi-millionaire Brock Tucker." He read fast. It was a society piece, mostly fluff, but referenced her humble beginnings and rumors of her past involvement with militant anti-fascist groups. His lips twitched. Interesting—not something he would have pegged her for.

Leo ran a search on her maiden name. Most of the results still pulled up Riley Miller Tucker charity work. He kept scrolling. Gave up and added militia to the search. And then his jaw dropped.

Western Pride Founder Andrew Miller Sentenced to Five Years in Montana

Had Riley been married before? He pulled up the article. Scrolled, scanning, until he found mention of her in the second paragraph.

> *Andrew's siblings, Riley Miller, Tanya Sones, Brandon Miller, and Randy Miller, were not charged, although all have been tied to the anti-fascist militant Western Pride group in the past. The Miller siblings lost their parents in a shootout with the ATF and were split up and raised separately in foster families. Andrew has refused to answer questions about his siblings' involvement or his unconventional childhood in an off-the-grid mountain compound.*

"Son of a bitch," he said. Parents then brother. Riley's past was ultra-conservative even by Wyoming standards.

His phone rang. Delaney. He answered it before the second ring. "I've been wondering how it's going for you with the girls. Any progress?"

Her voice sounded too flat. "Zero. They wouldn't let me talk to anyone. Just told me to prepare to present my case at the hearing."

"I can't believe this is happening."

"I can't believe Ellen Day pulled it off right under our noses."

"We'll get it straightened out. But I'm sorry."

"Me, too."

"Have you heard from Zeke?"

"No. Nothing."

"Me neither."

"But I did talk to Skeeter's attorney. And he had something for us. Something Skeeter passed on from Rufus."

"Rufus *Payne*?"

"Yes. He and Skeeter are locked up together. He said to tell us that he was working for Pete Smithers taking pictures of his cheating wife but that was all he was guilty of."

"What?!"

"Maybe he has pictures that could help us."

"Or maybe he killed Annabeth for Pete. Shoot. I forgot to tell you. A car registered to Pete Smithers was found abandoned in the Paintbrush Lodge parking lot."

She whistled between her teeth. "Sounds like Rufus had wheels. And that Pete might have been preparing for life without his wife's money."

"I have news, too." Leo filled her in on what he'd learned about Riley.

She appeared in the doorway. They hung up their phones at the same time. "Militia green. There's a stylish look for a charity maven."

"I thought it was interesting."

His phone rang. "It's Sugar."

"Put it on speaker."

He snatched it up and hit speaker. "Tell Delaney and me you've got something good."

"I've got something weird," she said.

"I don't like weird."

"Delaney won't either. I found her brother's fingerprints at Ellen's house."

298 PAMELA FAGAN HUTCHINS

After the phone call with Sugar, Delaney sank into the chair in front of Leo's desk. She hung her head in her hands with her elbows on her knees. "Liam. Liam's back."

"We don't know that. They could be old prints," Leo said.

"Then Ellen or her housekeeper do a shitty job at keeping her place clean."

"They finished their search there. There was nothing else connecting her to him. But I've asked for a warrant for her office. I should hear back from the judge soon."

"Shit, Leo."

"I know. I'm sorry."

"We can't just sit here."

"I updated our plans. Put together new ones for Ellen and Zeke."

"Is that supposed to make me feel better?"

"No. It's supposed to give you something to do."

She nodded. "I need something to do. Send me on an errand. Let me go arrest someone."

"I don't have those kinds of things for you yet, but we have a few to-dos on our list that are big."

"Drag Corey and Shaina out of their cells for questioning about Annabeth."

"That, for sure. But I want to keep us free to go search Ellen's office. Honestly, given her connection to your brother and all the ways her name has come up, it's my first priority."

Delaney sighed. "Agreed."

"I have more about Riley," he said to Delaney. He told her about his alibi checking, the missing days, and her friend's story about Riley's family."

"I remember that shootout. Happened when I was a teenager."

"You know, if no one saw Riley for two days, she could have left the hotel."

"Have you ever tried to fly from New York to Sheridan? It

takes a full day. And then to track down Annabeth in the mountains and do the return trip? It would be nearly impossible. Especially with the time change."

"Nearly but not completely?"

"We'd have to look into it further."

"In the meantime, we can see what the other friend, a Ms. Benson, has to say. The whole thing could be a dead end." Leo's phone rang. He frowned. "It's the hospital."

"Is Corey Castle still there?"

"Actually, I think so. I'd better take it." He hit ACCEPT. "Sheriff Palmer."

"Leo, it's Zeke."

Leo hit speaker. "Zeke. Where are you? Are you okay?" He put a finger over his lips and held eye contact with Delaney until she nodded.

Delaney stood, fist over her mouth and eyes wide.

"Thanks to your deputy, I am. He gave me a ride to the hospital."

"Did you have a wreck?" But they'd found his car at the Loafing Shed.

"No. Someone tried to kill me."

Leo reclaimed Delaney's gaze. She looked as shocked as he felt. "How?"

"Tricked me into giving her a ride home from the bar, claiming she was drunk. Only it was the other way around. She'd roofied me. Then she dragged me out of my car and threw me off a cliff. I woke up last night and walked out."

"Do you know who she was?"

"Some Amazon blonde woman who claimed to be a friend of Delaney's brother."

Delaney said, "Sounds like that warrant for Ellen's office just became a little more pressing."

"Is that Delaney? Delaney, I'm sorry. I—"

She reached over Leo's desk and took his phone. Leo watched her press END CALL.

"He's a crime victim. We have to get his statement." Although Leo could send someone else. And would. He and Delaney had enough on their plate already. Plus, he was afraid the meeting wouldn't go well.

She nodded. "It won't kill him to wait. And it will give me immense satisfaction."

FIFTY-EIGHT

The warrant for Ellen's office came in before Delaney had parked Shelly outside the county offices. She'd insisted on bringing her muscle car. Sometimes it was the only thing that made her feel better, and Leo had learned to roll with it. She suspected he secretly enjoyed it.

Leo read the email from the judge, then said, "It comes with a stern admonition. He doesn't like searches of government property. However, he likes the rash of murders in the county even less, and he's giving us some latitude. Or rope to hang ourselves with if we screw it up."

"And that's before the information from Zeke came in, even. I'm just glad he said yes. I'm not sure we could have sweet-talked our way in there."

They walked in together, served the warrant on the unhappy Administrative Assistant to the Commissioners, and headed for Ellen's office under watchful, mournful gazes. The AA unlocked the door and let them in.

"Do you want someone in here while we conduct the search?" Delaney asked. "I'll need in her computer."

"I'll send the county attorney and our IT manager right up."

"Thanks," Leo said.

As soon as the AA left, Delaney and Leo donned gloves and got to work. Leo started on the perimeter credenza and bookshelves. Delaney headed for the desk.

"Our presence probably feels intrusive. She just died yesterday," Delaney whispered. "Most people here probably only found out about it after they got to work."

"It's sobering. But she can't have been popular," Leo said, keeping his voice low, too.

Delaney lifted the blotter on the desk. Nothing. She rifled through the pages of a day timer. Blank and unused. Ellen appeared to like her desk surface tidy. There was nothing on it except a monitor, keyboard, and mouse on a pad. She wiggled the mouse, and the screen came to life. She struck a key. A username and password prompt appeared. That would be a job for IT.

The desk had five drawers. Two on each side and one in the center. She started with the center drawer. The one most people used for odds and ends. She pawed the contents. Chapstick, lipstick, breath mints, gum. Pens, pencils, sticky pads, paperclips, and the usual detritus. She flipped her hand and probed the space above the drawer. It was solid. She pushed her fingers against it and pulled outward.

An extension slid out. On its surface, notes were taped. Numbers mostly. Some looked like phone numbers, others accounts, and a few possibly passwords, as they were mixed with symbols and letters. Using her iPhone, she took pictures of each note. Then she pushed the drawer in and knelt, looking at the underside. Nothing. She returned the extension and did the same inspection of the bottom of the drawer.

An envelope was taped between the runners.

"Got something." She photographed it in place and peeled it off.

Leo joined her as she opened it. He smiled. "Photographs."

She spread them out and took pictures of each, trying to be methodical while ignoring the emotional impact of what she was seeing.

"It's your brother."

"Yes."

But it wasn't just Liam. It was Liam as his alter ego Larry Pilsner, naked. Then it was Liam with bandages on his face, asleep. A man that looked less like Liam, bruised and thinner. His muscles more cut. In a location that looked somewhat tropical. Pictures that showed the evolution of Liam Pace into a different-looking man altogether, until, finally, there was an ID photo showing a blond man who looked nothing like him, but a lot like each evolution documented by Ellen.

Delaney held the last one up. "So, this is who we're looking for now." If she had to put her feelings in one word it would be loss. She didn't know what to make of it. She'd lost Liam a long time ago when he became Jefe. How could she feel like she was losing him again now that he had become someone else? And why did she care? She looked at the ID photo again. "I've seen him before. Here. In Kearney."

"I think I may have, too. I'm not sure."

"But what does Ellen have to do with him? And how did she get all these pictures?"

Leo nudged a boarding pass among the photos. Ellen Day had flown from Denver to Mexico City. "Could he have gone to Mexico to get the work done on his face? Because she went there."

"It makes sense."

TAP TAP. The noise at the door startled Delaney, pulling her back from the tangle of emotions she was trapped in.

A pretty young woman said, "I'm from IT. You have a warrant to get into Ellen's computer?" Her voice was crisp. Efficient sounding.

Leo handed it to her. "I'm sorry to be asking it. I know everyone just lost a co-worker."

"If it will help you find a killer, I'm all for it. Because I don't believe it was suicide." She snorted as she came around behind the desk. Delaney moved out of her way. "Ellen was not the kind of person to kill herself. She was far too... too..."

"Ambitious?" Delaney said.

"That. And self-assured." She typed rapidly on the keyboard. "But who am I to say? No one knows what really goes on in people's personal lives." She stood back. "You're in. From here on out, the computer will track your movements, just so you know. If there's ever any questions."

"Of course. What about if it times out and we need back in?"

"Don't let it." The woman gave a barking laugh. "No, seriously, it won't. I'll be just outside. When you're done, I'll lock it back down."

Leo nodded at her. "Perfect."

"Do you mind if I take a chair?"

"Be our guest. And thank you."

She dragged a rolling chair into the hall. Delaney heard her settle into it.

Leo went to the desk chair. He plugged in an external drive.

Delaney stood behind him. He smelled good. She hated him for it and herself for noticing. Forced herself not to.

"I'll copy everything first. Then let's see what we've got," he said.

"You narrate. I'll keep searching drawers."

"Works for me."

Delaney began pawing through them again. The side drawers were much larger, and she found mountains of county records. Every now and then she glanced up. Leo was opening, reading, and printing emails to the printer in the office.

Leo blew a raspberry sound through his lips. "I'll have to do

a more thorough search later, but so far, nothing about a counselor, therapist, psychologist, psychiatrist, medications, prescrip-
tions, depression, sadness, suicide, killing herself. Not on her
calendar, not in documents, not in email. Nothing to suggest
financial trouble, romantic breakups, career issues, or a serious
health crisis. I wish we had her texts, though."

"Without her phone, we're at the mercy of the phone
company for them."

"Yeah, we'll just have to make do. I thought through this
when I was working on the investigation plan, and I'm pretty
much searching for anything related to Annabeth or Brock
and now also Liam by any of his aliases. Mitch and Zeke,
too."

"And I'm getting papercuts and a lot of dust up my nose.
Apparently some of these files haven't been opened in years."

Leo froze. "Oh my god."

"What is it?"

His fingers started flying again. "Oh my god."

"You already said that."

"Nothing for Zeke or Liam, but I've got communications
about Annabeth and Brock coming out my ears. And they're
with Mitch Stonefield, who wanted someone to convince Annabeth and Brock that her candidacy wasn't in the best interest of
the people of Wyoming."

"Self-serving, but not incriminating."

"No. Okay, I'm just scrolling now because these all look
good. Here's another string of interest. It's with Abe Dunkirk.
She's promising him permits if he helps with their mutual problem. A trail with Shaina Pham letting her know that Annabeth
was about to disassociate herself with the extremists. You name
a player in these cases, and Ellen was feeding them
information."

"Again, not incriminating. Machiavellian, though."

"She's a manipulative, evil woman. How did she even find

time for county business? Oh, shit. She sent pictures of Annabeth and Brock to both their spouses."

"I figured Pete knew, but Riley did, too?"

"She did if she opened these emails. She didn't respond that
I can tell. Pete did. He told Ellen to leave his wife alone. How
chivalrous."

"Maybe. I can't believe she used county email to conduct
this type of business."

"Trying to strong-arm people requires the color of
authority."

"And an enormous ego that's convinced you'll never be
caught because you're smarter than the rest of the world."

"That, too." Leo's voice pitched downward.

Delaney moved closer to hear. "What?"

"You know we're going to find the evidence we need to
exonerate you and get your girls back."

"That's not within the scope of the warrant."

"We can't unknow what we know."

"Put a cork in it. I don't want you doing anything that can
get you or me in trouble."

A whiny voice interrupted them. "This is highly unusual. I
can't believe the judge issued this warrant." Myer Patton, the
county attorney, was standing outside the door.

Delaney nodded at the man who came up to her shoulder.
The sheriff's department and county attorney were normally
allies. It felt strange to be on opposite sides of an issue. Adver-
sarial, although less than he might worry. This was all about
Ellen's private dealings, albeit conducted using county equipment and email. "We had compelling cause."

Myer held out his hand. He was looking for the paperwork,
not a handshake. Delaney picked the warrant off the desk and
took it to him, then resumed her file review. She had only a few
to go, plus the space above and below the last drawer.

She heard the sound of pages turning. "So, you're not looking into county business."

Leo said, "We have no reason to think her death had to do with the county."

"Or that it was suicide."

"It could be. Or it could not be. She was also a person of interest in two murders. Those cases didn't die with her."

"I have your assurance you'll ignore anything outside the scope of your inquiry?"

"With one caveat. If we see something that looks like trouble for you, I'd like to give you a heads up. Then pretend I never saw it."

He nodded. "I can live with that."

Delaney finished the last file and patted the space above the drawer. Then she squatted and slid her hand under it. It was a lower drawer, so she couldn't get her eyes on the space without removing the drawer altogether, but it turned out that she didn't need to. The county attorney was still watching her, so she played it cool when her fingers found a slim envelope taped to the drawer. At first she was surprised. Ellen had already used this hiding trick. Then she remembered what Leo had said about the best way to hide a weapon is to carry more than one, in the expectation that a search will end after the first is found. Had Ellen given away the photos on the more accessible drawer hoping no one would find and open this envelope?

Delaney peeled it off and set it on the floor by Leo's feet. She could feel him watching her in his peripheral vision. She opened the envelope silently, withdrew a folded set of papers, and unfolded them.

It was a lease, in Ellen's name, for a house she didn't live in.

"What did you find?" Myer asked.

Without a word, Delaney handed it to Leo.

FIFTY-NINE

Freddy repacked his earbuds in their case. His mom's asshat boyfriend had pulled over, finally.

"There are bathrooms in there." The jerk shoved the keys in his pocket and got out.

"This isn't the ski area, then?" Freddy's mom asked.

Freddy rolled his eyes. She was clueless sometimes. Others, she was straight up savage. He never knew which version to expect. His dad used to call her a handful. Uncle Leo sometimes called her Sybil, which he said meant she had a lot of personalities to choose from. Freddy just wished she'd act more like a mom. He worried about her. He wasn't old enough to take care of her, but somebody needed to. She'd been through a lot. They both had. Losing Dad and his grandparents. Moving across the country. But still, his mom needed to deal.

"No ski lifts or ski trails, Mom," he said, under his breath.

They followed Paul inside. "It's just a lodge. We still have a way to go."

"Oh. Well, thanks for stopping for me." She flashed a brilliant smile. Freddy knew she'd used the whitening strips on her teeth the night before. And a face mask. *So extra.* "I wonder if we're near where that woman from Jackson was murdered?"

Paul held the door open.

She obsessed over Uncle Leo's cases. She also listened to a lot of true crime podcasts. He heard her once telling Uncle Leo that it was her dream to host one of them. Freddy thought she needed to stay in her own lane.

"Probably," Paul said.

They walked into a bar. The only bar Freddy had ever been in other than the Loafing Shed. That one was western redneck. This one was dark and spooky AF with dead animals mounted everywhere. Bears, mountain lions, wolves, moose. And it smelled like a wet dog.

"Bathrooms?" his mom asked.

Paul pointed at a sign. Freddy had already seen it. His mom took off.

"Aren't you going?" Paul asked.

"Nah," Freddy said.

"Wait here for your mother." Paul walked to the bar where he started talking to a woman.

Heard: *No, thanks. I don't want a soda or anything.*

The woman walked away, but Paul stayed at the bar, messing with his phone. Freddy kept his eyes off the creep show animals. For a minute he watched TV. But it was some weather channel. Boring.

He looked back at Paul. Now the dude was pacing and mumbling curse words. Freddy walked up behind him. He wasn't trying to snoop, but he couldn't help seeing Paul's phone screen. He had the Google Home app pulled up and was watching video from his Nest camera. Uncle Leo used the same thing at his house. He had cameras at every door and window. Not that he was throwing shade or anything, but it was a little much in Freddy's opinion. Uncle Leo had said he had his reasons for them. And his mom had replied, "Yeah—

we met one of them before we left San Diego." Freddy knew they were talking about the undercover work he wasn't supposed to know about, and that some cartel was pissed off at Leo.

The crazy thing about Paul's phone though was that the video feed was showing Kat's aunt at the door. Then he switched to another camera, and it was Uncle Leo at another door.

Freddy frowned. "Why do you have video of my uncle and Delaney?" Then he realized it was an app connected to the internet. "Hey, is there WiFi here?"

Paul whirled. "Nosy little shit. This is none of your business. Come on." He headed toward the lobby.

Man, he went zero to salty in a flash. "What about my mom?"

"We're not going far. She'll catch up."

"Can I have the WiFi password?"

Paul stared hard at him for a second. He held out his hand. "Sure, I'll type it in for you."

Sweet. Freddy gave Paul his phone. Paul turned it off and put it in his pocket.

"What did you do that for?"

"So, you'd quit whining about it."

Freddy didn't want to go anywhere with Paul. But his mom would flip if he dissed him. He'd tell her what a jerk Paul was being later.

"Wait at that table." Paul pointed into the restaurant.

More dead animal heads. Freddy didn't think he could eat with them watching him.

"I'll be there with your mom in a minute." Paul went to the cashier.

Freddy sat down. A waiter brought a menu. He read it. Chicken fingers. Easy choice. His thoughts returned to Paul's phone. Why would Paul have Nest video of Leo and Delaney?

HER LAST CRY 311

His mom appeared in the doorway to the restaurant, wide-eyed and searching.

"Yo, Mom." Freddy waved.

She joined him. "Where's Paul?"

"Dunno."

She started looking around again, then waved. "There he is."

Paul started over toward them.

"Hey, Mom?"

"Yes, honey?" She wasn't looking at him.

"Paul took my phone."

That earned him a puzzled look. "Oh."

"And he's watching a Nest video of Leo and Delaney on his."

She frowned so hard that her forehead made bulldog lines.

Paul put his hand under her elbow. "We're all set."

"For what?"

"For a surprise. Time to go, Freddy."

Paul was pulling his mom along by her arm. They were walking kind of fast. Freddy hurried after them.

"What do you mean?" his mom asked.

Paul smiled at her, but it was tight lips, teeth, and a total fake out. It didn't show in his eyes. "I'll tell you in the truck. Freddy, you're in front this time."

"What?"

"Male bonding." Paul held open the passenger door. "Trust me, Adriana."

Freddy got in. He didn't trust Paul. But the guy scared him. Not like Freddy Krueger scared but at least sweating out the pits of his shirt scared. Paul opened the back door for his mom, and she climbed in and shut the door.

"Mom," Freddy hissed. "I don't like this."

"Maybe it's part of the surprise?"

Paul slid into the driver's seat. He locked the doors then

reached across Freddy and opened the glove box. He pulled out some duct tape and a gun.

WTF? Freddy shrank back. He was used to Uncle Leo's guns and had even gone to a range to learn how to load and unload a handgun. He'd shot it, too. It was harder than it looked, but he'd hit the target after a few tries. So, Freddy wasn't scared at the sight of a gun. Except in Paul's hand.

"Paul, why do you have a gun?" His mom sounded shook.

No lie, I feel shook, too.

"Here's the surprise. We're not going skiing after all." Paul backed the truck out but instead of driving onto the highway, he drove behind the lodge and down a snow-covered road.

"Where are we going?"

"We're going to spend some time together."

He drove to the last cabin on the road. The other cabins didn't have cars in front of them. A few had scaffolding and stuff around them, like they were being worked on.

Paul parked and pointed the gun at Freddy. Freddy's mouth felt sticky and dry at the same time. "You guys are going to walk ahead of me into our cabin." He tossed Freddy's mom a big metal key. "And then you're going to call your brother, Adriana."

Her voice squeaked. "Okay."

They climbed out. Freddy thought about running away or screaming, until Paul pressed the gun into his back. A roll of duct tape hung around his wrist like a bracelet, and he was holding a weird phone in his other hand. A big, bulky one.

Freddy's mom led the way to the cabin. She opened the door. It was cold and dark. They all filed in.

Paul turned on the lights. "Adriana, open the closet. Clear a space and sit down."

"Paul, don't do—"

His voice was harsh. "You don't want me to hurt Freddy, do you?"

She started to cry, but she did as she was told.

Paul set the phone down. "Freddy, put your wrists behind your back."

Freddy didn't want to. The gun wasn't digging in his back anymore, but it was still pointing at him, so he had to. He put his wrists behind him. Paul made circles with the silver tape. It pulled his arms so tight it hurt his shoulders.

Paul slapped a big piece across his mouth. "Don't start crying like your mother. Your nose will get snotty, and you won't be able to breathe."

Freddy wanted to breathe more than he wanted to cry.

Paul threw his mom the duct tape. "Two times tight around your ankles."

She sobbed but did as she was told, hands shaking so hard she dropped the roll multiple times.

"Now, I'm going to call your brother and hand you the phone. You're going to repeat after me. If you say anything I don't tell you to, I'll hang up, and then I'll shoot your son. Do you understand?"

She nodded.

Paul pressed buttons. He listened into the receiver. Said the F word. Pressed buttons again. Listened. Smiled. Then he handed it to Freddy's mom. "Tell him you're in trouble and that he needs to listen carefully without asking questions."

His mom took the phone, her eyes as big as an owl's.

SIXTY

Leo heard Delaney's voice on his speaker phone. He was watching the back door of the house Ellen held the lease for, while his partner knocked at the front. The house where they expected to find Jefe. The house where someone had left an overripe bag of trash by the back door. *Lucky me.* "We've given it ten minutes," he said. "He's not here."

Another call was coming in on his phone. He pulled it from his pocket and checked caller ID. Unknown. He declined the call.

"I think we should let ourselves in," Delaney said.

"Let's get a warrant." His phone rang again. Unknown, again. "I have to take a call. Don't do anything until I'm back on the line."

"I'm coming around back with you."

"Fine."

Leo took the new call. "Sheriff Palmer."

"Leo, it's me. Adriana. Freddy and I are in trouble. Don't ask any questions. Listen carefully." It was clearly his sister, but her voice was strained. Trembling. High-pitched.

It took a few seconds of reaction time for him to process her words. Something very, very bad was happening to his family. "I'm listening. What's going on?"

In the background, he heard a man's voice, low and commanding.

"Who's Jefe?" Adriana said. But not to Leo.

Leo clenched his jaw. *Jefe?* The voice rose and grew harsher.

Then Adriana said, "A man named Jefe has Freddy and me. He's, he's—" Her voice broke. "He's taking Freddy with him. He said you have to let him go. In a week, he'll send instructions on where to find him. But if you come after them, we'll never get him back."

Freddy. The boy of many interests. The one unafraid to stand up to adults who bullied his friends. Because of his job, Jefe had his wonderful nephew. He'd just thought it was bad when the cartel was closing in on Adriana and Freddy. This was worse. A million times worse.

He had to keep her calm, so he spoke in an even, reassuring tone. "Where are you, Adriana?"

The man spoke again.

"Leo, Jefe can see you and Delaney. On his security cameras. You need to leave his house. You need to leave him alone. You need to do what you're told."

Leo lowered his voice to a whisper. "Just give me a clue. Any clue. Where does he have you?"

But the phone went dead.

Leo screamed in frustration. "Dammit!"

A hand gripped his elbow.

He startled, then saw it was Delaney.

"Adriana. Freddy. Where are they? Does someone have them?" she asked.

"Your fucking brother has them."

"Shit!"

"He said if we come after him he'll kill Freddy. But he said otherwise he won't hurt him and will send pick-up instructions for him in a week."

"And Adriana?"

"I have no clue. No clue where they are." He felt like he was coming unhinged. His voice rang in his own ears. "No clue what he plans to do with her. Where he's taking Freddy. Nothing."

Delaney gripped her head by her temples. "But why? Why did he take them and why is he running now?"

Leo pointed above the door. "His security cameras."

"Clearly we're at the right house."

"Yes."

"I'm going in. Maybe I can find something that will help us. A name. Vehicle registration. I don't know. Something."

Leo's head snapped up. "Her laptop is at our house. She has the Find My app on iCloud. For her and Freddy. I can access it from her laptop."

"What if they're out of cell range? Or their phones are off?"

"Shouldn't matter."

"Do it. Take Shelly. Then get back here and pick me up. By then, we'll know whatever we're going to know."

Leo nodded.

She handed him the keys, and he sprinted to her car.

SIXTY-ONE

Freddy stared, unable to speak through the tape, as Paul took the phone from his mom and ended the call.

She shouted through her tears. "Why are you doing this to us?"

Paul put the phone down, then returned to her. He slapped tape over her lips. Freddy couldn't help it. Tears spilled down his cheeks. Paul grabbed her wrist and pulled it behind her, then did the same with her other one. She made a screaming sound that was muffled by the silver line across her mouth. Paul taped her wrists together.

Freddy's shoulders heaved. His nose was already getting stuffy. The tape smelled all chemical and disgusting, too.

Paul laughed. Then he dialed the phone. After a pause, he said, "I need your help." He paused, giving someone else time to speak. "Get your ass up to Bear Lodge. I have a situation." Another pause. "You sure as hell better already be driving." Pause. "If I had anyone else I could call, I would. But I need you to hide me." Pause. "With your brothers, numbnuts. And I don't know how to find them." Pause. "For as long as it takes. I'll explain everything when you get here. Oh, and I have hostages."

Pause. "If you're burned, you're burned. That's better than dead, which is what you'll be if you don't *fucking do what I told you.*"

He slammed the phone down on the table then walked to the window, breathing heavily and squeezing his fists. Paul's lips moved like he was talking to himself.

Freddy's tears had stopped. He began to notice little things. A ticking noise in the floorboard heaters like the ones at their house. The wind rattling something metal on the side of the cabin. The whine of an engine, far away. He picked up smells next. The ashes of an old fire from a small pot-bellied stove. Cold bacon grease. Freddy's shoulders ached. He realized that as scared as he was, he could barely keep his eyes open. How could he be sleepy?

Paul turned to Freddy. "Sit."

Freddy stared at him. He was sick of doing what this bully said. Maybe he should dive out the window and run back to the lodge. *But the gun. My mom.*

Paul laughed. "Whatever you're thinking is a shitty idea. I'm a much badder man than you're giving me credit for yet, kid." Then he jerked the tape off Freddy's mouth.

"Argh!" It felt like the tape took off half his lips. They were probably bleeding. "Where are you taking me?"

"Wouldn't you love to know."

He could try to finesse Paul. It probably wouldn't work, but it wouldn't hurt either. "Why does it matter? I'm gonna find out anyway when you take me."

"Maybe. Or maybe I'll blindfold you. Or drug you."

Freddy swallowed. "I just... it would help. If I knew, I don't think I'd be as scared."

"Nice try. It's a place you've never heard of with people you don't know."

Freddy didn't know what to ask. His brain latched on to one thing he'd heard. "What's your real name. Is it Jefe?"

"No."

"But Uncle Leo knows you as Jefe?"

"Curiosity killed the cat. Or, in this case, kid." Paul pointed at the couch. "Sit. And don't make this harder than it has to be."

Freddy hesitated.

"Do it now!" Paul shoved his chest.

Freddy stumbled back and fell onto the couch. Dust puffed into the air. Paul tore off a length of tape. Freddy knew what was coming and whipped his head side to side.

"Enough." Paul grabbed him by his bangs, jerked his head back, and smacked the tape over Freddy's mouth, covering it just as he cried out.

Freddy's heart was slamming at his ribs. He felt like he couldn't breathe. Like he was going to pass out. *No. I can't let him win. Mom needs me.*

Then Paul knelt in front of Freddy and stuck an end of tape to Freddy's jeans at his ankle. Wrapped it twice around both of his legs, pinning them together.

Freddy stared at Paul's face. *He's going to kill us. Both of us.* Because they knew what he looked like, and he was trying to get away. *I've got to go ham on this asshole.*

The man looked up. "What are you doing, memorizing what I look like? It won't matter." He tore the tape and patted the end to secure it, taking his eyes off Freddy.

It's now or never. Freddy jerked his knees up and to his chest. Before Paul could react, Freddy drove the heels of his cowboy boots right in the side of Paul's head.

Paul toppled like a falling tree. Freddy lunged and lost his balance on the couch. Pain shot through his shoulder. Worse than anything since he'd broken his wrist skateboarding. He ignored it and rolled onto his face then lifted his upper body and turned, until he was sitting upright and could see what was going on.

Paul was lying on the floor. He wasn't moving.

My kick did that? But what was he supposed to do next? Freddy couldn't use his hands or feet or voice. Neither could his mom. He didn't know how long Paul would be unconscious. *Oh, God. What if I killed him?* But as he stared at Paul, the man's back rose and fell. He was breathing. He wasn't sure if that was a good or a bad thing.

Freddy's eyes found his mother's. Hers looked... frightened... but something else. Proud. Hopeful? She nodded at him. He stood up. Maybe he could find a knife or something. He and his mom would figure out how to cut each other loose. Paul had a gun, but that wouldn't get them free, and he couldn't shoot it with his hands taped like they were anyway. He hopped. One hop, two hops, then he crashed to his knees and onto his chin. *Ouch!* He tasted blood. Maybe he'd do better sliding. He'd never been some super athlete with a jock's coordination.

He was near the fireplace, so he rolled over. His eyes searched for tools. One of those little axes would be Gucci. But there wasn't even a poker or a shovel. A quick glance around the room didn't help. Nothing sharp or pointy. The bulky phone was heavy—he could hit Paul with it—but they needed to get loose more, so he'd have to go to the kitchen. He inched across the floor like a worm. The effort pushed his sleeves up and ground dirt, little rocks, and splinters into his skin. Inching wasn't easy. It was like planking, which he'd done in phys ed class, but not very well. His abs burned. His kneecaps hurt. His progress was super slow. The whole time he kept imagining Paul jumping to his feet and coming after him.

Finally, he reached the edge of the short counter. He got to his knees then used the edge of the counter to stand, almost like a chin up. Those he had been able to do in gym. Something about being skinny making it easier to lift his body weight. He'd rocked the climbing rope, too. When he was on his feet, he jerked open the only drawer in the space. He groaned behind the tape. Plastic cutlery. He lifted his aching shoulders and opened the double cabinet. Plastic plates and bowls. A few coffee mugs and glasses. A frying pan and a pot. But there was something else. Something long and flat. And if it had been last summer when he was still a tadpole he'd have been too short to see it.

He pulled it off the shelf. It clattered to the countertop. *A knife with a serrated blade.*

And then something hard came down on the back of his head. Before he lost consciousness, he reached for the knife. His fingers found nothing but air as he crumpled to the floor.

SIXTY-TWO

Leo clamped a wig wag light from Delaney's trunk on top of Shelly, then drove as fast as he could through town, short of rolling the car. He made it to his house in five minutes where he raced into Adriana's room.

The laptop lay closed on her bed. He opened it and typed in her password. She thought he didn't know it. Everyone in the family had known her password ever since Freddy was born. Fr3dDy plus the current month and year, followed by an exclamation point. It didn't work the first time, so he subtracted a month and tried again.

It worked.

Fingers flying, he accessed her Find My app. It felt like forever until it pulled up a map showing the location of the laptop he was using and two phones. Adriana's and Freddy's. They weren't in the same location. They were near each other, but just far enough away to give him pause. Freddy's looked like it was in a building up in the mountains, and Adriana's seemed to be in a smaller building nearby.

He panned back to see if he could tell exactly where they

were, and suddenly it was obvious. They were at Moose Lodge. An hour away.

He tucked the laptop under his arm and sprinted for Shelly. Then he burned rubber on the way back to Jefe's house.

As Leo drove, he heard an Attempt to Locate go out on the radio. It was for a truck registered to a Paul Lester.

He called Delaney. "Is Paul Lester our ATL?"

"Yes. Liam's got a Dodge Ram Crew Cab 1500 registered to that name. Black. 2018 model."

"I'm on my way. And I know where Adriana's and Freddy's phones are. Or were. Moose Lodge."

"I'll meet you at the curb."

"I'll be there before we hang up the phone." He turned onto Paul's street. A woman was running from a house to the street. His partner. The woman who always had his back. Who was by his side now when his family was at risk. He braked hard, and she ran to the driver's side.

She pointed at the passenger seat. "Out."

He didn't argue. She was accelerating by the time he buckled in.

"Good you have the lights up top." She turned them on.

Leo pounded his fist into the dash. "They're an hour away from us. God knows where they'll be by the time we get there."

Delaney floored the accelerator. "They're forty minutes away with me behind the wheel. And before you start screaming, you're welcome. You can thank me later."

Delaney shot around a delivery truck.

Leo closed his eyes. He could have sworn they caught air on the entry ramp to the interstate. "Shelly has some get up and go."

"Eastern Wyoming Dirt Track Champion." She tapped her chest, where she wore the heavy medallion her father had won and given her under her uniform. "She's about to show us why."

"You aren't concerned about the roads or weather in the mountains?" Actually, the sky and pavement were clear at the moment. But things in the mountains could be radically different.

"She wears snow tires in the winter. I've got chains in the back along with bags of sand for traction. The only thing she can't handle is deep snow. If Liam's making a run for it, he's going to be shooting to put distance between him and Kearny. That means paved roads which will be plowed. If he's going into hiding, then all bets are off. Anything could happen. But we have one thing in our favor."

"What's that?"

"Moose Lodge rents snowmobiles. They also have tracks vehicles we could commandeer."

Leo remembered the last time he'd driven a snowmobile. "Great."

"And I know the owner. He'll let us use anything we want. He's got good conventional vehicles, too."

She zipped off the interstate. Shot over the bridge to Ranchester. Sped through town like a Grand Prix racer. Moved in a blur through the ranchland between Ranchester and Dayton. Blew through Dayton with tires squealing as she navigated the two curves on the far side of town.

And then she accelerated. Shelly laid rubber from thirty-five to eighty-five in the blink of an eye.

"Jesus God."

"I'm good, but I'm not that good."

Leo closed his eyes again. "My sister's been dating a guy."

"Yeah."

"Did you know his name?"

"No, but I'm guessing it's Paul Lester."

"Do you think he pursued her to get to me?"

"She's a beautiful woman, but it's a good guess."

Tires squealed. Centrifugal force shifted Leo toward the

door. He swallowed. "I did this to them. Again. First the cartel. Now Jefe."

"It's just as much me as you. He shares my DNA after all."

"He'd never hurt you, though."

"It's not your fault, Leo. Bad people making bad choices is about them. We do the best we can."

"That wasn't the story I heard from you last night when Skeeter was arrested, and CPS took the girls."

"I was wrong then. You're wrong now."

Leo tried to push his thoughts away. But they stuck in his brain until fighting off nausea replaced them. Storming the climb up Highway 14 with Delaney Pace at the wheel of a race car—even a retired one—was going to be something he remembered as a top five most terrifying moment.

He put his hand to his mouth. "My stomach is rebelling."

"No barf bags on this flight. Stay tough. I think we're going to be there even faster than I promised."

He tried opening his eyes and looking for a horizon. It didn't work and he closed them again. "Do we need to worry about animals in the road this time of year?"

"Always." Shelly's engine strained as Delaney accelerated on a straightaway between switchbacks. "I've been background processing on something. About Ellen being connected to Liam. And everyone else in our homicide cases. Do we like her for the murders?"

Leo welcomed the distraction. "These cases are like one of those thousand-piece puzzles of gray clouds where every piece looks the same and half of them are nearly interchangeable. And it's not until you find the right piece that you even see you've forced a wrong piece in."

"So, is Ellen a wrong piece? Or is she the right one?"

"Discovering she's connected to Jefe makes her feel a lot more like a right one."

"Except why would Jefe give a flip about Annabeth and Brock?" Delaney swerved.

"What was that?" Leo shot up, nearly bumping his head on the ceiling.

"Relax. False alarm. A moose who exercised better judgment at the last second."

The nausea returned. "I don't think Shelly would win in a jousting match with a moose."

She hit the steering wheel with her hand. "Of course. Mitch Stonefield."

"What about him?"

"If he has motive, it's transferable to my brother. They were best friends from their diaper days."

Leo remembered the smug, self-assured politician. "Mitch seemed solid in his belief that he bore no responsibility or connection to this."

"He could be lying. Even if he's not, there's a chance Ellen or my brother might have acted without his knowledge."

Shelly flew by the Paintbrush Lodge, where the car owned by Pete Smithers had been found. Leo was thankful no vehicles were pulling out now because there would have been no stopping the Chevelle. "It just seems like there are others with better motive."

"Motive isn't evidence."

"You can be really annoying."

"No argument." Delaney nodded. "But who had means and opportunity, too?"

Suddenly, she veered hard right. Again, his eyes popped open.

"Burgess Junction. Put your hand on your gun. We're going in hot in one minute. Do we know exactly where, though?"

"I got two readings."

"They have WiFi at the Moose Lodge. We can check again in there, and I can talk to the owner."

"Quickly."

"That's my middle name." She entered the parking lot at just below warp speed and nearly put the car on its nose stopping it, thanks to the snow tires. "Let's roll."

They ran side-by-side from the car and into the lodge.

SIXTY-THREE

The crusty owner of Moose Lodge crossed his arms. "I can't just open up my guest logs to the fuzz, Laney."

She ignored the childhood diminutive. "Jack, you go way back with my daddy. You've got to help me here. The sheriff's sister and nephew have been kidnapped and the last pings on their phones are at the lodge."

"Bring me a warrant. It's hard enough to make money up here. I don't want to get sued and give it away."

Behind him, a young woman in tight jeans and a shirt hanging off one shoulder popped a hip. "Are you talking about that woman and her son with the really hot old guy?"

"Old?" Delaney said. That didn't sound like Paul Lester. But she had a photo of him on her phone now, taken of the ID picture at Ellen's office. "Older than him?"

She smacked her gum. The strong odor of artificial watermelon scent mushroomed out from her. "That's him. He looked like Brad Pitt. Is he in trouble?"

"Did you talk to him?"

"He rented a room. Or a cabin, I mean."

"Well, there you go. Can't help what the girl saw," Jack said, eyes twinkling.

"Leo!" Delaney shouted. Her partner was sitting at a restaurant table with Adriana's laptop open. "Did you get a better marker for them? They rented a cabin." To the girl, she said, "Show me."

"Delaney, you gotta way'a pushing things." Jack grinned. "Just like your daddy. I think I'm just gonna walk out. Ignorance is always the best defense, and I've perfected that one."

Delaney hugged him. "Take care of yourself, Jack."

"You, too, Laney."

The girl shoved a laminated property map across the desk. "It's the most private one we have, back at the far edge of the property. He asked for it special." She traced the road from the lodge back past a line of cabins, stopping on one at a fence line.

Leo was looking over her shoulder. He held up his laptop to give Delaney a side-by-side view. "Adriana's phone is there. At that cabin. Freddy's is here."

"We have a lost and found. Someone turned a phone in earlier." The girl reached under the counter. "Is it this one?"

The iPhone cover was the San Diego Chargers.

Leo grabbed it. "Yes, that's it." He turned it sideways. "The SIM card is missing."

"It wasn't me." The girl held up her hands.

Delaney said, "Liam was covering their tracks. But how did he miss Adriana's phone? That has to mean something." She tapped the map. "Is there a back way to this cabin?"

"Not unless you go over snow. Skis. Snowmachine. Snowshoes. There's a trail that heads right behind there."

"Do you have cameras out there?"

"Not to, like, spy on the guests or anything. But just in case there's trouble. Outside."

"That's good enough. Pull up the outside camera that shows their cabin."

The girl typed on a tablet, then turned it around to show Delaney and Leo. The truck registered to Paul Lester was parked at the cabin.

Leo shouted, "They're still there."

Delaney was already heading for the door. "Time to turn the tables on my brother."

SIXTY-FOUR

Freddy jerked awake. *What had happened?* He was sitting up in a chair by the kitchen table. He jerked his legs, but they wouldn't move. Something smelled bad. Like when Kat's crazy dog had peed on the carpet. Only there was no dog. And he felt cold and wet down there. Humiliation washed over him. *It's me.* He wanted to cry, but he couldn't. He and his mom were in trouble. Bad trouble. He had to stay strong.

He leaned out for a look. His legs were taped to the chair.

"You don't feel so smart now, do you, kid?" Paul was peeking out the front window. He turned. He glared, looking pissed. "You're lucky I didn't kill you."

A knock sounded at the door.

Freddy struggled at the tape. *Maybe it's Uncle Leo.* His arms were taped to the chair, too.

Paul pointed his gun at the door. "Yeah?"

"It's me." A man's voice.

Paul lowered the gun and opened the door.

A deputy stepped inside. Freddy had seen him before, at the redneck bar for his uncle's birthday. He tried to scream.

Help was here. The deputy would see what was happening and save them!

"Took you long enough," Paul said.

"I figured you'd want me to look official. I had to run home and change," the man said.

"Might be good for me. But you'll be in hot water if anyone recognizes you in that."

"I'll be in hot water for anything if I'm seen with you, no matter what I'm wearing. Now, what am I doing here?"

"You're giving me your vehicle. By now, every cop in five states is looking for my truck."

"What am I going to drive?"

"You're coming with me."

"I can give you directions."

"I don't want just directions. I want an introduction. Then you can drive your own vehicle home."

The man gestured at Adriana and Freddy. *He sees us!* "What's the deal with the sheriff's sister and nephew?"

"She's staying here. He's coming with us."

"Whoa. That's a bad idea."

Yes! You tell him!

"You got a better one?"

"We bring 'em both. Look at her. She recognizes me. Don't you, Adriana?"

Freddy looked at his mom. Her eyes were wide and bulging. She couldn't be more obvious if she tried.

"Help me get them loaded then."

Freddy's heart sank. This deputy was *nothing* like Uncle Leo.

SIXTY-FIVE

Leo wasn't making the same rookie snowmobile mistakes this time. He followed Delaney and stayed in the packed trail. Daylight and regular snowmachine traffic made this time easier, and Leo's confidence increased as he gave his machine more gas. He felt lift, and then he was floating. Gliding. If it wasn't for the circumstances, this would even be fun. But the circumstances were what they were, and he was praying they weren't already too late. It had been an hour—maybe more—since the abrupt call from Adriana. If Jefe had taken Freddy and left, he could be on the other side of the mountains by now.

He and Delaney had a plan. And that plan was to maneuver the snowmobiles just past the back of the cabin, circle around to the front, and park at the property line, out of sight of the front door. Jack had said it would take them only a few minutes to get there. For now, they were on their own, but he'd called for backup from Kearny, Sheridan, and Big Horn counties from the lodge. The calvary would come.

Delaney signaled a left turn with her arm, then her snowmobile glided around a stand of trees. He was ready for it and stayed close. The snow was deeper here, though, and he felt his machine wobble and start to bog. *No, no, no!* Freddy and Adriana needed him. He was not letting this happen again. *More throttle.* He asked for the speed, and the snowmobile responded.

A moment later, Delaney pulled up. He stopped behind her. Shut his engine off. Struggled up to her sled in the snow. She'd turned hers off, too. The world was completely quiet around them. The pine trees smelled fresh. The air was crisp. It was peaceful, except for the fact that his sister and nephew were at the mercy of Jefe.

"Well?" he said.

"His truck is still there. But there's another car, too. On the far side of his truck."

Leo walked a few feet for a better view. He frowned. The car looked familiar. But surely there was more than one piece of shit silver Toyota Corolla in the area.

The front door of the house swung open.

Paul Lester emerged, one arm looped through Freddy's, a gun in his other hand. Freddy turned his head in Leo's direction. Duct tape covered his mouth. Freddy's arms—their angle. Leo swore under his breath. His hands were secured behind his back.

They'd just barely made it in time.

As he was about to signal to Delaney that it was time to intercept Paul, a second man came out with Adriana tethered to him. But it wasn't the sight of his sister that froze him. It was the Kearny County deputy's uniform the man was wearing, complete with a duty belt and gun on his hip.

SIXTY-SIX

"Oh, my god," Delaney breathed. For a crazy moment, she thought she was looking at Riley Miller Tucker in a Kearny County deputy's uniform. From a distance, the resemblance was striking. But it wasn't Riley.

It was her brother, Tommy Miller.

The blood drained from her face. How had she not realized Tommy and Riley were related? Sure, Miller was a common name. But their resemblance was uncanny. Details started zipping through her mind and lining up. Riley's violent past. Her dependence on Brock and his lifestyle. Ellen telling her about Brock's affair with Annabeth. The two crucial days she was missing from her girls' trip. Rufus's claim that he saw a tall, thin woman enter the cabin late at night.

The tall, thin woman who had killed Annabeth was *Riley*. And Tommy had killed or helped her kill Brock. But what did any of this have to do with Liam?

Leo swore. "Son of a bitch. Tommy is our dirty cop."

"That's not all he is."

Paul loaded Freddy in back of the Corolla and got in the

driver's seat. Tommy shoved Adriana in beside her son and climbed into the passenger side.

"What do you mean?" Leo said.

"I'll tell you later. Right now, we have to figure out how to get Freddy and Adriana back. From two armed men instead of one."

The Corolla's engine cranked over and caught.

"We need backup," Leo said.

"It's not coming. I'd suggest you get back on your snowmobile. I'll get in front of them and block their path. You come up behind them."

"They've got hostages."

"Then we'd have a stand-off. We could wait for that backup."

Leo nodded. "I can't think of anything better, except I'll intercept them. You find a position to fire on them in case you get the chance."

"I'm a better rider."

"You're also a better shot."

He had a point. She nodded. "Move fast. We want to isolate them out here. Not in the middle of the main lodge area."

The Corolla backed out and started slowly up the road toward the lodge. The other cabins seemed to be under renovation. Empty. That was unusual. The lodge tended to stay booked. But it was a relief. She didn't want to risk civilian lives.

Leo pulled around her. She waved him on. He shot forward, throwing up a thick tail of snow. She fell in behind him. He closed the gap to the car in seconds. Delaney stood up on her footrests for a better view as he veered around it and slowed in front of it.

The car honked. Delaney saw brake lights and the car's back end kicked up. Suddenly Delaney knew what to do. Her brother wouldn't lift a finger to save anyone in that car besides himself. If she pulled her gun on him and kept him from driving or shooting at Leo or her, it might give Leo time to do the same with Tommy.

She accelerated until she was even with the Corolla. She vaulted off her snowmobile toward the car as it stopped. Then she grabbed the driver's door handle, yanked it open with her left hand, and drew her gun with her right. Her body fell backward, but she kept herself partially upright with her grip on the handle. She yanked herself back up just as Liam ejected himself from the car and barreled into her.

This time the door didn't save her.

"You son of a bitch!" she screamed up at him.

"You've got to quit fucking up everything I do, Delaney," he growled in her ear. "Or I'm going to put a permanent stop to it."

She still had hold of her gun, but her hand was trapped under her body weight, buried in snow. She bucked and twisted. Felt him reach into a holster and draw his own weapon.

But then she felt something worse. The car engine revved, and the door scraped over her legs as it rolled forward. Tommy was behind the wheel. Leo. The snowmobile. They were in front of the Corolla.

A scream. It ripped her heart open.

For a split second, her brother stilled. It was all she needed. She yanked her gun hand out from under herself and cracked it against the side of his head.

"You bitch!" he yelled and twisted away from her.

But not far enough. She hit him again. And again. He slumped against the ground. A thousand competing priorities warred for prominence in her mind. Leo—he was hurt. Tommy. Was he getting away? Adriana and Freddy in the car with him. Her brother, who had more lives than a cat, and would not be incapacitated for long.

She didn't have time to dwell on her options. She needed to improve her odds.

Scooping under the worthless man who shared her DNA,

she rolled him and snared a wrist with a zip tie. She tried to pull his arms around to secure them in the back, but he was already stirring. Speed was more important than anything. She snugged his wrists together in front of his waist and tightened the restraint. He writhed and groaned. She fished his gun out of the snow and threw it as far as she could. Frisked him for more weapons. Found a knife on a belt holster. She tossed it away, too.

Then she turned to get a fix on the Corolla's location. It was fifteen feet away. *Past* where Leo had been. Past a tumbled and partially crushed snowmobile. And now the Corolla was accelerating.

She holstered her gun, high stepped to her machine, leaped on it, and gave it enough gas to launch it into outer space. Gathering speed, she pulled alongside the Corolla and steered into the driver's door, ramming the metal. The snowmachine's fiberglass windshield didn't survive the impact. In a battle between a snowmobile and a small sedan, the car wins.

But she wasn't trying to break the car, she was trying to break Tommy's resolve.

She squeezed the throttle flush and pushed at the car. It lost traction. *Should've put on snow tires, Tommy.* The snowmobile whined with effort, but it began to change the car's trajectory, pushing it little by little to the right.

Delaney looked into Tommy's wide, panicky eyes. He let go of the wheel with one hand. The snowmobile gained more ground against the car. His hand came up with a gun, and he pointed it at Delaney's face. She ducked, trying to flatten herself against the seat without easing up on the steering. *Please God let him not shoot my hands.*

The driver's side window exploded and rained glass on her.

She stayed low as Tommy fired one shot after another. BAM. BAM. BAM. BAM. BAM. *Come on. Empty your magazine.* But then she remembered the lodge. They were getting too near to it. Too near to people. People who would probably run outside to see what the shots were about—thinking it was hunters, most likely—not duck for cover. She pulled harder to the right with the steering with all her strength. She felt the car slide.

Then the world came to a jarring halt like she'd propelled her own body into a brick wall. Her hands were ripped from the steering grips. She flew over the handlebars and onto the hood of the car, where she slid into the needled lower limbs and trunk of a spruce tree.

Everything came to rest. She was completely covered in a canopy of green branches. She fought to regain her breath. Her lungs were frozen. Unworking. Just when she thought she was going to suffocate, she coughed, then dragged in a deep breath. It felt horrible and wonderful at the same time. There was no time to enjoy it, though. She scrambled off the hood, falling to her knees on the passenger side. She crawled, then bear crawled, then got to her feet with her hands braced on the roof of the car.

Falling against the window, she peered in. Adriana's frightened eyes met hers. Freddy was prone across her lap, but he was blinking up at her. Adriana gestured with her head. Delaney followed the instruction and saw Tommy. He was draped over the steering wheel, vomiting. Delaney felt for her gun.

She drew her gun and limped around the car and up behind him. Pressing the barrel of the gun into the base of his neck, she spoke in a low, calm tone. "It's over, Tommy. Put your hands on your head."

He stiffened.

She sensed it before it happened. And it wasn't a surprise, not really. Tommy had nothing to lose by trying.

He reached for a weapon as he wheeled on her, daring her to make good on her implied threat to shoot. She didn't know what he was planning to use on her, but it didn't matter. Her training had been clear. He'd used deadly force against her. She had reacted in kind, but with restraint. He was threatening again. And she could never, ever draw a weapon she wasn't ready and willing to use.

She was ready and willing.

But she couldn't shoot him point blank in the neck, which was where her muzzle was, no matter what some instructor in a theoretical exercise had coached her to do.

She lowered the gun, firing as the business end descended. Then she dove to the right, behind him.

Tommy jerked, screaming, as he fired a gun of his own. The shot went wide and wild. He tumbled out of the seat into the snow clutching his left hip with both hands.

"Freeze." Delaney pinned him with her gun. "Kick your gun away."

He looked up at her like a wounded animal. Wounded animals were dangerous. He spat his words. "I can't. You shot my leg."

She didn't see any spurting blood from his femoral artery. He would survive. And his bullet had embedded itself in the trunk of the car. *That close* to Freddy and Adriana. Her rage was blinding, but she willed it to settle. She had to finish this. "Use your other leg, or I'll shoot it, too."

He snarled and kicked, knocking the gun just far enough away that it was outside his easy reach.

She pulled a flexi-cuff from her belt. "Wrists."

"I need to put pressure on my wound." He dripped venom from his words.

"I'll cuff you in front. And I'll be fast. Which is better than you deserve." Leo needed her. She didn't have time for Tommy's antics.

He stuck out his quaking arms. He smelled like fear and adrenaline. She cuffed him quickly, and he jammed his hands back into his wound.

"Feet."

His eyes swore he'd hate her till his dying days, but he straightened his good leg and put it next to the injured one. She wrapped an oversized zip tie around his ankles and tightened it. Tommy gritted his teeth and didn't utter a peep.

"I'll be back," she said.

"Where are you going? I'm hurt."

"To see whether you killed Leo, you asshole."

She stood. One glance at her own snowmobile was enough for her to know it wouldn't be any good for transportation. She shouted at the car. "Adriana, Freddy. I'm going to take care of Leo. You're safe."

Then she ran through the snow, back to her partner. The accident site was further away than she'd expected. She rounded one curve and then another. Her lungs were searing. Her thighs were burning. She was lightheaded and near collapse.

Then she saw a human mound inert in the snow.

"Leo!" she screamed, but just that one word ended on a sob.

She broke into an awkward sprint. *Please, God, no. Please, God, please. Not Leo. He's my person. I need him.* She closed the distance between them in an instant that took an eternity.

Then she skidded to her knees beside him and shook his shoulder. "Leo! Talk to me!"

His voice was a croak, his eyes closed. "In case I'm dying, I love you."

She swayed. He was alive. *He is going to live.* "I love you, too." A laugh burst from her lips. "Tell me where it hurts."

He rotated his head toward her voice and opened his eyes. With a weak grin and a raspy voice, he said, "Have you ever been run over by a car?"

"Everything but."

"I'm fine. Get Jefe."

"I already did."

He gave a tiny head shake. His eyes crossed a little. "He ran off."

No! Delaney checked the area herself. She'd been so focused on Leo that she hadn't been looking for her brother. Sure enough, there was no mass murderer lying cuffed and helpless. "I can't leave you."

"Yes, you can." Leo coughed. He sounded awful, but not near death. "He's our most wanted criminal. He'll do horrible things, again. To you. To Kat."

She hated leaving him, but he was right. She leaned close to his face. "You promise you're fine?"

"More or less."

"Leo!"

"I promise. I'm sure my ankle is broken, but backup will be here soon."

Delaney rocked back onto her heels. "Okay. Tommy is hog tied. Adriana and Freddy are still bound in the car, but they're fine. Help will be on the way soon because of our shots." She got to her feet. "I'll hurry." She stood.

"Don't hurry. Be careful."

She nodded. She hated leaving him. Suspected he wouldn't have left her if their roles were reversed. But knew she had to do it. She didn't look back as she followed the tracks her brother had left in the snow.

Delaney ran. She ran until sweat soaked her clothes all the way through to her jacket. She ran until she heaved her breakfast and then ran some more. She ran until she thought she would never find her way back to the lodge again, but she kept running.

Where is he? He'd had a significant head start, but his arms were cuffed. His balance would be off. He wouldn't be able to pump his arms. His inhibited upper body movement would break down his stride.

But he was bigger. His legs were longer than hers. He was faster. Stronger.

So she kept running. Kept following his obvious trail. Her eyes burned from snow glare, wind, and ice crystals. Her chest hurt like she was about to have a heart attack. Her lungs felt like overused sandpaper. Her ears were ringing like cathedral bells. *I'm like a wounded elk, just right for an easy predator dinner.* She didn't care. Didn't watch out for the dangers of the mountains.

She had eyes only for Jefe's tracks. Jefe. Liam. Brother. No matter how she thought of him, she had to be ready to do what needed to be done. It was up to her. Her alone. The best and worst candidate for apprehending him. The best and worst person to take him down if he gave her no choice.

No one else.

She found inner strength she'd never realized she had, and she kept running.

And then she saw him.

He was standing still, looking downward at the edge of some kind of drop off.

Hallelujah. The terrain had turned on him. Knowing these mountains as she did, it was likely a sheer cliff. Rocks dominated the landscape. Sometimes spiring up to the sky, sometimes rising to form a wall half a mile across, sometimes descending straight to hell.

She slowed to a walk, drew her gun, and advanced on him. "Face me, big brother. I want you to see this."

He held his cuffed hands over his head. "You can't shoot an unarmed and cuffed man."

Her body cam was on. She couldn't shoot him if he was giving himself up. *I don't want to shoot him.*

He turned to her, sneering. "Congratulations on adopting my daughter. That was some trick, given that I'm still alive."

She kept advancing. "You're dead to her."

"Ouch. You wound me."

"Don't pretend you have feelings. It's past being funny." A blackout threatened, wavering on the edges of her vision. She stopped, trying not to show him how vulnerable she was. Acting like she was evaluating him. Waiting for his next move. But he made no move. When she had recovered enough to trust her strength, she waved her gun at him. "Time to walk back."

He laughed. "You need to focus on the bigger fish."

"Tell me about them on our little walk."

"That's not happening."

"That's where you're wrong."

Nausea engulfed her. The words. The words. What was it about the words they'd just said to each other? They pounded in her head like an echo chamber. As they continued to ring out, she recognized them. They were the words from the hall of the Loafing Shed. The words she'd heard before her father died. She and Liam had just spoken them to each other like some kind of farcical reenactment of her living nightmare.

"What's wrong?" Liam was watching her like a bird of prey.

She flicked the safety off her gun, blinded by sudden rage. The memory she didn't want to face. The voice in the hall. She couldn't turn away from the truth anymore. "You killed him."

He snorted. "You're going to have to be more specific."

Her voice came out as a skull splitting, throat ripping scream. "You killed *Dad*." She sank to her knees, drained by her own voice and crushed by the enormity of her emotions.

He threw his head back and laughed. Laughed so hard that his eyes ran. That his shoulders shook. When he stopped, he was shaking his head. "You only just now figured that out? The old man wouldn't get out of our way."

"Whose way?"

"Mine. My partner's. We had big plans for the future."

"You son of a bitch." She didn't care what her body camera

recorded. She'd gladly go to prison for killing this man. Her finger weight increased on the trigger.

"If you kill me now, you'll never get a touching reunion with our mother."

Her finger began to shake. "Our mother?! Is she alive?"

His smile was toothy and evil. "Very much so."

If she was alive, she'd left Delaney alone all these years, even after the death of Rudy Pace. With grandparents who didn't want her. A succession of foster homes, each worse than the last. Years spent running from the pain of loss and desertion. It meant that when Delaney came back to Kearny to care for an orphaned girl *who was her granddaughter*, she still couldn't be bothered to show up.

So why should she mean anything to Delaney? Answer: she didn't. This did. Delaney finally knew who had killed her father and had a chance to send his murderer to hell.

She pulled back on the trigger, almost to the firing point. A sense of peace came over her. *Yes. Yes. Do it.* At the last second, she thought, *Can I possibly see my mother again?*

She flinched, and her shot went wide. Her eyes had already filled with tears by then, so she couldn't see Liam anymore. She heard the impact, though. Bullet into flesh.

"You shot me!" he screamed.

She wiped her eyes on her coat sleeve. When they'd cleared, she watched Liam, feeling disappointment and relief at the same time. He was still standing, his left hand holding his right shoulder where her shot had hit. Not a kill shot. Just enough to make dragging him back to justice harder on her. *How ironic. How fitting.*

She said, "Come on, Liam. Game's up. Let's go."

And then her brother was backpedaling. Falling, sliding. The snow beneath his feet crumbling. A crack appeared, and the snow ledge he'd been standing on broke off.

He plummeted from sight.

"Liam!"

There was no answer.

She crept as close to the edge as she dared. Puffs of dry snow clouded the air. As they settled, she searched for him, hand over her eyes. But there was nothing to see below her. Her brother had been buried in a torrent of snow.

The walk back to Leo seemed to take days. By the time she reached him, two ambulances had arrived. The EMTs were taking Leo to one vehicle. Tommy was already inside the other. Adriana and Freddy had been freed from their tape restraints. The two of them were pressed against the rear of Leo's ambulance. Lodge personnel were hovering around them with blankets and hot drinks.

Delaney walked into their midst like a ghost.

Freddy saw her first. "Delaney! You're the GOAT!"

Adriana said, "Oh, my god. You're... you're... feral."

Delaney actually laughed. "I think the word you're looking for is amazing."

"That, too. Thank you. Thank you, thank you, thank you."

She threw an arm around Freddy. "You're both welcome."

Adriana pushed herself in to join the hug. "Are you okay?"

"I'm fine. Really. I'm so glad to see you guys are, too."

"Stop loading me for a second." Leo held up a hand to the two EMTs. "Sheriff business."

The EMTs exchanged a look but backed away.

"Delaney," he said.

She moved to stand beside him. He was pale. His face was pinched. If she'd made the right choice to leave him, why did it feel so crappy seeing him like this now. "Are you okay?"

"Still fine. What happened?" He dropped his voice. "Where's Jefe?"

"Mother Nature."

"What does that mean?"

"He forced me to shoot him. It's on my body cam. I wounded him and was going to drag him back in, but he was standing at the edge of a cliff. It turned out, he was on an ice ledge. It broke. He fell. I... I couldn't find him."

"He's dead?"

She checked to be sure no one was eavesdropping. "I hope so. He killed my father."

Leo's eyebrows stretched upwards. "He admitted it?"

She nodded. "And he tried to tell me some bullshit about my mom being alive and in touch with him. But, anyway... that's what happened."

"Oh, Delaney." He reached for her hand. She let him catch her wrist. Just that small bit of contact warmed her insides. Made her skin tingle. "I don't know what to say except I'm sorry."

She shrugged and ignored the sting in her eyes. "Thanks. Can I ride with you to the hospital?"

"Adriana and Freddy already claimed the spots." He licked his lips. "But I'm glad you offered."

His words came back to her. *I love you.* And hers. *I love you, too.* She let the silence stretch. Fear rose to a fever pitch inside her. *I can't. I just can't.* She gently pulled her wrist away. "About earlier. We said some things."

"We did." His eyes shone brilliant in his pallid face.

She forced the lie out. The lie that was best for both of them. "I love you like the brother I wish I'd had instead of the one I got."

The hurt in his eyes matched the pain she felt. "Delaney." He reached for her again.

She stayed just out of reach and forced a crisp, professional tone into her voice. "Also, Riley murdered Annabeth. Tommy either killed or helped her kill Brock."

It took a moment, but he nodded. "Yeah. I was thinking the same thing. I wish I could help. How about you go get her?"

"After you're settled and checked out at the hospital. You're the priority here."

He locked eyes with her. They said so many more things than the words coming out of his mouth. "Get Joe and bring her in."

"I'll be fine on my own."

He waved the EMTs over and pointed inside the ambulance. They each took a side. As they rolled him in, he said, "For once, pretend I'm your interim boss, and do what I am asking, begging, pleading for you to do."

And, so, for once, she did.

SIXTY-SEVEN

Delaney drove like a maniac from the T Bar O Ranch to the Sheridan County airport. She and Joe had struck out arresting Riley at her home, but a quick call to her pal Liza Wells had yielded gold. Riley had just dropped her dogs off to stay with Liza and was on her way to the Sheridan County airport. She was taking hers and Brock's private plane on a little trip, destination unknown. Thanks to Joe's quick work on the phone with the manager of the private terminal, they had learned the Tucker plane was being fueled up and their pilot was filing his flight plan at that very moment. The Sheridan airport wasn't large, serving only two commercial flights in and out a day, all to Denver. But private jets came and went on their own time, to whatever locations they wanted.

"Stall him," Joe said. "We're on our way with an arrest warrant."

"How?" the terminal manager asked. Joe had Harry on speaker.

"There is going to have to be a problem with the plane," Delaney said. "Your call on what that something is. But we need forty-five minutes."

Harry said, "I've been friends with Bernie for years. This feels all kinds of wrong."

"It's not Bernie we're coming for."

"Oh," he said. Then, "*Oh*. Her husband?"

"We're not at liberty to say. But consider Riley Tucker desperate, armed, and dangerous."

"I'm on it."

Joe ended the call, and Delaney pulled into the parking lot. She was hurrying, but she was mindful of civilians—and of calling undue attention to themselves. No squealing tires, wig wag lights, or sirens. They marched side-by-side through the parking lot of the Sheridan County airport. Delaney had taken some time on the drive down to Kaycee to update Joe and begin mending fences with him. It was necessary. They needed to rely on each other now, without hesitation.

Joe opened the door for her, and they entered the private terminal. Delaney had flown in and out of Sheridan many times. This was a different world. The seats in the public terminal weren't this plush. The artwork not original oil paintings. The smell not this spa-like, and there was no piped-in classical music for the hoi polloi.

Riley, however, was nowhere to be seen.

Joe whispered, "So this is how the other half lives."

"Apparently so," Delaney said.

A man in wire-rimmed glasses rushed over and introduced himself as Harry. "I think she's suspicious," he whispered.

"Where is she?" Delaney asked.

He frowned "She was here a minute ago. Sitting right by that window facing the parking lot."

"Shit," Delaney said.

Joe gestured at the ladies room. "Maybe she's in the head."

Delaney ducked in and threw open the two unlocked stalls. No one was in there, and there was no other exit. She emerged shaking her head. "We know she didn't come out the entrance. Where else can you exit this building?"

Harry rubbed his hands together. "Only out to the tarmac. My office looks out on it, and I didn't see her go that way."

The three of them turned toward a picture window with a clear view of the concrete apron and planes on it. No Riley. Two men were in a heated argument beside the closest plane, a low-wing white aircraft with swooping blue stripes.

Harry said, "That Cessna Citation is the Tuckers' plane. The guy in the bomber jacket beside it is their pilot, Bernie. He called bullshit on the mechanical issues. We aren't going to be able to hold him much longer."

Delaney said, "She's gotta be in the building then."

"What's she look like?" Joe said.

Delaney said, "Nicole Kidman."

His eyebrows shot up.

"I wish I was kidding." To Harry, she said, "Can the doors be locked from the inside?"

"No. It's a safety issue."

"All right. Can you make sure no one leaves the entrance without your knowledge, then? And, Joe, how about you man the door to the tarmac?"

Joe shook his head. "You planning on searching this building? Then you need backup."

Delaney thought about Riley's militia experience. About the fact that, if she was right, Riley had strangled Annabeth and smothered her husband before she put a bullet in his head. She was no less dangerous than any other murderers Delaney had apprehended. Including her own brother. Joe might have a point.

Harry cut in. "That mechanic. He's getting in the cabin of the Tucker plane." His voice squeaked. "Bernie's starting it up."

"Would the mechanic have any reason to be in it?" Joe asked.

"None that I can think of. He looked a lot scrawnier than usual, too. Something isn't right."

Delaney rushed to the window, only a step ahead of Joe. Bernie climbed into the plane. Seconds later, it started to taxi.

Of course! "It's Riley. It's got to be her. Do you have any type of vehicle we could drive to intercept them?"

"The fuel truck, but I wouldn't recommend it. We've also got a modified ORV our guys use to get around. It's right outside and the keys are in it."

Delaney and Joe were already sprinting out the tarmac door. Delaney reached the ORV first. Joe managed to hop on as she threw it in gear and accelerated after the plane. The Citation had reached the runway and had stopped.

Joe shouted to be heard. "They're not just going to throw out the welcome mat for us. If Riley's in charge, she's going to demand he take off."

Delaney nodded in agreement. She knew what to do. "Hang on." She whipped around the plane as it began to move forward again.

"Oh, heaven help us," Joe said.

"If I pull up too early, it'll just go around us. I need to create some space for a little game of chicken."

"Not a game of chicken."

"Got a better idea?"

"I wish I did."

The ORV rattled as she coaxed it up to sixty miles per hour. When she guesstimated she'd left enough clearance between them and the aircraft, she did a squealing U-turn and accelerated back at the plane.

"Whoooooa," Joe cried.

Delaney ignored him. From the sound of its engines, the plane was nearing take-off speed. It veered to go around her. She matched its path. It adjusted toward the other side of the runway. She adjusted in sync with it. Then she began to weave from one side of the runway to the other.

"If we survive, remind me I don't ever want to work with you again!"

Delaney held the accelerator to the floor and kept up her serpentine dance with the Citation. *Please don't lift off. Please don't lift off. Please don't lift off.* They were only twenty feet apart now. If she didn't steer into the grass soon, they would collide. She and Joe and the ORV wouldn't win that battle with the hurtling metal tube.

One more second.

Joe screamed.

The pilot blinked first, and the plane jerked hard to the right and hurtled off the runway, into the snow and underneath it the rough Wyoming grass of the apron. It bounced high. Delaney heard a creak and a pop, and then it planted itself nose down in the dirt. The sound of the propeller digging itself to a stop in the ground was like the screech of a dying animal.

Delaney whooped and steered toward them.

"She's been armed before," Joe said. "Has to be now."

Delaney pulled to a stop by the one door to the aircraft as it opened. She drew her gun, remembering Riley's past. Her parents' deaths in an unwinnable shootout with ATF agents. Information Joe didn't have.

"Joe, take cover." She dove out of the ORV into the snow.

Joe did the same to the other side.

The door swung part of the way open but not enough for her to see inside the Citation. *Shit.* Riley had cover and a clear line of fire at Joe.

Delaney's voice cracked. "Get behind the ORV." He hesitated, and she screamed, "Now!"

Joe scrambled his heavy body toward the rear of the vehicle, his hands and knees slipping and sliding in the snow. Delaney saw the barrel of a rifle emerge from the door like a snake.

354 PAMELA FAGAN HUTCHINS

She didn't have time to think because Joe didn't have time to get away. She stood up, waving her arms. "Riley. Over here."

The rifle swung toward the sound of her voice. Delaney dove forward into the snow a split second before she heard the distinctive CRACK of it firing. Blood filled her mouth. She spat it out. She'd bitten her tongue as she fell. As far as she could tell, Riley's shot had gone wide and high. The woman was firing blind. But Delaney expected her to correct quickly. That didn't leave much time.

There was only one way out of that plane. The same way in. Riley thought she had them pinned. She wouldn't be expecting a head-on attack, so, Delaney charged the door. Woman against woman. She could take her. She had to try.

"Delaney!" Joe hissed.

She didn't dare make a sound, just prayed Joe's law enforcement training was enough that he'd make the right decision. A few seconds later, the rifle cracked again. The shot made a PING noise as it hit the metal hood of the ORV. The aim had been better. If Delaney hadn't charged, it might have embedded itself in her flesh instead.

POP. POP. POP. Joe was firing his weapon. SMACK. SMACK. SMACK. His shots hit the fuselage. Riley's rifle barrel disappeared. As Delaney neared the belly of the plane, she put her feet in front of her and skidded underneath it. The pilot. Bernie. What if he was helping Riley? She wished she'd called out to him while she was still behind the protective hulk of the ORV. Then she would know whether she was up against one person or two.

Joe's gunfire ceased. She glanced back at him. He'd seen her. Wasn't taking a chance firing in her direction. She was glad, and not just because she didn't want to catch a round of friendly fire. The odor of jet fuel was strong. But Riley would catch on to the cease fire quickly. Figure out why—Delaney was on the offensive.

She had to act fast.

She crouched underneath the door. Whoever had opened it hadn't lowered the steps. By now Riley was searching for Delaney. Or Bernie was. Maybe stepping back to peer out the windows. She listened for the sound of footsteps. Heard them. Felt them shaking the plane as someone moved back to the door.

Delaney drew in a deep breath, braced her gun in both hands, and bounded in front of the door, balancing on the balls of her feet deep in a squat. She aimed upward, ready to fire.

And saw an empty doorway.

Without hesitating, she tucked her gun in her waistband and braced her hands on the plane's door frame, ready to vault in.

A heavy, booted heel stomped her left hand.

Delaney gasped and looked up.

Riley glared down at her. She swung the rifle toward Delaney's face, then fell out the doorway, landing on top of her and knocking her on her back.

"Watch out, Deputy!" A man's voice. Bernie.

She'd thank him later. Riley's weight had knocked the breath out of her. The woman's rifle made a soft PLOP in the snow to Delaney's left. By the time the daze of the collision had subsided enough for Delaney to catch her wits, Riley had risen onto her knees. Delaney tried to move her hand to her gun, but Riley punched her in the face, jumped to her feet, and stomped again, this time on Delaney's right hand. Then she took off at a run, away from the runway and the airport.

Delaney rolled over and stood, shaking her hand. Luckily, the snow had cushioned the impact of the boot or it would be broken. She snatched her gun out and aimed it at Riley's retreating back. "Freeze!"

Riley didn't stop.

Delaney looked from her fleeing suspect and the widening gap between them and the ORV. The vehicle was closer. She sprinted over, threw herself into the driver's seat, and jammed the gear shift into high as she hit the all-wheel DRIVE button and floored the accelerator.

"Wait for me!" Joe yelled.

Reflexes like a turtle. There was no time to wait. Delaney steered to Riley's left. As with the plane, her goal was to get in front of her, but not for a game of chicken this time. To cut her off so close that Riley would fall into her lap. Delaney knew she risked running over the woman, but she didn't care. It was better than shooting her in the back.

She pulled even with her, then past her, and cut sharply to the left. But Riley didn't tumble into the ORV. She'd thrown herself backward onto the ground. Delaney catapulted out of the seat and on top of her before she could get to her feet. The ORV sped onward.

"Riley Tucker, you're under arrest for the murders of Annabeth Dillon and Brock Tucker," Delaney shouted.

WHAM.

For a blinding moment, Delaney couldn't see, couldn't hear, couldn't think, couldn't feel. Then the pain in her temple started. Riley had hit her in the head with a rock, and she was wriggling out from under Delaney. Crawling free. Kicking off Delaney's hands.

Delaney let out a war cry. *Not. Getting. Away.* Not like her brother. Not today. She launched herself after Riley, clawing for a grip on her clothing. Reaching for her hair. Jerking her backwards off her feet by the red strands that had come free of the cap Riley had tucked them under when she'd been masquerading as a mechanic. Kicking out a leg to straddle the woman's writhing body.

With her adrenaline pumping, Delaney rolled her suspect onto her face and grabbed both her wrists.

"You don't understand!" Riley screamed.

Delaney growled. "Shut up until I read you your rights."

She heard panting and stamping that sounded like a buffalo, then Joe's voice. "Can I help?"

Delaney pulled a cuff from her duty belt and snugged it around Riley's wrists. "You can go after that ORV. I left it in gear and it's halfway to Buffalo by now."

Joe groaned, but the buffalo noises receded as he ran after their vehicle.

Then with enormous satisfaction Delaney spit the blood pooling in her mouth and recited Riley's Miranda warning.

SIXTY-EIGHT

THE FOLLOWING THURSDAY

"All rise," the bailiff said.

Delaney stood beside her attorney. She'd asked Wesley James to join her, after he'd made a good impression on her with his work that week for Skeeter. The skinny, bow-tied attorney looked like the law's answer to *Doogie Hauser* and smelled like a pull-open Stetson cologne ad from *Men's Journal*. She snuck a glance over her shoulder. The gallery was filled with people she loved. Mary. Skeeter. Clara. Joe. Leo waved at her, his crutches leaning against the bench seat beside him. He'd just been released from the hospital. Broken ankle. Severe concussion. Sprained wrist. Separated shoulder. And yet he was here.

The judge swept in, black robes swirling, and took a seat. Her steel wool hair stood on end at the crown, a natural mohawk. "Be seated. We're here regarding the adoption petition of Delaney Pace. For the state?"

The county attorney stood. "Myer Patton for the state, Your Honor." He'd refused to make eye contact with Delaney when she'd walked in. She was pretty sure that was a bad thing.

"For Ms. Pace?"

Wesley stood.

Before he could speak, the judge said, "Kid James, is that you? I haven't seen you since Little League baseball."

His face reddened. "Wesley James for Ms. Pace, Your Honor."

She beamed at him. "It's your petition, Ms. Pace, so we'll hear from Kid first."

Wesley cleared his throat. "Your Honor, this has been a most unusual, unfortunate, and damaging week for Ms. Pace and the minor children she is seeking to adopt."

"I'm aware of the circumstances."

Wesley steamrolled on. "Ms. Pace and her employee, Skeeter Rawlins, have been victims of a frame-up by a county official, now deceased, who planted false evidence in Ms. Pace's home, then called in a 'tip' to a now-incarcerated, dirty county deputy, resulting in the arrest of Mr. Rawlins, the removal of Kateena Pace and Carrie Hoff from their home and their placement in separate foster homes, the search of Ms. Pace's home by city police, and, as I suspect you'll hear momentarily from the county attorney, the state's opposition to her petition to adopt the girls that consider her their only family."

"That was a mouthful. Do you have evidence of this hatchet job? Or is this guesswork?"

Wesley swept his hand at Leo in the gallery. "Kearny County Sheriff Leo Palmer will be providing sworn testimony."

"Physical evidence, Kid."

"As a matter of fact, we do."

Myer jumped to his feet. "Objection. The county expects this so-called evidence was obtained illegally by exceeding the scope of a search warrant on county property."

The judge frowned. "You'll get your chance to argue against the evidence when Kid proffers it."

"Wesley, Your Honor."

She couldn't hide her smile. "Wesley. But it may take me some time getting used to it, Kid."

Wesley sighed.

"Myer, is it your intention to argue that the evidence *Wesley* will be introducing is factually inaccurate?"

Myer bowed his head. "Well, Your Honor, with all due respect, that's not the point."

"Excuse me? This is family court. The only point is the wellbeing of these two orphaned girls. Is the county opposing these adoptions?"

"We are, Your Honor."

"On what grounds?"

"The instability of the home situation for them, with Ms. Pace as their parent."

Delaney's fists balled. This was utter, unmitigated garbage, and she hated that she couldn't speak.

"And you base this on?" the judge asked.

Myer enumerated on his fingers. "Her job, her hours, her status as a single, first-time parent, her juvenile history, her—"

"Her what?"

"You want me to repeat the whole list?"

"Did you say *juvenile history*?"

"Yes, Your Honor."

"Since when is that relevant in an adoption petition filed by a thirty-five-year-old woman?"

"Well, Your Honor, there is also this most recent situation."

She pulled at her lips. "Let me ask you, counselor. Are you willing to provide a sworn statement that the evidence you are seeking to keep out of my court is untrue?"

"What do you mean?"

"I'll ask the inverse. Do you have knowledge that Wesley's assertion Ms. Pace was framed is *incorrect*?"

"I don't have to prove it's incorrect. I only have to keep improperly obtained evidence out of court. Your Honor has sufficient grounds to decide the petition in the state's favor on the other grounds I've mentioned."

The judge stood. "No, Your Honor does not. Because I won't be considering any of those other grounds. Here's what I'm going to do. I'm going to conduct an in-camera review of the evidence before I decide whether to rule it in or out. And I guarantee you, no matter how I rule, if it proves this county participated in acting against the wellbeing of two young girls, I will never, ever let you forget this day or this moment."

Myer swallowed and pulled at the collar of his shirt. Wesley held perfectly still. Delaney crossed her fingers.

Myer finally spoke. "There's reason to believe Ms. Pace was railroaded."

A buzz like a swarm of killer bees started in the courtroom.

The judge banged her gavel. "It sounds like this will require communication with the Kearny Police Department to convince them to drop charges against Ms. Pace's employee, given that the only witness is deceased and the information spurious. Am I right to assume this will happen later today?"

Myer seemed to shrink even shorter. "Um…"

"I didn't catch that."

"Yes, Your Honor."

Wesley pumped his fist.

The judge smiled beatifically. "Thank you. That wasn't too difficult. Now, this seems to have morphed into a normal final hearing on a petition for adoption. Is Ms. Pace's paperwork in order?"

Myer stared at the desk in front of him. "Yes, Your Honor."

"Did she fail to meet any of the prequalification requirements?"

"No, Your Honor."

"Have any parties raised objections to the adoption?"

"No, Your Honor."

"Do the minor children wish to speak about the adoption?"

Wesley stood. "They do, Your Honor."

"Well, then, Kid, let's bring them in."

Wesley cleared his throat. "Ms. Pace calls Carrie Hoff."

The buzz was softer this time, and the judge allowed it. The bailiff stepped into the hall and returned with Carrie. Her pink hair was woven in a single braid down her back. Her clothes were subdued. She waved and smiled at Delaney as she passed. Delaney waved back, eyes burning.

The bailiff swore Carrie in.

Wesley walked to stand in front of the teen. "Hello, Carrie. We've told the judge you have something to say and are willing to answer questions."

"Yes, please," Carrie said.

"What is it you'd like to say?"

Carrie took a deep breath. "This is a little scarier than I thought it would be."

The gallery laughed. Delaney smiled and nodded at Carrie.

Carrie rubbed her hands on her arms. "Okay. Well, here goes. I met Delaney and Kateena during the worst week of my life. I'd lost my mother, my twin brother, my boyfriend, and I had a miscarriage. Yes, I was a pregnant teenage cliché, and this was before I lived with Delaney. Back when I lived with my mom. It's true that Delaney works really hard. Her job is exciting and dangerous. That's how I came to her. She rescued me, twice. But she still finds the time to ground me when I break the rules, get me to and from school and stuff when I'm not allowed to drive because I'm grounded"—more laughter from the gallery—"make me stay with a babysitter even though I'm old enough to drive, and make me feel like I really am her daughter."

The laughter died. Tears rolled down Carrie's cheeks. "I had a terrible dad and a very good mom. I wish my mom hadn't died. But the second worst week of my life was this week when I was taken away from Kat and Delaney. I want Delaney to be my mom. I want Kat to be my sister. We are a family. We are a good family. And if it will make the court say yes, I promise to try my hardest not to get into any trouble again. But based on my track record, I'll probably mess that up. And I'll probably be grounded again. That would be okay with me. I love Delaney." She turned her head and stared right into Delaney's eyes. "And if there is any woman in the world I'd like to be like, it's not my mom. It's her."

Now it was Delaney's turn to wipe tears away.

"We pass the witness," Wesley said.

Myer half-stood. "No questions."

"Thank you, Ms. Hoff. You can step down," the judge said.

"Cool hair, Judge," Carrie said.

The judge smiled. "Thank you. I like yours, too."

Carrie left with the bailiff.

The judge leaned on her forearms. "Before we bring in Kateena, I'd like the parties to know that unless something new comes to light, I won't require additional character references. Myer, are you planning on calling any witnesses or introducing more evidence?"

"No, Your Honor." His rounded shoulders reminded Delaney of a cowering dog.

"Then, *Wesley*"—she winked—"it will be up to you."

"We do have multiple witnesses here who have offered to testify, but I'd prefer not use the court's time unless it's necessary to prevail on our petition."

"How about I let you know for sure after I hear from young Ms. Pace?"

Wesley nodded. "That's fair, Your Honor."

Kat sidled up to the witness box, looking more like a wraith than ever. She sat, and, before the bailiff could utter a word, she blurted out, "What happened this week was wrong and mean and stupid. I want to go home."

No one interrupted her. The gallery was rapt.

"I miss my dog. My dad is—I mean was—a criminal and my mom let him push her around. Nobody pushes Aunt Delaney around. She taught me how not to get pushed around either. She makes me feel safe. I love Aunt Delaney, and she loves me. I think my family deserves a big fat apology, and I wouldn't say no to a gift certificate to the Burger Barn."

Loud laughter erupted.

The court reporter said, "Your Honor, she wasn't sworn in."

"Let's do it this way." The judge turned to Kat. "Do you swear that everything you just said was the truth, the whole truth, and nothing but the truth, so help you God?"

Kat's big eyes lit on Delaney. "I swear. Aunt Delaney doesn't believe in lying."

"Just one question for you, then, Kat," the judge said. "What would you say if I told you that I approve of the petition of Delaney Pace to adopt Kateena Pace and Carrie Hoff?"

"Really?"

"Really."

Kat climbed into the seat of her chair and threw her arms open.

The judge stood and leaned over. She hugged the girl, then wiped her eyes. "Petition approved. Kat, you're free to go to your new adoptive mother."

Delaney met Kat halfway. She swung her in a circle hug. "That was beautiful, Kat."

In her ear, Kat whispered, "You can still call me Kateena sometimes. But only when there isn't anyone else around to hear it."

SIXTY-NINE

"Welcome back, Sheriff!" Clara said.

"Good to be back." Leo crutched down the hallway. A week off work had given him perspective, a chance to help his nephew and sister recover, and time for his body to heal, but it had not given him clarity on the decisions he had to make.

Once in his office, he aimed to land his tush in his chair. He succeeded, but without two feet to ground him, the chair rolled backwards and crashed into the credenza.

"You drive chairs about as good as you do trucks and snow-mobiles." Delaney was standing in his doorway, hands on her hips, softening the boxy edges of her tan and brown uniform.

He cocked his head. Something was different about her today.

She brushed the front of her shirt. "What? Did I spill my coffee? Dribble syrup?"

Then he realized what it was. He touched his hair. Hers was a waterfall of gold and chestnut streaks.

She shrugged and dropped into his guest chair. "I didn't have time to braid it this morning."

He'd only seen her hair loose a handful of times. It was like looking into the sun, if the sun smelled like maple syrup and coffee. He cast his eyes down and picked up a stack of papers, tapped them on the desk to align their edges, and returned them to their place. "How was your first weekend as an official mom?"

"We celebrated. They behaved. The honeymoon was over this morning, which is why my hair isn't braided and they're late to school. How are you and Freddy and Adriana?"

"Adriana is taking this hard. She's embarrassed she fell for Jefe's tricks. Freddy is worried about her and torn up that he couldn't protect her. I thought I got how you feel about Kat before, but I really do now. Down to the marrow of my bones. This kind of thing has a way of shaking up one's world view."

Delaney nodded slowly, rhythmically. "Speaking of things that shake up a world view, we never found my brother's body."

He sighed. "Why am I not surprised? Here we go again."

"Maybe. But he killed my dad."

"I'm sorry."

"I thought I'd feel closure when I found his killer. Instead, I find out it was my own flesh and blood. I've been hoping a mountain lion dragged him off and cached him."

"It would sure make all our lives easier."

A heavy sigh vibrated her chest. "I can't believe I let him go."

"You didn't. You shot him."

"I shot badly. And I'm not a bad shot."

Leo's heart hurt for her. "You want to find out what he knows about your mom."

Her face drooped, and her lips tightened. "It guts me that he's had a relationship with her all these years when she left and completely cut me out."

"He could have been lying. Working you over."

"Maybe."

"You gonna look for her?"

Her eyes were filmy. Haunted. "I think I have to."

Leo let the silence resonate. He'd help her. Whatever she needed. Right now, she needed for him to change the subject. "I still can't believe I didn't recognize Riley from the picture Tommy keeps of his family on his desk. It was right in front of me."

"I'd never even looked at it."

"I wouldn't have if he hadn't taped it to his damn tablet."

She chuckled, relaxing her lips. Color returned to them. "A picture frame. You have to admit that's putting it to good use."

"Ha ha." Leo shook his head. "Give me the rundown on Tommy."

She walked to his window. "Riley has hired them both the best attorneys money can buy. He won't say a word about Riley killing anyone. She won't say anything about anything. Joe and I have been working on putting the cases together for the county attorney—that asshat is lucky he has my help. I'd like to roast him like a campfire weenie. We have time-stamped pictures from Rufus's phone that put Riley at the scene of Annabeth's death. And we found a witness at Moose Lodge who remembers Annabeth coming in for a late evening drink and then seeing her with Riley. Which, by the way, solves the mystery of how Annabeth sent texts that night."

"Their WiFi."

"Correct. It might not be enough for Riley, but we have her resisting arrest and discharging a firearm at Joe and me."

"What about Ellen Day's death?"

Delaney turned to him, smiling. "Sugar is a miracle worker. She linked fibers from the floor in Ellen's bathroom to a balaclava we found at Tommy's. Plus, he took his phone with him to her house. Left it out in his vehicle, but it puts him there at the right time. If all else fails, we have him for kidnapping Adriana and Freddy and your attempted murder. Unfortunately, I doubt he'll flip on his sister even to deal down, though. The blood in the Miller family runs thick."

"It dumbfounds me that he was the dirty cop. That we had one at all."

"Me, too. But I believe we have a dirty politician, too."

"Can we tie Mitch to any of this?"

"We have him linked to Ellen, but not to any crime she committed. Yes, she attempted to murder Zeke, but Mitch had no beef with Zeke. As far as Annabeth and Brock go, all she did was feed information to their enemies."

"Speaking of their enemies..."

She ticked them off on her fingers. "Rufus took a deal for assaulting me. Pete Smithers is on the hot seat for stealing from his wife's trust. I suspect he'll take one, too. Corey Castle and Shaina Pham are looking at minimum sentences of three years each plus some hefty fines unless they plead out. My guess is Corey will pick up that bill with Abe Dunkirk, too. And Mitch came through for Abe, so whenever he is operational again, he'll have his mine."

"We'll keep an eye on Mitch. We know to watch him now."

"Still, it would have been nice to take him down. Link him to my brother's crimes. By the time we got back to 'Paul Lester's' house with a warrant, all his electronics were restored to their factory settings with clean hard drives. He ghosted us again."

"I suspect he wiped everything remotely when he saw us at his house."

"You're speaking Greek. And we're not tying anyone to anything through our dirty cop's bank records. They're squeaky clean."

"Cash transactions?"

"That would be my guess. But it's not just no record of money coming in. There's no evidence of money going out. He wasn't a spender. Nothing to arouse suspicion. Ten bucks says he was contributing to the family business."

"Western Pride?"

She nodded, arms crossed. "Riley made regular transfers to them from a private checking account."

"And yet neither of them stuck around to work for the cause."

"I think they were."

"How?" he asked.

"Funding the group. Feeding them information. And Tommy in law enforcement? That's perfect placement. They just need a family attorney, and they're a little Rocky Mountain Mafia."

"Bite your tongue."

She looked at her nails. "I saw Zeke tied the knot."

He raised his eyebrows.

"What? I googled it."

Leo nodded. "You okay?"

"With that? Of course."

The silence between them was charged now. "Listen. There's something we need to talk about."

"We've been talking."

"It's decision time for me."

She pretended to study one of Fentworth's old photographs on the wall. "You're moving back to San Diego, aren't you?"

"It's not what I want to do. But I don't want to stay here if you don't want to work with me anymore."

"I didn't say that."

"Well, you kind of did, before."

"Forget that."

"Are you telling me you want me to stay?"

She walked to the door, hair bouncing. Almost a strut or a sashay. Or maybe it was just wishful thinking on his part. She turned back to him, green eyes glowing. "You're a big boy, Sheriff Palmer. I think you can make up your own mind."

Then she disappeared, trailing sparks that ignited his biggest smile in a good long while.

It was a hard first day back, even leaving early per doctor's orders. His ankle was throbbing. His head hurt from information overload. Leo pulled up the collar of his coat and hunched under it as he crutched out into the wind and blowing snow. His private cell phone pealed. Only one person called it. His DEA handler, Natalie Amin, the woman who gave Special Agents an especially bad name.

He gritted his teeth and kept walking as he answered. "Natalie."

"Leo. It seems you've had developments," she said. *Just once, would it kill her to say hello?*

"One of which is being in the hospital. Another of which is helping my traumatized family in the wake of their abduction."

"Which is why I'm cutting you slack. I could have asked why I haven't heard from you."

He paused at his truck, resting on his crutches. "We nailed our dirty cop."

"I saw there was one in jail. What do you have on him?"

"Kidnapping and murder at best, attempted murder if all else fails."

"Any ties to bigger and better things?"

"If by that you mean Jefe, yes. He killed Jefe's lieutenant for him. The kidnapping was with Jefe. The attempted murder was part of the kidnapping."

"And Jefe?"

"Missing, presumed dead. His sister shot him, he fell off a cliff, and an avalanche buried him."

"I'd like a body."

"Only slightly less than I would. Now, what about our deal? Is this enough to sever my leash to you?" He opened the door and shoved his crutches into the passenger seat.

Natalie didn't respond.

Leo was used to her silent treatment. She alternated it with a sharp tongue and sarcastic remarks. Their conversations were a laugh a minute. He levered himself up into the seat and slammed the door. "I delivered the dirty cop. That's what you sent me to find."

"You did. But I'd like to make you an offer."

Leo let his head thunk back against his seat. "Yes or no. Am I free?"

"You're free. But..." She paused.

"Just spit it out, Natalie."

"You've proven useful."

"No thank you to whatever it is."

"I'm authorized to put you on contract."

"Another leash."

"A job. We pay you. You can even have a title."

"I have one. It's sheriff."

"For now."

"I stay in Wyoming for this job?"

"Yes."

"But I can say no? And move anywhere I want?"

"Even back to San Diego."

He thought hearing those words was all he'd wanted. They were nice, as a symbol of freedom. But his heart was fluttering at the base of his throat. Did he want to work for the DEA? If he didn't, why did he feel this adrenaline? "When do you want an answer?"

"There's one more thing. Well, two, really."

His senses went on high alert. This was the real reason for her call. He should have known. He started the truck, shifted it in reverse, and backed out of his reserved parking space. "What are they?"

"You have to run for sheriff."

"What's number two?"

"You have to bring us Delaney."

He stomped on his brake at the edge of the parking lot. *Not this again.* "What? She's not dirty."

"That's not what I meant. You bring her to me. I have a... counterpart... in another agency. He wants to pitch her a role."

"Why doesn't he just call her?"

"Because we hear you're the only person she listens to."

He snorted. Looked both ways. Accelerated into a turn toward home. "She won't do a damn thing I tell her to."

"Don't tell her to do it. Tell her if she does it, we'll give her back her mother."

A LETTER FROM PAMELA FAGAN HUTCHINS

Dear Reader,

You not only read *Her Last Cry*, but here you are reading this letter as well, you amazing creature! With all the choices for and demands on use of your time, I am honored that you spent hours of yours reading my words. Delaney Pace and I thank you, with all of our shared heart.

If you would like to receive email alerts of all my latest releases, just sign up at the following link. Your email address will never be shared, and you can unsubscribe at any time.

www.bookouture.com/pamela-fagan-hutchins

Her Last Cry was exciting to write, and I literally wanted to know what would happen next just as much as readers. I had no idea! As the story unfolded, so too did several ideas for new adventures in future books. Yay! I can't wait. There's just so much going on in the rugged Wyoming world of Deputy Investigator Delaney Pace and Interim Sheriff Leo Palmer. I feel lucky to be their scribe.

I hope you enjoyed *Her Last Cry* and, if you did, I would be very grateful if you could write a short review online. I'd love to hear what you thought about it, and reviews make such a difference helping new readers discover one of my books for the first time.

Writing is a solitary experience, and I am somewhat of a

hermit anyway. I split my time between two rustic homes. One in—you guessed it—Wyoming, on the face of the Bighorn Mountains, the other on a remote lake in Maine. My companions are my husband and our draft cross horses and sled/ski-joring dogs, with visits from our adult children and grandchildren.

So, I *love* hearing from my readers out there in the real world. You can get in touch with me via my Facebook page where I am fairly active, through Instagram, Goodreads, or my website.

Thanks,

Pamela Fagan Hutchins

www.pamelafaganhutchins.com

facebook.com/pamela.fagan.hutchins.author
instagram.com/pamela_fagan_hutchins

ACKNOWLEDGEMENTS

Sometimes life throws a few curves. This isn't always good, but it's not always bad either. While writing *Her Last Cry* and half of *Her Hidden Grave,* I spent seventy-five percent of the time away from home. The time I did spend there, our beloved Snowheresville, Wyoming experienced -60 Fahrenheit wind chill temperatures for long stretches and endured twenty-five feet of snow. I was snowed in and out every time I blinked. Our septic system froze. Our Boston terrier didn't want to go outside for *any* reason.

During the long, long winter with my husband mostly on assignment overseas and me forbidden to operate heavy equipment on our steep mountain road, I relied on the help of many people to keep our animals alive, our road *sometimes* plowed, and me able to work, maintain relationships with our kids, and travel to and from wherever Eric was so that he could stay strong for all the others who counted on him with the help of "Vitamin P."

Through it all, Eric and I racked up unwanted frequent flier miles and logged an eight-day cross-country last-second move with four dogs in our Jeep only to bid a sad and surprise farewell to our mountain girl—Belgian Malinois Georgia—in a desert far from her home but with her family around her.

So, thank you to my village. My parents, for a gorgeous, intermittent temporary abode. Tiffany, P1, and P2 for animal love and all kinds of help and oversight. Paul, Doug, Melvin, and Craig for that road. Melvin, Erik, and Glen for emergency repairs. Eric's boss for plane tickets. Dr. Cindy for working with us to heal our Alaskan Malamute Sibley's body and spirit. Friends for offering prayers and help over and over: Bonnie, Mandy, Sherri, Rosie, and Daisy. Alexis for taking over the Snowheresville rental business and Tia for managing the rentals at Mooselookville in Maine. Helen for understanding about missed deadlines and having faith in me to deliver.

I learned a lot about myself and what I am not scared of in the last year. Maybe someday those lessons will find their way into pages you will read.

A few years ago, my husband Eric posted that we were giving away rusty, fire-damaged barbed wire. One of the takers was Daisy, who showed up with her family to claim some to use for a project. We soon learned that she'd given up oil field trucking in North Dakota—and a side gig as a reality star— for taking over the family homestead, raising her second daughter twenty years after her first, and being a service to others through philanthropy and her physical labor. She was a key player in organizing one of the largest agricultural relief efforts in the history of the United States through a huge convoy of truckers, donors, and volunteers after historic fires devastated America's Midwest. She and her family raise (and butcher) a large flock of turkeys every year to feed 300+ people at a free community Thanksgiving dinner. Daisy's the one you want as your second in a knife fight, who could have been a model or actress instead of a rodeo star and extreme trucker, and she's the friend you can knock back a cold one with or take to meet your pastor (after you've done your best to prepare them for the encounter). If by some small miracle you find her in a church, you won't see her sitting in the pews... she's the one standing in the back. She was forged in the kind of volcanic upheaval that can result in smoking rubble or beautiful rocky mountain ranges. Daisy, through character and force of will, is the latter. If you enjoy Delaney as much as I do, it is because of my friend

Daisy. Daisy, thank you for agreeing to let me reshape you in fiction.

When it comes to creating a fictional law enforcement world, you have to start with the real thing. I am so lucky to have Police Chief Travis Koltiska of Sheridan, Wyoming in my corner for this. A fourth generation native of Wyoming (with his kids the fifth generation like Delaney), Travis is a bit larger than life. I know him as the generous guy with the heart for his family and animals, a big laugh, and endless stories, but trust me that you would *not* want to be the perp who faces him! Which is ironic since we met him through his wife after my husband accidentally broke into a house she was listing for sale. (It's a long story that ends in years of friendship, and I swear, it was an accident!) I've included anecdotes, quotes, history, and ideas from Travis in many books. I even have a Deputy Travis who shows up from time to time in several interconnected Wyoming series. This time, he took it a step further and acted as my beta reader and coach. Any mistakes are mine alone. He improved the Delaney Pace books immeasurably and put up with dumb questions in texts all hours of the day and night. Please email Travis some love through me as I am praying he wants to continue in this role!! Thanks, Travis, for your friendship and your help.

Huge thanks to my creative, firm, encouraging, brilliant editor Helen Jenner for patiently talking to me about these books for many, many months while waiting for her wisdom and experience with crime fiction to rub off on me and my writing for Bookouture to commence. Helen, you've pushed me through walls I didn't know I'd built to shelter deeply buried writing fears. I'm very lucky to collaborate with you on this project. I hope there are many more to come.

Thanks also to the wonderful team at Bookouture. As a rugged individualist/indie since 2012, I didn't think there was a publisher I would ever be willing to work with. Nimble, lean, flexible, strategic, mission driven, and reader centric, Bookouture is everything I was looking for, and I appreciate them taking a chance on me. The support has been incredible, in every step of the process.

Thanks to my husband Eric for brainstorming with me, encouraging me endlessly, beta reading, and much more despite his busy work, travel, and workout schedule. I will follow you anywhere, even Fredericia, Denmark and Bakersfield, California.

Thanks to our five offspring. I love you guys more than anything, and each time I write a parent/child relationship like the ones Delaney has with Kateena and Carrie, I channel you.

Finally, to each and every blessed reader: I appreciate you more than I can say. It is the readers who move mountains for authors, and you have done so for me, many times over.

PUBLISHING TEAM

Turning a manuscript into a book requires the efforts of many people. The publishing team at Bookouture would like to acknowledge everyone who contributed to this publication.

Audio
Alba Proko
Sinead O'Connor
Melissa Tran

Commercial
Lauren Morrissette
Jil Thielen
Imogen Allport

Data and analysis
Mark Alder
Mohamed Bussuri

Editorial
Helen Jenner
Ria Clare

Copyeditor
Janette Currie

Proofreader
Liz Hurst

Marketing
Alex Crow
Melanie Price
Occy Carr
Cíara Rosney

Operations and distribution
Marina Valles
Stephanie Straub

Production
Hannah Snetsinger
Mandy Kullar
Jen Shannon

Publicity
Kim Nash
Noelle Holten
Myrto Kalavrezou
Jess Readett
Sarah Hardy

Rights and contracts
Peta Nightingale
Richard King
Saidah Graham

Made in the USA
Thornton, CO
06/21/24 10:34:55

0a95b4fa-a0a2-45e8-b5bb-2316f0ea4b9bR01